REDNECK ELDRITCH

Edited by Nathan Shumate

Published by
Cold Fusion Media
http://www.coldfusionmedia.us

REDNECK ELDRITCH

Cover illustration by Carter Reid

Cold Fusion Media
http://www.coldfusionmedia.us

TABLE OF CONTENTS

A HOLE IN THE WORLD

IAN WELKE

The glass is empty, apart from a foamy film in the bottom. I set it down on the bar next to my lighter and my pack of smokes. I'd like to order a fourth beer right away, but I figure I better pace myself. Remembering the task at hand, I tilt my head to get a gander around the Jager display, past the pull-tabs, to where you and your friends are holding court.

I've seen your type plenty. Time was you were few and far between, but now you're all over the place like ants. It started with a trickle. Scouts looking for new territory. You came here 'cause houses were cheap, at least compared to the city. But our houses weren't good enough. So you knocked them down and put up those condo buildings. Then your businesses figured they could come out here as well, lower their overhead. And so more of you came out and bought houses and apartments, and the prices went up, and then the folks that lived here before couldn't afford it anymore and had to move away.

I always thought this bar would stay true. The Hole was a local dive for decades. But now it's more of a typical sports bar and most of the locals are gone. I see they have beers with names I've never heard. Some are dark and thick as syrup. The menu even has a veggie burger. The Hole I knew would never have stooped to this before you lot showed up in your Subarus. Some-times I wonder, *If this bar goes where will we find the people we need?* The bar's original owners are long gone; do their grandchildren even know where the bar gets its name from?

You and the after-work crowd have moved four tables together like you're expecting a large group, but there's just six of you, and I'm guessing most of you are too pussy to keep drinking, so that number will dwindle soon enough.

"Another beer, Ray?" Abby wipes down the bar and takes my empty glass. She's new, but I'm not one to complain about her. She's too good-looking to complain about and besides, she gets it. When one of the old gang is here, we get our drinks before any of you geeks.

I nod, though I should really slow down. It's not even dark out and I have a feeling it's going to be a long night. I reach for my pack of Winstons and the lighter sitting on the bar. Abby frowns. I know, I got to take it outside. Fucking gentrification. I've twisted a cardboard beer coaster into a totem-man. I leave him standing guard over my place at the bar. "I'll have that beer when I get back."

The sun is setting as I pass by the faded Monday Night Football Bud Light display and step out to the parking lot where they've relegated anyone who might want a smoke.

I wince at the glow topping the tree line. Do I have the right day? Late summer in the Cascades, the days aren't as crazy long as they were just a week or two ago, but they haven't given in to the dark months yet.

The whispers said this was the right day, or at least this would be the right night. I could swear it. Though who knows? It's not like they're known for their clarity. They expect that we're able to interpret. Sometimes it's more of a feeling than an understanding that guides our hand to appease them.

Once I've killed my cigarette, I reach into my kit bag for the bone pipe, carved from the femur of my predecessor's predecessor. I run my finger down the runes lining the pipe and then I trill a few notes. There's no response. Nothing. Not even birds singing. All I can hear is the dull murmur of the juke-box through the glass. I trill a few more, but still get no response.

Here goes nothing. I pull the shaker out of my jacket pocket. It's an old Indian prayer stick. It's got juju, but I've always sort of liked the rattle, magic or not. I play the notes with the flute again, this time with an accompanying percussion from the rattle. Smoke rises from the ash tray to my side and begins to swirl around me.

Quiet. And then in answer I hear it in the distance, a low rattle of a large, nasty, oil-burning engine. A beast of a GMC Suburban lurches into the parking lot otherwise filled with German sedans and your fucking Subaru.

They're coming. The apostles of the soil are on their way. Knowing I have the right date, I head back in for my beer.

Ricky and his brothers come into the bar with a full head of steam. Ricky's cap is pulled to the right side. His older brother, Austin, has put on some pounds since the last time I saw him. His gut hangs out from the bottom his shirt, sticking through his denim vest. The youngest, Wade, has never been a light one. Now he's pear-shaped. Touched in the head even more than the rest, Wade waddles side to side as much as he moves forward.

Your table hasn't noticed the new arrivals. I suppose that's for the best.

Ricky and I make eye contact through the gaps in the beer taps lining the bar. He grins, but doesn't come this far back. He takes a table at the front of the bar on the other side of the pool tables. They're far enough away that I can't hear when Nancy, the waitress working the tables, takes their order. She returns a moment later with a pitcher of beer. They all sit on the same side of the table, keeping their eyes on your group.

Even over the jukebox, I can hear Wade's donkey-bray of a laugh. For a moment, I'm worried it will give the game away, but either no one at your table notices or you don't get that he's laughing at you.

Ricky's too cool. He keeps his brothers in line, long enough to make sure that you finish your drinks and that you order again, before he goes to your table. Sooner or later Ricky will take my place. None of the others have the wits left to do it.

I can imagine what he says. The boy has a charm about him, but I notice that you cast wary eyes toward his brothers at the next table. When the waitress returns, Ricky does the talking. This should help fashion the lure. You've been looking at her tits all afternoon, and it's clear he knows her. Maybe he'll help you to get to know her. Ooh! He's ordered a round of shots. Good. This should speed things along nicely.

Two more rounds and you're playing pool with Ricky and his brothers. There are a couple of empty pitchers next to the pool table, and the waitress is returning with a tray of shot glasses.

The sun is down now and time is moving. You might have somewhere to be, I catch you glancing at your watch, and I sure hope Ricky catches it too. You say something to him. Probably something like, "It's getting late." Or "I gotta work in the morning, even on a Saturday."

This is it. Ricky's gotta give you the sell now. He'll size you up and figure what it'll take. A party somewhere with free drinks? Girls? Maybe he'll even lure you with the waitress and her friends, tell you they're coming after their shift ends. He'll take your comment about having to work Saturday and tell you to live a little. If you work hard, you've earned the right to play hard too.

You're considering and I don't think you're going for it. I'm out of my chair wondering if I'll have to step in when I see the look on your face change. You shrug and probably say something like, "I'll go for one drink."

I can tell he has you hooked. It's just a matter of time now.

We've lost two of your friends. Did they sense something? Or did they just have someone waiting at home for them? No matter. We can get this done with three of you, and we have four.

I wonder what you talk about on the way there. It's easy enough for him to get you into the great big Suburban. A bit crowded maybe, with seven adult men, but Ricky knows the way to the party. Besides, you've had too much to drink, don't want to risk getting pulled over, but it's okay for the redneck.

The race to get there will be close. You all are in the GM truck, but you have a longer route. I'm going on foot, more or less as the crow flies, but of course I can't fly and there are a mean couple of hills between me and where we'll meet up.

The hilly terrain, loose rocks, and fallen branches are all I can deal with on the moonless night. Time was, I could've seen the stars. But in recent years with the way your people have encroached on the land, spreading the halo of the city with you, the night's sky is dull background for my climb. At a clearing at the top of the first hill I have to struggle to make out the stars we need tonight, counting to make sure they're all in the place we thought they'd be.

The first of the sigils of concrete mixed with cigarette ash mark the ground, letting me know that I've reached the outermost perimeter. The breeze picks up and I hear the clanking beer cans and other totems hanging from the trees.

I turn my ankle in a dry creek bed on the downslope and have to limp and hop my way up the next hill. By the time I reach the site, you're already there and the boys have a fire going. You each have a beer in hand, and judging from the cans on the ground—nine, ten, thirteen—you're into the second twelve-pack.

Your voice carries to my vantage point at the edge of the clearing. "So you said something about a party…"

"In a while. There are more coming." Ricky snickers.

I worry the laugh will give it away, but you're pretty damned drunk now. You stagger and wave your beer can for balance. I almost wonder if you have an idea what's waiting beneath you, but no, if you did you'd run. I would guess you'd be the sort to panic and make a break for it. Though I have seen your kind freeze up. Stand there waiting for it to happen. Some even welcome it, I think. At least they don't have to go back to their desk come Monday.

You sit back on the half-stone. Do you notice the other stones in the ring? Most of them are broken and overgrown with moss and ivy, but you can't be so numbed that you're unable to feel the power in this place.

Your hands come off the stone. Electrical charge or just cold? Before you get a chance to ponder it, the first of the voices whispers across the wind. Your head snaps back and forth. Yeah. You caught that all right, loud enough that you wonder what it said.

The words are never in English, nor any human language, but as the language of the empty side, you're sure to feel its effects. The hairs on your arms must be upright. That twinging pinch on your intestines might be too much. We need to keep you here; if you start worrying you're going to shit yourself, you'll want to leave.

I remember the first time I was brought here, before I'd begun the training. The first time I heard them speak. I blacked out. I lost a week, like a bad binge. It left me with the same sort of damage. The shakes, bugs on my arms no one else could see, and it was days before I could stomach even broth.

"Hey, man, it's been great meeting you all, but I think I've got to get going."

Crap. You're clutching your gut. I knew it. The whispers, the great hollow empty spirit in the pit, have that effect even on those of us that are used to it.

Ricky steps forward, another can of beer in his hand. "No, man. Stay. Have another beer. The girls will be here soon."

You reach forward for the beer. Holy crap, it's worked. But Wade stumbles up behind Ricky, blocking the path. I watch your eyes look him up and down and at the path. "I… I am free to leave when I want, right?"

"Of course," Ricky says. He hands the beer to you with one hand and smacks his brother in the gut with the other.

You don't look convinced, but you take the beer anyway. "One more beer, I guess."

"Good man. And trust me, by the time you finish that beer, the girls will be here and you'll want to stay."

I still don't think you're convinced. You tilt that can back like you're hoping to down it, but you're not ready for normal beer, it doesn't have that flowery taste like the beers your kind usually drink, and it almost comes back up. That's good. You'll need a nipple for the second part of that can, you'll be drinking it so slow.

It seems like everything's cool, but when you step back the branches under you crack and you look down at the ground your standing on and you go pale. Shit. It's too soon.

Running through the woods in the dark is a good way to get yourself killed. Normally, I wouldn't advise it. But given what you're running from, I can't say I blame you.

And it didn't take you more than a moment from hearing those branches snap to taking off. I have to credit you with that much sense. I doubt you have any idea what's down there, but you have sense enough to know that you don't want to find out. You left your friends, doubled over and drooling on themselves. They don't have your sense of self-preservation, but the strong don't always survive. The strong are the main course.

The terrain is rocky as hell, but that don't mean you can spend all your time worrying about tripping. There are also plenty of low-lying branches to whip you in the face with those conifer needles, so you have to look up as well. Hard to do when you're running in the dark. I have an advantage over the rest of you. I need to hang back anyway, but I'm still doing my damnedest not to trip on loose rocks. Paying too much attention to my feet, I get swatted in the eyes with a dose of those pine needles.

I hope to hell the boys have a spring in their step. Ricky's spry, but Austin and Wade ain't exactly going to win any footraces. I'd tell Wade to stay put and keep an eye on your friends, but they're too out of it to go anywhere under their own power. You, on the other hand, might just get away.

Shivers shoot through me as I understand what will happen if we don't get you down that pit tonight. I wouldn't claim to understand it all or know what would happen if it went on indefinitely, but I'm the only one left that remembers what happened last time the hole wasn't fed. The effects on the world grew nastier and nastier. It started with just tremors. You ever been in an earthquake? You know how it reaches that point where you wonder if it's ever going to stop? At some point you start doubting you can take any more. The fear of that fear gets so bad, you actually do begin to go mad. It was like that. The tremors were followed by waking dreams and visions, and then the worst of the visions began to come true. We thought the world would end. We hoped it would end. It got so bad we wanted anything just to make it stop.

And that was when it was easier to get the sacrifice together. As more of your kind move out here, there are more cops to contend with, cameras everywhere. Time was, our sacrifices weren't missed any. But we catch you, you'll be missed. There'll be an investigation. We'll be lucky if it blows over in time before we need to do it all over again. And of course that's assuming we get this done right tonight.

A rock gives under my foot. I find myself sliding down the hill on my ass for several feet, then I burst through low-hanging branches and onto the grassy floor of a clearing. At least with the clearing I can see the stars over the city halo below. Cygnus and Aquilla are right where I'd expect them. Hot damn, would you look at that? The stars are right. And that means we haven't much time.

As if on cue, the world shakes and there's a primal shriek from the pit. My vision flashes rapidly, like someone switching channels fast on the television. When I can see again, those same stars shine red in the sky above and a layer of cloud funnels through the sky twisting and contorting into pictographs and words spelling doom in a hundred forgotten languages. One thing is clear, the pit is demanding to be fed.

Branches ahead of me break and you come plunging through. Doubled back? Clever, but not clever enough. It takes just seconds for me to grab a handful out of my juju bag and fling a blast of enchanted stripper's glitter into your wide eyes.

You writhe on the ground screaming while the boys return. This little excursion is over. It's time for the main event.

We're back at the pit for a while before you come to. Your eyes have been open, but there's no light behind them at first. Then I catch it. Clarity crossing your expression. You see where you are. You see what's happened to your friends. And you have an inkling just how fucked you are.

Your friends are draped across the branch screen covering the pit. They've been cut in the designs of the traditions, red runes mark their bare flesh, bleeding from as many spots as they can to whet the pit's appetite. But your friends are just appetizers. You're the entrée.

The tree totems clatter, dangling together on the fishing line suspending them. Just the wind? Or catching the spirits, dreams, your fleeting hopes? The hubcap is the best spirit catcher I've found. It's knocking against the air filters and the Skoal cans I enchanted to try and provide a final perimeter for the whispers from the pit.

I know it won't help you any, but I do my best to explain. "It'll keep getting worse. The last time it wasn't fed when the stars were right, feeding it one or two meals wasn't enough anymore. You've heard 'it takes a village?' It took a village."

You start to whimper and then to cry.

"I don't want to die." A bit of snot looses from your nostril.

"No one wants to die, son, not 'til they're real sick in some ways."

"Why are you doing this? We didn't do anything to you."

That's a doozy, but in your place, I get how you see it that way. "That's neither here nor there, son. Sometimes you have to consider the greater good. There's more to this world than you or me, and if we don't feed that hole there, it all goes to hell."

"What the hell's in that hole?"

"Son, the words for what's down there don't exist. Not in our language. It's too old for words. It's emptiness. The type that consumes everything around it. We can keep it sated, but that's the best we can do. And if we don't do that... You've heard the whispers. Its hunger will ripple outwards until the world devours itself in chaos."

You start to cry louder. Your face is thick with tears. It takes me a moment to make out what you say, it's so covered by crying. "But I haven't lived yet. All I've done is work."

Wow. I hadn't counted on this, that I'd feel bad for you. This hasn't happened in years. Usually, when of the hole's meals starts whimpering, I think of it the same way as any other animal and realize it's time to put the poor thing out of its misery. But there's something about that look in your eyes, something about the way you plead for your family.

I know what I have to do. I drop my kit bag to leave the tools for Ricky. I reach out to you, put my arms over your shoulders to comfort you, and I throw us both into the pit together.

I have no idea how long we've been falling before you finally stop screaming. You screamed through the first part of the fall, when we first entered the near dark, where the walls of the pit are slick with blood and caked with the decaying tissue of appetizers past. You kept screaming as we burst through the phlegmy membrane, the strands of mucus creating the veil between the false substance we inhabited before the fall, and the void that we now plummet endlessly through.

You stopped screaming momentarily, but just to vomit. Thanks for that. Waiting to wither to death and dust in this emptiness, your puke is exactly what I wanted to be coated in. I really feel that I made the right decision in taking pity on you and trying to comfort you in this time. No booze, only half a pack of smokes, this will be great.

To make matters worse, the moment you were done puking, the screaming started again.

I think you just screamed until you had nothing left. Your eyes dart about the black like they're expecting to find something to focus on. Either that or the emptiness is itself too much for you. I hadn't thought of that. That it wouldn't be dying, or more accurately, the loss of your life that would break you, but the emptiness.

Though it's not entirely empty. There is occasionally dust. Or other flecks. And some of these give off light.

When I look into your eyes again, that manic ping-ponging has stopped and been replaced by a strange serenity.

"Are you still alive?"

You smile. It's almost more upsetting than when you puked. "Yes. I am fine."

"Fine? You were screaming a moment ago."

"I know. I think I've been screaming for years."

"Then why are you happy?"

"As long as I can remember, I've been falling. There's always too much to do. I fell behind in school and screamed and fought to keep out of that hole. I couldn't catch my breath. There was no time between that pit and falling into the one at work. Seven-day weeks, only time off to sleep a few hours, maybe do laundry. Until I couldn't take it anymore and got drunk until I'd wake up the next day and do it all again, scraping by to keep out of a pit of debt and hopelessness."

"But why are you happy now?"

You grin. There are still flakes of puke adhered to your front teeth. "Because I get it now. There's nothing I can do. I'm always going to be falling until I'm dead."

I'm stuck with a philosophizer. I should have shoved you in on your own. But it's too late now. We fall and fall together.

RECORDING DEVICES

D.J. BUTLER

The old man's gnarled right hand stopped, springing into the air above the trembling banjo strings and freezing in clawhammer shape, index ever so slightly extended and thumb to the square.

The short sustain of the banjo meant the strings sang their final chord with power, but briefly, and then fell still and silent.

John Hanks reached over to stop the recorder and set the microphone down. He leaned back on the three-legged stool next to the open trunk of the 1937 Ford that held the bulky recording device and wiped sweat off his forehead.

The musician's name was Roscoe, wasn't it? Suddenly he wasn't sure. He'd recorded the songs and playing of so many of these hill folk that their faces and names were starting to fuse, Earl and Sunny and Andy and Roscoe. John's eyes and ears itched, and he rubbed them.

"Thank you, sir." He'd just avoid the name entirely, it wasn't worth wasting any time on it. "You sure that's the last one you know?"

The old man's head swiveled on his neck. His jaundiced eyes, punctuated with glittering dark irises, pierced through the trees surrounding his dog trot cabin and seemed to search out the entire knob of rock that in this part of the world passed for a "mountain."

"Waall…" The banjo player popped his neck by cranking his head in a circle and licked his lips. "Not all songs is proper to sing. Not in public. And some songs just en't proper at all."

John restrained a sigh. Instead, he dug into the cash in his waistcoat pocket and pulled out thirty-five cents. "There you are, Roscoe," he said. "Seven songs and tunes I haven't heard before, a nickel apiece."

"Name's Earl." The banjo player looked down at the dull change in the palm of his hand: two dimes, three nickels, ten pennies. "I got another, I reckon. It's gettin' dark, though."

John patted the microphone. "The folks hearing the recording will see you just as well in the darkness as in broad daylight," he cracked wise. "And if you're worried about me getting back down the… mountain," he swallowed the word in one bite, "the car's got headlamps."

"It en't that. It's only… iffen." Roscoe licked his lips again. No, Earl. "I need the money. Nickel goes a long way these days."

John let him think about it. Some of these old folks up in the hills couldn't wait to get someone to listen to their treasure trove of nursery rhymes, blues, ballads, and hymns. Others acted like they were sharing the most precious thing in the world, and had to be bribed, coaxed, reassured, and sometimes even tricked.

"You jest gonna record it on that... what'd you call it?"

John nodded and grinned. "It's a mobile recording device." The recorder was a chunky machine that ran off the Ford's battery and turned sound waves into grooves in a wax cylinder by way of a handheld microphone. It was state of the art, or at least as state of the art as you could reasonably be expected to drag up into the *hollers* of Appalachia.

"It en't dark yet," Earl decided. "You hold a red an' a white thread side by side, an' iffen you can't tell the difference, it's dark. En't that what them old presters used to do? Let's git this one down, an' fast." He leaned over his banjo to whisper to John, and his voice dropped an octave. "An' I en't singin' the words, not to *this* song, nuh-uh. But I'll play you the tune, an' I wager you en't heard it. That worth a nickel?"

"Has it got a name?" John turned on the recorder and held the microphone up to Earl. Still plenty of juice in the battery, he was sure—he had no desire to spend the night in Earl's dog trot.

"No, it en't." Earl squinted. He must know, from all the tunes he'd already recorded that afternoon, that John wanted some kind of label, a way to catalog any piece of music. "But it's a tune as old as the hills." As he said it, he was adjusting the tuning on the banjo. At first, John thought it was just tuning up, but then he saw and heard Earl drop the second string an unnatural amount, and when the wiry farmer ticked the strings off one after the other with his fingernail, the resulting chord sounded... off. Modal, but beyond modal. Microflatted. Intervals all wrong. Unearthly. "Old as the hills," the old man repeated.

"Let's hear it."

Earl played.

True to his word, he didn't sing. His tune was long and discordant, a double drone that must have been some sort of diminished fifth by way of interval, or maybe a diminished sixth, but it seemed to John that the distance between the drone notes grew and shrank as the sound moved through time. The drone was accented by choppy bits of melody on the first, third, and fourth strings, shreds of sound that seemed to John like voices.

Not human voices. And not singing.

Old Earl's drone felt like the thrum of earth moving through infinite time in mist and darkness, and as John's eyes seemed to fill with those mists, he would have sworn he saw standing stones jutting from the mists, and heard voices shrieking in joyous celebration. Only the voices weren't human—they sounded more like birds, but not any bird he'd ever heard sing before.

John wanted to rub the hallucination away from his face, but he had to hold his position very carefully or he would fail to capture the sound on the recorder. His eyes and ears itched and his legs felt asleep. Too much time sitting on this stool.

The banjo shrieked again, or was it a bird? Or was it Earl?

Or was it John?

The tune stopped, abruptly.

Darkness had fallen. Darkness as Earl himself defined it; John could no longer tell the white stripes from the red in Earl's old cotton shirt.

"The nickel," Earl said.

John fumbled for the coin in the darkness. "You say there are words?"

"I won't sing 'em. En't no place safe to sing 'em except mebbe in church on Christmas, an' then I reckon it'd be spittin' in Jesus' eye."

John found himself curious. No, not curious. He found himself craving. He had a strong and unexpected desire to know what words went with that strange, shuddering, atonal tune.

And publish them.

"What about written down?" he asked. "Would you write them? Or do you know where I could find them written?"

Earl was so still that for a moment, in the darkness, he was invisible. When he shook his head it was in a shudder, a sudden paroxysm of motion that almost knocked John backward. "I cain't."

"Or won't?"

"Difference don't matter." Earl stood slowly. His banjo was a light one, an old Sears Roebuck model with an open-back pot, but the slow hunch in which he rose suggested a heavy burden on Earl's shoulder.

Arthritis, John told himself. Bad nutrition. Inbreeding, maybe.

"'Cept mebbe one person," Earl said. It was an afterthought, spoken from the dark shadow of the dog trot running between the two cabins of Earl's house. "Up top of the mountain. Name's Hodder. He's got books, an' I reckon he might have the words written down somewheres."

"'Hodder.' Is that his first name, or his last?"

"All the name he has. He ain't got a clan, not like most folks."

"What do I ask him for? I can't just say 'the song as old as the hills,' can I?"

"The *call*," Earl said slowly. He had disappeared entirely into one of his cabins, and John couldn't even tell which. "Just tell him you want to know the words of the call."

"I don't really understand what you're doing."

John Hanks and Dr. Bender stood inside some sort of laboratory space belonging to the professor. He must be a professor of anthropology, John thought, judging by the twisted masks, dream catchers, untutored paintings, and oddments of wax and feathers that lay strewn on the great trestle tables.

"Oh, and isn't that just life?" Dr. Bender chuckled, chalking the floor around John's feet.

"I've heard stories about the faculty and their… interests. Look, if we're going to do something crazy here, can I at least sit down?"

"My dear Dr. Hanks." Dr. Bender straightened to his full height, looking down into John's eyes from a few inches away. "I mean, you're not technically a doctor yet. But you will be, and what are a few formalities and a sheepskin between friends?"

It was John's turn to chuckle. "Okay."

"I don't know what kind of crazy thing you're imagining we're going to do, but you're mistaken. This is just a little something that will help you remember."

"A mnemonic device."

"You could say. Yes, a device of memory, that will help us remember." Dr. Bender turned to light three candles. John didn't know what kind of off-brand wax they were made off, but they candles sputtered horribly and they stank. "A recording device."

"Us?"

"Mmmm." Dr. Bender handed John a mannequin—an unpainted wooden puppet that flopped all loose-jointed in John's two hands. "Here now, hold this."

From a pot on the trestle, Dr. Bender took a fingertip's dab of some kind of oil or cream and dotted it on the puppet's face in four places, where its eyes and ears would have been. He put a final dab on the doll's belly, and grinned at John.

"To give desire," he said.

The drive back down the mountain was physically no different from the drive up, but John Hanks hit the bottom harrowed. Three times, he nearly wrecked the car: twice over sudden precipices and a third time running it into a grove of tangled trees.

At the first cliff, he found himself tapping the steering wheel with the fingers of his left hand in a repetitive figure; at the second, he started a second pattern with his left foot. The two overlapping patterns felt familiar, deeply rooted in his being.

The recognition that the rhythms were the two entwined drone rhythms of old Earl's banjo was what nearly sent John into the trees.

Hawthorns. But there shouldn't be hawthorns on the mountain, should there?

After that, he found himself humming a melody. A drone, punctuated by birdlike cries.

John's hotel was a shabby boarding house called McCord's. He'd been staying there for three weeks while he tooled around the mountains, passing out nickels to the locals in exchange for any piece of music he hadn't heard before. Though he knew exactly where it was, McCord's still managed somehow to catch John by surprise and throw an azalea bush under the wheels of the Ford before he managed to stop.

Sheepishly checking for witnesses and seeing none, John backed the car up, rolled it around behind the boarding house, and set the hand brake.

He was drenched in cold sweat.

John dreamed.

He looked down from a great height. The height, he knew, was part of what would make him a god.

Although height alone would not do it. Nor would the birds circling him, whose eldritch cries spoke hidden wisdom into the torn and shredded sockets from which his mortal, worthless ears had been removed.

To become a god, you participate in the banquet of the gods. This was the feast of Tantalus, the feast of Atreus, the feast of Moses and the elders of Israel on the Mountain of the Gods.

John heard a low rumble, and the stone supporting him shook.

The gods came.

He let out a piercing cry. The cry contained the wisdom of the birds, the cry was the call that summoned the gods to the feast.

In the morning, John checked out of McCord's.

"Got what you came for?" asked the old woman at the desk.

He stared into her toothless mouth longer than was strictly polite while the question registered.

"Not yet," he finally said.

"Oh? What'cha gon' do, sleep rough while you git the rest of yer music?"

Her words seemed to come from far away.

"Iffen yer short on cash, Mr. Hanks, I reckon we could extend ye a little credit. You bein' a university man an' all."

"Oh, no." It was a cool morning, if humid, but John took a handkerchief from the breast pocket of his waistcoat and swiped at his forehead. "No, I have one more person to see. Up on the mountain."

"Old Earl? Earl picks a fine clawhammer."

"I saw Earl yesterday." John's hand trembled as he handed cash over to the proprietress to pay his bill. He must be sick. "If I could have a receipt, please. No, Earl suggested I see his neighbor."

"Earl ain't got neighbors." The old woman said it matter-of-factly, printing dates and numbers in large block letters on the top page of her receipt pad.

"Well, perhaps not his neighbor. Another resident of the mountain, further up."

The old woman shook her head. "Ain't been no one further up the mountain from Earl for twenty years."

"No?"

"Not since old man Hodder died."

The ground beneath John's feet shifted. Somehow, the old woman didn't notice. She finished printing his receipt and handed it to him. He tipped his hat, a deeply sweat-stained fedora that had once been dapper, and walked outside.

He tossed his valise into the back seat and stood beside the car to think.

He had many recordings. Surely, as many as Professor Bender required.

He ought to get in the car and just drive north. A couple hours' driving would get him to the highway, and from there it would be sunshine, breeze through the window, and cold Coca-Colas all the way back to Miskatonic.

He would do that.

He'd miss out on the words to the song Earl had identified as the song *as old as the hills* and the *call*. Would that be such a steep price to pay?

Instead, without quite ever making a decision to the effect, he climbed into his car, started it, and headed back up the mountain.

As he negotiated the steep switchbacks and narrow gullies that had nearly thrown him the night before, John remembered his first encounter with Dr. Bender and the man's project.

"You're not a musicologist?" John had asked.

"No, but you are." Dr. Enoch Bender had a shock of white hair like a duster, and when he moved or gestured he seemed to leave a cloud of chalk behind. "Or you will be."

"Well, I don't understand what it is exactly you're looking for. Just old songs?"

"Yes, exactly. And you can have all the publications."

That was music to John's ears, though he never would have been so low brow as to speak the pun out loud. "I get the credit? This is not how it usually works. Graduate students usually do all the work and get none of the credit. That's the deal. Indentured servitude, in exchange for a doctorate."

"I'm generous." Dr. Bender grinned, flashing very large teeth, deeply stained by coffee.

So much the better. If all the publications were to be his, John Hanks could launch his own professorial career with a bang. He could be the new James Francis Child, the musical James George Frazer of Appalachia.

"But... what *is* your interest, then?" It seemed too good to be true: his travel expenses would be paid by this small university, and then he could go back to Harvard with all—or maybe most—of what he had collected and make his career with it. "What exactly are you looking for?"

"The oldest songs. The strangest songs. Songs of doom and ceremony." Dr. Bender's smile disappeared. "Songs of summoning. I don't want to publish them, you see. I just want to know them."

***

John stopped briefly at Earl's dog trot out of a sense of obligation, but knocking on the doors of both halves of the cabin produced no response. Earl farmed, he had said, so he must be already up and in his fields.

The road that continued up beyond Earl's cabin was barely worthy of the name. Sometimes it was a track scarcely wide enough for a mule, let alone the Ford. He remembered Dr. Bender laughing as he'd handed over the keys: "Eight hundred fifty dollars, they tell me!"

"Well, maybe you'd prefer that I take another car," John had said. "That's a lot of money."

"However little I care about money," Dr. Bender had confided, "I care about cars even less. I don't know how to drive."

John stomped the accelerator pedal on the Ford, pushing it forward with increased strength as the path became more narrow. Saplings, bushes, and low-hanging branches fell to one side and the other or were torn out by the root as Dr. Bender's car charged through.

Then the mist.

Odd, to have so much mist on such a warm day, in late summer, at such high elevations. The mist was cold, too; it reminded John of British mist in the clammy way it crept in through the windows of the car and climbed inside his shirt.

He pulled up over the lip of a long slope and saw the cabin.

Braking, he pulled up in front of it. This was no Appalachian dog trot, it was something older and less comfortable, and John Hanks barely recognized it for a cabin at all. Slates had been piled up to make four walls, and there must be some kind of a roof substructure, a lattice of limbs or boards maybe, because the roof as he could make it out was a pile of turves. The cabin looked like the kind of thing you might find in some remote abandoned glen in old Europe, not within a hundred miles of Nashville. He wouldn't have been surprised to see a goat munching the grass growing on the roof.

But there was no goat.

Indeed, stepping out of the car, John noticed that he could see no animals at all. Not a chipmunk, not a bird, nothing.

"Mr. Hodder!" he called out.

Silence.

"Hodder!"

Still nothing.

Stooping to pass beneath a twisted lintel, John peered inside the cabin. It consisted of a single room, with a fireplace and chimney, a pile of wool blankets on a stone bench beside it, and a few shelves carrying necessities. There were books, as Earl had suggested there would be, but John's heart fell as he looked at them: *Anatomy: Descriptive and Surgical*, *Corpus Areopagiticum*, *La Cena de le Ceneri*.

Nothing that suggested it might contain song lyrics. Other than the anatomy book, the titles in fact suggested nothing to John. Latin and Italian? he guessed. Out of place in these hills.

He walked around the cabin. Hodder's home stood in the center of a small clearing, and the trees surrounding it were stunted, gnarled things. Maybe blighted by the altitude, John thought, but the trees didn't look as if they were blighted by any external force at all. They looked—John dared to think it— as old as the hills. They looked natural, indigenous, and twisted by their very nature.

They looked malevolent.

At the far end of the clearing from the cabin was a pile of stones. Twelve stones, rounded and rough, but piled together, and the topmost stone was flat and provided a table-like surface. The entire thing was stained dark, or at least the cracks and indentations in the stones were dark.

Maybe lichen, John thought.

Sitting in the center, on top of the mass of stone, was the skull of a bird.

He realized he was humming the droning sound of Earl's melody from the day before.

Like a didgeridoo, he thought. A drone, with yelping accents here and there to provide variety. Only the yelping cries punctuating the tune in his memory did more than just relieve monotony. There was information in them.

A summons.

He heard a cry overhead, and looked up just in time to see a bird appear from the mist, pass overhead, and disappear again.

"Hodder!" he called, one last time, and turned back to the car.

A man stood before him. Short, completely bald. Eyebrows thick as caterpillars and unnaturally wide nostrils.

"Yaas?" asked the short man.

There was something *off* in his accent. Not *non*-Appalachian, exactly, but *pre*-Appalachian. His accent sounded like the ur-Scotch-Anglo-Irish whine from which all redneck accents might have descended in the hundreds of years of the borderers' wandering in the Americas.

"Oh." John Hanks stepped back. He took a moment to organize his thoughts, which seemed to have fled with the passing bird. "Earl sent me."

"Don't know an Earl. Not a livin' one."

"He, ah, he lives down the mountain from you."

Hodder raised his eyebrows briefly but said nothing.

"Anyway, my name's Dr. Hanks. John Hanks." A lie. Anyway, a stretched truth. But the little man's stare made John feel the need to reinforce his own gravitas.

"Ain't sick."

"I'm not a medical doctor. I'm a musicologist, I collect songs. I'm a doctor of music."

"Looking for sick music, are ye?" There went Hodder's eyebrows again. John almost laughed at what must surely have been meant as a joke, except that he felt that on some level Hodder was speaking a simple truth.

Simple, and maybe horrible.

"You might say so. I heard a piece of music from Earl, and he told me you might know the words."

"I ain't a musician."

"He said you'd know this one. He said you'd know the words to the call."

"Did he?"

Moisture trickled down between John's shoulder blades. He couldn't tell if it was sweat, or the mist condensing on his body. "I'm paying a nickel. A nickel a song."

"Nickel's a damned small price to pay for somethin' sacred."

John found himself nodding. "Yes, yes indeed. And that's just how I'd treat your words, Mr. Hodder. Sacred. The university wants to collect them because they're important, and we think other people ought to be able to learn them." John had had this conversation with a hundred other informants, each reluctant to part with the special song grandpappy taught him, regardless of how tiny a variant the song might be on *The Jew's Daughter*.

Only usually a nickel was enough to bring a smile to their wrinkled, tiny faces.

Hodder still wasn't smiling.

The mountain man looked John Hanks up and down, and eventually nodded.

"I kin help ye," he finally said. "In the right time an' place."

"Very good." John stepped towards the car. "If you'll just step over here with me to the recording device. Would you mind speaking the words into a microphone? Or singing them would be even better, that would let us capture the melody."

"In the right time an' place," Hodder repeated himself. "Which ain't here nor now."

He turned and walked into the mist. Within three steps he had disappeared.

"Nuts," John muttered.

What kind of name was Bender, anyway?

Enoch was a biblical name, John had gone to enough Sunday School as a boy to know that. Old Testament, wasn't he the one who walked with God and disappeared? Lived to be old, but not as old as Methuselah and Adam and some of the others. A mere three-hundred-something years, John remembered.

But John had known his share of Jews at Harvard and quite a few more growing up in Brooklyn, and Enoch wasn't a very Jewish-sounding name. Moshe and Reuben and Judah and Shimon and... so on.

Enoch felt like a Puritan's name.

Bender? John had no idea.

Maybe it was one of those old English occupational names, like Smith, Taylor, Butler. Maybe it meant someone who bent things.

* * *

The car started on the third try, and John backed it around with a three-point turn that brought his bumper under the lintel of Hodder's front door. Keeping his feet hovering over the brake, he put the car into gear and eased back over the lip at the edge of the clearing.

To his surprise, after a small initial dip, the road climbed again.

This was wrong. He distinctly remembered driving up to the clearing. Maybe, he thought, his memory was tricking him, and at the end of a drive that was mostly ascent he had descended the last minute into Hodder's clearing. He stuck with the road.

But no, the road definitely climbed.

And it was too narrow to turn around.

"Wrong road," he muttered to himself.

He'd imagined, without voicing the hope, that speaking out loud would dispel the tight feeling in his chest. It didn't.

Ten minutes later he found a shelf of dirt and gravel. What he intended as another three-point turn became a seven-point turn as he rocked back and forth a few feet at a time before finally managing to rotate the car one-hundred eighty degrees. He kept his eyes firmly on the shelf the entire time, and resolutely looked away from the trees.

The trees, which stared at him with gaping sockets and open mouths.

"They don't warn you about this when you say you want to get a Ph.D." Putting the 1937 Ford into gear again, John drove back the way he came.

Inexplicably, the road *continued up the mountain.*

"Nuts." John put the Ford into neutral and pulled the hand brake. "Damn."

The fog felt like fingers under his shirt. He wanted to roll up the windows, but he knew if he did the windows would fog and then he would be blind.

As annoying as it was to worry that he was lost on the mountain, it would be much worse to drive off the mountain's edge.

"Okay." John tapped the steering wheel and breathed deeply. "Get hold of yourself, Hanks. You're just a little lost." He tapped his foot, too. "But you're on a road, and roads go somewhere. So just drive. Drive forward. You'll probably find Hodder's cabin. Or the highway. Or Earl's dog trot. Or anything.

"What's the worst that could happen?"

Still tapping his fingers and his foot, he drove.

The road climbed, and John thought the tire tracks he saw looked fresh. It might mean he was backtracking, of course, but still the sight heartened him. At least he was on the same road he had already traveled.

He began to hum, low and tuneless.

From time to time, when he felt the rhythm dictated it, he whistled a note or two of accompaniment.

Then the Ford climbed over a lip of earth and he was in a meadow. Before him, and slightly to the left, stood a waist-high pile of stones that looked familiar.

John set the brake and breathed a sigh of relief.

In that moment, he recognized the tune he was humming, the rhythms he was tapping out, the bird-like trills of ornament.

He wished he had never asked Earl for that last song.

Climbing out of the car, he approached the pile of stone. There they were again: the lichen in the cracks—but was it lichen, after all?—the flat stone on top, the bird skull.

"Right. So I got turned around, but I'm back." John looked about him. "Only I seem to have come up to the clearing by a different road this time."

He spoke out loud to reassure himself.

It failed.

"Hodder!" he cried.

Faintly, he thought he heard his own voice echo back to him. No sign of Hodder.

The cabin must only be a few steps away. He walked into the fog, looking for it.

"Hodder!"

No answer, and no sign of the cabin.

"Damn," John said again, and then he kept saying it, under his breath and once per step. He reached the edge of the clearing and followed it several paces in one direction, and then back several paces the other way.

No cabin.

No Hodder.

"Hodder!"

Overhead, the piercing cry of a bird.

John's breathing came fast and painful. He stopped walking to try to get control of his heart, which raced to match his breath.

The fog would pass. Hodder would return. He just needed a place to sit down and wait.

The car.

Looking down, John saw his own tracks in the grass, a darker streak where his feet had shaken the silver dew from the tall green stalks. Breathing easier, he turned and followed his trail back.

He had the oddest sensation that his legs were long wooden dowels, pinned together only loosely at the knees. He shook his head to clear the non-sensical thought, then pawed at his own eyes and ears to smudge away the persistent itch.

There was the altar, and the bird's skull. And there his path stopped.

There was no sign of John's car.

He was beyond cursing, beyond the power of speech. His heart raced so fast he feared he'd die of cardiac failure then and there. He tried to tell himself that he'd sit and wait for Hodder to come back, but the only sound he could make was a droning hum, marked by sharp whistles.

He was too old to whimper, so John Hanks bit his lower lip until it bled. Tasting the tang of iron on his tongue, he sat and leaned against the one landmark that remained to him, the rough stone altar, to wait out the fog.

* * *

John woke up.

He leaned against a massive trestle table and two men stood before him. They wore masks, outsized and shield-shaped, only the masks seemed to be made of flesh.

They were mobile, had expressions.

The man standing nearer John leaned in. His mask, lips thin and pulled as wide as possible, eyes bugging, hair a white shock that shed a cloud of chalk as he moved, looked like a mask of Dr. Enoch Bender's face.

As interpreted by some Polynesian tribe.

Using living flesh as a medium.

John blinked and looked away, his eyes stinging.

"The words, Dr. Hanks."

"What words?"

The second man, standing behind Masked Bender, also looked familiar. Blinking to look through tears, John thought his mask looked like the face of Earl. The banjo player, the man who had sent John on this wild goose chase around the mountain.

"The words to the song as old as the hills," said Masked Earl. "The call."

"Well, you know them, don't you?" John challenged Earl. He felt groggy, and had to fight to keep his chin off his own sternum.

"I don't. I en't ever heard 'em. You gotta hear 'em from Hodder."

"The right time and place," John said drowsily. "Only then he disappeared."

"Well, can you sing us the melody, at least?" asked Masked Bender.

"Sssssure." The soft hiss of his own speech almost put John to sleep, but he shook himself and focused.

Tapped his fingers on the stone floor under his thighs.

Tapped his foot in a second rhythm.

Started to hum.

John woke up.

The sky above him was the color of slate.

The fog was gone.

His back and neck hurt from lying against a hard surface. John turned to look about him and saw that he'd been sleeping against a rough stone altar, a pile of uncut stone with a bird's skull on top.

It looked familiar. He remembered sitting down next to an altar like this, although the memory was faded and seemed quite old.

And the altar was now red and slick with... blood?

John checked himself all over. He wasn't bleeding, and his breath came in big, cold gulps of relief.

He distinctly saw the limits of the clearing he was in. There was no car and there was no cabin. There were only the encircling trees and the rocky path climbing up.

John took the path.

He sang to pass the time, or he tried to. Whether he started with *Fatal Flower Garden*, *The Parson and the Clerk*, or one of the Robin Hood ballads, he always ended humming the same tune.

He squeezed his shoulders together to avoid being touched by the trees. At each step and on both sides, they seemed to loom closer.

He tried to curse and couldn't.

The path abruptly leveled and widened into a clearing. He must be at the top of the mountain, because he saw no more slopes up. He also saw no slopes down, and no sister mountains off in the distance.

For all the world, it was as if he had climbed a mountain and at its top found a flat plain, a featureless collision of blue-green grass and slate gray sky.

Almost featureless. Dotting the plain like rotted canine teeth were stone pillars. They were as tall as the skyscrapers of Manhattan but thinner, and hanging on the nearest, fifty feet off the ground, John saw rusted iron chains.

John's bones felt like ice.

Above, circling birds.

"The right time an' place."

John turned and saw Hodder standing at his shoulder. He shuddered, sucking in cold air to steady himself.

Then he looked past the bald man and saw no slope, but only more featureless plain. The mountain, with its paths and its trees, with John's borrowed car and Hodder's cabin and altar, was gone.

A bird called, sharp and short.

John fainted.

John hung on a wall.

There were pins under his shoulders; his arms tingled, asleep, from having their circulation pinched by the pins. His legs felt no sensation at all. His eyes and ears itched.

"So, then," Dr. Bender said, leaning in close to John's face. "Have you got words for us?"

Behind Dr. Bender John saw the cavernous empty space of the professor's laboratory. It seemed even larger than it had before.

"Not yet." John felt strangely remote from his body. His attention felt small and local, as if his mind were cleared of all other matters. As if he were simplified. "Soon."

Dr. Bender nodded, rubbing his fingers together. "Time to sleep some more then, John."

"Can I get down now?"

"And do what?" Dr. Bender laughed. "*Walk?*"

John Hanks looked down at his legs. His legs, his body, his arms—all of himself that he could see—was featureless wood.

"Don't worry," Dr. Bender said. "We'll speak again."

* * *

John hung on a rock.

It was a pillar, not a boulder. And there were no pins under his shoulders —he hung from rusted iron chains that were manacled to his wrists.

He woke to the sharp feeling of his head being punctured, and he shook it, dislodging something hungry and cold. He opened his eyes in time to see a large black bird, flapping slowly away. The bird didn't go far—it settled on the top of another rough stone pillar, within a stone's throw. At the peak of that pillar it perched and glared at John with a baleful yellow eye.

John couldn't feel his arms, and the pain in his shoulders was intense. He looked down, and saw that he was thirty feet off the ground. Below him was blue-green grass in a flat plain that seemed to extend forever; above him was slate-gray sky.

The wind blowing through the stone whistled two tones, one lower than the other. The skin on John's back prickled as he recognized the two drone notes and their strange interval, accented by the occasional cries of birds.

Before the pillar stood the man named Hodder. Hodder raised his arms to the gray sky and began to chant.

John had climbed the mountain for these words, and they burned into his consciousness.

amatim shikaram nipqid, he heard.

amatum sha belim anaku—

amatim shikaram nipqid!

shepum sha kalbim imratz!

The pain in John's shoulders dimmed as the old man chanted the strange words. The tingling sensation of sleep in his limbs spread up through the shoulders, into his chest, into his legs.

His head.

The next-to-last thing John thought he saw was Dr. Enoch Bender. If there had been anyone to take his dying deposition, he would have sworn he saw the professor standing behind Hodder with an ear cocked and a pen furiously scribbling notes in a stenographic notepad.

And then the sky cracked—

John understood the song—

and he was no more.

MINE OF THE DAMNED GODS

SARAH E. SEELEY

The echoes of her moans grew more distinct as I followed the abandoned mineshaft to the pit where my Pa held her captive. The cool, humid air tasted slick and dirty, like oil with a hint of rottenness seeping up from undigested victims long trapped in the bowels of the earth. Crumbling black walls of coal sucked the intensity from my headlamp, and smudged my t-shirt, jeans, and the industrial nylon of my backpack as I repelled foot-by-fist into the chamber no man had entered since the day they struck pure chaos nineteen years ago. She'd been here all that time. People'd heard her, sure enough. But nobody dared to wonder if she was more than a ghost or a warning to their ears for getting too close to a place where thirty-two men lost their minds, and their shit, and tore each other to pieces.

The infinitesimal significance of my own existence thickened on me as my fancy Mago Scarpas touched down on the floor of the pit. He was here. Probably hibernating until the time was right. I could see him looming in the shadows if I wanted, but I didn't go looking.

Naked and caked in soot, she stooped on a heap of coal and rubble. Left arm flung across her waist. Her slight form rocking as her body attempted to cry or scream. She couldn't manage it, though. Only those moans sighed out, soft and desolate, like a faun who'd lost her mama and was slowly starving to death. Except she couldn't die like I knew she wanted to.

She still looked a girl, not a day older than seventeen, with matted blonde hair that draped in clumps around her shoulders and hung halfway down her spine. Aside from her belly she was thin, but had enough meat on her bones to pass as healthy if she weren't so filthy. Clamped around her left wrist was the heavy, two-inch long metal cuff with strange symbols embossed on it like I remembered. I didn't know how it worked. I didn't know why she was special, why she hadn't gone stark raving mad long before I was born. I only knew I was almost a man now, and I couldn't ignore her pleading thoughts in my head no more.

"It's you." The cherubic whisper of her voice was thick from unseen cosmic static filling the air and blanketing her mind. Her right hand rested on her knee, clutching a rusty spike that dripped blood to a tiny splatter sunken in the dust by her foot. A long pink seam in the flesh of her swollen belly was the only testament to her desperation.

"You called me."

"Did I?"

"Yeah, Ma."

She turned her head slowly to meet my eyes, as to a great dark fiend, such as I was. Her lips quivered and stretched into a strange, limp smile. I couldn't quite discern from her thoughts whether her fear or her wonder governed this expression. Perhaps they were one in the same. "You're still alive. I haven't seen you in a long time."

"Twelve years," I said.

"How old you now?"

"Eighteen."

She swallowed. Her doe-brown eyes glistened and pinked in the light of my headlamp. Her voice hushed to a whisper, "I think she's coming tonight. Could you take her away with you? I can't stand to watch it again. Not this time." She held out a blood-caked hand to me. "Help me?"

I licked my lips. I didn't want to touch her, fearing I'd drive her mad if I messed with her head, even just to induce her and block the pain. But I couldn't say no. This was what I'd come for. "I'll try," I said. I took her hand and bled my thoughts into hers until she'd settled down on the ground, contracting in hushed, noiseless breaths.

The body came out first. It was full-term, but withered and blue, slimy with blood. Headless. The little she-thing wriggled and kicked in my hand as I pulled it to me in shock. The head came out separate a minute later, a tiny, faceless orb of overgrown skin, cartilage, and tentacles that had parasitized itself clean off. I suppose I shouldn't have been surprised, given that Ma and Pa were of vastly different species. It just wasn't right, wasn't fair.

"Can I see her?"

"She's dead, Ma," I whispered. "She didn't stand a chance."

The temperature of the air dropped, filling my chest with the tang of needles and turning my breath to mist. That eldritch force crawled across my skin like ants tearing flesh from a corpse one tiny bite at a time. I hated my flesh. My mother's conscience burned within me whenever my thoughts turned dark and apathetic. Her own suffering was so senseless, yet she called me back from the void of a universe that I knew felt nothing for the life it excreted into existence. I saw glimpses of it from time to time, but I cared only because I cared about her.

I let the two lumps of infant corpse slip from my fingers and pressed my palms, slicked in Ma's blood, to the front of my skull. If I didn't let myself molt, I'd go blind with rage and terror in about a minute. An icy burn seared my flesh as it melted into a rubbery, knotted texture like porpoise skin studded with grain-sized barnacles. My nails grew out, curled and blackened. Claws extended through slits I'd already made in the fabric of my shoes. The tentacles normally suppressed by my human genes snaked out around my lips and throat. Sliming my clothes was about as pleasant as shitting my pants, and equally humiliating. Coupled with the fact that human emotions were poorly adapted to handle shifts in physical identity, I could either cut them off or remain at the mercy of the greater fiend stirring in the darkness where I dared not make my presence obvious by looking.

Ma pulled one of my remolded, talon-like hands into hers and squeezed. "It's alright, Eustace. Go now. Go before he gets you."

The shrill hiss of steam made me leap up. A space opened in the surface of a sleek, black twenty-foot-long pod cocooned in the lowest layer of coal in the floor, less than a dozen feet away. A plume of dust and smoke swept out from that void, carrying a strange smell that reminded me of dead fish pickled in paint thinner.

Wet growls rumbled low and deep enough to vibrate my bones. A huge shape emerged from the void in the pod. I saw him in eye and mind. And he saw me. My headlamp flickered and buzzed until it popped, plunging Ma and me into total darkness. I could see in the dark when I wanted, but I didn't want to see him coming. I didn't want to listen to my Ma's submissive wails of disgust as he violated her one more time. If I left her here, I knew I'd hear her cry out to me as I fled. If I stayed, I knew he'd kill me.

Dust crackled as he slithered toward us. I slid the remnants of my infant sister into his path and hoisted Ma to her feet.

"What?"

"Come on." I pulled her arm across my shoulders and we ran.

"You can't take me out of here," she said, seeing my thoughts. "He'll hurt people, kill people."

"Don't care. He'd do it anyway." Claws didn't make my repelling rope any easier to tie on right.

The soft crunch and slurp of my Pa consuming the little corpse made Ma gasp out in grief. "No. No!"

He was coming. I left the rope and pulled Ma to my hip.

She shook her head and tried to pull away. "There's nothing left for me up there. The world's all changed and I ain't. I don't know it anymore."

"Listen." I kept a firm grip on her arm, willing myself not to numb her into a stupor. I couldn't carry her if she passed out. "You ain't no lab rat. You're my mother, and I won't leave this pit without you again." I couldn't see her face, but I sensed her thoughts grow cloudy and chaotic. I shook her arm to regain her attention. "Ma, please! You called me to come. Let me help—"

The Elder Thing struck a heavy blow to my chest, slamming me against the wall. I sank to my ass, gasping for breath. My fingers discovered four long shreds in my shirt, beneath which four slender cuts began to bleed. A huge, rough, slimy limb clamped around my neck. Unable to cry out, I thrashed and slashed at the Elder Thing, cutting his skin and making him roar. Claws clamped into the skin under my jaw. I knew he wanted to tear me apart, starting with my head. With my mind.

My reality shriveled as the void of dark, cold nothingness that was the Elder Thing's thoughts pulsed through me. I wasn't me anymore, but two creatures in one. My consciousness kept disintegrating, like the human and alien halves of my core identity were being ripped away from each other and liquefied a little at a time. Soon I felt only fear and spasmodic reflexes reacting to the pressure driving my skull and spine apart. He took pleasure at my torment. He left enough of my cognition intact to sense it.

As suddenly as the attack on my psyche had commenced, the Elder Thing released his grip both inside me and out. I got to my feet somehow. My mind was blank. I couldn't speak, couldn't move.

"Hold onto me, Eustace," Ma's voice pleaded.

I climbed onto her back and she began to scale the wall of the pit. He followed us up the wall all the way to the mouth of the mine. I wanted to scream.

She carried me out into the open, into the wooded hillside. He stopped following us there. Don't know why. I tightened my grip around Ma's shoulders and let my head sink against the crook of her neck as I slipped out of consciousness.

The smell of Clorox, and the fresh sick it masked, roused me. That, and the hand shaking my shoulder.

"Eustace," Ma's voice called.

Burning pain stung my chest. I clutched at bandages instead of gashes and blinked up at two male nurses dressed in green scrubs. My shirt was off. My pants were still on, still soaked in slime. I sat upright in the hospital bed, didn't see Ma, and started hollering for her.

One nurse, a dark-haired man about thirty with sea-green eyes and freckles, pressed a latex-gloved hand firmly to my shoulder and said, "Take it easy!"

Ma came from somewhere on my right, took my hand and squeezed. "I'm here, baby. I had to go away for a little while and get cleaned up. But I'm back now." She forced a smile, her eyelids drooping in a glazed, half-aware expression. I frowned, a little dumbfounded to see her in a white hospital gown with black polka dots and a matching pair of pants. Her long, straw-colored hair made a strange contrast against the pale blue undertone of her skin. I was looking blue myself, which happened sometimes after I molted. Thankfully, all my non-human features had gone dormant again.

Damn, she was pretty. If I knew anybody who could take care of her and resist the Elder Thing to protect her like she needed, I'd set her up on a date in a heartbeat. Except I knew that no decent guy her actual age would meet up with a girl who still looked like a kid. And the ethics of setting up a 36-year-old woman who looked and felt seventeen with a kid didn't sit none too right with me either. The horror of just how irrevocably messed up her life was twisted me up inside.

I scratched my face and found another set of bandages stuck over the punctures around my jaw. I stared at the bizarre bracelet on her arm for a while, wondering if anybody had asked her about it. Then I fell back onto the angled mattress and groaned, taking in the further complications that were bound to come from involving all these well-meaning hospital people in our escape from the mine. Someone was going to split us up, ask questions, go poking around where they shouldn't and get themselves in trouble. Though I'd seen too much of the underbelly of existence to believe in any sort of god, I prayed to whatever benevolent forces may be to bless my Ma's heart for doing it anyway, hoping to save me, or get me whatever help she thought I needed that we couldn't take care of ourselves.

Ma sat in a banged-up folding chair, teetering back and forth on the four uneven legs, frowning at the shriveled exoskeleton of a praying mantis on the windowsill of the outpatient office. It was a small town hospital with sixty-five beds on two levels. The unscreened window was locked open with about an inch of space beneath the sliding pane, letting in flies with the humid summer air that was only slightly cooler than the greenhouse heat inside the room. Clutched between the mantis's pincers and mandibles were a couple of wasp legs. Five slender white stalks topped with berry-red caps stuck up from the mantis's belly like a collection of mutant sewing pins. "I wasn't blue before the mine," Ma said.

"They can treat it, Ma. You've just got a little less oxygen sticking to your blood than normal."

"Who's gonna pay for... for treatment and things?"

"The good old state of Kentucky." I paced around the room, waiting for the town investigator to arrive and ask us a bunch of dumb-ass questions I couldn't answer in any way that'd make sense. To make matters more complicated, the hospital had found my driver's license in the wallet I kept in my backpack and called up my foster mother. She was on her way to meet us. She wanted to help us, but I didn't know what to tell her about the girl who'd rescued me from the mine a second time when I'd made up my mind to rescue her.

I wanted to get Ma as far away from this town and the fiend in the mine as possible, to give her back some chance for a normal life if I could. No more monster, no more suffering, no more dark energy to cloud up her thoughts.

"Wasn't so slow before neither," she lamented a little softer. Her mental fascination for the dead insect started to grate on my nerves.

"Do you have to stare at that thing? It's disgusting."

"Nah, its God's work."

"God's work? You're crazy."

Her frown deepened, hurt. "Least that thing's natural. I ain't seen natural things in a long time."

I sighed and pinched the bridge of my nose. "I'm sorry, Ma. If anyone can find God's hand in predators and parasites, its you."

We didn't say nothing for a long minute or two. Then Ma reached for the trash bin next to the office desk and scooped the dead insect off the sill. "Did you know he's superstitious?"

"Who?"

She swallowed. "The... that thing I lived with."

I looked at the back of her head while she gazed out the window.

"It's scared of us, you and me," she said. "It didn't want to spawn neither. It was looking for a way out. Out of the mine. It... it changed me, Eustace."

A part of me wanted to ask if she wasn't really just talking about herself, but I knew it was too callous to mention aloud.

She heard me anyway, and said, "Maybe you're right. But I know he's stuck down there, some reason. Thinks something inside me, in my head, holds the key."

Again I couldn't deny how strange it was she hadn't gone mad, lost her grip on reality to the point where her neatly evolved social wiring and moral arbitrations had disintegrated into cosmic mush. I knew she loved me. Didn't know how she could, or why she wanted to. A part of her feared me, and what I was or might become, just as much.

"You ever kill anybody, Eustace?"

I blinked in surprise at the question. "No, Ma." *But I've sure wanted to.*

She heard that. She turned in her chair, turned her distant, unfocused gaze to my face. "Me too," she whispered. "But I ran away instead."

"Really?"

She nodded slowly.

I squinted at the dark corner of her mind I'd never been able to read. "Was it the right thing?"

She shrugged. "Don't think it would've made things any different than they turned out."

The door swung open and a stocky, middle-aged man in a dark blue police uniform walked in. His white hair was buzzed short, and his cool blue eyes peered casually into the room behind a pair of black-rimmed glasses held together in several places with thin pieces of duct tape. A piece of gum that stank of nicotine popped between his teeth as he chewed. He clutched a manila file folder under his right arm.

Ma froze like a pea stalk in April, mind blank. The emptiness inside me when her thoughts withdrew was always unsettling. It meant something was wrong.

The old man's chewing paused. His eyes widened for a split second before they narrowed, darting back and forth as his gaze lingered on Ma's face. His eyes licked to me, then back to her. "Do I know you kids?"

I shook my head. "Don't think so, sir." I glanced at Ma. She was gone all right, eyelids drooped, barely blinking.

"Take a seat, son."

I rolled my eyes where the officer couldn't see and repositioned Ma's chair so she sat side by side with me. The officer pulled up another chair across from us and crossed his ankle over his knee.

"You the investigator?" I asked.

"Sheriff, son. Name's Roy Cummings. You can call me Sheriff Cummings." His bucktooth grin looked more like a grimace, and the yellow tobacco stains on his teeth didn't make him look any more appealing. He extended a hand to me and I shook it to be polite. He held my hand a little longer than comfortable and grumbled, "Rough hands. Must be a farmer's kid."

"I was raised on a corn field, sure enough."

He let go and just stared at me a while. Without even looking at the file in his lap, he asked, "Eustace Kelly?"

I clenched my jaw, but nodded.

"Your folks down in Karns have been worried sick about you. They say you ran away two weeks ago."

"They ain't my folks. And I'm eighteen—I can go where I want to."

The sheriff sighed and leaned back in his chair. "They treat you poorly?"

I shook my head. "They's good to me, sir."

"You eloping?"

My cheeks burned as I glanced at Ma. I'd taken her hand without realizing, and I didn't want to let go. "No sir. She's… she's my sister."

He nodded slowly. "If I didn't know my biology, I'd say you two looked like identical twins." He leaned forward just a little and opened the folder, thumbing through papers. I didn't know what the file was, but I suspected it contained some details on our stay overnight here at the hospital. "How'd you end up in here with those cuts, and her without a stitch of clothing?"

"It's a long story."

"I'd like to hear it." This was stupid. I shouldn't even be sitting here having this conversation with anybody.

"What's her name?"

"Uh…" I blinked, realizing for the first time that I had never known Ma's name. I wondered if she knew her name either, anymore. Not that I would want to give the sheriff her real name anyway.

The hesitation wasn't missed. Sheriff Cummings looked up. "I'm sorry, say again?"

"He don't know my name," Ma mumbled.

The sheriff laughed. "So the girl speaks after all? Guess she ain't mute *and* dumb."

I jumped to my feet, ready to smack the condescending leer from the man's face when Ma pulled back on the hand she still held. Reluctantly I sank back into my seat, glaring at him instead. "You here to help us, sir?" I asked as politely and bluntly as I could.

"I want to. Problem is, you don't have a sister, Eustace. Not that anybody knows of. And if I can't figure out who your girlfriend is, I'm gonna have to take her into custody until somebody claims her."

"What if nobody claims her?"

"And why would nobody claim her?"

"He found me in the mine," said Ma.

I looked at her, eyes wide.

"My name... it's Cassie-Jo Lyons. You know me, don't you, Roy?"

Sheriff Cummings stared at her a moment. He looked about ready to laugh again, but he frowned and leaned in closer to us, took off his glasses. "You ain't Cassie-Jo. It's not possible."

"I ain't dead." She reached out with the hand that wasn't holding mine and squeezed his shoulder. I sensed her fighting to break free of the inhibiting ethereal chaos in her head that no machine on earth could detect. "Look at me real close. I know I ain't right in the head no more, and I don't look right neither. But you gotta listen. This here is my son."

Sheriff Cummings uttered a nervous, high-pitched laugh, then coughed. She wasn't just telling him, I knew. She was showing him, opening up his mind and letting a little bit of that chaos bleed through so he'd have no more doubts.

"I know you feel bad about me, Sheriff Cummings. You know something's down in my papa's old mine. Something dangerous. If you want to put things right, you gotta let us go, and you can't let my papa know I got out."

In the morning, she smelled like that cheap no-name motel soap they give you for free. The whole world pretty much stank, but nothing on her ever did.

My foster mother wouldn't be able to make it into Thistleville until today, so she'd booked a room for this girl and me at the only halfway decent motel in town and told me to stay put until she got there. Our room had two beds, but Ma—Cassie-Jo—let me curl up next to her to sleep, she under the covers and me above them. She wore scrubs and underwear the hospital had been kind enough to let her keep, and I wore a pair of old shorts with a shirt from my backpack that hadn't been ripped to shreds. Since my one pair of jeans was still soaked in slime, I'd be wearing my pajamas till I washed them.

It had been a long time since I'd been close enough to see Ma's dreams. Though she kept still, her dreams were rough, full of longing, guilt, and confusion about the deformed thing she'd just given birth to and left to be consumed by the Elder Thing. I was the one who abandoned the two-part body, but even the unconscious recesses of her brain didn't think to blame me. After all, she'd tried to gouge it out of her own womb to hasten its entry and perhaps even its demise, hoping to spare it the fate that forty-three others had already endured.

She didn't tell me how Sheriff Cummings knew her or what he'd done to wrong her in the past. She didn't tell me about her parents, about her papa. All she'd said was, "Don't go digging up skeletons in the backyard, Eustace. It'll drive you mad." The summer's heat began to creep in through the window along with morning's first light. At least the wimpy little AC unit in the room worked. She faced me, form coiled in a tight fetal position with her knees squeezed up nearly to her chin, hand curled against my chest. Don't know if the hand was there to reassure me she hadn't gone missing in the night, or to keep a little space between us.

I watched her breathing, struck once more at how beautiful and vulnerable she looked. She had the softest snore I'd ever heard. Ma's psyche exuded nothing but sweetness and sorrow. She still hurt real bad. She still wasn't sure she had much to survive for. But there wasn't a bitter cell in her body. Compassion that I'd never known before, her own compassion, burned within me. I knew that as long as I lived, no wolves or fallen fiends from unknown stars would ever hurt her again. I just wished I knew how to heal her and make her happy. Maybe I'd have to start with me.

Ma's dream twisted, and I heard a strange voice call to her in a language I didn't know that felt as old as darkness. The Elder Thing. He wanted her to return to the mine. She jerked her eyes open and clutched her stomach, body rigid, mouth agape as she sucked in strained, wheezy gasps.

I flipped on the nightstand lamp beside her and took her by the shoulders. "It's changing me," she huffed.

"What do you mean?"

"I don't know." She writhed and her gasps turned to sobs.

"How bad does it hurt?" She said nothing, just clenched her eyes shut.

"Do you want me to take you back to the hospital?"

She huffed, "Don't think they can... help... help me."

I scooped her up into my arms, took a seat on the edge of the bed, and cradled her head against my shoulder.

"I don't know what it wants. I'm so tired of... of... Why won't it just let me die?"

She settled down after a while, and I felt sick inside. All that nonsense I'd thought about keeping her safe from Pa, and I didn't know how the hell to keep him out of her head.

Ma's crazy smile appeared, though it looked a little more genuine this time. "It's the bones," she said. "He can't change our bones. They're solid. We're... we're too tough inside." She laughed at her own metaphor.

"Ain't he got bones too?"

"Yeah, something like bones. That's why I can't change him neither."

I picked up her left wrist and took a closer look at the cuff. It was a simple cylinder clamped flush against her skin, with thick rims and a texture more like polished stone than metal. It resembled the same material as the sleek pod he slept in when he wasn't hungry. The nearly invisible black symbols felt as dark as they looked. Some kind of energy exuded from it. Buzzing through her. Buzzing through me. This was the thing that connected us. And this thing was messing with her metabolism. It had frozen her in time, in a way, or in age. I swore in shock. "Ma, did he put this on you?" The answer I craved lay in that part of her mind that was blocked to me.

Her lip twitched the smile away. She sat up and brought her cuffed wrist closer to her face, trying to focus her eyes on it. "No," she whispered.

"Where'd you get this? Did your papa find it?"

She shook her head, refusing to answer.

"This is what the Elder Thing wants, Ma. I'll bet its been keeping him alive for millions of years, and he needs it to… to get out of there, er… I don't know what."

She lifted her gaze to my face, brows furrowed, eyes wide. "What're you thinking about, Eustace?"

"He ain't getting it back. Or you neither." It'd been a long time since my voice had cracked at anything this way. I brushed her curtain of blonde hair out of her sweaty face to make eye contact easier. "I could try to break that thing off you. I don't know what'll happen, but…"

"I'll die." Despite the distance in her words I knew she was certain of the outcome.

I swallowed and said, "I don't want you to suffer no more. Tell me what you want me to do and I'll do it."

Her unfocused eyes searched my face, and I looked away. I was so afraid she'd see my dread of losing her and ask me to return her to the mine. Maybe I was selfish, but I couldn't bear the thought of her screams, or the details of her pain echoing in my mind. We were quiet a long time. "I didn't know you was seeing everything that happened to me," she said. "That's why I sent you to live with people, so you wouldn't have to see so much. I'm so sorry, baby."

I shook my head. "None of this is your fault. He's got no right to hurt you. You understand?" I took a deep breath and blew out slowly, stoking my fingers through her hair.

"I only feel the change when I get too far away, or when I use my thoughts to hurt him," she said. "It don't happen if I stay with him, if I don't use the… the dark noisy stuff."

"You did something to him the other night so we could escape, didn't you?"

"Yes." Trembling, she extended her arm bearing the cuff to me. "I don't want to go back, and I don't want it to change me. Help me get it off?"

I nodded and took the hand in both of mine.

She squeezed my shoulder with her other hand and I looked into her eyes once more. "I think I've been keeping him in there somehow," she said. "If you try to break this thing off me and something goes wrong—if it kills me to take it off—he might get out and hurt people."

I believed her. Maybe I was about to kill my mother and set this monster loose on this world, a world that wasn't fully mine, either. The weight of what I was about to do—and what could not then be undone—sank my facade of apathy and pride to the pit of my stomach. The fiend would kill me if it could, and I'd have to face him alone, without Ma's voice or her protection. I'd have to find a way to get him before he got me.

"I love you, baby. Know that I'll always love you." She kissed my cheek, then squeezed her eyes shut, bracing for pain.

I took another deep breath and closed my eyes, sending a tendril of my thoughts into her arm. I wrapped my will around and through that strange cuff to try and discern it, disrupt it, break the constant connection I'd always had to my Ma's mind. It had melded to her flesh, to her life-force. I pried at it, wedging the power of my own life-force in between and making the connection weaker.

The peculiar elements in the cuff hummed, provoking the things that lay deep and dormant within me beyond my human nature. A chill rippled across my skin and a wave of nausea squeezed bile into my throat, but I held back the molt. How long I could keep it back, I didn't know. The cosmic energy I diverted from the transformation was strong, ripping into me like a raging river current while it bled away from her.

Ma shrieked. I pulled her head to my shoulder, cupping my hand over her mouth to muffle her cry. She struggled in my arms. I reached into her mind and found this wasn't an ordinary pain I could simply numb away. This strange energy I tore at had become so intrinsic to Ma's existence I'd have to permanently muddle up her thoughts to stop it, or else cut her off and watch her shrivel in agony.

The voice of the Elder Thing called. He may not have known laughter like I did, but I sensed his twisted mirth and felt him reach across my mother's life force directly to me. He was helping me wrench the life out of her, and promised he would do the same to me. He would regain all that he had lost, he said, and would repair the damage to his broken vessel and broken body with an infusion of my hybrid essence to rise once more to rule the stars. My blood would run black with his curse, he swore, and my resistance to the change would make it thick and sweet enough to rejoin him fully with that force from which his unfortunate fall to our Earth had severed him. His hold on my will was fierce, draining me of my grip on the world like a spider draining a fly of its innards.

I thrust Ma from my arms and fell out of the chair, scrambling as far away from her as I possibly could to drive the Elder Thing's voice from my being. The connection broke, and I lay on my stomach, dry-heaving. The chill in my flesh wouldn't leave. I squeezed my eyes shut, willing myself not to lose control of the terrible thing that slept inside me. I didn't molt, but it took a long moment to calm myself and return to equilibrium.

What a fool I was. That cuff turned its host into an energy conduit, one limited just enough so that it wouldn't drive her insane. He could only leech so much from a crushed mind, and nothing from a dead one. A living mind, however, would continue to feed him a little at a time. Even then it might not be enough to nurse himself back to health. For that, he'd created his bastard offspring, hybrids with an augmented tolerance and connection to cosmic power.

But Ma had been more than a host to a cosmic parasite. She'd been a shield, standing between my natural energy and the thing that wanted to suck my living aura dry to give itself a kind of transfusion so it could regenerate. And now, because I'd wedged my thoughts right into his soul-sucking cuff, he'd managed to draw enough energy through me to break through some ethereal barrier that would have starved him dry if he'd left the mine. How had such a creature managed to injure himself so badly, let alone survive by hibernating millions of years since that coal bed was laid down, waiting for the perfect host to come along? And who or what had trapped him behind a cosmic forcefield? He hadn't siphoned enough energy from me to regenerate, though, and I knew with deepest horror that he was coming for us to finish the process. For me.

"I f—feel it too," Ma stuttered. She lay curled on her side where I'd dropped her, body shaking uncontrollably like she had just emerged from an unexpected plunge into an icy lake.

Shit. I wanted to leave town, lead the alien away into the hills and then hightail it outside his range again. But the further we got from the alien pod, the more violent Ma's "changing" attacks would become. "We have to... warn people..." I gasped and forced myself to my feet, then pulled Ma up after me.

I stumbled down the road ahead of an impending rainstorm, clenching Ma's hand in mine. The sky was half thick with clouds, allowing scattered rays of light through here and there. The temperature of the air had cooled, muggy though it was. When we reached the police station, I burst straight into reception. Sheriff Cummings knew something about the thing in the mine, and as much as I disliked him, he had the authority to immediately evacuate the town before that thing came round the mountain. I knew Ma was scared about what I was up to, but I assured her I wasn't going to look into anybody's mind without asking and she made no protest.

Inside I froze. The station was dead empty except for two people at the front counter. Sheriff Cummings spoke to a tall, lean man in his sixties with black slacks and a black-and-white checkered shirt trying not to look like a picnic blanket, long sleeves rolled up to his elbows. A faded cowboy hat sat atop thin, greasy white hair pulled back in a ponytail. He turned to examine us, a pair of muddy green eyes narrowing as they scanned us down and up. Dammit, this was him. I sensed it. Cassie's papa, my grandpa.

The corners of his mouth twitched into a slight grin. In a voice low and crisp like burnt honey he said, "That you, Cassie-Jo?"

An airy squeak escaped her. Her hand shook in mine. I squeezed her fingers so tight I had to be hurting her, but I didn't dare relax my grip and let her slip away from me in a panic.

Sheriff Cummings shifted his weight with his hands on his hips and looked at his shoes, smacking his Nicorette gum.

"And you must be Eustace 'John Doe' Kelly." The old man walked around us in a slow circle. I felt his eyes on me in a way that made my skin crawl. When he came round to face me again, he stuck out a rough-looking hand. "Earl Lyons. Chief executive of the Thistleville Mining District."

I glared at him a long time, refusing to take his hand. "Cassie-Jo don't wanna talk to you none, sir. What did you do to her?"

"What makes you think I did something to her?"

I didn't bother answering. Maybe it was the wolfish gleam in his eye. Or the fact that he knew my full name, or that he wasn't shocked to see her unchanged in nineteen years.

He retracted his hand and folded his arms, stroking the closely trimmed beard as he narrowed his eyes on me. "You're a bit of a troublemaker, ain't you, boy? Seems you've had a few run-ins for schoolyard fights, broken windows, violent threats, stealing…" He leaned closer and closer to me until his dill-pickle breath blew right in my face. "Unless you want to add kidnapping the disabled daughter I just learned I had to your juvie, I suggest you let her come with me and be on your way back to Tennessee."

I glanced at Sheriff Cummings. He watched us now, but he showed no intent to intervene on Ma's or my behalf.

"What do you want her for?" I asked.

"That's none of your concern." He had murder in his eyes. Learning why he hated Ma so much would take prying into his mind that I'd already promised her I wouldn't do.

"I pulled her out of that mine."

"For that, I thank you kindly."

"Tell me about that thing living in your old mine."

"What makes you think—?"

"There's a lot of coal in that mine," I said. "A lot of other stuff, too—artifacts. I'll bet it's worth a lot of money."

He flared his nostrils and stepped back, pacing in front of us. He was pissed, all right. And he didn't know nothing about me. He somehow hadn't noticed the resemblance that had been so obvious to the sheriff. He thought I was just another troubled boy who happened to come through town.

I looked at him serious. "You have a bit of a problem, and I'd like to help you out. I like hunting, see. An alien corpse like that'd make a nice trophy. Unless, of course, you'd like it incinerated to make the old creeper leave the town's consciousness alone for good. In that case…" I let my eyes flicker to Ma, then back to Sheriff Cummings and Mr. Lyons. "I just wanna get this slave bracelet thing off her wrist and elope."

The old man's eyes fell to my hand holding Ma's, where the cuff remained clamped on her skin. His grin widened and the twinkle returned to his eye. That lie about hunting resonated just a little too well with him, and I knew Ma and I were in for some serious shit. We had to run, but I needed to know what the universe wouldn't tell me straightforward about my Pa—how to kill him—and I had to save the town first. "Well well well, Sheriff, what do we know about the alien in the mine? This here kid wants to kill it for us." Mr. Lyons whipped out a pistol and pointed it at my chest. "I think he knows a little bit too much. What do you think?"

"You ain't gonna off your own boy right here in my office now, are you?" Sheriff Cummings settled his weight onto one leg, gum smacking, hands still on his hips as he spoke.

Mr. Lyons said, "What the hell are you talking about?"

"Take a good look at him, Earl. I bet if you took a paternity test right now, you'd come up positive."

"What're you saying, Roy? You think I...?" He laughed again, a hearty, gut-busting laugh that made veins pop out on his neck. "Well, I'll be damned! Lock him up. I'll deal with him after I've got that 'slave bracelet' someplace—"

Ma's fist flew up and caught Earl Lyons square in the crook of his throat. The movement was so sharp and swift I jumped. He gagged. Ma slipped from my grasp, screaming and slapping at the gun. It exploded. A cold burn seared up and down some nerve in my arm and I screamed, clutching a bloody hole that went clean through my bicep. She wrenched the gun away from the old man, pointed it at him. Panting. Eyes wide. Jaw clenched tight.

The sick old bastard put his hands up and smiled at her. Laughed at her. "You gonna shoot me, sweetheart? You gonna run away with our baby and make some more babies? I hear if you inbreed enough, they come out face-less."

"Shut up, Earl. Take an easy, Cassie-Jo." Sheriff Cummings had his own gun drawn, trained on Ma. His eyes went wide as he glanced to me. "What the hell?"

Too late, I realized I'd begun to molt. Watery mucus dripped off my skin as it changed texture and darkened to a rich blue hue. This time I welcomed the appearance of my claws and tentacled jowls. If either one of those sleaze-bags got close enough to touch me, or Ma, I'd scramble their brains up good.

Earl's nasty grin vanished, and he backed away slowly to stand by the sher-iff's side. The two men could sense the deeper shift of atmosphere in the room, the incongruity of my nature with the reality they knew. They glanced at each other, then back at us, like they'd both felt that kind of dissonance before.

"You ain't his only daddy, Pa," Ma said in that weirdly distant, almost listless voice. She smiled back and tried to laugh, except her lips quivered too much and she choked instead. In confirmation, three panels of florescent bulbs in the ceiling above us flickered with energetic interference.

I wanted her to shoot the two men, douse them in something foul-smelling and flammable, and burn the whole damn exploitation-of-justice office to the ground.

"Please don't make me do that," Ma whispered aloud, gun hand shaking. I didn't think I could make her do anything, not without touching her, but I was angry and foul enough in my head for her to see and sense it all clearly. "Please just let us go, Sheriff Cummings. You don't have to kill us. We won't tell no one about the alien in the mine. Or the others, neither."

Sheriff Cummings gave that nervous, squeaky laugh back when he decided Cassie-Jo wasn't lying about her identity. He lowered his gun.

"What are you doing?" Earl growled.

"I'm tired of covering your ass just to cover my own. You helped me off my ex-wife. I helped when you offed yours. The fire in Hell's been burning hotter and hotter with each body I've helped you add to keep things quiet around here about what's in that damned mine. Now the demon's come to get us, don't you see?" He laughed again, a manic, panic-stricken warble that wouldn't end.

Earl grabbed the sheriff's gun hand. "Just shoot them!"

Ma kept Earl's gun pointed at the brawling men. I took Ma's hand and she gasped. I wasn't sure if her reaction came from the slime or the energy. I tried to pull her with me, but she wouldn't budge. "Come on," I growled.

Sheriff Cummings finally pushed Earl away, stuck the muzzle of the gun inside his own mouth and pulled the trigger. Blood sprayed the silver-sheen desk, and his body fell backwards to thud against the bone-yellow floor tiles.

Ma dropped the gun from her hand, and I didn't take the time to retrieve it before we both turned and bolted out into the morning storm.

Warm rain beat down on us, and thunder rumbled beyond the hills surrounding the town. The stitches in my chest burned and oozed. I knew those wounds were bleeding again. The slime-saturated bandages slid off me, falling out from under my shirt as I ran. My legs burned from pumping them so hard, so fast, and I could barely hear anything except the throb and rush of blood in my ears.

We were almost to the motel when a bullet thudded into the back of Ma's ribs. She fell hard to her knees almost at the motel's front stoop. I tried to pull her back to her feet, but she hurt too bad.

"Eustace!"

I snapped my head around and saw a stout little lady, four-foot-eight, with a bob of bottle-blonde hair showing gray roots. Good Lord, it was Margot Polyston, the woman who'd raised me on a troubled boys farm down in Karns for eight of my twelve years in foster care. She stood in the threshold of the open door to the room where Ma and I had slept the night.

She whistled and screamed at me with one hand cupped around her mouth, the other clutching a rifle, "Get your ass in here quick!"

I wrapped my arm around Ma's waist and pulled her up, forcing her to run with me to the welcoming reprieve of the dank little room.

Margot cocked the rifle and aimed it at the old man. "Stop right there! Why're you shooting at these kids? Hey! I asked you a question! Where do you think you're going?"

I couldn't hear Earl's reply, if he gave one. I took Ma into the bathroom to get her as far away as I could manage from the window and the gun in Earl's hand. I let her sink to the floor, propped up against the wall. She choked and spluttered, coughing up blood. She clutched the front of her left side while a chocolate-brown spot seeped into the back of her hospital scrubs.

Margot slammed the room door shut and I heard two bolts click into place. Her footsteps stomped back to us. "How bad is she hit?"

"Bad," I called back. "She hurts real bad."

Ma's eyes were wide, her face streaked with tears, blood dribbling down her chin as she continued to cough and gulp air, one shocking breath at a time.

Margot cursed. I turned my head to see her standing outside the bathroom with her phone pressed to her ear.

"Who you calling?" I asked.

"Ambulance and the police."

"Wait—"

"Now's no time to worry about your molting. She's bleeding to death."

"That old man chased us out of the police station. He and the sheriff were going to kidnap us, right before the sheriff shot himself."

Margot's eyes widened. "What?"

"You can't trust the police in this town to stop that cuss, and you don't need to call an ambulance." I gestured to Cassie-Jo. "She's different. If you just give us a minute, she'll be fine."

Margot stared hard at me. She looked at her phone and dialed a different number before turning away to watch out the window, rifle in hand.

I took both of Ma's hands in mine and whispered, "You want me to hold it off until it heals?"

She nodded, and I did my thing. I went into her mind where she processed physical sensations, where it hurt, and numbed the pain. She didn't quit wheezing, but her body relaxed, her eyelids drooped in that half-conscious stupor that was her norm. I moved one hand to her shoulder to keep her from slumping over on her side. It took about thirty seconds for her punctured lung to reinflate, and two minutes more before I heard the clink of metal on linoleum as her body expelled the bullet.

Margot's anxious growl rumbled in the background. She'd gotten through to somebody on the phone, and her tone was fierce and animated. Then she cursed. Then silence.

When the hole in Ma's skin and insides was nearly closed, I pulled out of her thoughts as far as I could and let go. Her mind remained blank a moment, and I was terrified I'd broken her until I heard her thoughts whispering to themselves again.

I picked the crumpled bullet off the floor and looked it over in my palm before tossing it in the garbage.

Margot had returned to check on us. She stared at me, brows furrowed. "What you do to fix her?"

"It wasn't me." I held up Ma's arm to show off the strange cuff. "It's this thing. Came from the aliens." I let Ma's arm fall back in her lap and refrained from touching her so she could return to the few senses she had undisturbed. "Ambulance coming?"

"Couldn't get through. I called Bryan at home long enough to explain that some crazy fella shot at you and hit the girl that was with you, then I got cut off. It's like somebody's using a signal jammer." Phone out of sight, she waved her arm, sighed, and put her hand on her hip. "Eustace, what the hell is going on?"

"You won't believe me."

"Try me."

I took a deep breath. "This here is Cassie-Jo. She's my Ma. She's been stuck in the mine with my Pa—the alien—a long time. Or at least I thought he, it, was…" I finally had the time to process what Earl Lyons and Roy Cummings had said. And I'd thought the world I lived in couldn't get any more shocking. My mind reeled, numb. Ma had never had another boy. I knew because her mind had cried out to me every time that futile cycle of birthing, expulsion, and re-insemination had come to a peak. Her ill-fated spawn with the Elder Thing had always been female. Until now I'd chalked it up to statistics. It had never occurred to me I'd begun life with a complete template of human genes.

"That man chasing us," I said. "His name's Earl Lyons. He's Cassie-Jo's papa. I just found out he's my papa too, at least in part."

"I think Eustace is a… chimera," Ma whispered. "I think that's what they'd call that sort of thing. Don't know for sure, though."

Margot cocked an eyebrow, but her eyes were too wide, nostrils flaring too much to look skeptical. Her expression was more a kind of mixed sympathy, gut-felt knowing, and disbelief. She'd dealt with a lot of crazy family shit from kids she took care of, though I was probably the craziest. She knew things about me, knew there were things even I didn't know how to explain. "This the girl you kept saying was in your head?"

I nodded.

Margot nodded slowly in return. "You came here to get her out."

"Nah." I glanced at Ma, then back up at Margot. "You remember Bryan ended up in the hospital with a seizure last time I got mad. You know it weren't natural. He came out all right, no brain damage or anything serious. But…" I swallowed and rubbed my palms on my knees. I hated apologizing for something I wasn't sure I'd done. But I knew I'd hurt Margot worse if I tried to deny the terrible power of the thing inside me I couldn't always control, the thing that had gotten stronger and stronger over the years. "I didn't mean to hurt him. I don't want to hurt you two, leastways. You've been fair to me, taught me how to survive shit, how to get along with people and feel good about working hard."

The bathroom light flickered. Margot looked up at it, then let her gaze fall back on me. "Think I know what's jamming my phone signal." She sighed and looked hard at Cassie-Jo. "You affecting her too? She doesn't look quite…"

"All there?" I shrugged and looked at Ma. "The alien's affecting her worse. It's the cuff, see. It…" I didn't know how to explain exactly what it did. Wasn't sure how well I could sense and comprehend everything about it if I tried. I shook my head.

"The man you say shot himself," said Margot, face tight. "You make him do it?"

"I wasn't touching him."

"That ain't what I asked."

I took a deep breath. "I don't know. Wasn't trying to."

Margot turned away, pressing her fist to her mouth. The silence stretched on long enough I knew my guardian hurt as much as she was shocked and bewildered. She was afraid. Afraid for us. Afraid of us. "What am I supposed to do with you, Eustace Kelly? I came out here to talk some sense into you and bring you home. But this..." She waved her hand in the air once more. I reckoned she wanted to say it was too much, but she didn't.

Ma's eyes widened suddenly, and I heard the language of the Elder Thing calling in her head. I cursed and reached for her hand, then pulled my hand back and bit my knuckles, letting my facial tentacles weave and sucker around my fist.

Margot took a reflexive step toward us. "What's happening?"

I put my hand up to back her off. "The alien in the mine wants its cuff back. He's weak and needs the energy to leave the darkness, but he hasn't been able to break her mind in whatever way he needs."

"Seems like a mighty powerful creature." Margot dropped her voice to a whisper as though it made her question a little more discreet. "Why hasn't it killed her?"

"I don't know," I whispered back.

Ma gasped, "He's changing me!" She slid to her side and began convulsing on the floor.

Margot began, "What...?"

"I don't know what it means," I said.

The pale blue hue of Ma's skin deepened to the color of blueberries in a matter of seconds. That's what my skin looked like right before I slimed my-self, what it looked like now. "Holy shit, I think she's trying to molt."

Three calm raps at the door made Margot and me both jump. Cursing, she re-cocked the rifle and crept back toward the front of the room. She looked through the peephole, then slowly unbolted the door and left the chain in the top lock. "I'm armed," she called. "What do you want with these kids?"

"I'm Earl Lyons. The girl's my disabled daughter."

"If she's your daughter, how come you shot her?"

"I was aiming for the boy. He's trying to kidnap her. I just want to take my girl to the hospital and turn the boy over to the authorities."

I left Ma to her distress and poked my head out past the bathroom door frame. Margot glanced back at me a second before returning her face to the stranger. "I'm the boy's guardian. He's not going anywhere until the police get here."

"Let me take my daughter, please. I can hear her crying."

"I don't think that's a good idea," said Margot. "She's stable for now. I called the front desk and told them to get an ambulance. They should get here soon."

"Hospital's just down the street."

"Maybe you could go tell them to hurry it up."

"I ain't going nowhere until you folks give me back my daughter."

"We'll all just have to wait, then."

"Fine."

Margot closed and bolted the door. She picked up the receiver for the room phone and hit buttons on it, trying to dial out. She cursed, and I knew the connection was either lousy or nonexistent.

I turned back to Ma and took her hand. She was so scared. Something was happening inside her, something I couldn't see.

"Make it stop," she gasped.

"I can't." I didn't want to mess with her head any more than I already had today.

"Please, help me."

"What do you want me to do?"

She answered me with sobs. I sensed a part of her still just wanted the power in the cuff to release her so she could finally die a natural death, so she didn't have to put up with the crazy, endless, unchanging ungrowth her life had been since she'd been stuck with it. Another little part of her wanted to hope for a normal life again, wanted to live, and grow, and think without all the noise of an incomprehensible universe slowing her down. She wanted to feel safe. To feel loved.

I gripped her shoulders gently with my clawed fingers and leaned in close, pushing my lips to her wailing mouth. Her mouth promptly closed, pressing our lips together. At first I felt a twinge of cold dread in the pit of my stomach. In fairytales, kisses could cure poison. In movies, kisses could distract the good guys from pain and the bad guys from carrying out their nefarious plans.

I knew this wasn't a fairytale or a movie. This was my Ma. My Ma, whose life was very messed up, and who didn't need another reason to feel con-fused, to hate me or hate herself. I just wanted her to feel good. To feel loved. To feel like she wasn't alone in the cruel experiment of nature that had changed us from what we were meant to be and made us both into something grotesque. However time and space had managed to rob her of progress and hold her in perpetual stasis, she was still just a seventeen-year-old girl, and maybe always would be.

She tried to say my name. I tried to say, "I love you." I knew she heard me in her thoughts. Our lips moved together, and over each other. I'd never kissed before, and I was awful embarrassed at how sloppy I was. Her hand lighted on the back of my neck, and her thumb trembled as it stroked the hair behind my ear, back and forth. Electric chills and heat prickled down my spine. I could tell she hadn't kissed before neither, and she liked this. I let my-self relax on top of her, let my tentacled jowls caress and kiss the skin of her face and throat as they traced the contours of her cheeks, chin, nose, and ears.

"Eustace Kelly!"

I rolled off Cassie-Jo with a start and banged my head on one of the legs of the counter holding up the bathroom sink. I clutched the throbbing spot on my head, half-groaning, half-laughing as I scrambled to sit up. Judging by the unrelenting tightness in her face and narrowed eyes, Margot wasn't amused. I stopped laughing and cleared my throat. "I think her pain's gone now, or whatever it was."

Cassie-Jo stared up at the ceiling with an almost wistful expression, eyes a little brighter than they had been. She smiled. A real smile.

I opened my mouth to warn Margot she should leave us here, leave town without us before the Elder Thing got here. "Margot—"

The walls of the building shuddered, and the sharp pop of bricks and glass exploding made Margot and me both jolt. I jumped to my feet and stuck my head out of the bathroom. The now-crumpled front half of Margot's silver Ford F-150 stuck through the far wall where the window and door had once been, pushing the two queen-sized beds together and displacing the table a good five feet.

An arm with a colorless picnic blanket for a sleeve squeezed a bullet from his gun out the driver-side window. I pulled my head back in the bathroom and Margot ducked the opposite direction into the shallow closet space as the bullet thunked into the drywall between us.

"Shut the door and lock it!" She raised the rifle and fired two return rounds, shattering more glass.

I obeyed, slamming the bathroom door behind me and hitting the loose thumb lock I knew was useless. I took a step back, trying to think as more shots exploded in the room behind the door.

"It was me," Cassie-Jo said quietly.

"What was you?"

"I didn't think he'd kill himself. I just wanted him to stop and let us go, like I said at the hospital."

Margot growled, her voice muffled. Struggling.

I closed my eyes and licked out with my mind and my energy to find Earl's.

"Eustace, don't." Cassie-Jo's voice was so soft I barely heard her.

"He's gonna kill her, kill all of us," I growled back. I saw him in my mind, boiled down to a neon collection of particles in space and time. He wrestled my foster mother down while clamping an ether-soaked cloth to her face. When Margot stopped struggling, he let her slump to the floor. He picked up her rifle and pointed it at her head.

My stomach churned as my mind slithered into the nerves in Earl's skin, and I perceived his every sensation from the suppressed ache in his old knees, to the thumping of his heart, to the cold thrill of his frustration, rage, and fear. He feared being found out. He feared losing us and the secrets we knew about the mine to a world he only cared to exploit as much as he could make it bleed. He'd murdered many a man and woman, even before the mine. Some he killed in terrible, perverse ways. I couldn't see it all because his calculated fury at Margot's interference was so damn loud and hot.

I pumped my energy into him with the intent of subverting every rational thought in his mind until he couldn't remember his own name, let alone say it.

Nothing happened.

I felt his lips pull apart in a sneer as though they were my own. He laughed aloud, though I heard him in my head louder and clearer. "You wouldn't kill your own papa, would you, Eustace?" I squeezed my mental fist again, harder, and the connection snapped. Searing pain ripped through every nerve in my body and I fell on the floor between Cassie-Jo's feet and the toilet, writhing and shrieking in pure agony I'd never known before.

The eldritch tendrils of energy I'd put out folded back in on me. Reality and meaning were ripped from my mind, and I felt a maddening compulsion to claw my own eyes out and lobotomize myself. I wanted to numb myself to the things in the darkness of space I could not comprehend that I was being forced to comprehend. My fragile identity as a living thing with a rational form and delusions of indivisible qualities began to dissolve. I wasn't simply a tiny speck swirling by chance in the cold heart of space, I was a soulless blob of matter and energy bound to be liquefied and re-constituted in a near-endless variety of futile forms until the universe collapsed back in on itself or flung itself so far apart everything stopped cycling and moving altogether.

Cassie-Jo sat me up and wrapped her arms around me, pinning my clawed hands to my chest to keep them away from my eyes and rocking me as I continued to scream. I remembered her hiding me from the Elder Thing in little crevices of the coal-lined pit, suckling me, feeding me bugs and the occasional bat or bird that drifted inside until I was six years old. She never ate anything, but I was always hungry. Neither one of us had a stitch of clothing to share, and we were always sticky, cold, and covered in coal soot. She'd figured out that the Elder Thing hibernated good and deep right after it impregnated her, so she finally got the courage to leave the mine and take me into the closest town so I'd have a family to live with. Then she disappeared back into that hell hole to keep the monster amused, or satisfied, or whatever she thought it needed so it wouldn't hurt other people. To keep the cuff from doing whatever it did to her when she stayed away too long.

I heard Margot's rifle pop and knew Earl had finished her. He'd come for us next. I couldn't move, couldn't make my mouth form words. All I could do was weep and flail. Drool rolled down my chin.

"Maybe I'm not as smart as you, but I think it's a lie," Cassie-Jo said in that calm, distant voice as she rocked me like the babe I once was to her. "I'm scared, Eustace. I don't want to be something else. I want to be me. I don't want that thing to change me, but I know it's too late. But maybe if I let it happen, if I let all the change come, I'll still be me somehow, someway. Then we'll both know it's a lie, something the aliens use to drive us crazy and nothing more when they want things they can't have."

She pressed her clammy palm to my forehead, and I felt the chaos drain out of me. The pain in my head and its caustic effects on my body slowly faded. I felt heavy as lead in Cassie-Jo's arms, and twice as dumb. But her love for me buzzed through me, filling the void my own energy had ripped in my thoughts.

I'd never thought my being born was a good thing, or at least, that it had any kind of purpose. Now I wanted to believe I was born so Cassie-Jo wouldn't be alone. So she'd have a chance. It was ridiculous, preposterous. Just my short-sighted, human teenage hormones or whatever. But I felt she and I belonged together. I gave her a reason to keep living, and she gave me a reason to care, a purpose in fighting for our identities rather than letting us both get swallowed up by the dark. Because our circumstances weren't natural, Cassie-Jo and I were on the same level. We were the same species, becoming the same species, inside and out. If we faced the entropy of our lives together, we might just survive all this crazy shit and find some peace.

I heard the bathroom door shudder.

"I'm sorry," she whispered, her voice weak and rattled by the pain she had absorbed and managed to dissipate somehow. "I have to go now, baby, so Papa don't hurt you." Her lips kissed my forehead, and her embrace fell away as I sank once more into the abyss of unconsciousness and uncertainty.

My tentacles and bumpy skin were still expressed when I woke up. The cuts in my chest had healed over, though, so I clawed the sutures out. I found a couple of bullets lying next to me. Guess Earl shot me in the head for good measure. I'd never healed like this before, not like Ma did—like Cassie-Jo. Her healing touch must've helped me after she'd gone.

I opened the bathroom door to see red and blue lights washing over the walls and Margot's truck through the broken window. The room was dark, and light was fading from the sky outside. I'd been out a long time.

Margot's petite feet in fancy purple Chacos stuck out between the nearest bed and the wall separating the bathroom from the rest of the room. I couldn't stand to look at her, lying in gore with a bullet hole in her skull somewhere. Her death was my fault. I didn't want to face it, couldn't deal with it right now.

I didn't know why the fiend hadn't found me after so many hours, or why no one else had moved the car. I wrapped a couple of towels around my hands to protect them from the broken glass and climbed out between the truck and the window. I was poised to run away before the emergency people could catch me, but I saw that Margot's truck wasn't the only thing wrong in the little town.

A dead police officer lay cuffed to the wheel of his car, head slumped forward, with blood dripping off his dark hair. Two other police cars were empty, lights spinning, with no sign of where their operators went.

Smoke from fires on distant streets showed that the motel wasn't the only site of madness and violence, although it may have been its epicenter. People screamed and ran to and fro, some clawing at their heads and faces like something had gotten inside them that needed digging out. A woman walked down the street stark naked, covered in blood and gore, carrying a man's severed head and two smaller ones by the hair in one hand and a woodcutting axe in the other while she shrieked obscenities and gibberish. Then I realized it wasn't gibberish at all. She was trying to articulate the language of the Elder Thing.

I tried calling out for Cassie-Jo in my mind, but she didn't answer. The Elder Thing answered instead. A huge, moist paw seized my throat from behind, gouging the nape of my neck with its many-clawed fingers. It hoisted me off my feet and slammed me down on the cement so hard it knocked the wind from my lungs. My skin crawled with the icy throb of eldritch energy licking out from his aura. The Elder Thing made me sick to be alive, confused to have conscious thoughts, ashamed to believe that anything about my puny existence mattered or endured.

This was the first time I'd really seen what he looked like. In the twilight his skin was milky and grayish, slicker and crustier than mine appeared now. A long, thick beard of tentacles knotted on itself in betrayal of his exertion where it hung off his skull. A massive bat-like wing, or a pair, flapped and crumpled against his back in a way that made him look like a displaced aquatic dragon. Emotionless eyes the color of egg yolks peered at me and through me, directing his power into my mind, my being, and my very flesh. And he was damaged. He was a bipedal creature that had been reduced to slithering on his hands and belly instead of stalking upright.

"I only wish to be whole, to return to the stars," he whispered to my mind in that strange, old tongue. "Do not fear for your mother. No harm will come to her. She has been returned to me and will soon be made to bear me another fodderling in your place. Go now, and I will spare you."

"What happens to her when you become whole?" I asked in my mind. "What'll happen when you don't need her to feed you her babies no more?"

"The change will take her, and I will make her my queen."

"You ain't a good liar."

He squeezed my throat, and squeezed the tendrils of his will that he'd woven thick around my mind. "Your exploits and your thoughts have revealed to me the great error in my methods, and it pleases me that you may spread elsewhere the seed of the Old Ones that lies within you. But if you interfere again, I will suck away your life force to rejuvenate myself. Leave this place, and never return."

He released my throat and his harrowing presence withdrew from my thoughts. I rolled on my side, vomiting on the asphalt. Using his forelimbs and undulating the muscles of his torso, the fiend who had half-sired me dragged his shriveled hind limbs and tail in a labored side-to-side roll, like a snake, down the street until he disappeared into the untamed foliage where civilization ended.

Slime oozed from my pores. I gripped the waistband of my shorts to keep them from sliding off and forced myself to stand. I didn't know if I believed that the Elder Thing would spare Cassie-Jo like he'd said when he got what he wanted. Hell, I didn't know if he'd spare Earth. But all I'd been able to offer the woman I loved was a slow, agonizing death in answer to her pleas for relief. I'd been as cruel to her as he was. I'd known all along what I needed to do to set her free, but I'd been too afraid to face it. As long as that fiend lived, she didn't stand a chance. If I truly wanted to end her suffering, I'd have to kill him before he could regenerate, before he could kill her, or change her... whatever that meant. If I wanted it to end before he ravaged her again, I had to go now.

My thoughts called to her once more, "Cassie-Jo, where are you? Where'd they take you? Are you back at the mine?" I needed her. But she wasn't there. Her thoughts had withdrawn, and I couldn't feel her.

I found the naked lady in a pool of her own blood behind the gas station across the street, eyes and mouth wide open in a grin of terror. She'd fallen on her own axe. The heads of the man and two children she'd carried lay strewn next to her. She reminded me of my own Ma in the worst way, and I couldn't decide whose fate had been the lesser evil. I slid the unknown woman's eyelids closed and whispered, "I did this. I let the monster out of that mine. I'm sorry." I couldn't quite bring myself to promise I'd put things right again. It was too late for her and her loved ones.

The power struggle between my human and alien natures had always been bigger than me. But it had taken Margot's death and the destruction of this whole town for me to accept that I couldn't keep the seed of chaos within me from robbing others of their life and their peace of mind. The Elder Thing wanted me to spread that chaos. I vowed to myself that after I killed him, his destruction would die with me. I wouldn't procreate, and I'd spend the rest of my life helping my Ma cope with her muddled existence. If she found some peace, I might be able to live with myself. My stomach knotted with disgust and anguish as I twisted the axe free from the dead woman's abdomen to take with me.

The asphalt petered out into trees, and the small town faded behind me into the dark, wild hills of Appalachia. Twilight cast the woods in deep shadow, and everything seemed too loud to my senses. Insects blared. The nitrogenous stench of plant rot overpowered the sweeter scent of wildflowers, pine, and bleeding maples. Gritty soil bit into the strange skin of my feet through my shoes as I climbed.

The Elder Thing had left a trail of slime that gave off that fishy paint-thinner smell. I followed that trail, not even trying for stealth. He'd sense me with his aura if I got anywhere close to him. Sudden pain burst through my skull and spine before I could even see him. I stumbled to a halt, fighting to keep on my feet. His darkness squeezed me, seducing me to drop the axe and turn back, to embrace the freedom he'd offered me. But I no longer feared my own destruction. I feared for my mother, and for the world I'd betray if I shrank back from this fiend anymore.

He gurgled his final warning aloud. Then the foliage rippled with his movements and I heard the wet crackle of his skin as he continued to drag himself away. I remained paralyzed, shrieking my frustration after him.

I shut my eyes and squeezed at the Elder Thing's ethereal tendrils with my own. Another shock of pain seared through me. The axe slipped from my grasp and I stumbled sideways, wrapping both arms around a tree to keep myself from falling. Despite his physical injuries and whatever had severed him from the cosmic ichor he needed to survive, my own power was no match for his. How had Cassie-Jo managed to use his own power against him, to hurt him so we could escape the other night?

Earl had done it to me too, I realized, when I seeped into his thoughts and he'd turned my own crushing will back on me. Had the fiend given him some device like Cassie-Jo's cuff, something that protected him from the chaos? It seemed absurd. I hadn't seen any cuff on him, and the Elder Thing was too vulnerable to grant some mere vermin a power that could be used against him in any way.

I withdrew my tendrils and let the Elder Thing's will meld into my own. It was a gamble. If I lost my mind I wouldn't be able to stop him.

A terrifying sensation swelled around me, as if the earth shifted beneath my feet and I sank into an ocean of tar, cumbered, forgotten. The forest became a writhing jungle of black worms in my vision, snaking around me, stretching me, squeezing me, biting at my senses in jarring waves of heat and cold, light and dark. I let the vision envelop me. The pain ceased. The ground turned solid beneath me once more, and the black worms once more became leafy shrubs and trees silhouetted amid the orange light of the sinking sun beyond the hills.

The Elder Thing called me to come to him, his will tugging at me like marionette strings. I pulled away from the tree I had leaned against. After taking three steps forward I stopped myself. With a shiver of astonishment I took a step back. Then another. His thoughts jerked at my own, but just as I had been unable to crush him he was now unable to crush or control me. It seemed whatever the Elder Thing and my human parents shared in common, they couldn't pry far into each other's minds when they were calm and focused without taking a licking. If my prediction was correct, the fiercer and deeper we sank our vices into one another, or into a nearby entity that couldn't defend itself, the harsher the recoil when the defender interfered and those tendrils snapped. And snap them I did. With a cool, deliberate lurch of thought I withdrew from the fiend's grasp, and the weight of his aura lifted from my limbs.

Weary from the struggle, I swept up the axe—when had I dropped it?—and rushed toward his burbling roars of fury. He was a dark mass in the darkening forest. I swung the axe down where he might have a spine, hoping to paralyze him by degrees until I found his head and hacked it off his shoulders. The blade stuck fast in his flesh. I wrenched at it, but he flung me away and I slid on my back, plowing twigs and soil. I rolled and pushed myself up to my knees, then ducked as the axe whizzed over my head and its blade flashed out of sight.

His form groaned and struggled in the darkness. "You are magnificent," he whispered in my mind. "But you are weak. You fear the change, as all things do."

I glanced over my shoulder to search for the axe. The rope I'd stolen and used for a belt had come off, so I gathered the waistband of my slimed shorts once more and scrambled to my feet. I found the axe head, broken clean off the handle near the rocky outcropping it had hit..

The Elder Thing's flesh scraped the ground as he dragged himself toward me. I left the axe blade and ran on. If I got Cassie-Jo out and kept her away from him long enough, it might buy us some time to figure out how to manipulate that cuff against him. Maybe we could cut him off from her thoughts and her connection to the cosmos, starve him to death.

"Go on to the mine, my foolish spawn," he goaded. "Fate and I will meet you there."

"I don't believe in fate." The lie twisted at my heart, knowing how I'd felt after kissing my Ma. I withdrew my thoughts from the fiend's once more and ran on.

Trees grew thicker, the shadows darker and deeper as I came down and rounded the hill. The wooden skeleton of some old structure loomed over the mouth of the mine. I clambered past it and braced against the logs and rusted iron struts in the wall, gasping out like a dying man choking on his own spit. I knew she was inside. She had to be. If she wasn't, I'd be dead and she'd be trapped with him forever. "Cassie-Jo!"

I heard nothing except the moan of the breeze through the dirty tunnels.

"Ma, please be here! It's me, Eustace. I need… I need…" My shorts slid to my ankles and I fell forward into the dark. My face and knees slammed into rocks and grit, smarting my skin and bones. I rolled and writhed in the soot, fighting my mind and my body as my molt penetrated deeper than ever before, threatening to alter me in ways that might be irreversible. The energy had become so strong in this place, a kind of energy that conformed to it what it didn't destroy.

I didn't know what I was becoming, but I didn't want to lose my humanity. If I couldn't shift back, couldn't keep the energy inside, I couldn't return to civilization without destroying it. I couldn't touch Cassie-Jo or anyone else ever again. I'd be alone. Alone was not something humans had evolved to cope with. Alone would kill me—the two-thirds of me that could care. Now I knew what she was so afraid of when the Elder Thing called.

Something rapped me hard upside my head, sending a burst of pain through my skull and slashing my right eye. I screamed and clapped my clawed hands to my eye as hot fluid rolled down my face like tears. A second blow above the temple knocked me nearly unconscious. A hand clenched my hair and dragged me deeper into the darkness and the chaos. My shorts slipped off completely. I was too disoriented to fight back.

The hand hoisted me to my feet and its owner slammed me back against the iron struts in the wall. I gasped in shock and clutched at an iron pole jutting out between my ribs. I couldn't scream. Could barely breathe. Laughter echoed off the round walls, ghoulish and triumphant. "Well well well, if it ain't my little boy Eustace. I thought I killed you."

I jerked my body left and right, desperate to dislodge myself, to crawl off the pole. Earl's shoulder slammed me back again.

"It's nice of you to meet up with us here. I've gotten myself into a bit of a predicament, you see. The Old Thing wants me to knock her up again. Much as I'd like to, I ain't as young and perky as I used to be."

He punched me hard in the balls. My knees buckled and I curled over, dry-heaving. My flesh tore and my ribs cracked from bearing all my weight on the pole. I was scared shitless and I couldn't even cry out. This was it. I was born in this mine full of misery, and here I would die.

The sleazy old man caressed my head as I wept from agony and hysteria. "Don't be afraid, my boy. I'm doing you a mercy. It's not like you was gonna have any kind of a life among good normal folk with your tenties hanging out all the time." He yanked one of the tentacles expressed between by nose and upper lip, jerking my head and tweaking my neck at an awkward angle. I heard a clicking sound, like a knife flipping open. I wanted to lash out, try to claw at his eye or his hands. But I held back. Any attack I made wouldn't stop him, just make him madder and meaner. I couldn't see nothing. My gored eye still hurt like hell, and I kept the other one squeezed shut.

"Where's... Cassie-Jo?" I wheezed.

"Oh, she's here. She's just being a good girl, holding still and keeping her mouth shut like I told her to."

"What did you do?"

He chuckled. The blunt edge of a hunting knife scraped back and forth across the suckers on the tender underside of the tentacle. I tasted the iron tang of blood on the blade and knew without searching that it was hers. I winced but refused to plead with him to spare me pain or spare my dignity. He said, "There's a lot of mysteries hidden in the ground ordinary men wasn't meant to find. But I ain't ordinary. I know my place in the universe, and I knew about the technology and power of the Captured Ones long before I found me a live specimen. I heard his pathetic call. I dug him out. I made a deal with him. If I healed him, he'd serve me, like a genie in a bottle. But he tricked me. Suppose I knew he would."

I felt and tasted his musty breath hissing right in my face as he curled the tip of my captured tentacle between his fingers. "I took material from his damaged pod, his ball-and-chain, his Webowax—that's the name for it. I forged it into a brand-new, smaller Webowax, that slave bracelet thing, and I brought my daughter to him as an offering. But any new artifacts I forged to take command of his power wouldn't take the script because of one extra little symbol he added to her band. Oh, he told me I couldn't take control until after he'd restored his body and rejoined himself in full to the pulse of the universe, that it were the only way it worked. But I knew he was trying to escape his own bondage. So I trapped him in here by carving a few little symbols of my own into the walls of this mine that'd suck his energy away so fast his brains would shrivel up before he could shake a wing if he ever tried to leave. Thanks to you, though, he broke out of my trap. Fortunately, the little slave bracelet breaks easy enough, too, if you just cut it off from its host."

"Cassie…" I coughed, choking as my own blood rose in my throat and filled my mouth.

Earl spat in the darkness. "There's still a way I can fix this. I've already carved new command symbols into the band. Unfortunately for you, my boy, you're his one mistake, and his last desperate chance to reclaim that connection and regenerate. When he comes for you, I'll be waiting. The Old Thing will be my slave, and his power will be mine at last."

"It ain't as easy to control as you think," Cassie's voice called with its familiar quivering distance from the shadows. "It'll change you eventually, and you'll be alone. Alone with the ghosts like he was."

"Keep your mouth shut, bitch, or I'll cut your legs off next."

The familiar crackle of wet flesh on gravel, and the cold, electric prickle of the Elder Thing's energy sent a shockwave of panic through me. I wriggled, scraping my shoes against the ground and ripping fabric as I gripped Earl's shirt with one hand in a futile effort to pull myself forward off the pole.

He tore away from me, laughing full from his belly. "Come to me, Papa Mayhem. I'm—"

I heard a loud crunch, followed by his body thudding to the ground as he shrieked in pain. I opened my good eye to see him cradling his right knee while he shuffled toward the slight figure I made out as Cassie-Jo, knife swishing as he swung his fist through the air. I wrapped my thoughts around his once more, hating every inch of his vile carcass. Instead of snapping my connection like he had in the motel, he spun and waved his blade at me like he might throw it. He was in too much pain to throw me off.

She shoved into his back with her shoulder. He threw himself on top of her, pinning her throat with his arm and raising his blade. Something exploded inside me. I kept his raised hand from sinking the knife into her until he pulled himself off her and dropped it.

He crawled toward a black bag and unzipped it. He drew out the metal cuff fused tight to the flesh beneath the hand he'd cut from Cassie's arm. As he pried at the Webowax, he wheezed, mouth gaping open and closed in fury and astonishment. I relished watching the life quickly bleed out of him and his body growing still, and I thanked the careless stars that whatever power he had stolen wasn't deep enough to save him.

The wet crunch of the Elder Thing persisted. A softer sound drew my eye back to the darkness where Cassie-Jo's figure crawled toward me. She let her papa's gun slip from her hand and retrieved his knife, cutting away a length of skinny nylon rope around her waist that pinned her arms to her sides just above the elbows. A second knot of rope binding her ankles came off just as quickly. Her left forearm ended in a dark stump where her hand and wrist had once been. I couldn't see her face well, but I heard her breath quiver, weak, suffering some kind of torment I didn't understand that I suspected had something to do with being severed from the Webowax.

She used the pole slicked with my gore to climb to her feet. Without a word, she drew my arms around her shoulders and pulled at me until I walked myself off the poll. I collapsed on top of her. Instead of pushing me off, she kept her arms around me, entwined the fingers of her right hand in my hair and held on. "I'm so sorry," she whispered. "For everything."

I groaned and shook my head.

"I just want to go home to my mama," she whispered, "but I know she's gone. Papa killed her. I've got no one left but you." A sob caught in her throat. "I can't watch that thing do it one more time. Not you." She took several quavering breaths. "We can still stop him."

"How?" I croaked. I knew she was talking about the molt, or that change beyond the molt that neither one of us could return from if we gave in. But based on what Earl had said, I wasn't sure either one of us could survive much longer without the Webowax, let alone fight and kill the Elder Thing.

"I still have a choice," she said. "I know I'm shriveling up fast inside, but…"

The Elder Thing's burbling growl shuddered through me, and I caught a whiff of his fishy paint-like stench. I closed my good eye and clung to Cassie-Jo tight with both hands as the aura of impending doom squeezed in on me. "I warned you to go," his voice whispered in my head. "But you couldn't stay away. Now, you will die. Submit to my will, and your suffering will be short." The wet-smack of the creature older than the dinosaurs who had fallen to Earth from across some distant darkness drew toward us in a weary shimmy. He'd known Earl would be waiting for him, and he'd set us up to incapacitate each other before he returned.

I was afraid to die, and I knew Cassie-Jo was afraid to lose me to this fiend's appetite. She said, "If I go through with this, Eustace, it'll change us both."

"It's… your choice. Either way… I… love…" I couldn't say no more. All of my breath had escaped through the hole in my gut.

My mind screamed like I sank once more through some bottomless abyss, drowning, deafened with the roar of the cosmos, surrounded by blackness. I felt the chaos bend around us, felt the cold of the universe sink into me deep, and sucked in a full, pain-free breath in shock. I reared up and clutched my side as the sticky hole in my flesh sucked shut. The torn flesh of my eye sealed over like a scar mass. As if in answer, the eyelids of my good eye sealed themselves together too, and the seam melted from existence. Both the organs I'd once relied on to sense light and chase out my fear of the dark were liquefying. There was no pain, only a hot draining sensation, but the change horrified me. I screamed and rolled away from Cassie-Jo, thrashing and clawing frantically at my face.

Her hand clutched at my arm, nails digging into my flesh. Her screams and her horror of the change were just as frantic as mine. "Help me," her voice pleaded in my mind. I took her wrist to pry her fingers from my arm and interlaced the fingers of my hand in hers. Her skin was slick with slime and grew knotted like toad flesh in my grasp. Her nails grazed my knuckles as they lengthened and twisted into claws. My hair tore away from my scalp like a slimy carpet of grass and slumped into a pile beneath my head. My ears sank into my skull, leaving canals that attuned themselves to disturbances deeper than sound. The seam of my lips grew tight as it, too, began to shrink. My tongue stretched and forked into three separate wormlike tendrils inside my mouth, the attachments pulling deeper into my throat as if my tongues had become rubber bands. Two of the new tongues flickered out among my lengthening mane of tentacles. Where the tentacles continued to increase in chemical sensitivity, the rubbery tongues had numbed and become enlivened instead by the thick, inky character of unnatural energy in the air. A strange hunger enveloped me, an urgent thirst for the poison of the deep things.

The scientists say nature doesn't strive toward a perfect form by evolution or crude mimicry. But I was being birthed again, birthed into a form, the only form, that could eat the darkness and live forever. I knew now what the fiend feared, because he'd not faced the prospect of death for some time, back when he was whatever he was before he became a god. Gods like the thing I was becoming were nature's bastard slaves.

My throat contorted to turn my screams into a deep, wet, gurgling roar, damning me forevermore to utter none but the cursed speech of that dark force which conforms or destroys without mercy. A mass of wet, bristly flesh slammed into me, tearing my hand from Cassie-Jo's. The Elder Thing's claws tore at my thighs and stomach. I kicked back and lost my shredded shoes, blind and deaf to all but the forces older than light, heat, and matter that buzzed through every particle of my body. I scrambled back the way I'd come only to meet with the wet wall and another slashing strike to the head.

He snared my tentacles in his talons, and I roared as his other paw of needle-sharp claws plunged into the back of my neck and his own tentacles constricted around my throat. He wanted to twist my head off, willing me by his cosmic voice to submit to the pain of his invasions into my mind so he could leech the energy out of me when my sanity broke. He might succeed in terrifying me out of my mind if his claws managed to pierce my spine and paralyze me.

His weight bore me down on my stomach. I swiped to cut his tentacles and he thrust my arm back, nearly breaking it out of its socket. Cassie-Jo's aura wrapped around his, wrenching his crushing thoughts away from me with a burst of pain, and his supernormal screech rang through my head. His voice withdrew and his weight eased enough that I wormed out from under his grip. I lashed out with my claws and another set caught me by the wrist. "Don't hurt me," Cassie-Jo said in my head. "I'm trying to help."

"I can't see!"

The claws jerked away. I opened my mind and let my thoughts lick out all around me. The extrasensory feedback was vivid and staggering. I clutched my bald, leathery skull as a giddy sort of high wrenched reality wide open. There was so much beyond what my eyes could have ever seen. Light revealed so little of all that swirled and pulsed in that living blackness where my foe had been entombed for an eon that seemed so minuscule now. The past spread out flat, smooth, and featureless behind us like a cartoon horizon, while the future of things bore steadily toward us, crumpled, dense, and ever obscure until it hit us and unfolded as things do. The endlessness of time was incomprehensible to my human psyche, yet the full force of that actuality threatened to explode my will to exist like a firehose bursting down my puny mental esophagus.

She was there, fighting claw to claw and mind to mind with the fiend our human papa had unleashed upon us both in his twisted ambitions, the fiend who'd made us the unwilling victims of this sickly energy that was quickly ripping our humanity away from us. There was no other way to stop his wave of destruction, and no other way to survive but to let the dark elements take us, and that sinking sense of doom became something more everlasting and profane than death. Time had warned the fiend about the perils and futility of creating fodderlings to escape his demise. Time had groomed me to carry out its consequence, the full extent of which remained obscure to me.

A dull ache seized me deep in my bones, and I felt a thousand things pop at once. I was growing, twisting, my whole body distorting. The change accelerated. My ribs bulged and my shoulders sank, lengthening my torso and extending my neck several inches. My guts crawled around as they rearranged themselves, and my muscles slithered and swelled. My slime-saturated shirt grew constricting and I tore it away.

My arms and legs stretched. My fingers and toes elongated, and the flesh between them melted back, splaying the meaty digits wider. I yanked my hands to my chest and curled them against me in futile defiance when two extra fingers budded up between the fingers I already had and the breath of my paws expanded. My spine flexed, crackling and jarring me with strange chills as the bones there multiplied. A tail budded and snaked out past my feet, hardening and rippling with new muscle like the rest of me. A pair of feelers teased up from the fibers of my spine, worming around under my skin until they found their mark and sliced out of my back into a pair of wonderfully gruesome spines.

Fine, leathery webbing climbed across my many digits. The same sort fanned out across the hardened fibers of my spine, which had jointed and bulked with muscle so I could stretch them, flap them. I tasted chemicals and the inky energy together in a peculiar rush of something more sophisticated than sensation alone. The ease and grace with which I folded my new antennae/wings flush against my back nearly convinced me I'd become the dark god this hellish universe intended to make of me. I staggered to my doglike feet with webbed, taloned toes and threw myself at the fiend to tear him off

Cassie-Jo. My body felt powerful. I stood over ten feet high. My foe was closer to twelve feet in length from head to toe, and his limp tail put him at about fourteen feet in all, but he could only raise his torso about four feet off the ground in his present wormlike stance.

The wounds he'd inflicted in my flesh knitted together, leaving no trace. My skin thickened and crusted with dense little spines everywhere except for a varying line from my head to my thighs, and under my arms. Every movement I made felt like I was sheer brawn encased in rubber. But I was disoriented, and I battled the nausea of madness that came with losing so much of what I'd known and had been in so little time.

It startled me to discover a sensitive nerve network had materialized within the whole swath of skin across my fingers and palms when I reached for Cassie-Jo's arm to pull her away from her battle with the fiend. There was a bizarre sweetness to her skin, both energetic and material, that was utterly unlike the taste of sugar, and I shivered. She was cut up, fighting back her own revulsion and terror at what was happening to us. She couldn't scream either now, and her bones were going to crack any second. I knew she might lose her shit then, and the Elder Thing would have his way with her out of sheer spite if I couldn't buy us both a few minutes of reprieve. I pulled her after me, and we ran deeper into the mine, collapsing near the mouth of the pit that had once been my home and her prison.

It would be our prison forever afterward, I realized. The Webowax had warped the natural flow of cosmic energy coming out of the pod to make it more accessible to lesser, undamaged hosts. When Earl broke that connection so violently, much the way he had broken my thoughts out of his head, that energy had wrapped back in on itself. The energy had fled to cling to the bowels of the mine instead, turning it into one giant Webowax and reactivating the commands he had used to trap the Elder Thing. When Cassie-Jo drew on that energy to embrace the change, she unwittingly trapped us under its influence. I knew well the boundary where the anomaly of energy ended, where I'd fallen on my face in the soot and the old bastard had dragged me inside. The mine created us, and the mine would cut us off from our sustenance and from each other's thoughts if we ever left its confines. Further still, it would draw energy away from us back toward itself and leave us as desiccated corpses if we ever set foot outside again.

The terror of it, the whole gruesome picture of this dead end, was too much. A shockwave of pain ripped through my head. I clutched my skull and roared. I thought it was the crippled god tormenting me until my skull cracked in several places and my head expanded. Oh, the bliss when my emotions fell away from me like ash from burning wood. The energy older than matter and time itself would purge the last of my crude and superfluous morphology, right down to the genes, the atoms, and the subatomics. I fought the lightless stuff no more but accepted that I'd become one of its chosen clay. I'd been born to it in part, after all.

Everything inverted on itself. The irreparable pain of my warped condition filled me with exquisite satisfaction, and the pureness of my devastation and inconsolable terror cemented my stability and invulnerability. I was Papa Mayhem now, as Earl had put it. My skull bulged and broadened, fanning out into bony processes like a cuttlefish's. The little opening that remained of my shrunken lips closed completely, and the mad part of me reveled in the retraction of my nose and the dissolution of my teeth, palate, and jaw behind the sealed flesh that had once borne a face.

I couldn't breathe, and I learned I didn't need to anymore. I still had lungs, or something like lungs. These drew the stale gases trapped inside me back and forth in reflexive spasms until they quieted and fell dormant for a short time. The energy had freed me from my need for material sustenance. I no longer itched for breath, food, or water, except to indulge in the bodily experience of such consumption.

The musculature of my shifting skull drew my tentacled mane deeper into the cavity of my mouth, closer to my esophagus. Then the new jawless ring gummed and teethed until a hexagon of skin sank to meet it and the circle of emerging teeth cut a wide new hole. More constrictable rings of teeth formed a fleshy cone tube behind it. I salivated, chewing and sucking new air, and the corpulent nest of tentacles bobbed and smacked with a twisted sense of glee at the perfection of this hideous orifice.

I rose, physically blind and inwardly unable to blink, to face the thing I'd once trembled to call "Pa" as his withered aura and broken body slithered forth to decapitate and eat me, if it could.

"You should not exist!" his cosmic voice cried. "You are a paradox I created, and a paradox I must destroy or the natural balance of things will be forever altered. Surely you've sensed how out of place you are, both in your natural state, and in joining the Old Ones."

Ma made a strange vibration in my new senses that I took for a sort of sobbing as she wriggled and clawed the clothes off her own twisting form with the only hand she had. I raised my hands to the sooty ceiling and took command of the living Webowax, the mine, and my mind churned the words of the curse with which the dark heart of space had transformed me toward my foe.

I hunched down and gripped the Elder Thing by the throat. His cries of agony shrieked across my mind as I sucked away every last particle of the chaos from his form. At last he curled into a fetal ball before me, clutching his skull until his brain imploded and his aura scattered like dust into the writhing knot of energy thrumming through the tunnels. Later, I would eat his corpse.

I reached for Cassie-Jo's shoulder and joined her back to the flow, splitting the power to draw its sustenance between us. When, at last, I collapsed beside her, numb as ice, her hand licked out across my arm, searching for mine. I took her hand but we both pulled away with a start at the intensity of sensation. A thing as human and natural as holding hands had warped into something bizarre, intimate. It unsettled me, like we'd held onto something I didn't care to know about anymore because it contradicted what I'd become.

She did that sobbing thing again, and I reached for her, cautious to avoid her hand. Her skin was smoother than mine, knotted though it was, and its slime still bore that strange inner and outer sweetness that wasn't sweet. She brushed my face, fingers feathering over my mane of tentacles. I drew her hand in toward my strange lips and kissed the back of her knuckles with my mouth and suckers. I traced the contours of her broad, hairless skull, and she returned a cautious kiss to my hand with the shorter mane expressed about her own mouth. I pulled her to me in an embrace.

She still had breasts. It surprised me, considering all the deep changes we'd been through. I checked and found I still had all my parts, too, and they weren't like those of the thing I'd destroyed. I'll be damned, I thought. Then a part of me roared back in disturbed amusement the fact that I was already damned. Skin and bones aside, some of the most fundamental components of our humanity had remained unaltered by cosmic conformity.

Somewhere inside me I still knew lust, and beauty, and disgust, and I still knew it wasn't right to want Cassie-Jo, her being my Ma and all. I didn't want to hurt her. I wanted her to stop crying, to help me accept the hell of our fate for what it was and tell me it was going to be all right anyway. That meant some part of my head was still human, too, that some part of me still thought about things like the color of sunsets, and wars, and video games, and still cared. I laughed, if you could call that strange gurgling purr I made in my throat laughter.

That's when my skin receded back around the sockets in my skull and my eyes came back into existence. They weren't special. I thought they were use-less at first, because they saw only darkness where my mind saw the energy and Cassie-Jo, and the two dead bodies we'd added to countless others that had decayed into the now-living tunnels of the mine.

My new eyes soon perceived shapes, and they took in the young sliver of moonlight kissing the hills of Appalachian wilderness just beyond the thresh-old of these cursed tunnels. It hurt more than I could hope to describe in any tongue, old or human, knowing I'd never be able to bask in the light or warmth of day again. The frigid slime of deep space would ooze from me forever until the day something broke my connection to the dark elements and finally obliterated me like my two fathers. I could still feel after all, and I knew there was still one way I could bring Cassie-Jo a measure of peace.

She still wanted babies, babies that were whole, babies that weren't con-ceived to be eaten or destroyed. With control, we could have offspring more human than we'd been, with enough of the Elder Things in them to withstand the chaos in the cradle, who could leave this mine unharmed when they were grown. Immune. Natural. Free. This was the change the Elder Thing had feared, the paradox, the shift in cosmic balance time had warned him about. After us, there would be no more Deep Things, or Elder Things, or Captive Things.

My new eyes shed tears as I turned them on the girl in my arms. She

quaked against me with the shared knowledge of the endless, unnatural torment she'd elected to bring upon us in an effort to save me and stop the fiend
who would have destroyed us and others still. She would never grow old.
Neither would I. We were damned together. I wanted to love her so the two
of us could forget.

Her enlarged eyes met mine, looking far more cephalopoid than human.
But surrounding each rectangular pupil in the pale lick of moonlight that
graced us was a doe-brown iris, a familiar trace from a past form and a past
life we'd forsaken. Her gaze was no longer glazed and distant, but sharpened
and dark with the affliction of our understanding. They glistened with the
same tears, the same inverted terror and apprehension I knew.

"This ain't how things is supposed to be," she whispered in my mind in the
language of the damned. "You're my baby. Not... not..."

"We're gods now," I replied. "The rules is different for us, and it's too late
for us to turn back. Cassie-Jo, I think I always wanted to kiss you. You've become more magnificent a fiend than all the predators and parasites that do
what nature made them to do. You're the first and only She-Thing I'll ever
think to love. Will you marry me, the son who adores you and shares your
condemnation?"

She shook with that same purring laughter I'd made. I drew her strange
mouth toward mine and kissed a strange kiss, our tongues and tentacles
snaking around one another in a natural delight I'd thought the dark had
taken from us. I took her hand, and we took back our humanity in the only
way we still could.

BLOOD

STEVE DIAMOND

Her entrails still steamed in the cool March air. Franklin Mercer wiped his eyes for the thirteenth time since he had walked into the house with his bouquet of flowers.

The woman's name was Rebecca Mercer, and she was his wife.

Franklin pulled a pocket watch from his jeans and checked the time. Nearly two in the morning. Which meant it was officially their anniversary. Ten years.

Her beautiful red hair now lay thick with blood where it had pooled around her in a crimson halo from her cut throat. So much blood. Franklin wasn't any stranger to blood, but it still shocked him how much had escaped from his Rebecca.

When he'd walked into his home with the flowers, he'd hardly crossed the threshold when the smell assaulted him. Blood, yes, coppery and thick in the air, mixed with the indignities of death... but under it, the familiar smell of sulfur. Franklin knew that smell, an odor that spoke of old rites and summonings. He and his brothers had witnessed more than their fair share of "normal" atrocities in Vietnam, and then some. Most members of Franklin's family could see things. They could sense when the Elder Gods' own were near. Many had taken up the cloth in some form or another to warn humanity against the things of the night—things even the night was afraid of.

But not Franklin. And not his brothers.

What was the point of warning people when you had the means to send evil back down its hole?

Besides, Franklin knew that as terrible as the Elder Things were, human beings were just as capable of evil and selfishness. He knew he wasn't free of those failings either.

Franklin crossed the room to the kitchen table and sat down. He carefully placed on top of the table the flowers he'd cut from outside. His eyes were drying up; he was running out of tears. For a moment he was glad their children hadn't lived to see this. No child should see their mother in this state.

After a few deep breaths to steady his nerves, he pushed himself back to his feet and retrieved a sheet from their bedroom to drape over her. He paused only long enough to close her eyelids. Those green eyes had looked so terrified and shocked.

He went back to the room and opened the closet—he'd built the armoire himself, just like the rest of their home—and pushed aside the shoes on the floor of the closet. Using the small hole in the back, left corner, he pulled up the floor board to expose the false bottom. Snug in the recess was a box, the top inlaid with carved stars and runes.

Franklin pulled out the box and opened its lid. More stars and old, arcane symbols covered the inside surfaces. The only thing inside was a single Colt Peacemaker.

Franklin knew what would be coming his way, and there wasn't much time. Blood and sulfur always called the Old Ones and their minions.

He ran his fingers over the runes—ancient words from a dead language— carved into the grip of the Peacemaker and etched along the barrel. It could kill what normal guns couldn't. As he walked out of his home, he spared a glance to the shrouded form of his wife.

He'd go to Hell and back for Rebecca. Do anything for anyone or *anything* for her.

Franklin took one step outside his front door, pulled the lever back on his pistol, and fired it into the air. There weren't but five homes in the vicinity— all built by him just three years ago—and that gunshot would bring their occupants running. And they'd come armed. He expected no less of his brothers.

Franklin Mercer didn't have to wait long. His brother came—guns ready— into the clearing in which his home had been built. They each carried a pistol similar to his own, all passed down from the Lieutenant.

"Heard the shot, Franklin," Jeremiah said. He was the youngest of them, with dark hair that had no chance of ever being tamed.

"It does my heart good to know you still know the sound of this here gun." Franklin held up his pistol, then flipped open the cylinder to pull out the empty casing and replace it with a fresh one.

"What happened?" asked Henry, only eleven months Franklin's junior. Henry looked a bit like a bulldog. He'd been the only one of the brothers to inherit their father's looks.

Franklin gestured inside. "You'd best go see."

They knew better to question him. After all he had done to get them through the war, they accepted his words without a fuss.

Franklin waited outside as they all filed in silently. He didn't plan on going back in there himself until this was all finished.

Stephen came back out first, followed by his twin, Alan. They weren't much for talking, but Stephen put a hand on Franklin's shoulder. He didn't say a word. Didn't need to.

"Condolences," Alan said. He did most of the talking for the twins. His eyes were wet, and Franklin figured this was the first time he'd seen his brother weep. "Any idea who did it?"

"Oh, I think I have a general idea," Franklin answered.

Jeremiah and Henry followed the twins out. It was a few more minutes before Daniel walked out, his brow furrowed in concentration. Daniel was the smart one, the one that people had to be careful around because he never missed a trick.

"How much time we got?" Daniel asked.

Franklin pulled out his pocket watch and examined it in the moonlight. "Half-hour or so."

"I don't get it," Henry said. "Who'd want to kill Rebecca? And why?"

"That ain't the question," Jeremiah said. "Why are elderspawn involved? That's what we should all be asking."

"Indeed," Daniel agreed. "But now's not the time to ponder on it."

"And I don't intend waitin' here for the *things* to converge on us," Franklin said. "I plan a lot of death this morning."

"For Rebecca," Alan said. Stephen nodded his agreement.

"For Rebecca," Franklin echoed, looking each brother in the eye in turn. He had their attention, just like back in the war. If they did what he said, Franklin knew everything would be all right. "Here's what we are going to do."

"Should have stayed all together," Jeremiah said. He ran a hand futilely over his hair, then check the cylinder of his revolver for the fifth time.

"We don't know exactly what manner of creatures are being sent," Franklin said. "Hell, we ain't even sure which god is sending them."

"Which is why we should be together."

"If I were a snake-handlin' man," Franklin said, "I'd bet that by splitting up we divide the focus of whatever god had a hand in my Rebecca's death. Those Elder Gods don't really understand us humans. They underestimate us. They don't quite fathom how far we're willing to go for our kin. Believe me, this is the way it needs to be for Rebecca."

Jeremiah sighed and said, "You say so..."

"I do. Now keep your trap shut. I need to listen."

As they watched the woods, their breaths visible in the air, Franklin again ran his fingers over the etched runes on the barrel of his Peacemaker.

It had been passed down, generation to generation, from his namesake, Lieutenant Franklin Mercer, who served under General Lee in the Civil War. Franklin had taken this pistol with him to 'Nam, and had made good use of it against the things no one wanted to believe—or admit—existed in those jungles. He put it away the day he got home, hoping to never use it again. But here he was. He glanced at his brother, who eyes scanned the woods for foreign movement. The irony of the moniker of the pistol, matched with what he intended on doing with it, wasn't lost on him.

After a time, Franklin noticed the silence that had settled heavily on the woods. Absent were the sounds of wildlife, and even the rustling of leaves and branches. It reminded Franklin of those moments when the jungles of Vietnam would go absolutely still right before some monstrosity would literally tear some of his platoon in half.

The creature burst from the vegetation to their right. Franklin was knocked off his feet and into the air. His back slammed into a tree, the only thing that kept him from flying into the next county. When he regained his footing—thankfully his own revolver still firmly in his grip—he saw Jeremiah wrestling with the monster.

It was dog-shaped, but with massive claws and a mouth that opened all the way from snout to chest. Where its eyes should have been were clusters of small thrashing tentacles. Four barbed tails waived about, as if they were watching the creature's six.

One of Hastur's hounds. Just as Franklin had privately reckoned.

Jeremiah tried lifting his pistol, only to have it batted away. His eyes, wide and wild like a doomed rabbit, found Franklin's.

Franklin lifted his pistol, but already his brother and the hound were tangled together. He didn't have a clear shot.

The hound sank its teeth into Jeremiah's arm, then ripped it from its socket with a wet popping sound. Jeremiah's scream shattered what was left of the silence in the forest.

Franklin knew he only had a few more moments before the hound killed his brother. Then, in the briefest of moments, he saw an open shot. Franklin aimed and fired without thinking. The bullet from the enchanted Peacemaker punched through the leg of the hound, and then took Jeremiah in the chest.

The hound loosed an ear-shattering wail, then bounded away, leaving Franklin with the still form of his brother. Franklin stumbled to Jeremiah's side and fell to his knees. He pulled his brother's head into his lap and ran a hand over the unruly hair.

"I'm so sorry, Jeremiah," Franklin said to the body. "I never wanted it to be this way. I wanted us all to live. I wanted…"

In the distance, from the direction of Alan's home, came that soul-tearing howl. The hound was letting Franklin know where it was going next.

"Rest easy, brother." Franklin gently let his brother's head fall to the forest ground. "This ain't over yet."

Franklin could still remember the first time he'd laid eyes on Rebecca—then still wearing the last name Young. It was the second day of September, 1973, and the U.S. was officially done with Vietnam.

He'd been on his way home, still in uniform, with his five brothers—they'd managed to stick together and survive the war—when they'd passed her on a street in Atlanta, burdened with enough groceries to feed a platoon.

No hesitation. Franklin crossed the street to her side and offered to help her on her way home. Seemed like only yesterday that she had flashed that beauty of a smile his way and had gladly handed over a single, light bag. She had a reputation to maintain, she said.

He remembered Alan being the first of his brothers to really welcome her.

He and Rebecca had stayed close, like a natural brother and sister.

Rebecca would have hated seeing Alan the way Franklin now did. He'd been late getting to Alan's side, and the hound was already about its business.

Franklin ran as fast as he could, covering the distance to the house he'd helped the twin build. All his brothers' homes were the same distance from each other, but running the direct route at night through the woods held its own dangers. Alan was the younger of the twins by three minutes. When Franklin arrived, most of his brother's body—and the elderspawn feeding on him—was obscured by trees. The hound was tearing into Alan's stomach with wet crunching and chewing sounds.

His brother's mouth moved in silent screams, eyes staring wide up at the forest canopy. Alan's body jerked as the hound ripped entrails from his middle. He'd be dead soon, and the hound would devour him. Franklin's chest felt hollow. He raised his gun again, and aimed at the only clear shot he had.

Alan's head.

He would not let his brother suffer needlessly.

Franklin squeezed the trigger and felt the revolver buck in his grip. The round caught his brother in the right temple, killing him instantly and ending his pain.

The hound bayed again and fled, its direction easy enough to guess. Franklin knew the other twin, Stephen, stood no better chance against Hastur's spawn.

"I'll come back and give you a proper rest," he said to Alan's still form. Yes, Rebecca would have hated this sight. "You haven't died for nothin', I swear on my Rebecca's soul."

He actually arrived at Stephen's home before the hound. Stephen wasn't the smartest of the brothers, and he'd left his lights on. Franklin knew it was because the brother likely thought he could see better this way. The fool had been dipping into his own shine too often. Now anyone could see him with far more clarity than Stephen himself could see out with.

How many times had Rebecca chided Stephen, telling him to be more responsible? Telling him to give up those habits and find himself a woman? To educate himself? Stephen hadn't said but a couple of words to her, but those couple of words were more than he spoke to anyone else. He could tell Rebecca's advice came from a place of love.

Now she was gone, and Stephen didn't have much time left of his own.

He was still alive, though, and that was a small blessing. The hound couldn't be far off. Hastur's minion was following a pattern, taking each of the brothers in turn with a method. It was a method Franklin understood, and likewise understood his role in.

Franklin heard a huffing sound to his right.

There stood the hound, yellow ichor draining from the hole Franklin had put in its leg. Where it dripped to the ground, steam rose and the fallen foliage wilted and crumbled to dust.

It looked from Franklin to the illuminated windows, then back again. The hound lifted is head and howled into the night. The sound scraped across Franklin's nerves, and almost immediately he saw his brother's silhouette as he came to the window to look outside for the source of the noise.

The hound again looked at Franklin, huffing again with impatience.

Franklin sighed. This was the only way he could bring Rebecca back.

He raised his rune-etched Peacemaker, aimed for Stephen's head, then fired.

Rebecca had had long, thick, red hair and the greenest eyes. It was love at first sight. They'd married as soon as they'd been able, and moved outside of Atlanta where they could get away from everyone but family and like-minded individuals. Where they could hunt or grow their own food. Make their own liquor. Stay away from the attentions of a government none of them cared for.

Franklin's mind kept coming back to his wife. He tried focusing on the more immediate concern: his brother, Henry. The problem was that each of his brothers reminded him of his Rebecca in a different way. She'd brought out the best in all of them.

"Franklin? Hey, you listenin'?"

He blinked hard, forcing himself to see the present rather than the past... or the future, depending.

"Sorry, Henry. It's been a dark night for our family."

"Heard shots. What happened?"

Franklin shook his head, his Peacemaker help loosely in his right hand. "One of Hastur's hounds got 'em."

"*All* of 'em?"

"Jeremiah and the twins."

"So it's just you, me, and Daniel left?"

"'Fraid not." Franklin lifted his pistol. This wasn't the path he had wanted to take, but for his Rebecca, this was the only choice.

Henry's eyes widened for a brief instant before the first round hit him in the chest. The next went through his left eye and erupted out the back of his head in a geyser of brain, blood and bone. Like a puppet with its strings cut, Franklin's brother collapsed to the floor, his blood spreading out in in a small lake around him on the generic linoleum of the kitchen floor.

Franklin walked to the front door of Henry's home and pulled it open, then went back to the kitchen to sit down. Within a few minutes the hound entered the house. It walked straight to his brother's corpse and began lapping at the pooling blood.

This was all part of the ceremony, Franklin knew, but that didn't mean he had to enjoy it. He averted his gaze, though the sounds of the elderspawn drinking couldn't be as easily avoided.

Henry's table was nice. People thought him unintelligent because of the Confederate flag tattoo on his left shoulder, or because he spoke poorly when he managed to put together more than a few words. It was true, to an extent. Henry wasn't the best at expressing himself with his limited vocabulary. But he had no peer when expressing himself through carpentry. Franklin ran a hand over the smooth surface of the kitchen table. Henry had made it himself, and had made one for Rebecca as a wedding present. It was one of her favorite possessions in this world. Now all that talent was gone.

But for a reason, Franklin told himself. *For the best of reasons*.

The hound finished its drinking and left the house.

Only one more left.

Franklin knocked on Daniel's door.

"It's open," came the words from inside.

Franklin pulled the handle down and went inside. The home was dark, and it held an air of resignation. Of bitter acceptance.

"It was you."

Not a question, but a statement filled with sadness.

"How'd you reason it out, Daniel?"

"I hadn't *totally* reasoned it all out 'til you just now confirmed it. Still don't get why."

Ah, Daniel, so damned clever. The thought actually brought a fleeting smile to Franklin's lips.

"You was always the smartest of us," Franklin said. "Rebecca always said so. Warned me so."

"Maybe. But I'm not the one who fooled his brothers into thinking someone else had killed your Rebecca. I assume the few shots I heard weren't directed at whatever was summoned, but at our brothers?"

Throughout the exchange, Franklin hadn't been able to pinpoint his last, living brother's location. His eyes still hadn't fully adjusted to the utter darkness in the home, so rather than walk around like a blind fool, he decided to hold firm in the middle of the entry room.

"They are all gone," Franklin said.

Behind him, the hound entered the house through the open door. It paused in the small square of moonlight that shined in through the doorway, sniffing the air. Its horrid visage turned to the left and stared there.

"Ah. One of Hastur's," Daniel said. "So you made a deal of some sort. What was it you asked for? What was it you killed your wife for, then all your brothers? What did the Unspeakable One promise you in return for your deeds?"

"Daniel, for all your intelligence, sometimes you just don't see what's actually happenin' in front of you." The hound growled, deep and feral. Franklin stepped in front of it, between it and the sound of his brother's voice.

"What you mean?" Daniel's voice was unsure, and Franklin knew how much it had to gall his brother not to know everything.

"You have it all sideways. I'm doing this *for* Rebecca. As much as I love you, and the others... I can't bear to be without her."

"Then why'd you cut her throat?"

"Daniel, she was already dying. She was diagnosed with cancer a few years ago. Right before I built all your homes. Terminal. Five years, tops. It's a miracle she lived long as she did."

"But... but she never..."

"What?" Franklin asked, angry now. "Never stopped and whined about it to yerself? Rebecca wasn't a whiner. She didn't want none of that chemo garbage, neither. If she was gonna go, she wanted to go without the supposed 'cure' makin' her feel worse that the thing killin' her. Her choice. That's why I built your houses for you. Picked perfect land for them."

"Our... homes?"

"You never noted they was sittin' in the shape of a pentagram? Thought you would have. Was worried about it, although with the trees in between it's hard to see right-off. I found a rite, Daniel. An *old* one. To bring her back. To bring her back forever. Wish I would have known about it when our kids passed."

"You needed our blood."

"I do, brother. I'm sorry, I truly am. But I need Rebecca back. I ain't nothing without her. With her help, I prepared the rite to bargain with Hastur. Then I cut her throat with my own hand. I laid her down on that floor, then I went out and cut a bouquet of her favorite wildflowers for her."

"Then you killed us all. I'm the last."

"You're the last."

"I could fight you, you know."

Franklin looked down at the hound that was now impatiently pawing at the floor. The time to finish the rite was slipping away.

"Yeah," Franklin said. "You could."

There was a long sigh, then the sound of a match being struck, followed by the blooming light of an oil lamp. "Does the blood need to be split unwillingly?"

"I... don't think it matters, brother."

"All right." Daniel set the lamp down, then dropped his own revolver to the floor. "Believe it or not, Franklin, I understand. I really do. So get it done with."

Daniel closed his eyes.

Tears streamed down Franklin's cheeks. Not of sadness, but of happiness.

"Thank you, Daniel. She'll live forever because of your blood. Yours and theirs."

Franklin, for the last time, lifted his gun and fired.

Franklin followed the hound back to his wife's dead form. The sacrifice required to bring her back was steep, and he knew he'd miss his brother's terrible-like, just like he missed his children. But seeing Rebecca alive would prove that his brothers weren't gone for nothing.

The hound padded into his home, then looked alternately between the bloodstained sheet covering his wife's body, and Franklin himself.

He bent down and pulled the sheet away.

Rebecca was so pale, and her skin looked like wax. With so much of her blood gone, he could see more of the yellow, diseased tint to her skin than before.

The hound moved forward and began licking Rebecca's face. It paused to make a hacking sound, then ran its tongue over the ragged wound on her throat. Wherever it licked, it coated the skin in blood.

The blood of my brothers, Franklin realized.

The hound licked every inch of exposed skin, then went over all the areas again, completely coating his dead wife in the blood of the sacrifices.

Suddenly the beast shuddered, then collapsed on top of Rebecca's corpse. It lay there, unmoving, for several minutes. When Franklin had finally worked up the courage to get closer to see, Hastur's minion had begun to *melt*. The process was slow at first, then quickened with each of Franklin's hammering heartbeats.

Within a minute, the beast was gone, leaving behind a yellow mess that covered his wife.

That was when he noticed that the wound on his wife's neck was gone.

Then her chest moved. Once. Twice. Three times.

Rebecca sat up with a gasp.

Franklin leapt to her side, and pulled her to his chest, weeping.

"You brought me back," she said. Her voice was dry and soft. It was the most beautiful sound Franklin had ever heard. "It worked."

"It worked," he said, kissing the top of her head, heedless of the filth covering her from the hound's tongue and from itself. "I had to kill them all, Rebecca. I had to kill them all for you. And I'd do it again."

"Franklin?"

He looked down into her eyes, glowing a putrid yellow. The yellow of corruption and decay. Then the color was gone, and her bright green eyes stared back at him.

"We can bring them back," she said.

"Who?"

"All of them. Alan, Jeremiah, Stephen, Henry and Daniel. We can bring them back. Hastur showed me how. Franklin, we can bring our *children* back. *Forever.*"

"How? Tell me how. Anything you want. As long as you're with me."

"It will take more sacrifice."

"How much more?"

Rebecca smiled.

"Everyone."

OSTLER WALLOW

Nathan Shumate

I aint had the dream abowt the corners for long years. I didnt no I misst it. Wen I first had it over and over, way back in the bigining, the corners fritened me so bad I almost left the wallow and wats here. But now I no that the corner cuttin into you is the only way corners can embrace you.

The first I heard that the old bastard was dead, I was down at Roy Sadley's store on a Tuesday morning; on top of the normal things Beth had sent me for, I needed a new mattock blade, as I'd sharpened the old one down to a nubbin I could shave with. Roy Sadley saw me come in, and the first thing he said was, "Phineas, your grandpap's passed on."

At first I thought he meant my grandfather Grandin, my mother's father—he's the only one I ever thought of as "my grandpap"—but that good man had already been been seven years in the Lutheran churchyard in Timoree. But Roy just went on.

"It was my Jude that found him," he said. "We hadn't seen Ephraim for a few weeks past when he said he'd be in, and I had stuff for him, so I sent Jude to truck it up to him in the Wallow, and that's how he found him in the cabin."

Ephraim. So that would be Ephraim Joel Ostler, my pap's pap. I didn't really know how Roy expected me to react, so I just shrugged.

"All gotta go sometime," I said, just to be saying something.

"True 'bout most people," Roy agreed, "though I ain't sure I figured it applied to Ephraim. He's still up there—Jude just barely got back, and he didn't know what to do—so I guess you'll want to go up there for him?"

I said, "Why?"

That took Roy back a step, and his bad eye rolled in surprise. "Well, he is your own blood kin—"

"I only set eyes on the old bastard three times in my life, and never spoke a word to him ever. I'm guessing if there's someone who wants to take the effort to gather him and put him 'neath the dirt, they're welcome to. I've got other things to do."

Roy was so shocked that both his eyes looked straight at me, up and down. "You listen here, Phineas," he said in a rough voice, "I don't say you gotta make up and like him now that he's passed, but there's some family responsibilities you gotta take as the eldest, the man of the family. Obligations, even, no matter love nor hate."

"So let my cousin Walter deal with it," I said. "He's older than me."

Roy looked at me like I'd started speaking in tongues. "The oldest *Ostler*," he said in a voice like you'd speak to an idiot child. "Walter can help with the funeral and the like, heck yes, but he's a McKinnon. You're the last Ostler, and that means something."

I didn't like the look in either of Roy's eyes, so I glanced around the store to give myself a break from them. Sadley's is a comfortably shadowy old store, with windows hazed over with dust and smoke so that sunlight coming through softens and blurs all around. There were a couple of old-timers by the small stove with the coffeepot, playing cards with a deck that I knew for a fact was missing the three of hearts. They kept their eyes on their cards and played right ahead, but I could tell all the same that they were both listening to Roy and me. Sadley's hadn't had a working radio since a tube blew in October, so there was nothing else to listen to.

"Fine," I said. "I need sugar and coffee and a new mattock blade, and ring up an extra dime so I can use your phone to call Walter anyway."

Roy's face softened, and his bad eye went back to looking at whatever it wanted to. "Ain't no need of that, Phineas," he said. "You go right ahead and make the call."

Sometims I feel like I got a therd eye in the back of my hed that dosnt see all the normal stuff that the Ssun shows becus it dont need lite to see by. It can see by the glow of the Edjes that are all around us, fillin the distans bitween all the things. The eye aint alwaz in back of my hed, somtimes its too the side or rite up top, but becus it dosnt see with lite it dosnt go blind with the Sun. And somtimes I dont no were it is, but it sees down, strate down, to all the things I love, and it sees so much it openss my Mouth and lets out all it sees in words and notwords til I got no breth left.

Most families around these parts have their own mountain or hill. When I say "have," I don't mean that they've got title to it, with fancy pieces of paper and something written in a book down at the county courthouse away in St. Stephen. Those families have been up here since before there was any county courthouse, or any St. Stephen, and we own what we own because we own it, not because a paper says.

Like I said, most families got a mountain or something. The Ostlers, we've got the Wallow.

It's away west off the land we live on, right in the crotch made between Blair Mountain and the Godfrey Ridge, a low spot where the rain runs down and makes a huge soggy puddle with inlet and no outlet, always in damp shadow because the sun don't shine there except right at midday. It's like our own little swamp in the hills, with plenty of frogs but no fish because there's no way for them to have gotten there. In the middle of the Wallow is a hump of black rock with moss growing up all sides, and on top of the rock is the hunting cabin put there by my great-great-great-grandfather Ostler.

That's where old Ephraim Ostler, my grandpap, had lived since the night that he killed my grandmother and got driven out of the house—the same house I live in now—by my pap, Eliazar Joel Ostler, when he was all of thirteen years old.

I think I heared its Name in my dream last night, but it wasnt ear-hearin, I only heared it with somethin deep in the senter of my head, a part that almost doesnt no how to hear because it hasnt heared for so long, for ages and ages back throu Fathers and Sons. But I heared it with that somethin in my head, I heared its Name or mabe only part of it becose it felt like its hole Name wouda bin too big for my head to hold it in at onct. And becose it warnt ear-hearin, its nothin I can say with my maoth, but thats okay becose I dont think its somethin I have a right to say. Names is presious, and even the little bit I got is presious, and I am to keep it safe and presious.

Walter had a telephone in his house, and his wife Clara picked it up after two rings. Walter had grown up here in the hills but Aunt Rose had let him go away for school when he was fourteen, and he never really came back. He'd gone off to the war—he was in the Pacific, though he never saw any fighting —then went to university and came out a Doctor of Divinity. Now he lived down in St. Stephen and was the pastor of a Methodist church. Clara said he was out and she'd have him ring me back as soon as he got in, but I knew Beth would be wondering where I'd got off to if I stayed down at Sadley's too long, so I told Clara the main points about old Ephraim's being dead—main points being all that I knew myself—and told him to call back and talk to Roy if he wanted to help me clean him out the cabin in the next couple of days.

Roy was listening, and as I hung up, he said, "Don't you think you oughtta go up there right away and collect him?"

While I'd been putting the call through, Roy had pulled everything on my shopping list to the front counter. I hoisted the bags up and balanced them on my hip.

"He'd dead already," I said. "A day or two ain't gonna make him any more or less dead, is it?" I pushed out the door without waiting for an answer. From what I'd been taught by my pap, anything short of leaving the old bastard to turn to bones by himself in the Wallow was more than he deserved.

The mushroms are bitter this spring. I dont know if that means thers somethin els in the Water, or mabe there was too littl snow and more flaver comes from Underneth. I dont mind the bitter. Its a good bitter. Somtimes bitter can be sweet if your tung is reddy to change. And the Frogs are getting meaty alrady.

My pap never actually told me about that night, when the old bastard had killed my grandmother Hannah right in front of him and Aunt Rose, or about why no punishment ever caught up with old Ephraim—even out here in the hills, where you can grow to an adult without ever once seeing a police uniform, there's still law, whether it's government law or our own law. I once asked Aunt Rose about it—that was back before Walter left for school, when we still played and hunted together and help each other with big chores—but she said that she had only been nine, and things were a little hazy in her memory.

"This is really your pap's place to tell you, not mine," she said, "but what I really remember from that night was his voice. It was so loud—not just shouting like they were having an argument—it's like he was a preacher, praying or preaching clear for the back rows. I don't know what he said, I didn't know what it was even back then, but he bellowed like it was something he'd practiced, and then he grabbed my mama's head. And then..."

Aunt Rose cocked her head in memory. I'd heard my pap describe her as "a slip of a girl" when he'd become the man of the house, but since then she'd plumped up, especially on her hips, so she looked like a sagging pear sitting there in her favorite chair.

"...And then," she said, her eyes looking past me into the past, "he grabbed her head on both sides, and just... he squeezed, maybe. I don't know what he did. But her eyes, they just..." Her voice trailed off. "And then he smiled. Like he was so proud. He smiled at me, but mostly at Eli. Your pap."

She shook herself then and put her eyes back on me, like she just realized who she was telling these details to. And that was all we ever talked about it.

Off to Sadleys today with deer skins to trade. Need more salt and a new pikax.

It was the middle of the next morning, while I was trying to replace a fencepost at the corner of the sheep's pen uphill from our house, that I heard a car horn and found Walter pulling up to the front porch.

Walter was dressed like he'd never even been to the hills before, much less came from here. His shoes were in two colors of leather, he wore a jacket and tie, and his hat looked like it had never seen a raindrop. He wore the same round eyeglasses he'd been wearing ever since he came home from school the first time. I don't think he needed them to see, I think he just wanted everyone to know he could read.

"Good morning, Phineas!" he hollered with a wave. I waved back with the hammer in my hand and went back to pounding the nail down to hold the barbed wire looped around the post. The country in the hills was too hilly for much farming—most people had a little family garden plot and nothing else—and the downhill ends of pastures were always bearing the brunt of snow and rain, and pulling the fences over to let sheep out.

At least Walter wasn't over-protective of his shoes as he left the pebbled area in front of the porch and waded uphill through the long grass to where I was. He crouched to check the line of the fenceposts I was repairing, and nodded in approval.

"So," he said. "The old so-and-so finally passed."

"That's what they tell me," I said. "You go say hi to Beth and tell her to hitch up the cart for us. I'll be down as soon as I'm done here, and we can go out to the Wallow."

"Or we could just take my car," he offered.

I squinted at his sedan, its white-walled tired gleaming with the morning dew they'd picked up from the road. "Do you even remember what the track back to the Wallow is like? Your rig'll barely get through, if at all—and it surely won't be pretty when we get back."

Walter shrugged. "Whatever you think it best. You're in charge."

I snorted and swung the hammer, and Walter retraced his steps to where Beth had come out on the front porch, Kezzie on her hip. I caught the murmur of their pleasant voices as I finished up. The sheep in that enclosure had retreated to the far side when I started hammering, and they still looked at me with stupid suspicion while I gathered up my box of nails and coil of spare wire.

Last night was a new dream I think, I dont remember it before enyway. There were big things like Lizzerd-pigs runnin around snortin, and trees that looked like big fethery mold. And there was the Rock, same as it oways ben. The lizzerd pigs lay down in front of it and sounded like Cats. They did this all day and when the nite came, the Moon was so big like it was close enof to touch, and still they made their cat sounds to the rock. I wonder how thos lizzard-pigs taste.

I had only met the old bastard once, and seen him two other times besides. The first time I saw him was once when Walter and I, both teenagers—him just about to move away for school, me just twelve or so—had trekked over to Ostler Wallow to try some hunting. Everyone from my pap on down had told me that the hunting in the Wallow was thin and dire; the deer just didn't go there, and the rabbits and other small animals were stringy and sour-tasting. But we wanted to shoot something where we didn't have to ask some other family's permission first, and I'd never been to what was supposed to be our land, so off we two went.

Even though the Wallow was ours, it wasn't connected to the land on which we lived. A lot of places were like that; a family would have a homestead and animals on the land easier to get to, and then a place that was theirs further on back in the hills that was like their own game preserve. The track to Ostler Wallow—even us hill people didn't call it a "road"—wound between a few other families' mountains and ended up with us looking down on the soggy cesspool in the hills, where the lump of black rock supported the old grey cabin. We didn't want to go down there anyway—nothing we wanted to hunt lived in swamp water—so our plan was to circle the slopes around the pit of the Wallow, seeing what we could flush out.

From just about everywhere we moved, all around the Wallow, we could see the cabin except when the trees blocked it out. I wasn't there to finally see my own grandfather, and I don't think Walter was either, but our eyes kept returning to the grey box of wood, slumping with its age, perched on the wide black rock. Out back were upright racks made of unmilled wood with pelts nailed to them, some from deer that definitely hadn't been caught in the Wallow. There was nothing that looked like an outhouse, not that one could dig a hole for it on that solid mass of rock.

About third of the way around the edge of the Wallow—we had heard things rustling in the bushes, but hadn't seen anything worth shooting at—we saw movement at the cabin, and both Walter and I stopped without saying anything and watched. We could just make out a pale human figure—skinny and naked—walk out of the cabin and stretch in the sunless daylight. He went over to a spot where the flat top of the black rock fell away steeply, and squatted, backside sticking out over the air.

When business was finished, the figure stood up again without wiping, stretched some more, got onto its knees like he was kissing the rock, and went back inside the cabin.

Walter and I finished our circuit around the Wallow, but I don't remember that we shot anything.

There are dayz I cant work atal because I feel it so much and I cant work for lovin it. I just haf to lay meself down on the Rock like I want to hold it all, the hole Rock and bineeth it, I just want to hold it and get holded by it til it crushes me into it like a Fly draonin in hony.

I would have just ridden or walked with Walter up to the Wallow that day, but we'd have to bring back the old bastard's body, so Beth hitched the horse up to the small cart I use for hauling sheep shit, and I threw in a couple of worn-out canvas tarpaulins and my two shovels. Beth made us each a sandwich and gave us each an apple—she didn't listen when I said for God's sake, we weren't off on a picnic—and away we went. The air was wet, and the sky threatened rain weakly.

We rode in silence for a while until we passed the old Shurdy place—the last Shurdy had died a decade ago, and now the place was nothing but a mound of falling-in greenery—then Walter cleared his throat.

"Kezzie's sure getting big," he said. "She got to be two, now?"

"Coming up in a month," I said.

"Funny how you always feel like people shouldn't get older when you're not watching."

"Like the old bastard himself."

"Well, Clara's doing well," Walter said, "though she gets awful tired these days. Doctor said she might be anemic. That means her blood doesn't have enough iron in it, so it can't carry enough oxygen."

"I know what anemic means."

"And Velma and Walter Junior are healthy and doing well in school," he continued. "And the church is growing, of course."

"Of course."

The track wound through a tight spot on the slope of a steep hill, and I slowed the horse down and watched for loose stones. It wasn't that I didn't want to talk to Walter, but there wasn't a lot that we both knew about and wanted to hear about, these days.

After the next few miles, Ostler Wallow opened up in front of us. If it had changed any since I'd seen it last, I couldn't tell: it dipped into wet shadow, like a mossy sheet suspended from the mountains around it, weighed down in the middle by the black rock. The cabin was still there, grey and lichened, surrounded by drying racks now empty of skins.

I nudged the horse and cart as far as I could down the track, now no more than a footpath, until we reach what I reckoned to be the last flattish place wide enough for all four wheels. Then I grabbed the tarps, and Walter and I descended the rest of the slope.

The air got colder as we went lower, until it felt like two in the morning when we reached the edge of the water. The bottom of the Wallow was a swamp, with slimy branches and yellowed grass reaching out of black pools. All the air had that sweet, metallic tang that stagnant fresh water gets. A white frog's head stuck out of a pool a dozen feet away, watching us as we tried to find a way across. Another frog was beyond that. There may have been more, but it was hard to tell them from the clumps of white mushrooms at water level.

The old bastard had built or rebuilt a ford of fallen logs just above the water level, and we tottered our way across the slick old wood onto the black rock.

It wasn't just a rock. It was a mass of black stone, maybe a hundred feet at its widest. There were no cracks in its surface, although it was rough like sandpaper and seemed like it should have had cracked and weathered with ages and ages of frost expansion. Because there were no breaks or crevices, nothing could grow on it except blotches of lichen, and moss clinging to the sides. And right in the middle of it was the cabin.

The oldest wood in the cabin—the greyest, most weathered wood—was milled lumber, brought up to the Wallow probably more than a hundred years before when great-something-grandfather Ostler first built the cabin. Since then, other wood had become attached to it, not to expand it except for a small lean-to, but just to maintain it: fresher but still old unpainted lumber, and untrimmed logs from the hills around supporting each of the four corners, with split logs laid at the bottom of the wall all around it, and against them all around were animal skulls—deer and bear, with smaller ones thrown in, all facing outward. I first thought that the dull red barn door was the door of the cabin. Only after I couldn't find a knob or pull on either side did I realize that it was part of the exterior wall, scavenged and nailed on. The actual door, slumping on rope hinges, was on the far side of the cabin. It stood a foot open, probably just as Jude had left it.

I set down the tarps, pulled my leather gloves out of my back pocket and put them on. Then I took in a breath and held it, grabbed hold of the edge of the door, and pulled it wide, standing as far back as I could. The daylight in the Wallow had no direction and didn't push very far into the cabin, and there was only one small, high window in a wall on the opposite side. I waited, squinting, Walter beside me, until the dark blur inside began to divide into lighter and darker parts. Then I finally saw him.

The floor of the cabin was mostly just the surface of the black rock, with a rag rug and a large cowhide thrown on spots. The old bastard was stretched face-down across the cowhide, arms toward the door where we stood, feet just barely off the bed built on split logs against the far wall. He was less naked than the first time I had seen him here, at least; his lower half faded away into the shadows, dressed in something like canvas trousers. His upper half was bare, and even with shadows on top of shadows we could see the light-and-dark splotches where rot had set in. The air rolling out of the cabin probably wasn't much worse than it had been while he was alive—every smell that a man can make, folded in on itself and stewed together for decades, along with woodsmoke and old meat, all on top of that wet, stagnant tang. It was only when I leaned in to grab the edge of the cowhide and pull it toward the door that the rot-smell hit me: rich and roiling, fertile as old manure, thick as a cloud of gnats riled up as the body was moved.

Walter backed up and covered his mouth and nose as I dragged the corpse out into the valley's light. The old bastard had been skinny to begin with, and now he was little more than leathery skin on bones. His greasy white hair, long enough to tuck into his belt, was tied back into a matted tail, with small bones woven through—bird bones, maybe. The blackened skin on his shoulders was speckled with huge moles and spots, running into and over each other. The fingers of each hand had become claws of callus and scar tissue with months' and years' worth of dirt ground into each wrinkle and pock.

"Turn him over," Walter said behind his hand.

I lifted the edge of the cowhide and tried to roll him, but in the days—weeks?—since he had died, his rotting skin had molded into and around the bristly hairs on the hide. After a couple of tries, I made sure my gloves were on tight, grasped his shoulder, and peeled him back from the cowhide. It felt like stripping the hide from a buck.

His face was blotched from the blood inside him that had settled downward and started to rot. His eyes had leaked and dried, and now each eye socket was filled with dried tar that had hairs from the deer skin stuck to them. His belly was probably bigger than it had ever been in his life, jiggly from all the gases still trapped inside. Around his neck, under his grimy beard, was a string of small skulls—frog skulls, which is probably also where the bones in his hair were from. Maggots had burrowed underneath where the moisture had collected between him and the hide, and now his chest and belly writhed sluggishly like bubbling oats.

Walter took his handkerchief out of his pocket and laid it across the old bastard's ruined face, making sure not to touch him. "That's him, sure enough," he said.

I nodded and let the corpse fall back onto the hide, squashing maggots and making the smell puff out. I flipped the edges of the hide up over him, then picked up a tarp and shook it out. Walter grabbed one end, and we draped it on the surface of the rock beside him. Then I nudged him with my foot over onto the tarp, and between the two of us we rolled him up tight. All sorts of flies buzzed around us, knocked away from the corpse and anxious to get back.

I made to pick up one end of the rolled-up tarp, but Walter said, "Hold on —let me get some fresh air first." He walked away from the bundle and the cabin, and I did the same, meandering around the edges of the rock that the old bastard had called home for something over forty years.

I glanced over the edge of the rock where, decades before, I had seen him taking a crap. It was still his outhouse, and his trash pile; dried, crusty shit striped the rock down to the water's edge, and below were odd bones from his meals, along with a rusted, curled shovel head and what few other things hadn't been worth fixing or burning, all coated in a fly-covered mound of shit. I saw tiny bones mixed in with larger ones from raccoons and deer, and wondered how many of the albino frogs he had eaten over his lifetime.

I took the rest of the turn around the stump-like rock, back to where Walter had steeled himself and returned to the tarp bundle. He gathered up the head end, I gathered up the foot end, and together we hoisted it and hauled it back the way we had come.

In between watching my footing over the swampy area around the rock, I saw maybe a dozen white frogs watching us with their deep black eyes just above the surface of the water. I wondered if they were going to have a population explosion without the old bastard around to keep their numbers down.

We got his old bones back up to the cart and hauled him into the back. The horse shook her head and blinked like she couldn't believe the smell. I looked at the satchel of food that Beth had made for us, caught Walter's eye, and motioned toward it with my head. He shook his head rapidly.

"I'm not eating nothing anywhere near this smell," he said.

"I thought not," I said. I stretched out my back after dropping my load, stripped off my gloves, and fished two cigars out of my shirt pocket. "These might fit the bill better," I said as I handed one to Walter, who took it easily. I bit the end off mine, then pulled out my matches and lit first Walter's and then mine. They were old, stale cigars—I don't smoke much — and they hadn't been that great when I first got them at Sadley's for cheap, but they were a damned sight better than the air we had been trying not to breathe too deep as we came back from the cabin.

"So," Walter said after two or three good cleansing puffs, "should we come back up later today, or leave it until tomorrow?"

"Why'd we want to come back?"

"Clean out the cabin, of course."

"I was thinking just burn it down," I said. "I got the matches."

"I'd not just Ephraim Ostler's cabin," he said. "His own grandfather built it, and came up here to hunt plenty, I heard. Ostlers are the only family that doesn't have a cabin to use, since Grandpap came up here to live."

"Ostlers been doing fine without one," I said, looking at the grey, wooden husk sitting alone on the black rock.

"Well, I'd like to be able to come up here with my family," Walter said. "Take a vacation week for some camping sometime."

"Fine," I said. "We can come back to clean it out." I looked up, where a bright spot in the cloud cover showed where the sun was hanging at midday. "But probably not today, once we get him planted. You're welcome to stay over, of course."

"Thank you. That'll work out fine."

"Then let's get along," I said, still puffing as I climbed up into the front of the wagon.

Today I changed thinkin abowt how long this will take. I no someon will haf to chip away for ten thowsand thowsand years and that oways galled me, but today I unerstood that the Years is part of the blesing. You love what you searve. And mabe wat you searve cant help but love you back. Even if your the ant. How could it not love the Ant wat searved it for ten thowsand thowsand years?

Not for a minute did I think of burying the old bastard behind the family home, where my mother and father and my murdered grandmother lay. Even if I'd thought to dishonor them all by planting him between them, I have to half-believe that they would have risen up together and kicked his skinny carcass out of their fellowship.

If I had still wanted to give the old bastard a full, proper burial—with a headstone and flowers and crying people dressed in black—we could have taken him down to the Lutheran church in Timoree, bought a fancy box, and paid to lay him in the churchyard where they keep the grass cut short and the trees neat.

But mostly what I wanted was to bury him deep where we could forget about him, and waste not too much time and absolutely no money doing it. So instead we took him to the old graveyard just down not too far from Sadley's, where the old log church used to be a while back. The church isn't there any longer—church-going folks decided they could ride a ways further to sit on varnished pews in a sanctuary with electric lights—but nobody was going to move the dead people already in the churchyard, so it's still there. I don't know as anybody new had been buried there for ten years or more, but there wasn't no law against it, and it was free. So that's where we went.

Walter took off his tie and rolled up his sleeves while I picked a spot for the old bastard, and the two of us dug until we had gotten about four feet down. The turfy was soft from the roots of the grass clumps, but creepers from elm trees wove through it like old baling twine, and half the time it felt like we were cutting a grave instead of digging one. I hadn't chosen a spot close to the old graves, which were still marked with leaning headstones or simple granite rocks with names etched in and lichen patterned over, spreading out from the old log church that now looked like a deadfall. A lot of those graves had dips in front of the stones, where the old boxes the dead had been buried in had rotted or been eaten by worms and the earth fell in, so I didn't feel too bad about burying the old bastard in nothing but an old tarp. I didn't feel bad at all, to tell the truth.

Once we had laid him in the hole we dug, Walter insisted on stopping and saying a few words. The old farts from up at Sadley's had seen us at work and were now at the edge of the graveyard, far enough away to respect any privacy we wanted but close enough that they could tell their wives what went on. I leaned on my shovel while Walter wiped the sweat from his forehead with his sleeve and calmed his breathing.

"Dear Lord," he said, his chin tilted up into the low-hanging clouds, "we commit to the earth the mortal remains of Ephraim Joel Ostler. May his soul receive whatever justice and mercy Thou hast chosen for him, and may his children and children's children redeem the wrongs that were done in his name. In Jesus' name, amen."

"Amen," I said, my first shovelful of dirt hitting the body before I was done with the word.

By the time we had all the earth packed back over the body, a light rain was coating us, keeping our sweat from drying and leaving us stickier than flypaper. Walter patted the last few shovelfuls down with the flat of his shovel and said, "We going to put up some sort of marker?"

I shrugged. "No hurry, I expect. I'll get to putting a slab here with his name before the grass grows back and people forget he's planted here." Even in the wet air, dust from our digging had gotten in my mouth and mixed with the dried-out spit that was all I had left. I gathered what I could on my tongue and spit it out to land on the grave.

I alwaz thot someone of my Blood wood carry on. Thats why I done it, to git her out from bitween us and let me raze him right for the Work. I thot that was wear my own Pap done it wrong, just leting me find out on my own after he was gon. Mabe his pap fore him did the same, I guess. But how much time has bin wasted that way? Hole tens of Yeers when I coud have been workin here. Evry year wasted is a year some one is gon haf to work.

The second time I saw the old bastard was when I got married. It was down at the Lutheran church, with me in a borrowed suit and Beth in her mother's dress. When we came out of the church with family and friends all lining the steps and throwing rice, I saw an old skinny man with a beard that hid half his face, standing just outside the black iron fence, wearing a feed-sack shirt that came to his knees. When I leaned over to kiss Beth I asked if if was someone I didn't know from her family, but she said it wasn't. I was planning to ask my mother—Pap was already dead from coughing up blood by that point—but before I got there, Roy Sadley said, while shaking my hand, "Don't that beat all? There's your own grandfather standing yonder."

He didn't look like he was planning on coming in, so I just kept watch out of the corner of my eye while being kissed and handshook and congratulated. Before we ran out of people wishing us well, he had shrugged, turned, and walked off with stiff steps.

This week I bin dreamin throu the Rock to whats bineeth. My lord. Its not alive, not like anything I ever new was alive, but its not Dead nither. Its keeps from dyin by dreamin. I dont unerstand it but its still the Truth. It dreams to itself to keep itself not dead, and it dreams to me and I dream back. It thinks long, long thouts in Dreams that last so long it was dreamin long befor the lizzerd-pigs worship it. It can stay in its dreams for the ten thowsand thowsand year itll take me and mine to reach it.

Beth and Kezzie loved having Walter over for dinner. Beth had Walter say grace, and it was a simple, beautiful, not-too-long prayer that asked blessings on our house. Over mutton and potatoes, he told Kezzie all about her cousins Velma and Walter Junior—Kezzie had never been down out of the mountains as far as St. Stephen yet, so she'd never met them—and promised her that, once we had cleaned out the cabin, their whole family would come for a vacation visit sometime soon. He also told her that her name, "Keziah," was from the Bible, where it was the name of one of Job's three daughters, the other two being Jemimah and Keren-Happuch. Kezzie was only two and didn't understand a lot about vacations and namesakes, but she got a kick out of his talk because she knew a girl named Jemimah just a few miles away.

Once Kezzie was in bed and Beth was washing up, Walter and I sat by the banked fire.

"It'll be good to reclaim that cabin," Walter said. "It'll sort of be like reclaiming the family name from what he did. I know I'm not technically an Ostler, but still—what he did hangs over all of us of his blood, no matter if we get it from our father or our mother."

"I'll trust you on that, I guess," I said. "Me, I just want to bury everything he done along with him."

"Problem is that nothing stays buried forever," he said, and chuckled like he had amused himself. Then he slapped his knee. "Well, no offense, but I need to turn in. I may have been raised a mountain boy, but I've got lily-white hands these days—" he turned his palms toward me, as if to prove it "—and I put more back into today than I normally do in a month. I'm just hoping I can roll out of bed in the morning."

Turned out for him that that wouldn't be a problem as such; the only other real bed we had in the house was the one we were holding for when Kezzie outgrew her pallet and it wasn't long enough for him, so we fixed him up with some blankets on the couch.

I guess I do regret killin my Wife. I thot I was doin somthin that would get fences out of the way and let Eliazar and me do the Work up here together. I thot I was smarter then my Pap had bin, and his Pap, and his Pap afore him. But Eliazar turnd aginst me, and now its just me here in the Wallow doing the work, and when I go, there wont be no one. And whats bineeth the Rock will stay bineeth the rock.

The one time I actually met my grandfather was only about a year before he died. Ma was gone by that point, too, from something that kept her from caring to eat or sleep or, eventually, breathe. I was down at Sadley's picking up some new bolts for the wagon's axle. As I walked in from bright sun to dusty shade and stood still waiting for my eyes to adjust, a skinny shadow stepped up toward me, a shadow that smelled like it had been sleeping in old ashes and deer guts.

I blinked, as much at the smell as to clear my eyes, and could finally focus on the old man in front of me. He was wearing a rabbit-skin vest over a bare chest and canvas trousers, and his eyes were small and watery—eyes that were searching me up and down. In his arms were a bag of salt and a shiny red pickax. Everything about him was lean, spare, and tough.

The murmur from the old timers always at the table in the corner died. Roy Sadley was leaning on his counter, watching us, over a roll of cured deer hides.

"Morning, Phineas," said Roy finally, and his voice broke the silence like a rock through pond ice. "Your grandfather was just here trading..." He trailed off.

My grandfather. Ephraim Joel Ostler. The old bastard himself. He was staring at me still, but for some reason I could only focus on his hands, spotted and papery on the backs and held together with scars. Maybe I was seeing if my grandmother's blood was still there for all to see.

The old bastard looked me up and down, examining me like a horse for sale or a spring crop. He pursed his lips. Then he shook his head with... was it sadness? Disappointment?

"Coulda been," he muttered, and his breath stank of rotten teeth. "Had hopes."

I stood stock still like an animal waiting for the situation to change so he'll know whether to fight or run. I was almost curious to know what I would do if he had tried to introduce himself, to put his hand out to shake mine or to hug me. I think I would have watched myself like a spectator as thirty years of learning to hate the old bastard had let loose like a thunderstorm.

But instead he slipped past me in the doorway like a outhouse breeze and went out. I couldn't help myself; I turned to watch him go. He was trudging slowly back up the direction of the Wallow, his shoulders slumped as if he was sorrowing for something.

So high you cant get overit
So low you cant get under it
So wide you cant get raond it
O rock omy sole

I don't dream much, and when I do they're boring dreams not worth remembering, just repeated bits from my daytime life—tending sheep, shoveling snow, felling trees, feeding horses. I wasn't surprised when I woke up in the morning having had dreams with the old bastard in them; the trip out to Ostler Wallow was not an everyday thing that blended into the background. All the same, as I sat on my stool milking the cows before sunup, I couldn't help going back over and over those dream images, even though they made less sense than they had when I was dreaming them.

In one, the waxy mushrooms were the size of trees, and I watched the old bastard stalking a deer through the white trunks. He didn't have any gun or anything in his hands, but I knew that he was dangerous anyway, deadly to whatever he caught. When a deer wandered out into his line of sight, the old bastard just pointed his finger at it, like a little boy playing cowboy. He didn't say "bang," though. When he opened his mouth, my dream-ears popped like they do sometimes when I go down-mountain when I have a cold. The deer flopped over dead. And then the old bastard looked at me, and I realized that suddenly he could see me, whereas before I'd just been outside the dream, watching it. That woke me up.

In another dream, I was inside the little cabin on the black rock, but the walls were all smooth like plaster. I had a lantern in my hand—it was night outside the cabin—and I was trying to read black letters that had been written all over the walls, up and down and sideways and crisscross. They weren't like any letters I knew, but in the dream I was convinced that if only I could find where the whole string of letters started—and it was just one string, wound around and around the inside of the cabin like a ball of yarn—then suddenly it would make sense to me. But the old bastard's corpse was just outside the door, right where Walter and I had first dragged it to turn it over, and it was slipping toward the edge of the black rock, and if I didn't stop trying to find the start of the letters, the body would slip over the edge and... the frogs would get it, or something. The dream faded out then, or faded into something else.

There were other things too, little bits and images that got foggier the more I tried to thing about them. Voices out of empty areas, a feeling of time passing like a grandfather clock that went for hours and years between the second-hand ticks that sounded like metal on stone, a longish number that seemed to mean "hate"... All of these were dream-scraps that didn't want to sit still for my woke-up brain to figure them out, and by the time I was done milking I had almost given myself a headache trying.

Walter woke up groggy after the rest of us were up and the oatmeal was on the table, and he rolled off the couch like he was a generation older than me. He said he was fine, but I could tell that he wasn't used to anything near the work we had done yesterday. His spoon hand shook as he ate his oatmeal, and I could see the red spots all over the palm of his hand. But he was in a good mood, complimented our couch, and said that he wanted to make an early start of cleaning out the cabin so we wouldn't be rushed by the shadows that fell early in the Wallow. He even helped a bit as I went out to take care of the sheep, and tried to make it look like he wasn't being careful of his shoes.

Low clouds had moved in overnight, the kind that sit right down on these hills and layer everything like wet cheesecloth. Walter didn't complain about leaving his car to sit for another day while we took the horse and cart back toward the Wallow. I had loaded up the cart with a few old feed sacks to haul away whatever the old bastard had crammed into his living space.

"Well, Kezzie sure seems to love you," I said as the horse plodded up over the hill.

Walter shrugged, but he looked pleased. "Around here, seeing anyone new is exciting, at least once Mama and Papa show that they're friendly. She'd probably love to come down and visit Velma and Walter Junior."

"Or you could bring them up here, I guess—once we've got that cabin cleaned out. That's what you're thinking, right?"

"Yeah, sometime," he said. "Although I don't know how many that cabin can fit." He stretched he shoulders back, trying to relax a kink in his back that had been bothering him since he climbed up into the cart. "So, do you get your family out to church often?"

I grunted at the change of subject. "Sounds like 'Cousin Walter' just turned into 'Pastor McKinnon.'"

"One and the same, Phineas." He smiled. "I just thought that Kezzie might have other friends there, children her age and such."

"Well, someone needs to tell the clodhead reverend at the Lutheran church not to start services so early," I said. "He starts at eight sharp, and most mornings ain't no way I could get chores done that gotta be done each morning, plus get everyone all clean and dressed and all the way down there to Timoree before he starts sermonizing."

Walter smiled. "He's old enough now—that's the Reverend Staheli, isn't it?—he's old enough that he probably wants to get his sermon out of the way before he feels his midday nap coming on." He laughed. "Maybe another benefit of me being a pastor is now *I'm* the clodhead, and can start services whenever I want to walk the dozen yards to the chapel!"

I laughed with him, and we rode along in comfortable silence for a bit.

"To tell the truth, though," he started up, "I'm jealous that you could go to Pastor Staheli's church. This up here—" and with his raised eyebrows, he took in all the misty hills around us "—is truly God's country. If I could live up here and serve at that church down there... That would be ideal."

"You'd have to switch from Methodist to Lutheran," I said.

Walter shrugged. "Changing teams, but playing the same game," he said. "As long as I didn't have to be a Baptist." We laughed again. "But I don't know how well Clara would do up here. Her health, you know. Anyway, it's a good dream, even if that's all it is."

Mentioning dreams brought back some of the images from the night before that had lodged in my head. The old bastard's corpse sliding toward the edge of the black rock. Long numbers as hateful as a mad dog. Big empty spaces that had a bunch of angles in them you couldn't see, but you could feel. I wiped the drizzle off my face and watched the clouds that had come down to fill the spaces in the mountains.

Its in the Bible that the honnors of the World are nothing unless thats all you want. Fokes that go to Church think they unerstand what that means, and they think the Paster's so smart when he repetes it for them. But they unerstand so Little they cant even unerstand that they dont unerstand. Theyr there in the little world of the Church, with its honnors, and they dont unerstand that those are all the honnors theyll git.

Ostler Wallow looked just the same as we'd left it, except for the puffs of fog. The white frogs kept their eyes on us as we made it across to the black rock with our empty bags. The mushrooms were little congregations of waxy white.

We'd left the door of the cabin open to air it out, but it still stank of everything that had ever gone into or come out of the old bastard. It would take more than one night of good air to clean it out. I didn't think that even Walter's grandchildren would be able to come up here and not get nightmares from the old bastard's stink, but I didn't say anything.

Walter tried to open the small window to get the air moving, but it was just a piece of salvaged glass anchored over its hole with nailed scrap wood. It was already broken, and the hole in it was covered with oiled brown paper.

The fireplace, at least, was clean—as clean as fire can make it. I searched around the lean-to for wood that hadn't been drizzled on, and used the old bastard's flint and steel to start a fire to clean the air and try to hold back the damp from seeping into our bones.

We started by hauling the bed out, the two of us struggling to turn it far enough to get it out the door. It didn't look it had been moved since the old bastard had originally come to live in the Wallow; the corners at the back behind the split-log bedframe were filled with dust, threads, small bones, and mouse droppings, which had all solidified in each corner, like mortar. I hadn't thought to throw a shovel in the back of the cart today, but the old bastard had used a rusting spade-head, as his one fireplace tool, its edge split and its wooden handle broken at the end of the iron, and I used it to carry three loads of corner crud out of the cabin at arm's length to drop over the side of the black rock into the water.

Walter was still just looking at the bed, put together with logs and sagging ropes. I don't think the bedclothes had ever been changed; it just looked like whatever secondhand castoffs the old bastard had scrounged just went on the top of the stack, turning into a layered, matted mattress over the decades.

"That sure doesn't look like it's even worth hauling back," Walter said. "And I'm not excited about trying to carry it across the Wallow back to the cart."

I said, "We should probably just set fire to it right here. That's all we'd do with it anyway, once we got it home."

"What, right here?"

"You're right," I said. "A little farther away from the cabin—I don't want to smell the smoke when it goes up."

Walter was reluctant, but together we dragged it to the edge of the rock as far as we could get from the cabin, and I used the old bastard's flint and steel again. It took four tries before a flame would stay lit, everything was so greasy and damp, but eventually the fire started growing on its own, and I moved back to the cabin so I wouldn't get a face-full of the oily, yellowed smoke.

"I guess if there's anything else we want to get rid of," I said, "we ought to haul it out here while the fire's still going."

There wasn't much. On a shelf that probably doubled as his table beside the fireplace was his "larder"—dried smoked strips of meat wrapped in oily deer-hide, an old Mason jar with dried mushrooms, a tin bowl of what had probably been fresh-picked mushrooms when he died and was now nothing but a tarry slime puddle in the bottom. All of them went into the fire.

Hung on the wall above the bed was a faded, smoke-stained blanket hung against drafts. Into the fire it went.

His clothing was hung on pegs on the wall and piled in a heap beneath it: ash-colored undershirts, a pair of trousers that had torn through around its leather patches, a couple of wrapped pelts that likely worked as his boots in the winter, several lengths and patches of cloth that had started as specific garments but which were now nothing but wraps and shawls. Under it all was a bear pelt that had been tied so it could function as a wraparound cape. We piled all the clothing on the pelt and carried it out to the fire.

The only other shelf, above the head of the bed, held his few personal items: a penknife, a tin drinking cup, a Bakelite comb that probably hadn't been used for years, and a stack of composition notebooks, the kind children use for their assignments in school. There had to be a dozen of them; the bottom one was obviously the oldest, and the top one was only half-used. I flipped through a couple. The writing was blockish and cramped. Some of it was written in lead pencil, and had faded to clouds on the old paper. Other parts were in ink using a bird-feather quill, but a lot of the ink had been watered down and mixed with ash to make it last longer, and was nearly as faded as the pencil.

Walter looked over my shoulder as I was puzzling over the composition books. "Granpap left a diary?" he asked. "Those definitely shouldn't go in the fire."

I turned and handed him the stack. "Then they're yours, because I don't want 'em."

He took them outside and looked at the dark sky. "Gonna open up soon," he said. He brought the composition books back in and set them just inside the door. "Don't let me forget."

The only things left inside were the old stump he used for a seat, and the rag rug in the center of the floor.

"The stump looks pretty new," Walter said. "It might still be useful as a seat."

Outside, the first solid raindrops hit, splashing so loud they sounded like the frogs jumping. The fire, now on the downhill side of its burn, steamed and spit as the rain hit it.

I stuck my head out the door. The dark clouds above us were being followed by black ones, rolling slowly over the lip of the Wallow.

"Let's go back," I said. "Is this clean enough for you? There's still whatever's out in the lean-to, but…"

Walter nodded, then took one of the burlap bags and wrapped it around the composition books. "Let's close it up," he said. "I'll try to get back another day this year to finish."

"Suit yourself," I said. I grabbed the unused bags while Walter pushed the door shut and made sure that the rope latch caught.

By the time were were halfway back across the Wallow toward the cart, the sky had opened up and was dumping bucketfuls of rain on us. The soggy puddles at the bottom of the Wallow frothed in the rainstorm. But the frogs kept their white heads above water level, watching us with their black eyes.

Sometimes I can see myself from far away, and Im so small that I can almost ferget Im even ther. But other times when the Glory is apon me and eyes and ears and tung become usseless becase they dont tell me what can be told, then those times I see maself in the midle of the endless distanse of time from all Eternetty to all Eternetty and I realize that Im being held by all of Creashion, that everything that is and was and will be is embrasing me.

It kept raining all the way home, and Walter and I agreed that the whole road down the mountain would be nothing but a mudslick straight down to Timoree, and that he should stay until morning

That night, I went to bed but I couldn't sleep. I listened to the rain keep coming down, and I tossed and turned until I was worried I was going to wake Beth up, so I finally went downstairs to the kitchen to find something to eat.

I poured myself some water and got a piece of cheese to nibble on. Over the sound of the rain I could hear Walter snort occasionally in his sleep on the couch in the next room. This wasn't a thunderstorm, but something still felt electric, about the air or about me. Even after my snack, I could tell that I still wasn't going to get to sleep anytime soon.

The door in from the barn was at the back of the kitchen, and that's where Walter and I had come in after we'd put away the cart and taken care of the horse. On top of the boot rack with our muddy shoes drying on it was the burlap bag that Walter had brought in, full of the notebooks.

I lit the lamp in the kitchen and bought the bag over to the table. The books all still smelled like the smoke-rot-sweat of the cabin. I riffled through their pages, then chose one at random near the center of the stack—careful to keep the rest of them in order—and flipped it open.

The entries were undated, and sometimes ran into each other where the only way you could tell them apart was the different darkness of the ink or the change to pencil. The old bastard had had even less education than I had, and trying to figure out what letters his scrawls were supposed to be, and then what words they were lumped together to make, was somewhere between finding a maker's mark on a rusty plow and imagining animal shapes in the clouds. But I got myself another drink of water and set to it, determined that my grandfather couldn't do anything that was beyond me.

It wasn't a diary, at least not like those I've heard of. The events of his life weren't much mentioned; I suppose his life routines would have been boring even compared to mine. But he rambled on about dreams and visions, about what "truths" he thought he'd discovered sitting out there alone in the Wallow, eating mushrooms and listening to the frogs.

After reading as much of the first three pages as I could make out, a word popped into my head to describe it: "religious." What I was looking at was the journal of a religious man, although not much I read sounded like anything I'd heard from the Holy Book or a holy man. I couldn't even hardly make out what it was the old bastard was religious *about*—his notebooks had been for him, I guess, and he didn't need to explain for anyone else the things that he would understand when he re-read them.

Reading there by the lamplight, even though I was wide awake, I still entered a kind of dreaming. As the old bastard's handwriting got easier to my eyes, I skimmed along the rows of text, not so much studying it out like before as just absorbing it. The old bastard hadn't simply taken up in Ostler Wallow because he had nowhere else to go; this was where he'd wanted to be. In that greyed cabin perched on the black rock, ringed by a moat of sog and frogs, he'd put his mind back into the past so far he couldn't see the speck of himself when he turned to see where he'd come from. He'd thought himself up into the sky past everything that was tolerably warm, to where nothing but great burnings and freezings existed, and the only things that thought and moved were too hot or too cold, or too much of both at the same time, to ever be anyplace a man could live. He thought down so deep beyond the dark of coalmines that the weight of all the blackness pressing down turned into sparks of blinding light, like the spots you see when you press on your eyes, but instead if his eyes it was his soul being pressed upon, and he laughed and named the spots and bowed to them and worshiped them and worked for them, chipping his tools and his life away in a great work that would take ten thousand times ten thousand years to accomplish...

When I came to myself—when I could see the lamp wick flickering low and feel the oilcloth table covering beneath my forearms and hear Walter snorting in his sleep in the other room—four whole composition books were turned onto their fronts beside me, finished. I didn't remember even finishing one and moving on to the next, but there they were. We didn't have but a single clock in the house and that was out in the front room, past where

Walter was asleep on the couch, so I didn't know how long I had sat there straining my eyes at the old bastard's penmanship, but my head throbbed with the effort and my buttocks told me, when I stood up, that I had sat in that wooden chair far too long.

I replaced the books I had read in their spots in the stack and set them on top of the burlap sack on the kitchen table, blew out the lamp, and went back upstairs to bed.

I lernd a new Word today, I smelld it and tasted it because it wasnt an ear hearin word, and it was so Good for me and delisios. And only after I lovd it, then I faond out that it was me, not my name but Me, all of me in the one word that coud go on forever in a saond that cant be made.

I know that I dreamed from the time I settled back onto the pillow until the time that the roosters called my cottonish head to come and do my chores, but I only remember one dream distinctly:

I was in, or above, the clouds, although I couldn't see blue sky above me —just a greenish-grey haze that seemed so much higher than the sky ever was. Around me, to as far away as I could see, were clotted clouds, crawling on their own without any wind to push them.

And the only thing I could see, aside from haze and clouds, was the old bastard, a black dot against the churning cotton.

He walked toward me, and his gait was weird—I couldn't figure out why his steps all looked awkward, until I realize that his legs were long stilts that reached down, down, down. I only realized this when I leaned to one side, or stepped, and discovered that my own legs were stilts too, so long that the earth down below was as unknown as the bottom of the ocean. Part of my own body had turned against me and trapped me up here, disconnected from soil and water, alone with nothing but the old bastard coming toward me with herky-jerky movements. Smiling.

"Phineas," he said, smiling as wide as the frog skulls on the string around his neck. "Glad you could be here."

"This is a dream," I said, and my voice sounded like distant wind in my own ears.

"Course it is!" he crowed as he got closer. "But that don't mean it ain't *real*. It's as real as time, and distance, and all the things we're at the center of."

He smiled wide, and his teeth were like little shards of mirror.

"It's as real," he continued, "as a big black stone from out in between the stars—so black it's almost like it was cut right out of the star-shadows— thrown here to pin something holy down in the earth. Now that's *real*, boy. Compared to that, you're a dream and I'm a dream and everything you ever known is a dream's dream."

The green hazy light bounced from his glittering teeth.

"Know what, Phineas?" he said as he finally got within arm's length. "I mourned you, boy—but I don't need you anymore. Not anymore."

And he shot out his arm and shoved my shoulder.

Like a tall tall tree falling when you've sawed through its stump, I could feel myself slowly start tipping, and just as unstoppably as that tree, I fell further from him, slow at first like I was falling through water, then faster and faster, and I could hear myself screaming and the old bastard laughing as I pinwheeled back into the clouds, faster and faster, knowing just how impossibly far it was to the ground, how I could fall forever and ever before hitting, like the black stone that pinned a god deep into the earth—

And then I woke up, with the rooster outside just starting to warm up his voice.

Evry Lord seys the same thing come unto me and Forsakke all others and I will give you evrythin. Evry Lord seys it but not evry Lord can give it. Some Lords lie.

I crawled out of my bed in the dark, feeling like a stranger in my own skin. My eyelids were gritty against tired eyeballs. I was so half-brained that put on my boots, went out, did the milking, and came back in before I noticed that Walter's shoes, which had been right beside my boots last night, were gone from the boot rack. The stack of composition books on the kitchen table was gone too, along with the burlap sack.

The sun was just beginning to glow behind the mountains when I walked out on the front porch and looked at where Walter's car had been for two days. The sky was clear, though the air was still sodden with yesterday's rain, and his tires had made deep furrows in the clinging mud as he'd backed his car and turned it around. I couldn't remember him saying anything about needing to get an early start in the morning; I hadn't imagined he would leave without saying goodbye, or getting some breakfast.

As I stood there I heard the echoes of a distant motor from down the mountain, and for a second I thought that Walter was coming back from some errand. But as the noise got louder, I realized that it was too rough and worn-edged for Walter's new sedan. I waited, and a few minutes later Roy Sadley's narrow old truck sputtered and growled its way into view, on the road that passed my house and continued up the mountain.

I put up my hand and stepped off the porch, and the truck slowed to a stop, chugging like a bulldog pulling at the leash. It's wasn't Roy Sadley's boy Jude at the wheel, but Roy himself, chewing the end of his pipe.

"Morning, Phineas," he said once he got the window cranked down. "Say, it was good the way you and Walter treated your grandpap t'other day. I know there's no love to be had, 'specially from you, but there's things gotta be done. You'll be back with a headstone sometime, right?"

"Sure," I said. "Where are you off to?"

Roy angled his chin so that his pipe pointed up the road. "Widow Laughton's expecting some chickenwire," he said. "Jude, well, he ain't such a good hand at the wheel when the roads might be slick. And they are, I'll tell you —slick as snot."

"I don't doubt it," I said. "Tell me, did you see Walter head back down your way this morning?"

"Nossir," Roy said. "You know can't but one motorcar fit on this here road all the way back to my store, and I've been alone all the way up."

"I guess he could've gone earlier," I said.

"Not likely. I been up with the gout since, oh, probably three-ish. Definitely before four." He rubbed his elbow meaningfully. "If he'd gone by, I'da seen it, or heard it. 'Sides," he twitched his pipe to the other side of his mouth and used it to point out the open window to the road, "ain't no tracks like that all the way down. Car tires don't look like wagon wheels, you know."

He chuckled at my scowl as I looked at the road. "Don't be frettin'," he said. "Walter may be cityfolk now, but he can't have forgotten the mountains altogether. It ain't likely he's gotten hisself lost. I gotta get along now afore I sink up to my axles."

He put the truck in gear before I remembered what his truck reminded me of. "Say, Roy," I said, "the day Jude found the o— found my grandpap dead, what was he going up to deliver?"

"I think it was a barrel of sauerkraut, and a new shovel and pickax," he said, tapping his chin, his bad eye rolling thoughtfully. "Might not have been the sauerkraut, but definite 'bout the others. Be seeing you, now."

Roy rolled up the window and put the truck in gear, and I stepped back so I wouldn't get sprayed by the gluey mud as he spun back into motion. I stayed there by the road, looking back down the mountain as the sound of Roy's truck faded up it.

There were tire tracks going down from my place. They were as clear as plowed furrows until the road rose and fell a few dozen yards on. But if Roy hadn't seen any down toward his store—and he swore he'd have noticed the car go by, anyhow—then that meant that Walter had turned off this road somewhere not too far from here.

Say, turned off onto the road out toward the Wallow.

My sole is swollowd up and I am forever being digested, hallaluia.

I tracked through the house, called up the stairs to Beth that I wasn't going to be around for breakfast, and went out the back door to saddle up the horse to ride. Long before the sun finally climbed up over the peaks around us, I was off down the road, letting the horse take her time feeling her way in the slick mud. On my way out of the barn, I had noticed that my pickax was gone.

A blind man could have followed Walter's tire ruts, and yes, they turned off toward the Wallow. I almost coulda swore the horse sighed when I nudged her up that track—the third time in as many days that she'd trudged out to Ostler Wallow, though at least this time she wasn't pulling the cart.

By the time the sun was throwing our shadows in front of us, I had seen several spots where the track hadn't been wide enough for the car, and Walter had pushed his way through, breaking down bushes on the verge.

Well before the Wallow, but a lot farther along than I would have guessed, I found the car itself. Where the track curled around a heap of rock, the tires had all slid sideways in the mud and ended up pinned between two hemlock trees, with the car's own weight holding it snug where it was wedged. The car was empty, and the prints from his two shoes—now ruined far beyond cleaning, I guessed—led off toward the Wallow.

The horse slowed to a stop right where we'd parked the cart on the last two days, even though she could have pushed further down into the Wallow. I just slipped off where she stopped and wrapped the reins around a small cedar. The sun hadn't followed us into this valley, and yesterday's rain had chilled everything down to the temperature of a root cellar.

The walls of the valley around us and the boggy bottom of the Wallow soaked up sound, so it wasn't until I was halfway across the soaked ford to the black rock, under the glare of the frogs, that I heard it: *Tink. Tink. Tink.* The sound of metal hitting stone and not doing much to it.

Before I got all the way up onto the rock, the sound had stopped, and Walter came around the corner of the cabin from the door. His shirt was open, his glasses were off, and he was breathing hard through a smile. In his hand was my pickax.

"Good, you're here," he said. "Let me show you." He motioned me around the corner of the cabin, and I followed.

The door of the cabin was open, and the rag rug—just about the only thing we had left when we had cleaned it out yesterday—was thrown back. There, under the rug, was a spot in the rock that looked like lead. When I stepped closer I saw what it really was: a spot where metal tools had hit against the rock over and over, not just this morning but for years and years. The tools had taken a beating; I thought of the broken bits in the outhouse pile over the edge of the rock, and the rusty spade-head with the split edge that the old bastard had used for his fireplace. Inside the cabin door was the burlap sack with the composition books, and in the back corner, where the bed had been, was an old but clean army blanket.

"Where'd you get the blanket?" I asked.

"I had it in the trunk," Walter said. "Sometimes the heater doesn't work." He still smiled wide, almost proud. He hadn't shaved since coming up earlier that week, and his blond whiskers looked like a teenager's first effort to grow a beard. "But you're missing what's really important. Take a look."

He pointed back to the spot on the rock where dozens of tools over the decades had beaten themselves out of shape. I crouched closer, and as he stepped out of the light, I saw it.

A crack.

It wasn't much, just a hairline that wasn't even as long as my hand. A crack that thin in a clay bowl wouldn't leak any. It didn't mean anything. Except it did.

When I stood back up, Walter was chewing on a mouthful of white mushrooms.

"Thanks for the loan of your pickax," he said around the mushy white bits.

"You need to go home," I said. "Back to Clara and Walter Junior and Velma."

He shook his head without concern.

"I am home," he said. "This is home. I never knew it, but it's always been here. We could have worked together, he and I, but..." He looked around at the sides of Ostler Wallow, crowding over us wet and green, in this place he had called God's own country. "All my life, I've been waiting for something to worship. It's like I was made to be worshiping. Now, here, is the thing that needs my worship like I need to worship it."

I looked down at the crack. Forty years, maybe, of hard work and hard worship. Plus however much time the old bastard's pap, and his pap, and his pap had put into this. All for this single crack that you couldn't even see if the light wasn't right.

Ten thowsand thowsand years.

"'Scuse me," Walter said, stepping into my space and edging my aside. "Gotta get back to work."

I didn't argue with the man holding a pickax. He could stand just outside the doorway and swing the pickax down at the rock. *Tink.* He could do that in rain or shine, even when there was snow on the ground—just clear himself a spot, and he could work on the spot that was protected just inside the cabin. *Tink.*

Out in the boggy land surrounding the black rock, the white frogs were all watching. *Tink.* Maybe they needed to worship something, too. Maybe they needed to worship whatever worshiped whatever was underneath the rock. *Tink.*

"What should I tell Clara?" I asked.

Walter shrugged while swinging the pickax, an impressive accomplishment. "Doesn't much matter," he said. *Tink.* "She won't come up here after me, not with her health." *Tink.* "At least I didn't have to clear her out of the way, like Grandpap."

I left him then. It was either leave him, or hit him. I just walked away, down off the black rock, across the soggy land, back to my horse, and out of Ostler Wallow.

NIGHTMARE FUEL

DAVID DUNWOODY

Sheriff Betty parked on the shoulder of Creek Road—well, "shoulder" was a generous description, given that her cruiser was practically in the woods, and that she had to force back knee-high overgrowth just to get her door open. Most of these back roads were only roads in the sense that they were slightly wider than walking trails. That made this little phenomenon with which she presently faced even more puzzling, the one she was eyeballing in her headlights as she kicked her way through tangled grass.

She'd come upon another derelict. This one was a four-door sedan that looked like it might be a couple of decades old—she wasn't certain of the make or model at first glance, and walking around the abandoned vehicle didn't offer any answers. The paint may have been cream-colored in a past life; now it looked like the skin of a bloated corpse, mottled and sickly. The sheriff aimed her flashlight through the driver's side windows. The interior was brown leather—there might have been a small stain in the driver's seat, she couldn't be sure. Doc Spence kept telling Betty she needed a prescription for her eyes, reading glasses at the very least, but she hadn't budged in her refusal. A woman cop took enough crap as it was, no matter who her daddy had been. She didn't need bifocals compounding the issue.

The sedan's plates were a mystery unto themselves. There was no indication as to what state they were from. No registration stickers either—the sheriff could only assume that they were fakes, and bad ones at that. No wonder the car had been ditched out here just south of Timbuktu. Whoever had been using—or misusing—this rolling eyesore must have finally figured out that the vehicle was a little too distinctive in its absurdity.

Betty knelt and leaned in to get a good read on the plates. The block lettering said NV-GO. Or maybe that last one was a zero, not an O. She scowled and grabbed the radio mic clipped to her shoulder. "Dispatch, wanna put me through to Jared or Abel? Got another ghost car."

She recited the car's limited description, along with the plates—November Victor Golf Oscar, or maybe Zero on that last one—but she didn't expect the dispatcher's computer to get any hits off that, and she was right. Meanwhile, she imagined, Jared over at the salvage yard was being awakened by a middle-of-the-night phone call. A few moments later he was on his

CB and being patched through to the sheriff.

"Where you at, Betty?"

"Creek Road. It's an odd looker if I've ever seen one. Not sure what else to tell you."

"You said Creek Road?" Unintelligible muttering followed. Betty needn't be able to make out the words to know they were colorful. Then Jared grunted, "I'll see if I can get the truck out there. Creek Road. Damn."

While she was waiting, Betty tried the doors. All stuck fast. Trunk too. The locks themselves were weird. She'd never seen these yawning triangular key-holes. Betty went to take a good look at that possible stain on the driver's seat. It was there, all right, but it didn't scream "blood" any more than it did "coffee" or "beaver fever." That last one was the nasty byproduct of drinking creek water, and it in and of itself may have justified abandoning a befouled vehicle.

When Jared's rig came trundling along, Betty had to return to her cruiser in order to try and move it over further, providing the tow truck enough clearance to situate itself in front of the mystery vehicle. Jared managed to make his way past the other two cars, although from the sound of it he took a few low-hanging branches with him. The bearded, bleary-eyed man slid out from behind his wheel and walked back to have a look at the derelict. He cast a glance Betty's way, arching one bushy eyebrow. Jared wasn't a day over thirty but he already looked like his old man, both in countenance and posture. He pulled the hook and chain down from the boom arm on the rear of his truck. Betty got out of her car to join him.

"Wanna see if you can jimmy it open and put 'er in neutral?" Jared asked without looking up. He knelt with a grunt and began slinging the tow chain around the derelict's bumper. "Hope this bumper holds. Can't reach that axle with all the goddamned thistles under here," he muttered. "Pardon my French."

But Betty only half-heard him as she headed back to her car to retrieve a slim jim, then started working on the driver's door of the derelict. Couldn't find the lock mechanism inside the door. She moved the slim jim back and forth and it seemed like there was nothing at all to catch onto. Was this thing even a car?

That seemed an odd thought, yet it stuck in the sheriff's mind as she circled the vehicle.

"Can't get any of these doors open," she finally said with a sigh. Jared shrugged and turned on the winch attached to the boom. The derelict's front end lifted out of the underbrush and its foremost tires settled on the truck bed's rubber mats.

"We'll see what happens," Jared said, returning to his cab, and a second later he started to ease forward. Would the derelict's rear wheels lock up and fight him? Betty waited for the screech of metal. Blessedly, none came. The derelict rolled after the truck without any complaint.

Jared braked and leaned out his window. "You want to come by tomorrow to process 'er? I'm dead on my feet right now."

"That's fine. Good night." Betty watched as the two vehicles, moving in tandem like mating junebugs, crept down Creek Road and were eventually swallowed by the trees. Betty felt plenty bushed herself. Tomorrow she'd spend the morning poking through that car. Until then, dreamless sleep. At least that's what she'd hoped for.

No, Betty awoke several times during the night, and each time her heart was pounding—each time, the misty fragments of some ungodly nightmare hung in her consciousness for a few nanoseconds before fading. She tried to grab onto those threads and remember what had so shaken her, but each time she found herself unable to remember a damn thing. Something about... junebugs? In space? Lord, no. That was more akin to the nightmares she'd had as a little girl. Young Betty had read too many issues of *Sci-Fi Shriekers!* and been prone to dreams about being an astronaut adrift in deep space: numb with soundless horror, no clear point of reference in the void, no sensation of forces acknowledging and acting upon her paralyzed body. Nothing, just the distant smattering of dim points representing dead stars. The doomed spacewoman may as well have not existed at all. That was the idea that had always haunted her upon awakening, the feeling that had caught in her chest and coiled up in there, promising her no sleep until dawn warmed her bones and made her real again.

With that rosy memory to keep her company, the sheriff gave up on sleep at four in the A.M. and sat in the kitchen with a pot of coffee. Around the time she was making the second pot, the sun bled through the forest that was her backyard and she went to shower. She'd grab breakfast on the way to the salvage yard. That second pot of coffee could wait until she got home—she was feeling jumpy enough without it. As Betty stood under the shower, she tried again to dredge up some remnant of her most recent nightmares. Nothing doing. She couldn't help but think it had something to do with that car, though. Just another abandoned car, sure, at first glance; but nothing at all about it was typical. She had a feeling that researching the thing was going to take up most of her day.

Betty finished her McMuffin just as she pulled into Jared's salvage yard. The derelict was parked in the gravel right in front of the office, itself a box on wheels. She tapped her horn and got out of the cruiser. It looked as if the driver's door on the derelict was slightly ajar. She hoped Jared's brother Abel hadn't been rummaging through it for keepsakes. She wanted every bit of material evidence associated with this car laid out in front of her.

As she drew closer she saw that, indeed, Abel was seated behind the wheel of the vehicle. It didn't look as if he'd noticed her presence. Staring straight ahead through the windshield, Jared's younger brother was mouthing something and stroking the scruff on his chin. Betty pulled the long flashlight from her belt and prepared to rap on the glass. She froze in mid-swing as she saw all of him.

All of him. Rather, all that was left. Abel stared through her, continuing to make soundless shapes with his cracked lips. He stroked his beard and nod-ded as if agreeing with someone she couldn't hear—or see—and beneath his ribs there was nearly nothing to speak of. The bottom of his ribcage was plainly visible, sticking out from beneath the tatters of his old corduroy jacket. Beneath that no stomach, no lap, no legs. A congealed, snotty mess hung from his open body cavity. They didn't look like any organs Betty had ever seen, those quivering tubes of tissue which hung from Abel—Abel, whose back had to be fused to the car seat, otherwise how could he just be reclining there above the cushion? Dully, the sheriff noted that Abel was buckled in. Had he been trying to start the engine? Drive the thing into the back of the lot? As if in answer, the seatbelt tightened across Abel's chest. That belt alone, though, wasn't enough to hold him in place like that. No, he was struck fast to that seat. Betty was sure of it.

The mess of guts that unspooled from Abel's insides and rested on the seat cushion pulsed, then collapsed. To Betty, still frozen in place, it looked like they were deflating. They were—he was—

It's eating him.

"That just ain't possible," Betty breathed. There was no response from Abel. The entire surrounding area, in fact, was silent as the grave. Where was Jared? Those abominable hounds who patrolled the property? The clouds of gnats?

From the corner of her eye Betty saw the derelict's trunk lift just a bit, then settle back into place. She was rooted to the spot where she stood. But she didn't want to look in the trunk anyway. Not until she'd processed the horror in the front seat, a gibbering torso in the process of being absorbed into the upholstery.

There were a lot of thoughts racing through her mind. Some were about her radio, others about her gun. One particularly vivid impulse, which was looping through her brain with some urgency, involved Betty running scream-ing from the lot and never looking back.

Something else, too, less a thought than a feeling—that one they called *déjà vu.*

Something I dreamed. The nightmares.

She'd asked herself last night whether this thing was even a car. Now it looked to her like a Venus flytrap. Nothing seductive or alluring about it—fact of the matter was, the car was unremarkable from a distance—but some-thing was at work underneath that hood and now she felt, rather than heard, the hum of it. Working on her. Trying to ply her from the fear that held her in place—protecting her from it, but already beginning to wane. It had worked Abel over real good. Had it gotten Jared first?

This time her question received an answer. A burst of static from the car's stereo jolted her enough to awaken her limbs, and she was turning to run when the voice from the stereo made her stop cold once again.

"Betty. You can't go.

"You found it, after all.

"You can't just GO."

Her hand found the butt of the revolver on her hip and she faced the car again. "J-Jared?"

"*I'm not tired anymore,*" said the radio. "*We're going on a trip. Not one you could take in any ordinary car. But you know this ain't a car, don't you?*"

It couldn't have been so much as a minute since Betty had first come across Abel, and yet she felt like a petrified tree that had spent an eternity trembling before this thing. *That* was it, the terror from her nightmares—the feeling came flooding back to her, and it was just as crazy and just as unde-niable as it had been in the realm of sleep. The terror was somehow knowing the agelessness of this *living thing* that had masqueraded as an early-nineties eggshell-hued sedan gathering rust on Creek Road. That something so old and intelligent had assumed this form... but what else should she have ex-pected from a wolf in sheep's clothing? Lights and whistles? It was a bland, innocuous imitation whose otherworldliness was only sensed through the scrutiny of someone who knew her cars.

And, perhaps, someone who wasn't altogether unfamiliar with a certain sort of terror. This ancient thing was sister to the void from her childhood dreams. It was endless, and cold, and uncaring.

Jared must have sensed something in the derelict too. He must have broken in to get a better look—all along he would have thought the tug in his mind was only his own curiosity at work, not some infernal mechanism under that battered hood.

Sheriff Betty was feeling the car's tug, and its invisible hooks probed deeper with every squawk of the radio. Jared's voice was a flat monotone but she knew it was him nonetheless, not the thing parroting him.

"*It's not bad. It doesn't hurt. Look at Abel. He ain't feeling a thing. It doesn't eat you, Betty, it just takes you in. And then we'll all go for that big star-ride.*"

"*Come on, Betty. Get in.*"

"This can't be right," the sheriff moaned. "How—"

"*It's right as rain.*" Static interrupted Jared for a moment, and he faded. Then he was back and clearer than before. "*You see this ugly old clunker? And how she blends right in 'less you give 'er a good once-over? She blends because this old heap is all this world has to offer us. Under the shell, though, where I am—where we are—it's all stars, Betty.*"

The car pulled hard at her mind and she stumbled forward in spite of her-self. She threw her left hand out and struck the hood. The sound of her palm against the eggshell was a sharp crack. The hood didn't feel like metal at all. It was brittle and rough. It felt like the carapace of a crawdad. A *shell*.

There was a scraping sound beneath Betty's hand and she jerked it away from the car. A radio antenna emerged from the place where her palm had rested. As she pulled away it craned forward in pursuit.

The horror of that sight was what gave Betty back full use of her limbs. Now she knew she could outrun the psychic tug of the thing beneath the shell. And that was all she needed to know in order for her to plant her feet and draw her revolver.

The car *shivered.*

Its paint job shimmered, and a ripple went through it like wind teasing linens on a clothesline. The ripple went from back to front and the headlights suddenly came on. The light was unlike any Betty had ever seen on God's green Earth. *Starlight, baby.* That was Jared's voice again but this time it wasn't coming from the radio. He was in her head. The antenna wavered, danced like an Indian serpent.

Betty summoned the strength to speak loud and clear. "Wherever you're going, friend, I can't come. Don't want to." *And get the HELL out of my mind.*

"You're just afraid." The radio again. *"It's not really fear though, Betty. It's wonder. It's like what you'd feel if you ran smack into the good Lord walking down Main Street. Don't lose out. GET IN."*

"Nothing doing." Betty took aim at one of the glaring headlamps. "Let them go," she said to that gleaming eye.

"Can't undo what's done," said the radio.

"Not talking to you, Jared."

The car shivered again and released a rumbling cough from under its hood. Was it about to rush her? Would it run her down or suck her in?

"It's alive, Betty. Smart. It can make itself look like anything at all, and it came here and it chose us. How about that? All it wants is to take us home with it."

"I'll bet."

"This isn't a creature feature. It's not gonna kill you." Static crackled through Jared's voice. He was sounding tired now. Betty focused again on her aim. She trained the barrel of her gun on the license plate. NV-GO, or maybe zero. Actually, she could see it a lot clearer from this distance. Damned farsightedness. She made herself a promise that she'd get the stupid bifocal prescription that afternoon.

Then she pulled the trigger, and the plate reading MI-GO warped as the bullet punched right through that center dash. The noise that came from the car in no way resembled the workings of a combustion engine. That was the sound of a pissed-off wasp and the wasp sounded like it was the size of a damn dog.

She fired again. The bullet struck the hood and cracks webbed out from the point of impact. Something pink and wet puffed out from the cracks. The car shook from side to side, then back and forth.

Betty took a sidestep and shot the front left wheel. More pink goo bloomed as the tire erupted.

"Stoooooooooooooop!" the radio blared. It wasn't Jared anymore. It was a hundred buzzing wasps. Betty doubled over and clutched at her temples as the sound filled her skull. Staggering back, she glimpsed Abel's torso slumping forward in the driver's seat and then flopping from view.

The car reared back like a spider, front end rising and folding down towards her, its membranous paint job rippling and then *flapping.* Peeling away from the derelict body and beating the air, three great pairs of translucent wings stained pink with either pain or fear or rage. Betty realized she'd lost her gun but didn't bother looking for it. Whatever was about to happen was about to happen.

The thing, which now only vaguely resembled a car, the thing whose pulsing undercarriage was ribbed flesh, lunged at her. Just before it would have taken her head off it tore upward and over her with a sound like a jet plane. Betty fell on her back and felt her head land hard on the revolver. Red light flooded her vision. When it cleared there was a dull ache, a ringing in her ears, and a clear sky overhead.

She rolled over and searched the horizon in every visible direction. It was gone, all right. She knew she'd only been out for a few seconds after smacking her head. It couldn't have reached the cover of the clouds that quickly. It had taken some other route, something as alien as it was itself, and she imagined that now it was somewhere out in that void. That awful void.

Yet Jared—and she still believed it was his actual self speaking through the radio—hadn't been shaken at all by the notion of surfing among the stars. She supposed it was all relative. Her idea of oblivion had, to him, seemed a boundless wonder. Maybe it was because she was content in her own skin. That made her flesh crawl a bit.

MI-GO. Her daddy would have seen that and pinned the whole thing on the Koreans. The thought made Betty laugh, and something about the unabashed cry of that laughter was liberating. Betty was able to lie prone in the gravel and regain her strength, to ponder, unafraid. Unafraid but hardly wonder-struck.

Regardless of that, she hoped that Jared would have a good trip, and that it would prove to be all he'd dreamed.

THE SWIMMING HOLE

THERIC JEPSON

I never wore shoes in July until 1987 when I was seven years old. No kid in our town did. I suppose if my family hadn't moved to California, I would have stayed barefoot all summer every summer until the boys came calling. But instead I found myself in Sacramento with nothing but brimstone-hot asphalt to walk on. What I missed the most was not the air between my toes or the lack of constraint, but the calluses. Calluses so thick and hard that once I checked my foot to see what had been pressing into my heel the last block and found a bent-over thumbtack. Now *that* is true freedom. The freedom to walk anywhere you wish, just as God made you.

Funny how clear the memory of those calluses is to me even today. Most memories of my rural Oklahoma childhood have fled. I remember my gran-mammy—she kept glass chickens filled with either hard candy or Brach Milk Maid Royals in every room. And even though I never cared for horehound, their location in the bathroom meant I didn't have to ask permission. That memory that came flooding back when my husband brought home a bag of horehound candy last year from the farmer's market. I still don't like it, but it tasted like Oklahoma and that was worth something.

One thing I don't remember is religion. Which is funny because my parents were about the most religious people I've ever met. I used to joke with them we must've moved to Sacramento for the name. First thing they did when we moved in was sign me up for a Baptist home school. This in addition to pub-lic school. On Sundays we were Methodist. Holidays we did Catholic. And anybody who knocked on the door teaching some version of Jesus was set right on the couch. Though the Mormons stopped coming after my mom tried to get one of them to take me to prom.

My parents passed away shortly after Ben and I were married. My father had a heart attack while driving on the 80. The car drifted into a truck carry-ing tomatoes. The spectacle became one of those stupid internet meme things. It still pops up. Ultimately, I had to quit the internet. My husband keeps an eye on my email (released to galleries only) and I stick with my old flip phone. But I never get online anymore. I barely touch the computer at all.

Ben and I have been blessed with two bright kids, ten and eight, a boy and a girl. Or, rather, our youngest manifests female. She's hermaphroditic.

The doctors urged us to give her a surgery as a baby, decide for her, but we couldn't. She'll just have to decide for herself someday. When she's an adult. For now she's happy being our little girl and we're happy to have her.

When I received a certified letter from Boktussa, Oklahoma, I didn't know what to expect, but certainly not that my granmammy had passed, leaving me her only heir. Her passing wasn't the surprising part—I hadn't seen her in 30 years and she had to be about a hundred—but that I was the only heir. My mother had a slew of brothers, six or seven, and I remember them having fertile wives. Nostalgia for my cousins has always been the prime temptation for getting back online in the age of facebooking and twittering and such. To learn that they were all… But how was it possible? My cousins would have kids by now—some of them I assumed would be grandparents! Clearly that detail was wrong, but for some reason Granmammy left me her property. Maybe the rest of the family had also moved away and I was the easiest for the small-town lawyer to find? Maybe Granmammy had had a falling out with her progeny? Or maybe she was trying to heal whatever mysterious rift had sent my parents west in the first place.

I didn't reply right away. I had to decide my own mind before sharing the news with Ben. One thing to know about Ben is that he loves two things: staying home and monotonous travel. He doesn't care where home is—just that it's his and his family is there. His only complaint about Sac is that its airport's only a half-hour's drive from our place. Even with traffic it never takes an hour, and that's hard to say about anywhere in Sacramento. I would say we're lucky, but he loves being alone in a car or a bland hotel. He usually works at home, parked in front of his PC ten hours a day, then they'll send him on long tedious trips to field offices to sit in front of someone else's computer for ten hours a day. I went with him once about a decade ago and it was the worst week of my life. But I love my boring husband. I wouldn't change him. I need someone plain and unimaginative. I suppose, a hundred years ago, a well-meaning doctor would have called me "nervous." I used to call it "rich" in college. Being twenty and an art student with more ideas than time to paint is rich, isn't it? These days I've settled into a defined subject matter, a "morbid hybrid of the insane unearthly and every sort of Christian iconography" as the *East Bay Express* described my recent Oakland show. I don't sell much of my work, but that's because I keep the prices high. I make enough to afford a small studio space to work and show in. What more could I need?

That was the question raised by the letter. With the lower cost of living in Boktussa, I could easily travel to Oklahoma City, a happening burg from what I've heard, or anywhere in Texas for that matter. And Granmammy's property has sufficient outbuildings for me to have any sort of studio I pleased, with some remodeling.

As for Ben, he wouldn't care either way about the house, but he would love his new drive out of the middle of nowhere. In fact, that alone might have been enough for him to say yes right off. So the real question was the kids.

What would Taggart say? What would Andee say? And would they be guessing right?

I suppose the six-week debate with first myself then my family doesn't matter anymore. We decided to leave behind a lifetime in California and move to a place I barely remembered. Carpe diem.

With Granmammy's house furnished and our kids past the age at which they destroyed furniture, we sold or donated nearly all our furnishings and books and linens and clothing. We kept our newest kitchenware and my painting supplies. The kids filled six boxes apiece. Some odds and ends. We packed one smallish moving truck and said goodbye. As we crossed over into Nevada, I surprised myself by bursting into tears: heavy, cracking sobs. Everyone asked, but I couldn't answer. I had always hated Sacramento, or at least said I had. Maybe it was just feeling my childhood and my parents fall away? I don't know. Anyway. Our California era was over.

The drive was a blur of hotels and fast food and roadside attractions. I barely noticed. As we left the mountains and came down to the plains, I started to recover what it felt to be a child. The long horizons and featureless distance filled me with nostalgic dread. The sense that you can walk forever and never get anywhere, never be found. Before I moved to California, such exotic places as the ocean and mountains and Disneyland seemed like Stoppard's conspiracy of cartographers.

We passed through oil fields, the mindless bird-heads of the pumps going up and down, sucking energy from deep in the earth. We saw cattle aligning themselves with the compass. Once, we upset a massive flock of small birds that fled in undulating waves of blackness and sky, a living stain until they slipped away too far to see, dissolved into the emptiness. I began to pinch my eyes closed with one hand, my other gripping Ben's thigh. I kept telling myself that these days we can have everything we want shipped to us. Or Ben can drive for food—he loves driving. I never even have to look out a window. I can pretend the landscape still has landmarks. I can pretend space is still finite.

We drove into Boktussa late at night. Our truck had had a flat which had left us on the side of a small two-lane county road for half a day, so we missed the lawyer's office hours. We passed one ratty motel when we first entered town, but kept driving, hoping to find something better. The buildings ended much sooner than we expected, and as Ben turned the truck around we saw the moon rising over a landmark I had forgotten, the one landmark in the county: Boktussa Butte—a decapitated hill, really. Half the moon lay atop it like some luminescent organ atop a platter, or like God's egg in its nest. It was... painterly, and this, more than the horizon or the benighted buildings, provided me specific remembrances. From here, the butte looked true, plateau-like. But I knew it was hollow and filled with sulphuric water, the smell growing stronger on hot days. We children would tromp up the hill and swim. When we returned, our parents would hose off the white layering our skin, and the smell, before we went inside to watch *Wheel of Fortune* and

Jeopardy! and the city news out of Oklahoma City and getting hustled off to bed. I wondered if the water was still there. Or had the adults finally found a way to exploit it? Fracking is a thing in Oklahoma, right?

I was stirred from my thoughts of the murky waters of childhood by the sound of the emergency brake. Ben walked into the motel lobby. He dinged a desk bell and an older man came into the room. He was strikingly asymmetrical. One eye pinched shut—perhaps gone?—his mouth twisted to one side, even his wrinkles were uneven. He and Ben spoke, then Ben was given a key; he came out and handed it to me, then reached in the back to lift one of our sleeping children. I rushed ahead, opened the door, pulled back the sheets on one bed, and went for our bags.

After Ben had tucked both of them in, we sat out on the curb and watched our shadows cast by the moon. Finally, Ben broke the silence. "I never realized how small a town of six hundred people actually is."

I nodded.

"It's so quiet." He let out a contented sigh. "That fellow said we took three minutes two seconds from first passing him back to parking in his lot."

"He timed us?"

"Said he knew we'd be back."

"And we took three minutes."

"And two seconds. Dum Dum?" He handed me a sucker, compliments of the house. I tried to take off the wrapper but the candy had melted into the paper.

"He must have had these when I moved away."

Ben laughed and pulled me under his shoulder. "We made it," he said, and kissed the top of my head.

In the morning, after getting everyone showered and checking out, we drove carefully down the main street, watching numbers. The office of Barrett and Holmes, Attorneys-at-Law, was marked only by aged gilt letters on the privacy-glass window of a weathered wooden door which stuck when we tried to open it. Ben was about to shove with his shoulder when a voice cried, Wait! Wait! The door closed fully again then opened with a moan. A prune-like man with frightened eyebrows and more hair poking from his nostrils than the sides of his head gestured us inside.

"The trick is lifting while turning. Simple, really, once you know how. The Reever family, I presume?"

"Yes," I said as I moved the children to a couple of plastic chairs beside a table with some celebrity magazines from the late '80s. "I'm Tabatha and this is Benjamin."

"Ben," said Ben as he shook the man's hand. "Mr. Barrett or—?"

"The very man. Old John Holmes has been dead these twenty years now, but I can't bear to scrape his name from the door. They will have to scrape our names off together. Please, sit! Sit!"

We sat on the proffered chairs, their old, cheap leather catching on my skirt. Mr. Barrett clattered on about the pleasure of welcoming his good friend's granddaughter back to town after so many years. I smiled and nodded and waited for his effusives to run their course. Then it was paperwork and paperwork and more paperwork. We understood that the entire inheritance was wrapped up in the property but the property did not become ours legally until we'd lived in it for two years. We understood that we could move in today. That he had anticipated contacting the utilities on our behalf, so nothing to concern ourselves with there. That he would be happy to drive us out. That the keys were right here in his desk.

And so on, swinging back and forth between legal matters, practical matters, and nostalgia. I learned more about my grandmother than my mother had ever told me. She had run the local women's organization until quite recently. After receiving the insurance money from her husband's death, she'd let the farm lie fallow as she became a librarian at the elementary school. As other old folks moved or passed on, she'd grown her property until she owned everything southeast of town including the butte.

"The butte is ours?"

"You possess it, and in two years you own it outright."

"It still has water in it?"

"Oh, yes. You'll have kids up there all summer."

Mr. Barrett did not lock his office door as we left. He drove an old LeSabre and we followed him south of town a mile, then east to a low-lying brick home. To my surprise, it wasn't familiar at all. As Mr. Barrett unlocked the door, I asked if the house hadn't used to be much larger and ornate, perhaps even turrets and towers—a Victorian castle?

He laughed. "No, no. It did burn down about ten years ago and she rebuilt smaller and closer to the butte, but her previous home wasn't that spectacular. Visions of childhood, I'm afraid."

We walked inside. I remembered more furniture, but perhaps Granmammy hadn't felt a need to replace it all. What did exist—a sofa and two recliners and an old TV perched on a too-small table—were covered in plastic jackets. The room felt remarkably clean, considering how long it must have been sitting empty. No dust to speak of. No musty aroma.

"It's nice," said Ben, which the kids seem to interpret as permission to run around opening doors. Further surprises awaited. Granmammy's mattress was the same as our $4,000 Stearns & Foster I'd tearfully watched Ben give up for $400 on craigslist. The basement had two rooms, each with an unused mattress. When I asked, Mr. Barrett could only imagine that my granmammy had planned for our coming long before her passing. How she knew the details of my family—down to the butterfly bedside lamp for Andee and a bucket of baseballs for Taggart—

The pantry had relatively recent Dinty Moore, blue boxes of Kraft mac and cheese, and a few large Hershey bars, a bag of marshmallows, and a box of graham crackers. I shot a glance at Mr. Barrett who just smiled and shrugged.

That night the kids were satisfied with the macaroni, and we microwaved some smores before readying for bed. Later, Ben and I sat on the front steps watching black clouds covering and revealing distant stars. So many more stars than I remembered seeing. Ben leaned over to kiss me, blotting out the sky. "I can't believe you were a child here." His hand crept up my thigh and his mouth moved up my cheekbone. I pushed my hands through his hair and raked his scalp. I felt my knees spreading of their own accord.

"Meet me inside."

I mumbled an affirmative.

As he slipped back inside, I stood and walked a few steps away from the house and looked about. The clouds seemed to have fled. The sky was just brilliant with stars. I turned slowly and saw stars spreading from the horizon to the apex of heaven. Then the butte: a sudden, melted rectangle looming over our house, making a large, square, bite-like wound in the sky.

I realized I wasn't breathing. Suddenly cold, I rushed inside to Ben, desperate for him to rewarm me.

In the morning, we unpacked the truck of our meager belongings. Each trip back to the house placed the butte in my sight. By daylight, that moment alone seemed absurd and I laughed at myself. Really, I was happy to have it breaking up the horizon. Finally: something to look at, to provide bearing —the butte would keep the plains from overtaking me. For lunch we went into town and I regaled the children with mostly invented stories of swimming in its bowl as we had hot dogs and frozen french fries at the town's lone diner. Instead of driving directly back home, we walked up the street and looked in storefronts. Many were closed, abandoned, but those remaining appeared healthy enough. A few seemed even familiar. The pharmacy with the jokey caps for sale. The alleged bakery that displayed fishing equipment in its window. All the while I listened to my mouth tell greater and greater yarns about swimming atop the butte until it was no surprise when Ben gave the kids the rest of the day off when we brought in the box with their swimming things. He told me to walk up with them and he would finish unloading on his own.

The butte was much closer than it seemed. The amorphous horizon had made it too seem far away, but in fact it was not more than a few hundred yards and, though steep, an easy enough walk to the top. We stepped over the ridge and into mud. The center was still filled with water, though I was taken aback by its blackness. Even in the brightness of early afternoon, it did not seem to accept light. Or, rather, perhaps, it invited light in only to swallow it whole into its deep and inescapable maw. But these morbid thoughts were my own and before I could fully articulate them even to myself, Taggart and Andee had run screaming joyfully to the water, touching it with their toes then jumping in and splashing each other. My unwelcome imagination now saw my children frolicking in the pupil of some great beast's eye. I turned away from them and looked down at our house. A ball large enough not to get trapped in divots or shrubs could easily reach our yard. I found a dryish spot and sat down to force myself to read the book I had brought with me. I read long enough to lose track of the sun, but I couldn't tell you a word of its matter. I was aware of nothing until I heard my children approaching me, laughing and screaming in the way they do, screeching for me to look at them. I turned and looked and dropped my book. I forced myself to laugh, trying to match my expression to theirs. Their toothy smiles shined bright within their chalky faces. Their hair too was matted and white. Taggart's trunks and Andee's skirted suit were caked with white. Their arms and legs were drying, cracks forming in the whitewash covering their bodies.

"I—I had forgotten," I said. "I had forgotten."

"We're so white!" said Andee.

My eyes traveled through the mud along their footprints back to the black water. "We should go home," I said. "You should bathe."

As I dried Taggart's hair, Ben asked, "And you're sure it's safe?"

"I suppose. Everyone swam there. No adults, but that's hardly surprising."

"It's unpleasant stuff."

"Ergo, no adults. We care more about such things."

"I certainly can't see myself enjoying its pleasures."

I snorted. "Andee! Are you done in there?"

"I just wish we knew what it was."

I shrugged. "Some alkali or something. Nothing that won't just wash off."

"Weird."

"You wait," I said. "It's summer. We'll see plenty more kids."

And perhaps I would, but Ben was called away two days later, first to work in the Madison, Wisconsin office, then to help install new infrared cameras at the Madison airport. Since no airport was "closest" to us anymore, Ben decided to fly out of Topeka. He kissed us, all three, then was gone. I stayed home to arrange our old belongings in our new home while the children went to swim. And so it went the next three days. I stayed home on some pretense while they climbed the butte to swim.

The third day they returned without swimming. Taggart carrying a small dog in his arms, its neck bleeding. In a rush, they told me of it being roped to a stake, straining and trying to pull away from the lake. I helped remove the rope and we treated its neck as well as we could. At first it was jumpy and anxious but by bedtime it seemed to have reached an equanimity and I allowed it to sleep with Andee.

The fourth day my children again returned in the early evening, white save for their irises. The dog—now christened Teddy—had stayed with me and cowered until they were out of sight, then he followed me to finish setting up the barn I was making into my studio. When they returned, I asked if other kids were showing up and they shrugged. I asked what the other kids were like and they said fine. I asked what they did with the other kids and they attempted a joke about baptism. So I pointed the hose at their heads and rolled my eyes and we went in to dinner.

I don't always sleep well when Ben is gone, and that was one of those nights. I arose and went to my almost-studio. I took a stretched canvas and painted the top third as black as the sky I'd walked under. I absently began to add stars as I imagined they might look reflected off the butte's water. I painted an old woman in a dark brown hood and cloak, her face gazing out of the painting, as if judging what she saw. Granmammy.

I awoke in one of the front-room recliners with early morning sun in my eyes. I showered slowly, letting the heat push into my muscles to loosen me up. I shaved my legs with the idea that I might swim with the kids today, and if not, tomorrow we should go see what the local churches were like so why not get the legs done now. First, though, we needed more food. The kids debated a while but decided to stay home while I drove into town to Dell's, the six-aisle grocery store. At checkout I got to talking with the older fellow running the register. "Oh yes," he said. "And you have the little boy and girl, don't you? My grandkids mentioned them to me. They enjoying themselves?"

"Oh, sure, climbing the butte and going swimming—what could be better?"

He paused almost imperceptibly in packing my bags, then nodded and chuckled as if to say kids would be kids and kids do swim the summer away.

The conversation felt dead, its hole of silence heavy. I said, "What I don't understand is how my granmammy could afford to buy all that land around her property."

"Oh," he said, his eyes unfocusing for a moment—or, rather, focusing about a mile beyond me, "I wouldn't say Bethelsda 'bought it.' More like she come into it, say."

"How do you mean?"

He shrugged and finished packing my groceries, placing the last plastic bag on the dogfood in my cart. "Just, she had a way with people. That'll be eighty-nine forty-four, there."

He ran my card and excused himself to sweep. I walked to my car and sat for a moment behind the wheel. Then, deciding the milk and eggs and such would be fine, drove to see Mr. Barrett. I lifted the door as I turned the knob and walked in. A buxom forty-something sat at reception and greeted me.

"Is Mr. Barrett in?"

She frowned. "No... May I take a message?"

"I—suppose. I'm Tabatha Crosby—Bethelsda Olney's granddaughter?"

"Oh," she said. I didn't know how to read her tone, but she promised to tell him I'd stopped by, then began tapping at her keyboard.

"Well," I said. "Thank you." I stepped outside and took a breath of air as I looked up the main street. Not one week ago we'd driven in just there. I turned my head slowly, talking it in, when a hulking mass in my peripheral vision startled me and I swung my head to see the butte, looming over the town. I squinted. From ground level its hollow top was hidden from me, but I could see a couple small humanish forms going up the townward side.

Based on my meager memories—possibly invented by California stereotypes of Oklahoma since I certainly never heard my parents speak of here—the economy of Boktussa is farming. Or ranching. I'm not sure if there's a difference. Other than open land, however, I hadn't seen much evidence of this, so it felt almost vindicating when a tractor came put-putting up the street, distracting me from the butte. Obviously an old machine, perhaps as old as the overalled man driving it. And—look!—his boots and denim below the knees, though dry, were caked white. I watched him pass by, my only clear thought curiosity. Had this man lost a dog?

I had put the food away and was just about to go see the painting I'd begun work on when the children came home for lunch. I hosed them off, careful to place them downwind to keep the sulfur smell away from me, but didn't make them shower as they told me they planned to swim more before bedtime.

"You never swam this much when we had a swimming pool," I said as I handed them grilled-cheese sandwiches.

Andee, whose hair and scalp were deathly white, replied, "Chlorine makes your hair smell funny."

"Besides," added Taggart, "in Sac we had AC. So it was easier to watch TV. It's not as hot here, but still."

"And it's, like, nature." Andee took a big bite of her sandwich, melted butter gathering at the corners of her lips. Through the sandwich she said, "Dere's shtuff."

I sat down and looked them over. With their faces still framed in shock white after their cursory washing, they were rather cinematic. One of these times, instead of hosing them off, I would have to have them pose for me.

"How many other kids were there today?"

Taggart shrugged. "Only two. But a bunch of grownups too."

"Oh. They swam?"

Andee giggled. "No, they just walk around singing to the water."

"Yeah, they said they have to do it in daytime."

"For safety."

"Yeah. For safety."

"For safety," I repeated. I should be going with them. "Did you take the dog with you?"

Both shook their heads—disdainfully? "He won't go. He's scared." Then they bye-mommed me and hugged me and were gone before I could offer to join them. I waited a moment then went out to watch them climb the butte. The dog was watching them also and whining, the white fur around his neck still slightly rusty with blood. I sat down and examined his scab, then scratched his back and together we watched them till they disappeared into the maw. "Well," I said. "Well."

The dog dozed off. I gave him a pat, then went inside to wash my hands and head out to the barn. I propped open the door and started placing some old 2x4s to hold open the swing-up shutters on the windows. I was on the sixth and last when a sudden gust of wind knocked loose three shutters on the butte side and they swung down with a synchronous, clapping bang. That noise was followed by a hollow, tinny clunk. A tin can had fallen from one of the beams and was lying at the foot of my easel surrounded by cigarette butts. In the remaining sunlight, ash fluttered downward. Onto my wet oils. I ran over and grabbed the easel, pulling it toward the nearest open window to get the best light for cleanup.

The left side of the painting was untouched, the brown-cloaked figure of my granmammy's memory staring darkly from its shadows, her figure looking out from a blocked-in landscape of dark green and clotted red-browns. The ash had fallen onto the right side which I had left dominated by a massive white block. I hadn't decided what it was to become—perhaps Jesus arriving triumphantly from heaven—but, wait.

My breath fell heavily in my chest, as if I had inhaled argon. The cigarette ash had lighted on the taller peaks of the white paint creating, undeniably, two clear faces. The first, Andee, somber, staring, unkind. The second a death's head complete with hollow eyes and naked teeth. I had no memory of painting any such things last night, white on white. But here they were now, outlined clearly in the black gray of ash.

I stumbled backward and fell on my rear, unable to stop staring at the faces. I had never seen Andee's visage filled with so devastating a purpose. And that skull! What did it—? Was it threatening Andee? Was it prompting her?

I pushed myself back, away from this horror. My eyes never left Andee's —not for full minutes—which is why it took me so long to realize that the green and brown blocking I had done on the other side took the form of the butte. Or that my granmammy and daughter were in perfect balance on opposite sides of the canvas. That the skull, for all its mythic weight, mattered less, and faded from my view.

Ben called after the children were in bed. His hotel, he was certain, maintained most of its decor from the '70s and '80s, but the mattress was firm and he liked it. As we spoke, he was fiddling with an infrared camera the company had given him to test and experiment with. Eventually they wanted to connect them to folks' phones and such to allow for distance viewing of home-security footage. He currently had it connected to his laptop and, though glitchy, said he could see the draft at the bottom of his balcony door, and the two red and white bodies sitting in the next room watching a glowing orange box.

"You can see through walls?"

"Yes. I mean—this is a lower-end model so I can't see into the hotel room down the block from here, but I can see through wall singular and *then* down the block."

"Wall singular." I looked at the kitchen wall facing the studio. "Still kind of creepy."

Ben grunted. "Which is why they only sell the better ones to airports and oil rigs and the FBI and stuff. Still. Vastly more interesting than my last assignment."

"C'mon, Ben. You like boring." I turned on the TV. Just a staticky picture from the broadcast signal out of OKC, but better than the unblinking walls.

He laughed. "True enough. You miss me?"

"You know I miss you. I always miss you."

I was surprised by the emotion in my voice, but Ben didn't notice as he abruptly started cursing.

"What happened?"

"Just dropped the camera. Damn it."

"It's broken?"

"Seems like it."

"You should go to bed anyway."

"I'll pretend this pillow is you."

"Don't get too confused. I have plans for your return."

The conversation turned more and more suggestive, but soon I was alone again with a bad TV signal and questions I couldn't answer. I stood a long time in the bathroom debating whether to take melatonin or not. Its guaranteed sleep comes with guaranteed dreams.

I took it.

I awoke in the morning rested, but filled with memories of the butte drawing nearer and nearer, pulling our house up its banks until it, with me inside, slid into the water, while all the time Andee, naked and caked white, urged me to join her and a skeleton who stood beside her, wanting to speak but unable. The story had wound around and around my sleep in as many iterations as there are hours of night. I was glad to leave my bed and make a homey breakfast of scrambled eggs and toast and feed it to my children. I told them to dress nice and together we drove into town to seek a church. I knew there were none on the main drag but in a town the size of Boktussa, it wouldn't take long.

We drove up and down streets for half an hour without luck. I slowed and rolled down my window to talk to an elderly woman in a house dress. I asked her where to find a church.

"Church?" She looked at me, then in the backseat at my children, then back at me. "You're Bethelsda's little gal, ain't'cha?"

"Yes, ma'am. I am."

"Hmm. Bethelsda never was one much for churches."

"You knew her, then?"

The woman smiled, revealing small brown teeth. "Oh, sure I did. Sure I did. Now Bethelsda, when she wanted to worship, she just headed on up the butte."

"They hold services on the butte?"

"Now and then they do. They're overdue, I must say." Her eyes traveled to the back again. "Boy and a girl. Isn't that nice."

"I'm a boy *and* a girl! I'm both!"

I was too surprised to say anything. We'd never told Andee to keep anything secret, but she'd never shouted it out before either.

"Um, yes," I said, trying to pull the woman's attention back to me. "Hey, since you know my mother's family, what happened to the rest of them?"

The woman looked at me a long time. As her brow furrowed, her eyes shrunk into shining black dots. "Couldn't say," she said, and walked away.

I was too unsettled by the exchange to keep looking. I took the children home and we read of Jesus' visit to the Gadarenes which, I admit, provided less comfort than I was looking for, so we pressed on, reading of the raising of Jarius' daughter and the woman with an issue of blood, then starting a new chapter. Finally Taggart and Andee tired and after Jesus fed the five thousand, I let them go. After a half-hour downstairs, they came up dressed to swim in their crusty white swimming gear. Andee's skirt had hardened up. Something about her earlier declaration drew my attention to her small bulge and I wished to rush over and correct her skirt.

I hadn't moved from the sofa in their absence and now I gripped the Bible tight. "Aren't you bored of swimming yet?"

Oh no, oh no.

"You really enjoy it that much?"

Oh yes, oh yes.

"Maybe I—I should come with you."

Oh no, Mom. Oh no.

So again I watched them go. And I sat there. And I pressed my fingers into my mother's Bible. The Bible of the mother who took me away from here. A place where my children's bodies are mapped in layers of white.

My phone rang and I jumped up to get it. Ben.

"Ben!"

"Hey, hon... Something wrong?"

I hesitated.

"Hon?"

"Sorry, no, nothing. Nothing's wrong. I just—I guess I miss you."

"Well then you'll be glad to hear I just landed in Tulsa. I'll be home before dinner."

"Oh, that's great." I was surprised to feel tears in my eyes. "I'm—I'll look forward to you."

"Good... Look, though. I'm only home long enough to connect the cameras to our computer so I can test them while I'm finishing up in Madison. I fly out again tomorrow evening."

"O-okay. It's—it's still better than no Ben at all."

I could tell he wanted to ask me more about my state of mind, but I couldn't let him. What would I say? Looked at rationally, was anything actually wrong? No. A couple of weird things, but... So I cut him off, said I was going swimming with the kids. But first I ran to the barn and hid the ash-Andee. Then I considered changing out of my church clothes, but instead I just hurried up the hill, calling their names. They met me at the ridge. I looked over their shoulders and in the water I could see, like white polka dots in the black water, the white-encrusted heads of other children. They all seemed to be looking at me, keeping their heads so low in the water I wasn't sure they could breathe.

"Mom?" Taggart looked at me perplexed.

"Your father's coming home. I need you to come clean up before we eat."

Andee sighed. For a moment, she became the teenager she too soon would be. "*Mom*," she said. "We were *doing* something. And he hasn't even been gone that long."

"That's true, dear. But it's his first return since we moved here. Come on."

She huffed and dragged her feet, but she followed me. I told her to shower first—and to start her shower in her suit to clean it up as well—and had Taggart feed the dog. Ben was home sooner than my most optimistic estimations and held me from behind as I stirred a sesame-based sauce into my stir-fry. He grabbed two trivets and carried over the rice as I brought over the vegetables.

Ben sat down and reached out to grab mine and Andee's hands. As we made a circle around Granmammy's small table he asked Taggart to say grace.

Taggart looked at Andee before closing his eyes. "Dear… God. Thanks, um, for this week. And that we're all here. Thanks that we're all here. Amen."

Ben raised an eyebrow at me, then stood to serve everyone rice.

As soon as the kids were in bed, we were too. I clutched Ben desperately —almost fearfully—as we made love. Afterwards, he tried to ask me what was bothering me, but he couldn't find a question I could answer. All I could say was that I felt better with him here. That when we were together, then I felt whole. But even with that clear truth that I'd told him before less fervently, I trailed off, thinking of the myth—was it Hindu—that at first we were all created like Andee, but the gods split us apart and our lives were spent looking for our other half. I had found this idea romantic in college, and before finding Ben, androgynes had found their way into the backgrounds of many of my paintings. I needed Ben. Did we, having found each other, need anything else?

My thoughts rattled on, getting less and less coherent. Ben held me tighter and tighter, but his body relaxed into sleep before I found anything to say aloud. Focusing on his breathing calmed me. And soon I joined him.

In the morning he set up four cameras outside the house, wherever there were outlets. I didn't leave him but held the ladder, then came inside with him and sat beside him, letting my hand rest on his thigh as he checked the feeds and made sure they fed to his phone. "Just don't turn the computer off while I'm gone, 'kay?"

"Sure."

"It's nice that the kids haven't messed up my desktop for a change."

"They just swim now."

"All day?"

"Every day."

Ben turned his head to look at me. I felt my lips quiver. He held my face and kissed my forehead. "We've always wanted them to spend more time outside."

"Yeah."

We watched each other's faces for a while. I don't know what mine showed, but it caused his to show concern.

"They're okay."

I nodded.

I was just about to wrap my arms around his shoulders when his phone buzzed. "Hold that thought. Ah, crap."

"What?"

"Some storm's moving into Kansas and they're expecting tornado warnings tomorrow. They want to know if I can fly out of Tulsa tonight."

"Oh."

"I'll tell them I can't do it. They'll get me another flight."

"No, no. It's fine."

He looked at me. I hadn't seen him this skeptical since... I don't know. "No," he said. "I'll stay tonight."

"No, Ben. Please. I'm a big girl. It's fine."

"Maybe *it's* fine, but are *you* fine?"

"I'm fine. Go."

He didn't move.

"I wanted to go swimming with the kids today anyway. I'll tell them goodbye for you."

"No, I'll go up there first."

"No, no. They'll be fine. And you've got a plane to catch."

"Not till nine."

"Go. Just call me when you get there."

He nodded. "You need this, don't you?"

"Yes," I lied.

"Okay. I'll call you when I get back to Madison."

"It's a deal."

He kissed me, then went to grab his travel case. Then he returned and we stood in the doorway and kissed. Although I had told him to go, I knew my mouth was telling him something else. But he'd already texted them to buy the ticket so it wasn't long until he was backing up and, with a small wave, turning away and driving back towards Boktussa.

I felt tears creeping up so I slammed the door and started disrobing as I ran to take a quick shower and make a haphazard pass over my legs. I put on my one-piece and some shorts, grabbed a towel, and went outside. I looked up at the butte and a whine drew my attention. The dog was peeking around the corner of the house. "Hey, Teddy. How'd you get outside? You want to come with me?" I squatted and scratched his head. I grabbed the leash off its hook and attached it to his collar then took a step towards the butte. Instantly Teddy sat down and started pulling back. "C'mon." I pulled; he pulled back harder. Soon I was pulling as hard as I could and this little dog, his eyes bulging, would not budge. So I let go. "I'm sorry, buddy." I held his face with both hands and let him lick my face. "I'm sorry." I took off the leash and dropped it on the ground. Then I stood up and started walking, trying not to hear his whimpers.

The walk seemed to take longer this time as I imagined scores of Bok-tussa's best and brightest stained white, turning to stare at me as I crested. But when I reached the top, I saw only Taggart and Andee, playing at the shore. Already they were white below the armpits. I stood at the edge and watched them building in the mud.

But *what* were they building?

At first I saw walls, but as I realized their undulating mounds radiated out-ward from a central point, that paradigm seemed inadequate. Some… star? A sea-star? And why the rocks at the ends of these squiggles? Little piles of —But no, not rocks—people. My breath stopped at this sudden insight. In-stantly, I was convinced. People attached to a central—what? At the center was nothing but the hole they'd dug to supply the waving mounds of mud, radiating outward. They worked with an intense focus, adding squiggles and people until, apparently satisfied, they stood and looked at their creation. Without a word, they turned to the lake, filled their hands with its black water and began filling the center hole. The motions seemed automatic as they walked back and forth, back and forth, scooping water and pouring it into the hole, while I remained silent, unmoving. When they'd filled the hole, they dipped their fingers into it, then they sucked off each finger in turn. I tried to cry out to them, but nothing arrived but a low moan, and they did not regard me.

In the next moment, all was well. My two children were laughing and jumping and splashing and running through and destroying their careful cre-ation, seeming unaware of its presence. I hailed them and they greeted me joyously, running to me and pulling me to the water. I laughed in return and ran with them, but as my forward foot hit the water, I collapsed into the mud in pain, yanking my foot out as if it had been burnt.

"What's wrong, Mom?" asked Taggart.

Andee looked at me almost medically. "She was chosen once," she said. "She was chosen and she chickened out."

"What? No—! I—Andee?"

"It's okay, Mommy. We still love you. And I'm better anyway. I'm com-plete. You didn't even have a brother."

"Yeah, Mom." Taggart slung an arm around me and squeezed. "Andee's special."

"We're… all special."

They rolled their eyes at me and helped me stand up.

I tried to lick my lips without biting my tongue. "Let's—let's go back down and watch a movie or something, okay?"

"It's my turn to choose!" yelled Andee, and she took off running for home, Taggart slipping as he tried to follow her. I closed my eyes and imagined sitting with them and the dog in front of the TV and nothing else. That was enough future for now.

That night, after they were asleep, I returned to the barn. I had to decide whether to paint over what I had started—maybe strip it back down to canvas—or to finish it. Or destroy it. Or just . . . abandon it. Start something new. Start something... with a large cross. Yes. Start there. Let it fill the canvas. Yes...

I set up a new canvas and began by blacking out the negative space, the corners, leaving the canvas untouched where the cross would later be. I put the paint on thick, thick as would hold, then grabbed a palette knife and began to scrape in vines and flowers, gouging them deep. As my work grew more detailed, I began to zone out my periphery, seeing no more than the square inch I was sculpting. When I'm focused like this, hours can pass without notice. And so they did this night. The sky was lightening when I came out of my reverie and took a step away from the easel. My back, I began to notice, was stiff and complaining about the final hours as I worked on the lower half of the painting. I set down the knives and stepped back again, stretching my arms then pushing into my hips with my thumbs. I walked over to open a pair of windows, then turned off the lights. The predawn sunlight lit the paint's contours in a satisfying way. I walked around it in a half circle. Seeing the different details reveal themselves, small leaves and blossoms and—

A certain overall pattern was established in each quadrant. One slightly larger blossom or leaf in the approximate center, the rest attached to vines trailing from the center in—

The precise mode of my children's mud sculpture.

I had painted their tentacled maw in utter black with greenery the color of death as decoration. I reached backwards with both hands; they crashed into my various tools—brushes and so forth—one grasping a roundnose chisel. I turned it in my hand and, as if by instinct, raised my arm to stab downward when a calm voice behind me said, "No, Mommy."

I spun around and there stood Andee, still in her pajamas, the door closed behind her. "How—! How long have you been here?"

"A while."

"Where's—where's Taggart?"

Andee walked past me and leaned up close to the painting, her nose nearly touching the larger blossom of the bottom-left quadrant. "This is very good."

"Um. Thanks. You're up early."

"I know."

"It's not even dawn."

"I know."

"Andee—" I rubbed my eyes. "You let Taggart sleep?"

"I don't know."

I sighed. "Well, should we go have some early breakfast?"

"Yay!"

"Yay."

Andee measured out the Malt-O-Meal while I got the water boiling. Then I let her bring a chair over to stand on so she could stir it while I threw together some instant coffee.

"I think it's done, Mom."

"Great. Yeah, that looks great, honey. I'll serve it up—you want to go see if Taggart's up yet?"

"He's not in bed."

"Did you hear him?"

"He's gone."

"What do you mean he's gone?"

"He's not here."

"What do you mean—you said—you said you... didn't know... if he was sleeping."

"Right."

"Because he's not here."

"Right."

I dropped the wooden spoon and stared at her. "Why didn't you—"

I left the rest of the question in the kitchen as I ran to Taggart's room. His pajamas were hanging over the same chair his swimsuit was on. "Taggart!" I ran through the house and outside, yelling his name. Where could he be? Where would he go? He hadn't gone swimming. He hadn't been anywhere else. Would he walk to town? He couldn't—could he?

I ran back in. Andee had served the Malt-O-Meal into two bowls and was putting too much brown sugar on hers. "Where did he go, Andee? Did he go to town?"

"Why would he go to town?"

I hurried to the front room and dialed 9-1-1.

"9-1-1, what's your emergency?"

"Hello, yes, my son is missing."

"I'm sorry, ma'am. And when did he go missing?"

"This—this morning, I guess. I don't know. Maybe last night?"

"Ma'am, I don't seem to be able to pull up where you are located."

"I'm—I'm in Boktussa. Well, outside Boktussa, actually."

"Ma'am, I'm going to patch into the deputy based in Boktussa while I'm talking with you. I'm not going away. I am still talking with you while that call is happening. Do you understand?"

"Yes. Yes, of course. I understand."

"Very good. Now, ma'am, while we're waiting, what's your name?"

"Tabatha. Sayble Tabatha Reever. Of—of—of just outside Boktussa."

"That's good, ma'am. That's very good. And your son's name?"

"He's—he's Taggart."

"Spell that, if you please."

"T-A-G-G-A-R-T."

"Very good. Now, ma'am, I have the deputy on the other line. I'll still be able to hear you, but it'll be a moment before I patch you over to him, okay?"

"Th-thank you."

The line went silent. I could hear Andee scraping the bottom of her bowl. "I'm going to eat yours, Mom! So it doesn't get cold!"

"Ma'am, I'm turning you over to the deputy now."

"Okay."

"Here he is."

"Miz Reever?"

"Y-yes?"

"This is Deputy Malone, Miz Reever. I understand your little boy's gone missing. He's the older child?"

"Yes. You—know them?"

"Why, Miz Reever, in a town this small what else has the law to do but gossip? So I've heard a bit about your children, yes. When did he leave, do you think?"

"He—I put him to bed around—around—before nine. Now his pajamas are in his room but he's—he's gone."

"I see. You don't reckon he just run off somewhere? Your dog still there?"

"I—I don't know." I covered the mouthpiece. "Andee! Is Teddy still here?"

Through a full mouth: "Yeah!"

"The dog's still here."

"Well, Miz Reever, you know it's only eight in the morning and I have a hard time calling a boy out of doors at eight a.m. a 'missing' boy."

"Yes, but, you see—" I took a breath. "He tends to sleep in. And." I didn't have anything else.

"Well, of course, I could always come out, but—"

"Would you please?"

"Well certainly, if it would make you feel better. 'Bout half an hour be fine?"

"Sure, yes, okay, thank you."

He arrived just past nine o'clock. My nerves were no better, but they were not as exposed. Deputy Malone was an older man, probably in his seventies, but with a gut and swagger that suggested he began and never left a midlife crisis of fast cars and faster women.

"Place looks about the same as I remember it."

"Oh. You knew—you knew—"

"Bethelsda? Course I knew her. I may have known her better than most. I don't suppose it's inappropriate to admit that as a young man I found her the most beautiful lady in the county. I remember being thirteen and 'magining your grandfather passing and taking his place. Heh. Course, by the time he did pass I was married up myself."

"Taggart—sleeps downstairs."

"Good place for a boy. Less noise for you, that is to say. 'Course, I remember your mother too. For some time I thought she might marry my Charlie, but she never was one for sticking close to home."

"Oh. Right. So Taggart—"

"I remember you too, of course. Little Sayble. You were always Bethelsda's favorite, I dare say. Shame you were gone so long."

"His clothes—"

"Little Sayble…"

"I—I go by Tabatha now."

"Ah, yes. Well, that was Bethelsda's mother's name, you know."

I hadn't known.

"Now about this boy of yours—"

"Oh, yes! He's—"

"He's in no trouble, Miz Reever. No trouble at all. I'm surprised your daughter didn't tell you."

"Andee?"

"You know, 'bout the moon and Mars and such. You probably remember from when you were little."

"I was seven when we left."

"Yes. Just before you turned eight. I do remember that." He rubbed his hand on his chin and I could hear the stubble against the calluses. "I tell you what I'll do. I'll keep an eye out. Mention to folks you're looking for him. But I betcha you'll get this thing all sorted out yourself real soon. Ain't that so, Andee?"

I jerked a bit to realize Andee was at my elbow.

"Yes, sir!"

"That's my—" he coughed into his shoulder. "That's my girl."

When he left, I turned to Andee. "How do you know him?"

She rolled her eyes. "He's been to the butte, Mom. Obviously."

"Ob-obviously." I watched her walk off then busied myself cleaning the kitchen, vacuuming, washing their swimsuits and other clothes, cleaning the bathroom. I was trying not to think of anything but of course I was failing. For one thing, I never stopped being aware of where Andee was. In the basement. Getting a yogurt from the fridge. On her dad's computer. In the basement. And so I also could not stop rerunning all of my conversations with her.

At four o'clock it hit me. I went to find her. She was playing jacks, legs crossed under her on the bed, bouncing the rubber ball off one of Taggart's *Harry Potters*.

"Andee."

"Yes, Mom?"

"Do you know where Taggart went?"

"Yes."

I took care to breathe slowly. "Why didn't you tell me?"

"You didn't ask."

"You knew I was looking for him."

"I guess."

"Andee."

"I'm on fives."

"Look at me."

She raised her head for the first time and looked at me.

"Andee?"

"Yes."

"Is Taggart—are you—is Taggart okay?"

"I don't know."

"Where did he go, Andee?"

She bit her lip. "The butte."

"But he didn't have his suit."

She laughed at that one. "He wasn't going swimming! Don't you remember *any*thing?"

"Where is he now?"

She looked back down at her jacks. "I dunno. Still there?"

"All—all day? Without any food?"

She shrugged.

"He's on the butte…" I started to leave, but Andee cried out. I looked back at her. "What? What is it?"

"You can't go yet!"

"What? Why not?"

"You just can't!"

"Andee. What is going on?"

"I need him."

"What? Why?"For a moment, I felt I almost remembered something. I felt dizzy and sat on Andee's bed. She pulled my head down onto her lap. And somehow, somehow, I slept…

I jolted awake and ran upstairs, spinning around house. It was nearly dawn again. No Taggart. No Andee. Just Teddy hiding in the bathroom. I went out the back door and could see a mist that had formed over the butte's pool, spilling over the edge and sending a tattered blanket down the sides of the butte, like the tendrils I had painted, reaching toward me. Taggart. I took a breath and set my face, then began the march up.

I stepped over the first fingers of fog, then a leg, then I punched into a chest-high wall which overwhelmed me like the tide. I stumbled as my feet became less visible. I had to lean forward and use my hands to scout a path up the butte. I don't know how long it took me but when I crested the top, the sun had risen into the sky. The fog still obscured most of my vision. The sun was a flat white disk before me, like the dead eye of a god that saw little need to impress with glory.

I struck for the water, a sense of panic building in me. A cry—my son? a bird?—and I lost my caution and ran forward, losing one shoe in the mud. At that moment, the fog cleared just enough to let the sun blaze through, blinding, sliced from the sky in unholy white, its clean edges turning the world from nondescript gray to legions of shadows, of which one—one was Taggart.

"Taggart!" I screamed and ran towards him. The sun dimmed again and I fell on my side in the mud as Taggart disappeared, a dark air swirling around him and seeming to lift him up. "Taggart!"

I repeated his name over and over as I pushed my way through the mist until my voice cracked and bled and faded to a ragged whisper.

When I became aware of myself again, the sun was high in the air and the sky was clear and blue. I was covered in muck, hair to foot. I pushed myself up.

"Oh, there you are." Andee looked down at me, her jeans stained white from the knees down.

"Where's Taggart?"

"He'll be back."

I struggled into a sitting position. The mud had largely dried on my skin, a whitish, fecal brown like old dog shit in a backyard but I wasn't able to care. I just looked down and concentrated on breathing. In. Then out. In. Then out.

"Mommy?" I heard her feet move. "Mommy, you should go home."

"Why is this happening, Andee?"

She paused, then spoke in sounds impossible for a throat as young and as human as hers to make.

I did not look at her as I stood, as I turned to the edge and walked over it. I kept my eyes on the ground directly in front of me. I showered, staring straight at the tiles, not blinking away water or soap. I stood most of an hour in the kitchen. I walked to the barn and stared at my mockeries. I returned to the house, stood by Ben's computer. Sat in front of it. Stared at its black unblinking eye. Reached to turn on its monitor. It blipped then came to life. I clicked on the icon for the cameras and all four views came to life. One looking across the backyard. One in the same spot, positioned up to the top of the butte. One on the driveway. One towards the entrance of my barn. In the late summer heat, everything glowed in shades of red and orange, a hell-scape of oscillating edges and fiery nondistinctness. The only contrast, a blue-green cap atop the butte.

On I stared, my eyes unfocused, all four views present in my vague con-sciousness; as the day drew on, the reds turned orange and the oranges turned yellow, but the top of the butte waged battle, getting bluer, then black-er, then black—just black. On the driveway camera, the dog with its white core and red legs paced back and forth. I should have let him inside. But I could not stand. I could not move.

At some point, the oranges stopped lightening. The ground returned to red. Night had fallen. Dark purple tendrils crept from the top of the butte, reaching downward. The dog ran out of camera and I could hear it scratching at the front door. The barn's temperature began to drop, drop. From its door, a mi-asma of black leached out in cancerous curls.

The tips of the butte's fingers drew nearer. At the front of each stood a fig-ure, black, outlined in blues and purply greens, cold, ghastly creatures—I could not tell if they were merely coming close enough to recognize or if these humanlike forms were solidifying before my eyes as they staggered forward.

The unreality of this horror shocked me from my stupor and I gripped the desk in front of me. Black-cold beings, approaching the house, growing in number. A sound like an uncertain earthquake rose and fell then rose and fell again. As it repeated it grew in volume and clarity until I recognized my own name—*Sayble... Sayble... Sayble... Sayble...*

They called me. I wished to close my ears but they called me. Dozens, hundreds of voices called me. Hundreds of individual voices. My granmammy called me. My son called me. Generations of my Boktussa blood called my name. I gripped the desk and watched the green-black figures multiply, generations of souls swallowed by the butte and then, walking among them, ministering to these frozen spirits as they turned to worship her, the white-hot body of an eight-year-old girl. As she walked through them, the chant began to change until the voices solidified, lost their individual characters, and chanted, *Mommy... Mommy... Mommy... Mommy...*

I stood up, straightened my knees, and let go of the desk. I stared at Andee's glowing form, radiating light among the bruised creatures surrounding her. "I'm coming," I heard myself say. "I'm—"

The phone rang. The phone rang? It rang again. The absurdity of such a normal, pedestrian sound shattered whatever spell I was under and I laughed, I picked up the receiver and, laughing, said, "Hello?"

"Hey, babe. You should answer the phone sometime. You been painting or something?"

Still laughing, I said no, no. "It's just Andee, she's—there's there—you see—" My inability to form a sentence made me laugh stronger till I was lying on the floor, holding my stomach, and my sobs of laughter turned to weeping, and I wept.

"Tabatha! *Tabatha!* Are you—? Are the kids all right? What—what—?"

I tried to answer, but my breath caught. In the silence, I realized the chanting was no longer. The world was quiet except for Ben's barky confusion.

"Ben... Ben, I'm okay. I need to go check something, though. Will you stay on the line?"

"Of course, Tabby. I—"

His voice faded as I walked away, leaving him on the ground. I heard the sliding-glass door open. I closed my eyes for a moment then opened them again and walked forward. Andee stood on the mat, naked save for the white crust staining her hair and face and body. It seemed to be caked so thick that her form was obscured and she looked neither young nor old nor small nor wide. The only aspect of her that seemed living were her burning black eyes.

"Andee—?"

I hate you.

She hadn't said anything, but I felt as if she had.

"Andee..."

For a moment, her shoulders quivered such that I knew she would break into tears and run to my arms as she had hundreds of times in the past. But she was not that Andee anymore. This Andee steeled herself, lowered her chalk-white brow over her depthless eyes and said as calmly as reciting the two-times tables, "That was my chance to be a god." Then she walked past me to the stairs and I heard her descend to her bedroom. I forgot about Ben waiting on the floor. I stepped outside into cool summer night air. Mars was barely visible to the left of the full moon. The night was still, no insects, no birds. I walked to the butte. Halfway up, Teddy joined me and together we crested to the top. The silver light of the moon made shadows of human-shaped impressions scattered through the mud. Teddy ran ahead and found Taggart in one, staring blindly at the stars. The dog licked Taggart's face, making skin-colored stripes in the white. Taggart sneezed and blinked. "Mom?" I made a burst of sound and pulled him into my arms. I carried him down the hill, bathed him, put him to bed in my own bed. I held him tightly, uncertain if I would sleep.

In the morning, I stepped on the phone. Ben was snoring and no yelling could wake him. I hung up and began to pack the car. We would make sure several people in town would know we were heading to Oklahoma City for a minor-league ballgame. Yes. And then we would drive to Oklahoma City. And then we would turn east and keep driving till we found the Atlantic. We would find a nice place to disappear. I would call Ben's home office and give him a phone number. And his imaginationless soul would come find us, would be a salve to our broken souls.

I stopped at the grocery store to buy jerky and licorice and peanuts. I chatted loudly with the girl at checkout about our baseball plans.

"You know," said a voice behind us, "you are the last of Bethelsda's line. You can't just leave."

I turned. Mr. Barrett smiled at me in a grandfatherly way. I laughed, I hope brightly. "We're not *leaving*. We're just going to watch a baseball game."

"What a coincidence," he said, his voice as cheerful as mine but his eyes dark as Andee's had been. "I'm heading to the city myself. I do love a bit of ball in the summertime."

"Oh... good. Maybe we can sit together."

"I would be honored, my dear."

As we left town, we led a caravan of seventeen cars. All headed to Oklahoma City. All in the mood for a baseball game. All planning to caravan there together and to caravan back together, always together.

I stared at the road ahead. Pointed my mirrors down to the pavement so I could not see what was behind me. And drove and drove and drove.

IT CAME FROM THE WOODS

Jason A. Anderson

Their second date had gone very well so far. Stan, not-quite star athlete at Shadow Valley High, and Billie, not-quite Prom Queen, had spent over an hour at the Brookbank Falls, deep in the mountains that ringed Pine Bow County. During the winter months, these mountains drew skiers from around the world to challenge its white-capped slopes. In the early summer, like now, the hills took on so much green they almost blended together, making it about impossible to tell one range from another.

Billie looked up at the lengthening shadows. Years of camping with her father had taught her a little, and though she wouldn't consider herself a "mountain girl," she knew enough to know how quickly daylight could descend into night on the mountain.

"I didn't realize how late it is," she called across the creek to where Stan was investigating something wedged between two large boulders.

Stan looked up at her and smiled, then leaped from stone to stone back to her.

"We should get back to the car," she said. "It's still a couple miles' hike to the road."

Stan shrugged and said, "Don't worry, I'm sure we'll make it before dark."

"If we leave soon, I'm sure we'll be fine," Billie redirected, and tried not to pull away when Stan put an arm around her shoulders. then the two of them headed down the dirt path.

"What were you looking at?" Billie asked as they walked.

Stan's hesitation drew her attention to him. He looked slightly uncomfortable.

"Uh," he finally said, "it looked like what was left of a coyote. It was pretty mangled, so it was hard to tell for sure. But it was fresh."

"Hunters?" Billie asked.

"No, it looked like something with teeth."

Suddenly nervous in the waning afternoon light, Billie glanced around, her gaze trying to pierce the heavy forest and foliage, looking for the telltale signs of predatory wildlife.

"Do you think whatever killed that is still around here?" Stan wondered aloud, sounding intentionally aloof.

"We should be fine, as long as we can get back to the car before dark," Billie replied.

Without a passable road to them, Brookbank Falls enjoyed an exclusivity that helped preserve its pristine location. At the same time, with the tall peaks surrounding them, the afternoon and evening sun took little time to fade, enveloping the young couple in deep shadows and making the trail so treacherous that they eventually had to slow their progress.

"I don't think we're going to make it to the car before dark," Stan said, his nerves beginning to show in his voice.

Billie decided not to comment on the obvious and pulled a small, powerful flashlight from her belt. It cut through the heavy darkness, allowing them to continue forward, until she stopped without warning.

"What is it?" Stan asked, watching Billie shine the line around them, then shining it up the path, then back the way they'd come.

"Did we pass a split in the path without realizing it?" she asked, hitting him in the face with the beam of light.

Stan put a hand up to shade his eyes and said, "If we did, it couldn't have been too far back. Why, are we lost?"

Billie illuminated the way ahead, but her scowl didn't inspire confidence in her date.

"I thought you said you've been here before," Stan accused, doubt and aggravation trickling into his voice.

Not rising to the bait, Billie said, "I have, but never after dark. You know how woods all look alike, once the sun goes down."

Before she could say more, something crashed in the darkness a ways off the path and in the distance a coyote howl echoed out at them.

Stan snatched the flashlight out of Billie's hand and played the bright-white beam back and forth in the direction the sound of movement had come from, but couldn't see anything. He held his free hand out to Billie.

"Come on."

Scowling, the girl took his hand and the two of them hurried along the path.

They made good time, until another howl jerked Stan's attention from the path. His left foot snagged against an unseen tree root. He cried out in pain as he fell, twisting his ankle so far Billie was surprised she didn't hear a *snap*.

"Are you okay?" Billie asked, kneeling down beside him.

The two of them carefully straightened out his wrenched foot, Stan wincing, but putting on his "tough football player" face instead of crying out a second time.

Billie took her mobile phone from her small handbag. After glancing at its screen she pursed her lips, then said, "No signal. How about you?"

Stan managed to extract his mobile phone from his back pocket without a whimper, but his mood didn't brighten when he looked at the screen. He held it up for Billie to inspect.

Her eyes fell on the complex spider-web of shattered glass that now took the place of the shiny, smooth glass surface. "Oh," was all she said.

He tried a few times to start up, but when the device refused to respond, he growled in frustration and tossed the phone a few feet away.

Billie hurried over to pick up his phone, but just as her fingers touch the metal case, something rustled about a stone's throw away and a low growl drifted to her on the breeze. She froze. When the growl faded away a few seconds later, she snatched the smartphone out of the damp dirt and ran back to Stan.

"Come on, Romeo," she said and hoisted him to his feet, ignoring his grunts of pain. "We gotta go."

Once she had Stan upright, it emphasized the height difference between them. In order to keep him from slumping to his left, she strung his left arm across her shoulders, pressing her right and his left side tightly together, for support.

As one, they hobbled as quickly down the dark path as possible, their progress hindered by the increasing pain in Stan's foot. It originated in his ankle and radiated up his calf to behind his knee, and any weight on it sent pulses of stabbing agony nearly to his hip.

"Keep it up," Billie encouraged him, "you're doing great."

Stan could only grunt in response.

A few hundred feet further on, the couple paused to rest. Stan managed to lower himself to an unearthed tree stump and shut his eyes while catching his breath through clenched teeth.

Before they were ready to move again, Billie heard faint growling behind them. She turned and scanned the path behind them, but couldn't see anything. There was, however, a thick, gnarly branch lying nearby. It made a solid weapon in her hands. As if in response to her new-found ability to defend them, the growling increased and she could've sworn she could now see a faint sickly greenish-yellow glow trickling between the leaves and branches of the thick woods.

"Um, Stan?" she stammered, backing away from the edge of the trail, her eyes still on the faint glow.

"What?" he demanded, not opening his eyes or making a move to stand.

Billie hurried back to him and, amid his grunts of protest, she managed to get him moving down the path, using her branch as a crutch to support her as she supported him. Several times she hazarded a look behind them, noticing that the sickly glow didn't get closer, but hadn't faded away, either.

Suddenly they reached the edge of the woods. The trees and underbrush didn't taper off, they stopped at the edge of a vast, empty field. The path they were on continued, snaking through the knee-high white field grass, in the direction of a motorhome or camper trailer permanently parked on the far side. Squinting in the gloom, Billie could make out several items surrounding the motorhome—weird statuary made from sticks and branches.

"Uh-uh," Stan told Billie. "No chance."

"Unless your cellphone has magically repaired itself and gets service," she said evenly, "we don't have a choice. We need a phone and someone there may have one. Plus, you can get off that ankle."

After a few seconds, Stan nodded reluctantly.

"Good man," Billie agreed and the two of them continued along the path.

Billie's anxiety increased as they approached the dirty tan motorhome. The strange icons woven out of sticks and bound together with twisted field grass turned out to be much more complex than she could see from a distance. Several were free-standing latices, with handmade runes woven into them made from sticks, twigs, several different colors of hair and strips of animal hide. She had seen similar items in horror movies over the years.

Her confidence really began to wane when the motorhome's doorknob started to rattle before they had gotten close. The teens halted just outside the perimeter of trampled dirt that made a large circle around the motorhome and that appeared to be the "front yard" outside the vehicle.

Like frightened animals caught in car headlights, both of them stared at the flimsy motorhome door as it opened outward and the biggest man Billie had ever seen angled himself out of the vehicle, stepping two feet down to the ground. The motorhome rocked back to a level stance.

In less than a second, Billie estimated the distance between the giant and them and determined that if the two of them decided to run, it wouldn't take long for the man to build up a big enough head of steam to catch them.

"Um…" she said, then hesitated.

The large man stopped, staring at them long enough for Billie to form a second impression as he stood before them in his tattered denim overalls. He had the look of a retired sports-entertainment pro wrestler: massive size, most of which had migrated from his upper-body to his sizable girth; a scruffy complexion that may or may not have concealed a few facial scars; piercing, attentive eyes that almost seemed out of place.

"I's just fixin' ta make supper," the man said, his voice lisping slightly through a few missing teeth.

"Can you help us?" Billie managed to ask, trying to adjust the weight of Stan, who seemed to be leaning on her more by the minute.

"T'ain't no one fer more'n a mile," the man said, turning away from them and crossing to the open pit fire that illuminated the area.

"My friend's hurt," Billie said. "I think his foot's broken."

The man glanced over at them, then bent over the large stew pot perched over the open flame. A few seconds later, he motioned toward a beat-up armchair that may have once sat in a upper-class casual room, but now looked out of place sitting out in the dirt.

With a grateful sigh, Billie said, "Thanks," and stepped from the path onto the dirt area that surrounded the motorhome. With effort, she managed to get Stan over to the chair, who grunted in pain as he was unceremoniously deposited onto the low cushion.

Billie straightened and took in a deep, cleansing breath. "Do you have a phone I could use?"

The man only grunted, but it was obviously a negative grunt.

"I need to call my family. We need a ride to the hospital."

"No phone."

Before Billie could protest further, the man dipped a fire-blackened ladle into the bubbling cookpot and fished out a piece of cloth about two inches long and over two feet long. Billie got her first whiff of the aroma coming from the pot and gagged at the noxious stench. What she had initially assumed was the "supper" he mentioned was obviously not. She hoped.

Carrying the strip of cloth on the end of the ladle, he crossed over to where Stan sat. He nodded down at the teen.

"Shoe. Off."

"Uhh..." Billie hesitated, then said, "Okay," and knelt beside Stan's injured foot. After working his shoe loose with several apologies along the way, she sat back on her heels as the big man knelt in front of Stan. He took the injured foot in one of his massive hands, lifting it slightly to get a better look. However, instead of rotating it to examine it while he squatted in place, he leaned and stretched around the stationary foot with an agility that defied is size. It reinforced her opinion that the man was faster and more flexible than his size first indicated.

Nodding to himself, the man gently wrapped the smelly strip of cloth around Stan's injured foot, the entire time muttering so softly Billie couldn't tell what he said. Within a few seconds, the lines on Stan's face began to soften, the pain receding from his eyes.

Billie resisted the urge to hug their benefactor Instead she settled for saying, "Thanks."

Before she could say any more, an eerie howl echoed out from the nearby woods.

Lurching to his feet, the man turned and headed for the edge of the dirt circle, detouring only to grab a staff along the way, half-again as tall as the branch that Billie still held. It looked like it had started out as a regular walking stick, but the decoration of carved runes, several small sticks and what appeared to be bone fragments, and the large clear stone attached to the top of the staff now hinted at a darker, sinister function.

"That's what was following us when Stan hurt his foot," Billie said to his back.

Another howl brought the attention of all three of them to the edge of the woods, where the greenish-yellow glow had begin to halo the tops of the trees.

Staring at the woods several hundred feet away, the large man rattled the totems tied to the top of his staff, muttering softly again. Billie felt a static charge push through her, but without a storm cloud in the sky. From the direction of the woods a rush of wind swept out at them, tossing Billie's hair. The stench of rotted flesh, far worse than the contents of the big man's pot, made her gag against bile rising to the back of her throat.

Billie heard the big man grunt against the wind's impact and saw his feet stumble back a couple inches on the hard-packed earth.

A moment later, the violent wind switched directions, creating a swirling dust devil which grew in seconds to more than an arm's length wide, then burst apart, bending the field grass, striking the area of the woods where the wind had originated. The tree branches twisted back violently, accompanied by a much louder, heartfelt howling.

Then the space between the huge man and the edge of the woods seemed to come alive with movement in the grass and from the edge of the wood, a flickering of shadow and debris in the conflicting wind currents.

Though the dust storm and flurry of raging breezes lasted less than a minute, to Billie it seemed to go on forever, especially when she saw the large man react to a particularly violent blast by falling to one knee. His breath came in labored gasps and sweat streamed down and dripped from his scruffy chin. His exertion had caused his skin to flush, accentuating the pale, thin scar that ran from the corner of his right eye down to the right side of his chin. Though he looked winded and worn, his vision was clear and with a mighty grunt, he stood and pushed out with his staff, sending a large energy blast outward.

The electricity in the air spiked and Billie almost applauded when a single sphere of ball lightning flashed from the clear sky and crashed into the woods; the sickly halo began to flicker. She ran over to the man and said, "Now's your chance! Kill it!"

A weird crackling sound began to emit from the woods.

"Kill it!" Billie nearly screamed in terror.

Flicking her fierce gaze on her, the man growled, "No killin'!" And instead he grabbed hold of her arm and stood upright, his staff raised over his head. His shout came out sounding to Billie like a mix of several different languages. The moment his bellowing ceased, a jolt ran through her fiercer than what she had already felt, this time taking most of her strength with it as it passed. She swooned for a second, but never diverted her eyes from the glowing woods.

An animal shriek unlike anything she'd ever heard flowed around them, then with the roar of a cloudless thunderclap, the ominous glow winked out of existence.

This time the large man dropped to both his knees, his staff resting across them, his head forward so his chin rested on his collarbone.

The silence around them felt so enveloping Billie declined to speak for fear of shattering the moment. Just as she reached out to touch his shoulder, the faint sound of a dog barking reached them and the man's head snapped up. He immediately whistled in response, which sounded like birdsong mixed with delicate wind-chimes.

A moment later, motion at edge of the trees caught Billie's attention and she watched in stunned silence as a small white animal raced down the path, disappearing in the tall field grass.

The whistling continued until several seconds later a tiny white dog emerged from the grass and leapt into the man's cupped hands—so tiny, it almost disappeared in his massive mitts. Billie couldn't believe this little creature had been the cause of so much distress.

"Where ya done been, Precious?" the man asked, softly caressing the small dog with a meaty finger.

The dog yipped up at him and Billie watched as he carefully extracted a handmade talisman that had become tangled in the dog's collar.

"I done told ya not to play in my stuff," he said, but his scolding held no anger, only affection. Without looking at Billie, the big man stood, turned and walked over to Stan. The young man's eyes were clear, without any sign of pain or discomfort.

After setting the small dog on top of what looked like a floor-standing heater but had a white glow pulsing inside the two-foot-tall metal cylinder, the huge man pulled his long hair back behind his shoulders and squatted down to scrutinize Stan's foot. Nodding to himself, the man slowly removed the smelly wrap and this time he took Stan's foot and moved it, bending it left, right, up and down. It seemed tender at the extreme angles and Stan flinched as a result, but other than that, and a disturbing green stain thanks to the noxious concoction, nothing seemed amiss.

Satisfied, the man stood, gently retrieving Precious as he did, then waved in the general direction away from the woods.

"Town's bein' that-a-way," he growled, then he reached down and flipped a switch on the side of the odd cylinder. As the light powered down, Billie felt static that made the hair on the back of her neck stand up, then relax. In her pocket, her mobile phone chirped, indicating it had a signal.

Excited, she took out her phone, satisfying herself that it had a full signal. Then she glanced from the cylinder to the large man, standing beside the motorhome's doorway.

"Not evvethin's magic," he slurred.

"Um..." Billie said, then hesitated. "Could you give us a ride into town?"

The large man gestured to the back of the rig with his free hand.

The motor-home was supported on blocks under all four wheel hubs, and there was no other vehicle in the yard.

With a final, gentle smile, the huge man took Precious into the motorhome, causing it to sway a bit, closing the door behind him.

With a smile of her own, Billie turned and walked over to where Stan stood, testing his weight on his injured foot.

"Amazing," he said. "Who'd have thought a miracle man would be camped out by the woods?"

Billie helped Stan turn, so he wouldn't tweak his foot at an odd angle again, and the two of them headed toward the mouth of the path that looked like it snaked toward town.

"Gotta admit," Stan said as they walked, "that was a pretty exciting second date."

Laughing, Billie nodded. "No argument, there."

After a few more steps, Stan said, "What'd'ya think—third date?"

Billie smiled up at him and nudged him with her shoulder.

"We'll see, Romeo," she said. "We'll see..."

Hand-in-hand, they walked into the starry night.

Inside the motorhome, Bubba-Ray watched the teens as they slowly made their way down the path that lead to town. His initial feeling of pride at fending off the dark entity in the woods paled now as he spotted a flickering shadow that had attached itself to the young couple. He had done what he could. It would be up to others to take care of the rest.

He turned his attention away from the teenagers and crossed down to the back room, to the window where Precious stood on the small counter, staring out to the woods. With conscious gentleness, he scratched the small dog behind her ears. She leaned into his touch, but didn't take her eyes off the edge of the wide field.

"You done good, this time, Precious," the big man rumbled, causing the dog to look up at him with big, soulful brown eyes.

"Too bad we ne'er saved t'others," he said and as if the dog could understand his thick drawl, Precious looked back out across the wavy tan grass. There, among the regular shadows of the trees and foliage, even darker shadows could be seen, swaying among the trees.

Bubba-Ray knew it wouldn't be long before those same swaying shadows would stand swaying among the high field grass at the perimeter of his campsite, the only bastion of defense for the distant town.

"We best be gettin' ready," he said.

Precious looked up at him and yipped in agreement, then they both turned their attention back to the deep darkness of the woods.

LAKE TOWN

Garrett Calcaterra

Jody dropped the tailgate on her K5 Blazer and hoisted herself up to enjoy her Slim Jim and Red Bull in the Gas'N'Go parking lot. "Breakfast of champions," she muttered, but mostly because she didn't feel bad about it. She'd earned it. Besides, it was too damn hot to be doing coffee and donuts. It was only 9 and pushing ninety degrees already. In November. Earthquake weather, if you believed that sort of shit. Jody didn't.

"Hi, hi, Jody."

It was Ted shambling through the parking lot, looking rougher than usual, gaunt and clammy, his nose and lips all red and chapped to hell. You'd never guess by looking at him that he was only a couple of years out of high school.

"Hey, Ted. You're up early this morning."

He gave a high-pitched wheezy imitation of a laugh. "Oh yeah, I guess. Hey, what are you doing?"

"Right now, I'm just having my breakfast. What's it look like to you, Ted? You high?"

"Oh yeah, I guess."

Jody shook her head. Ted had been a nice kid when they'd been in school. They'd even dated for a while and gone to formal together their sophomore year. Now Ted was just another Georgebrook casualty.

"Listen here," Ted said. "There's a big party tonight down by the lake, at Spider Camp. Gonna be a bonfire. Everyone is gonna be there. Come."

It wasn't so much an invitation as a command. Not exactly the way to win Jody over. Still, Ted was a good guy. Lost, maybe, but not a bad person, and she didn't have the heart to reject him flat out.

"I'll think about it. But do me a favor, Ted, will ya? Take it easy down there. Pace yourself."

Ted stared back at her blankly. "Come," he said again, and then the Gas'N'Go door jingled as someone else walked out, and it was as if Jody no longer existed. Ted shuffled toward the man. "Hey, hey," he said. "There's a big party tonight."

Jody had seen enough. She hopped down from the tailgate and walked to the driver side, safely out of sight from Ted. *Poor fool,* she thought as she fired up the Blazer. She guzzled down the last of her Red Bull and slapped her cheeks to make sure she was fully awake, then gunned it out of the parking lot onto Main Street, headed for home to put in a few hours on her psych term paper before crashing out.

"The Pride of the Mountains," read the engraving on the stone archway out front of the Town Hall. Jody rolled her eyes as she cruised past it and all the other historic buildings lining Main Street. Georgebrook might have been the pride of gold country back in the 1850s, but these days it wasn't the pride of anything. Apart from the architecture in old town Georgebrook, there was nothing here that interested her anymore. She couldn't wait to get out. One more semester at the JC and working nights at the animal hospital, and she was gone.

Once clear of old town, she laid into the throttle and sped past Georgebrook School, where she'd attended grades K through 8, and then Georgebrook High right alongside it. A mile beyond, she slowed as she turned onto Oxbow Spring Road, and then she was in the thick of the evergreen forest. Evergreen was another misnomer these days. More than half the ponderosa pines had succumbed to drought and bark beetles and stood brown and brittle, ready to go up like a tinder box at the slightest provocation.

The dead trees made Jody think of Oxbow Lake, itself withered away over the last several years of drought to finally reveal its forgotten secret. She considered driving out there again, but then she thought of what Ted told her, about there being a party out that way tonight. She remembered, too, how disappointing her last visit to the lakebed had been.

"Nope, going home, gonna knock out a few pages on my paper, and going to sleep." She wasn't even self-conscious about talking to herself out loud anymore. She'd grown accustomed to talking to the dogs and cats at the pet hospital as the only night attendant, and it had just sort of carried over into her daily life.

"It's time to go out and pee, Jack boy."

"Looks like that bandage is leaking, Dobie. We best change it out."

"I'm right here, Ms. Mittens, washing my hands. I hear you."

"Why is my mother texting me at two in the morning about praying for me? What doesn't she understand about the word 'no?'"

"The u-joint on the K5 has been clanking pretty loud the last week or two. I best swap it out this weekend. Won't do myself any good if the axle busts loose."

"Gonna knock out a few pages on my paper, and go to sleep."

It was like she was narrating her own life. Once she said something out loud, it became reality. That was certainly the case now—she was going home and straight to her room, hopefully without having to speak to her mother. Even so, the thought of the dried lake made her slow down as she came to the turn-off for it. She peered out the passenger window down the dusty tract between the trees, and was surprised to see two figures standing there, no more than twenty yards away. They waved their arms when they saw her.

Jody pulled to the shoulder and braked hesitantly, figuring it was meth-heads, but these guys weren't the local flavor. The older guy—middle-aged, graying, with the start of a gut—was wearing a pink polo shirt, khaki cargo shorts, and some serious-looking hiking boots. He even had trekking poles. The other guy was a skinny Asian dude in just a t-shirt, jeans, and Converse sneakers. He had a big DSLR camera hanging from his neck. The two of them couldn't have been more out of place in Georgebrook if they'd tried. Jody rolled down the passenger window as the Asian guy trotted toward her.

"Hey, thanks," he said. "You think you could give us a ride back into town? Our car is stuck and phones aren't working. Can't get ahold of Triple A."

Jody regarded the two of them. No way she could leave them out here to fend for themselves. Most of the other locals would probably help them if they happened to pass by, but not all of them, and not many passed by at this time of day. So it looked like no sleep for a while.

"Cellphones don't do much good out this way because of the hills," she said. "Tow truck would take pretty long to get out here, anyway. I have a tow rope in the back. If you want, I'll pull you out for twenty bucks."

The Asian guy glanced back at the older guy, who pulled out his wallet and checked it. "Sure," the old guy said. "That thing you're driving is big as a tow truck."

Jody smiled and motioned for the two of them to hop in. The Asian guy deferred to the older man and let him take the front seat. Jody was still trying to figure out what their relationship was.

"Thank you," the old guy said. "We truly appreciate this, young lady."

Jody turned down the dirt road. "No problem. You stuck out on the lake bed?"

"No, we didn't even make it that far, I'm afraid."

He wasn't lying. Jody rounded the first bend and there was a late model VW Bug sitting halfway off the dirt road.

"Yeah, not very far at all," the Asian guy said with a laugh.

Jody had to laugh, too. She pulled over in front of the VW and killed the engine. "So who the hell are you guys?" she asked as she hopped out to as-sess the damage. She'd had a brief glimmer of hope they were with the BLM, but no way, not in that car.

"I'm Doctor Hallward and my associate here is Steve."

Jody got down on her hands and knees to peer under the VW. "Like a doctor doctor?"

"Not an M.D., no. I'm a professor of anthropology at University of the Bay. Are you a real doctor? A nurse?"

"I'm calling 'dental hygienist,'" Steve, the Asian guy said.

Jody stood up and brushed herself off. She'd forgotten she was still in her scrubs. "Ah, no, not a doctor either. Just the night attendant at the animal hospital. Name's Jody. Looks like you got yourself high-centered on that berm."

"I told you," Steve said, eying the professor.

"No, I believe you 'called' I was a dental hygienist," Jody said.

"No, not that. I told Dr. H he was going to get high-centered and that he should have let me drive. I may be Asian, but I'm actually pretty good."

"No matter. You should have brought a different car. You're never going to make it down to the lake in that thing. The road gets pretty rough."

"What makes you think we're headed to the lake?" the professor asked.

Jody hefted a stone from the side of the road and wedged it under one of the VW's front tires. "Because that's the only place this road goes. Besides, you're an anthropologist, and he fancies himself a photographer. Where else would you be going but Lake Town?" She wedged another stone beneath the other front tire of the VW.

Steve shot a glance at the professor. "You know about Lake Town?"

"Everyone in Georgebrook knows about Lake Town now. Here, take this end of the rope and crawl under the front of that Bug." She handed Steve one end of the tow rope and attached the other end to the tow-hitch on the rear bumper of her K5.

Steve did as she said and laid down in front of the VW to peer beneath it.

"There should be a hook mounted on the frame somewhere back behind the bumper," Jody told him.

"Yeah, I got it." He pulled himself up and dusted off his hands. "You by chance know someone who goes by the handle 'LoreMiner?' You know, on Instagram, Tumblr, Twitter, that sort of thing. Not sure you've got the Internet all the way up here."

Jody turned away from him, half-annoyed, half-excited by his question. He knew about the LoreMiner posts. First things first, though, she reminded herself. "Hop in your car, Professor. Turn it on and put it in neutral. When I start tugging on you, steer yourself to the left, back into the center of the road."

"Okay, sure, but shouldn't I put it in drive?"

"No, don't put it in drive and keep your foot away from the gas pedal. Just steer and then put on the brakes once I pull you loose. Got it?"

"Got it."

She hopped into her vehicle and the professor into his, leaving Steve to scramble off to the safety of the opposite side of the road. It took only one good tug to pull the VW off the berm onto the road again. The professor was all smiles as he got out of his car. He reached for his wallet and the twenty dollars as Jody removed the tow rope.

"Look here," Jody said. "Keep your money. I have a better proposition. You guys obviously want to see Lake Town, but that car of yours is never going to make it down there. Even if you manage to not get stuck on the road, you've still got a half-mile of muddy lake bed to get across. The lake is dried up, but it ain't dry. How about you follow me? There's a turnout another hundred and fifty yards down the road. You can park there, then hop back in with me. I'll give you a ride down there and give you a tour of Lake Town."

"In exchange for what, if not the twenty dollars?"

"Depends. You got tenure at the university?"

"Of course. I'm very well-established in anthropology, really."

"I'm sure you are, Professor, but it's not like you're at Berkeley or Stanford. We're talking University of the Bay. Don't get me wrong. U Bay is good enough for me, and Berkeley and Stanford aren't easy schools to transfer into anyway. Consider the ride and the tour an audition of sorts. If I do good, you help me get into your program at U Bay."

Professor Hallward stared back at her wide-eyed, a coy smirk painting his face. "Well, you are a delightful surprise, aren't you?"

Steve stepped in. "No offense, but that doesn't seem fair. Sure, you have a big-ass truck, but LoreMiner is the one who put this place on our radar with his photos and research. If Professor H. were going to help anyone, it'd be him, not you. No offense."

Jody suppressed the urge to punch Steve in the face, keeping her attention on the professor instead. "Look, you don't have to make any promises right now. Let me take you down there, and if you're impressed with what I have to show you at Lake Town, then you do me a solid and help me get out of this town. Either way, I'll get you in and out safely. No hard feelings."

"Deal." The professor stuck out his hand to shake on it.

"But what about LoreMiner?" Steve protested.

"Grad students," the Professor said, winking at Jody. "Don't be a dunce, Steve. Our guide here *is* LoreMiner."

"But she's a..." He cut himself short.

"A girl?" Jody finished for him.

Steve's face turned red. "Shit, sorry."

"Feel stupid?" Jody asked him.

"Yep."

"Good, now let's go."

Oxbow Lake was a quagmire of mud crisscrossed with 4x4 tire tracks. A narrow creek running through the center of the muck and a piss-yellow pond at the base of the earthen dam was all that was left of the lake itself. Far in the distance, beyond the neck of Oxbow Valley to the east, were the Sierra Nevada Mountains, blue and hazy with no hint of snow on the peaks.

Jody locked the hubs on the front wheels of her K5 and traversed into the muck, sticking to the tracks where other 4x4s had gone before, weaving in and out of the debris pockmarking the exposed lake bed: tires, tin buckets, beer cans, plastic water bottles, and even an old Studebaker rusted to the same brown color as the mud.

"It was a couple of fishermen who first saw the tops of buildings poking out of the water at the beginning of summer," Jody said, as the straight lines of the town before them came into focus against the rolling backdrop of the lake bed. "By August, the lake was dry enough to expose the whole town. I used my waders and got in to take the pictures you saw online when there was two feet of standing water, so most everything was still untouched."

"I didn't actually see your pictures," the professor admitted, "but Steve assures me they're quite good. He also says you gave a preliminary date to the town?"

"Well, the town definitely dates back to around 1870, when prospectors found placer deposits with a lot of gold along this creek. It was a bit of a haul from Georgebrook back then, I guess, so they built a town here in the valley alongside the creek. The town was actually called Growlersburg. The mysterious part is when the dam was built and why."

The town was in full view now, a ghost town in the mud comprised of fourteen buildings, seven to either side of what had once been Main Street Growlersburg. The buildings were all wood planked one-story affairs with square-topped facades, but with steep pitched roofs behind the facades to handle winter snow. Two more of the smaller buildings had been knocked over since the last time Jody had been out there, and someone had stolen the wheels off the stage coach in front of the saloon. At least the saloon itself and the church looked to have been largely untouched.

"Here it is, or at least what's left of it." Jody came to a stop and they all hopped out. Steve immediately had his camera to his face, scrambling around to snap pictures.

"Careful," Jody hollered after him. "Everything is covered in a couple of inches of silt. It's slicker than shit."

The professor walked into the town at a statelier pace, trekking poles out to steady himself. Jody strolled at his side down main street between the buildings. She wished she had some rubber boots, but there was nothing for it now. Her sneakers and scrub pants would be stained forever.

"It's in amazing shape," the professor remarked. "The water must have been deep enough that oxygen levels were too low to allow decomposition. It's almost as if we stepped into a time machine and entered Growlersburg the moment before it was buried beneath a lake in the 1940s."

"The '40s?" Jody asked.

The professor shrugged. "Just guessing. This is not as uncommon as you might think. During the Depression, the Civilian Conservation Corps was building roads, bridges, and dams all over the country. Probably what happened here. Gold was long dried up and the richer town of Georgebrook needed a steady water supply, which meant they needed a reservoir."

"I don't think so. I looked in all the buildings and there were no artifacts from that time period. It's nothing more than a primitive mining town. I think it was drowned before the turn of the century."

"Perhaps it was abandoned long before it was flooded then."

"Possible," Jody admitted. "Still, I don't think so. The buildings wouldn't be in such good shape if they had been abandoned for decades before the valley was flooded. On top of that, the reservoir has never been used for drinking water or irrigation. It's just a big fishing hole. I did a bunch of research, but I couldn't find much. It's like people purposely chose not to write about it. All I could find were offhand references to the town and the Oxbow Mine in newspaper archives. Around 1898, any mention to the town disappears in the papers and you start to see references to Oxbow Lake instead. I don't know what to make of it."

"Haunted," someone said behind them.

Jody yelped and spun around to find it was only Steve.

"Sorry," he said sheepishly. "Didn't mean to sneak up on you." The professor seemed unperturbed. He stepped through the dilapidated doorway into the saloon. Jody and Steve followed behind him. Enough of the roof boards were gone to let in a few beams of sunlight, but it was still dark and dank inside.

"Shit, I didn't even hear you come up behind us," Jody whispered to Steve, embarrassed to have been startled so easily. "You're like a..." She caught herself.

"A ninja?" Steve finished for her. He winked. "Thank you, but I'm of Chinese descent, not Japanese."

Jody had to laugh. "I guess we're even now. Sorry. Were you just joking about the haunted thing?"

Steve paused to take a picture, and his flash lit up the entire bar. Even covered in a layer of black silt, the bar top was amazing, a full thirty feet long, like something out of the Old West. Jody shook her head in disgust, though, when she saw that all the liquor bottles and glassware had been destroyed. Even the bar-back shelves had been smashed to hang akimbo from the wall.

"I'm sorry, the local dispshits have been in here looting and thrashing the place," she said. "That was all intact when I first came in here."

"The ugly underbelly of human civilization," Steve said. "Ignorant people always destroy what they should appreciate."

"A bit of a broad generalization, but true in this case," the professor said. "You were saying something about the town being haunted, I believe?"

Jody hadn't thought the professor was paying attention, but there seemed to be more to him than she initially surmised.

"Yeah, after seeing Jody's Tumblr posts, I did a little research of my own at the university library," Steve said. "Like she said, there's not much out there, but I found a reference to the Oxbow Mine in a book about murderers and ghosts during the Gold Rush era. It was hardly more than a footnote, but there were rumors at least that some prospectors disappeared into the Oxbow Mine, presumed dead, only to show up a few months later to start killing people. The book tentatively dated the events to right before the turn of the century. Same decade Jody came up with."

"Interesting," the professor said, and he led the way out of the saloon back into the sunlight. It was near noon now, and the sun glared overhead in the clear autumn sky. Jody was a sweaty mess beneath her scrubs, not to mention muddy as hell.

"It wouldn't be the first time a town was abandoned due to a heinous crime or even superstition," the professor continued. "I'll need to examine a few more rooms to ascertain that the town indeed dates back to the Gold Rush, but even if not, I think it's a worthy site for investigation. I'm not much for field work these days but, Steve, if it's an expedition you'd like to lead, it would be perfect for you and some of the other grad students. Maybe some of the advanced undergrads."

The professor stopped at one of the smaller shacks, what looked to be a home, and tugged on the door. It opened with a squeal of water-bloated lumber and rusted hinges and he stepped inside. Before Jody could step in after him, the professor came sprawling back out the doorway to land on his back in the mud.

"The fuck are you?" a man bellowed, stomping out of the shack after the professor, fists clenched.

Jody gasped in surprise and jumped forward to stop the man raging before her. "Brad Boy! Hey, it's me, Jody."

Brad Boy came to a halt, but just barely. He was tall and lanky, with a feculent beard, ratty jeans, and no shoes. Worst of all, he smelled like an outhouse. His neck cords were taut and his jaw moved like he was chewing a piece of gristly steak.

"Jody, Jody?" His eyes were rimmed with red and he could barely focus on her face as she held him at bay.

"Yeah, Jody. Remember, we went to high school together? You're a few years older, but you dated a couple of my friends."

"Jody, Jody." His eyes darted back down to the professor and then at Steve, standing behind Jody.

"Yeah, easy. They're okay, they're with me. We're just checking out Lake Town. We didn't realize you were in there."

"My house."

"Okay, sure. We won't go in there. We'll get out of here, in fact."

He blinked, once, twice, three times, and then came to. Sort of. His eyes focused on Jody's face and he quit gritting his teeth, but she could tell he was still whacked out of his skull. "No, stay," he said. "Bonfire tonight. All gotta be here. Stay. I will find Preacher Wilson."

He spun on his heel, then sprinted off through the mud, down the muddy tract between the shack and the adjacent building, up the hillside towards the tree line.

Jody reached down to help the professor up. "Sorry about that. One of the local meth-heads."

"Fucking inbred redneck," Steve muttered.

"I think the preferred terminology around here is 'white trash.' I wouldn't let Brad Boy hear you say either one, though. He's known to tote around a .38 in the back of them Levis."

"Charming fellow," the professor said, scraping the muck from his hands and rear. "I'm beginning to have second thoughts about sponsoring a survey here. Who exactly owns this land, anyway? It's not Brad Boy or this Preacher

Wilson, is it?"

"Nah, Preacher Wilson is just the local pastor. He tries to save these meth-heads with the Bible, but more often than not, they just turn into meth-head Jesus freaks. On paper, this land is all managed by BLM. That's who I was hoping you guys were when I first saw you. I called the sheriff about the looting when I first realized it was going on, but they said they don't have jurisdiction, so all I could do was leave a bunch of messages with the BLM. I've never heard back from anyone."

Professor Hallward frowned. "I'll have to look into it and discuss the survey proposition with the university administration. Right now, I'm inclined to get out of here before Brad Boy comes back."

"Not yet," Steve pleaded. "Let's at least look inside the church before we leave. I want to get some photos. It'll help make our case if we can provide visual evidence of an intact building with cultural significance."

"Fine," the professor relented, "but let's make it quick."

"This way," Jody said, glad that Brad Boy hadn't ruined everything. "The church is the easternmost building now, but in all likelihood there was a whole city of tents and temporary buildings at one point, lining the creek up toward the Oxbow Mine. Most of the prospectors wouldn't have had the money or time to build something permanent."

"Makes sense," Steve said, but the professor seemed not to hear Jody's words. He was staring at the church.

It was modest by modern standards, single-storied and made of rough-hewn wooden boards. The only things that distinguished it from the other building in town was the fact that it was longer and had an iron crucifix at the apex of the roof.

Jody pushed her way through the double doors and came to a halt as the others walked in behind her.

"What the—?"

Piled high at the center of the pulpit was a heap of—for lack of a better term—treasure. Jody didn't know how else to describe it. There were vases and bowls, coins and medallions, and even what looked like nuggets of gold. The hair at the back of Jody's neck stood on end.

"That stuff wasn't there last time I was in here. I thought the looters were just *stealing* stuff. Why would they bring anything here?"

They walked warily past the moldering pews toward the pulpit, even Steve, who had been running around like a little kid the whole time.

"Take a photo before we touch anything," the professor said.

Steve did as he was told and they all moved in closer. Jody stopped several feet away and let the other two examine the treasure. Something wasn't right. It reminded her of something… a *déjà vu* moment just beyond the reach of her memory. A wash of senseless fear. She couldn't remember when she had experienced it before, but she felt it now.

"My God, this can't be," the professor said, holding up a gold coin to examine it closer in the dim light.

"What?" Steve asked and he zoomed in to snap a shot.

"I've seen this pictograph before, but it was on the wall of a cave in Africa where Holocene-era humans once resided. We're talking over ten thousand years ago. It makes no sense for it to be here, on a coin crafted in the late nineteenth century."

"You're sure it's the same pictograph?"

"It's unmistakable. The ten-armed serpent. The arms are all bent at right angles along the perimeter of the pictograph so they touch one another, and they're connected in the center by a spiral-like eye."

The professor grabbed another coin from the pile on the pulpit, and another, and then a wooden bowl, which he flipped over to examine. "All of it has the symbol, in one variation or another. How is this possible?" His voice was little more than a whisper. After a moment he stood, the first coin still gripped in one hand. He turned to face Jody.

"The mine. Where is it? Does it still exist?"

"Yeah, I guess so. It's at the opposite end of the lake from the dam, not far from here. Why?"

"Take me there." The professor was already striding back the way they had come. Jody and Steve followed in his wake, out of the church and through Lake Town toward Jody's Blazer.

"Whoa, whoa," Jody said. "Five minutes ago, you wanted to get the hell out of here. Ten minutes ago, you weren't even interested in any of this. Now you want to go look at the mine?"

"That's right. I must see it."

"But it's barricaded off with barb wire, and even if you get past the barb wire, it's just a vertical shaft filled with water."

"It *was* filled with water," the professor corrected her. "If the lake is empty, so too is the mine."

"Okay, sure, but what does the mine have to do with anything?"

They had reached Jody's Blazer and the professor was already climbing up into the passenger seat, heedless of the mud that covered his backside.

"Goddammit, what did I get myself into?" Jody muttered to herself as she pulled herself into the driver seat.

"I need to see the mine," the professor said when they were all in. "There must be the same pictographs on the walls. If so, I don't know what that means. It could be that everything we know about early human migration is wrong."

"I don't know, it seems a bit tenuous," Jody said.

The professor slammed his fist down on the dashboard. "Do you want my help getting into my program or not? Take me to that goddamn mine!"

Both Jody and Steve stared at him in shocked silence. After a moment, he let out a sigh and shook his head. "I'm sorry, I didn't mean to yell at you. I am going to that mine, though. You either take me there or I'll walk and find it myself."

Jody regarded him for a moment. He seemed himself again, but he was still gripping the coin from the church in one hand, rubbing it absently with his fingers. Her gut told her to let the guy run off on his own if he wanted, but she'd promised she'd get him in and out of Lake Town safely. Brad Boy was out there somewhere, probably with his .38, and then there was that party tonight that both Brad Boy and Ted had told her about. Spider Camp wasn't too far off from the east end of the lake, where the mine entrance was. It was still several hours until dark, but who knew if the local meth-heads weren't milling about already? If the professor went wandering around alone in his pink polo and khaki shorts, he was bound to run into trouble.

"All right," she said at last. "Let's go."

Jody pulled the Blazer to a halt thirty yards shy of the mine entrance, hidden in the trees in case anyone from Spider Camp came hiking down toward the mine. She swiveled in her seat to address her two passengers.

"Now listen, I'll take you guys up there for a quick look, but it has to be quick. There's some sort of shindig going on just up the hill from us. Brad Boy and all his sort of ilk will be there. That means we need to be fast and quiet. When I say it's time to go, it's time to go. Am I clear?"

"Crystal," Steve said, and he jumped out of the car with the professor. Apparently some of the older man's excitement had leeched into him. Jody lingered inside for a moment and reached beneath the driver seat where she fished around to find the last gift her father ever gave her, a Ruger 8-shot .22 revolver, loaded with bird shot. She double-checked that all the chambers were filled and that the safety was on, then took a page from Brad Boy and tucked it into the rear waistband of her pants, making sure that the drawstring on her scrubs was pulled tight. The little pistol wouldn't do her much good if it slid down into her butt crack or dropped into one of her pant legs.

Satisfied that she was as ready as she could be, she hopped out of her K5 and led the way up the hill toward the mine entrance. She could tell right away that something was different. It had been years since she'd last been here—since middle school, probably—but she remembered distinctly that there had been warning signs and two separate fences around the perimeter of the mine opening. There were neither anymore.

"Something's not right," she whispered, but the professor had already caught sight of the mine entrance, and he and Steve rushed past her. She followed slowly behind and with each step was consumed by the same sense of dread she'd had in the Lake Town church.

The fear and the sight of the mine before her brought it all back, the *déjà vu* moment. She *had* felt like this before. It was the last time she was here at the mine. She and some friends—all boys—had snuck out one summer on a dare. She hung back at the first fence, but the boys climbed through to stand at the perimeter of the second fence and throw rocks into the mine shaft. She still remembered the sound of the rocks echoing as they ricocheted off the sides of the shaft for three, four seconds before finally plunking into the black water a hundred feet below. While her friends dared each other to climb past the second fence and look into the mine, she found herself mindlessly climbing through the outer fence, moving toward them from behind, intent on pushing them in, compelled to do so without any conscious effort. Thankfully, her friends had chickened out and when they turned in her direction to get out of there, she snapped out of it. She'd forgotten about it all until this moment. She had fully intended on pushing her friends down the mine shaft. *Why? Why would I even think to do that? Dad was still alive still. There was nothing for me to be angry about. I liked my friends...*

"I'm going in."

"What?" Jody came back to the moment and saw that the professor was lowering himself into the shaft. "No, wait! What are you doing?"

"It's fine," the professor said. "There's a ladder, freshly made. It's perfectly safe. Aren't you coming, Steve?"

Steve snapped a photo, but Jody saw that whatever excitement he'd had a few moments before was gone. He glanced from the professor to Jody and then back to the professor again. "I think I best wait up here, you know, in case something happens. You give us the all-clear when you get to the bottom if everything looks okay, then I'll come down."

"Suit yourself," the professor said and began climbing down into the shaft.

Jody tried to say something to stop him, but she couldn't. She couldn't even bring herself to get within five feet of the mine. Steve glanced up at her again and then gazed down into the darkness after the professor. The only sound was the professor's boots scraping on the wood steps of the ladder, but even that sound slowly receded to nothing. Overhead, the sun had passed its zenith and continued its inexorable journey to the west, no more than a few hours from sundown. It didn't seem like they had been exploring Lake Town that long, but Jody must have lost track of time. It was so warm, it was hard to remember that it was late fall and that the days were shorter.

"Seems to be a day of dispelling stereotypes," Steve said after a while. "The anonymous Lake Town blogger I've been following turns out to be younger than me, and a woman. And my gay professor is the only one of us with big enough balls to go into the mine." He forced a wry smile.

The joke cut the tension and Jody found herself able to think again. "He's gay? I mean, I sort of figured he was with the pink shirt and the VW Beetle and all, but I didn't want to jump to conclusions."

Steve grinned for real this time. "He's as gay as a unicorn shitting Skittles. Great professor, and he's been a good mentor to me. His boyfriend split up with him recently. When I heard, I thought I'd invite him on this trip for Thanksgiving break. I was already planning on coming up solo. Didn't think he'd actually agree to come."

"Are you..."

"Gay? No. Pretty not gay, in fact."

Jody returned the smile. "So not gay, and not a ninja. Got it."

"Exactly. And I'm no good at math and know how to drive."

They both went silent again. It had been several minutes since the professor went down, and they had heard nothing. No "all-clear," nothing. Jody summoned the courage to step forward and kneel down next to Steve so she could peer down the shaft. The sunlight still illuminated the ladder and walls about ten feet down into the shaft, but beyond that it was pitch black. There was no sign of the professor. *Should we call down after him?* The thought of speaking down into the hole terrified her almost as much as the thought of going down into it.

Suddenly, Steve's head cocked to one side. "You hear that?" he whispered.

Jody leaned down closer to the mine shaft.

"No, it's not coming from down there," Steve said. "I hear voices behind us."

"Shit, get down," Jody told him, and she scrambled on her hands and knees toward the cover of a nearby manzanita shrub. She could hear the voices now, too. Rowdy voices, making no effort to be quiet. They were coming from Spider Camp up the hill. Jody craned her neck to get a better view and spied several faces she recognized in the distance, clomping toward the mine through the ponderosa pines. There was Brad Boy and Ted. And Preacher Wilson. *What the hell is he doing here?* She didn't have time to ponder that question long, because the next thing that caught her eye was the glint of Brad's .38 in his hand.

"Shit, shit, shit," Jody hissed, scrambling back to Steve. "They're coming this way. We have to get out of here. Come on."

She waved him in the direction of her Blazer, but he shook his head. "We can't ditch Professor H. We can hide down there."

Before she could protest, he lowered himself onto the ladder and disappeared below. She stole a glance back into the trees and saw that Brad Boy and his group were getting closer. Everything in her told her to bolt, but she just couldn't do it. She couldn't live with herself if she abandoned the professor and Steve. Besides, she'd waited too long. Brad Boy and the others would see if she made a break for her Blazer now.

"Shit, don't do this," she told herself, but she did it anyway, sliding her legs over the edge of the precipice into the shaft. Her legs swayed helplessly in the void for a moment, but then one of her feet found purchase on a ladder step. She let out a deep breath and began the long descent, hand after hand, foot after foot. Above her, the sound of voices receded and the daylight shrunk into a sphere of light that was swallowed in the darkness. Her hands and arms began to ache and she panicked for a moment, certain she would slip and fall to her death below.

Steve's voice broke her panic. "You're almost there. Keep going."

She glanced down and saw the blue LED light from his cell phone illuminating the way. She only had another eight feet to go. With a relieved breath, she climbed the rest of the way down and set foot on solid, if mucky, ground.

"The professor?" she asked.

"I don't see him. He must have gone that way." Steve shined the light from his cellphone to their left, dimly illuminating the shape of a horizontal shaft sloping away from them. "Only way to go except back up."

"Let's find him then, and get the hell out of here."

Steve led the way, leaving Jody to trail behind in darkness. She cursed herself for not bringing her own cellphone, or the Maglite she had in her truck toolbox. The thought of her cellphone made her think of her mother, who was probably wondering where she was, why she hadn't called. Jody didn't get along with her mother these days, but she was all the family she had. The thought of getting trapped down here—her mother never knowing what happened to her—was almost too much. It was as if Jody was certain she was never leaving this mine.

"Shine the light on the ground to see if there are footprints in the mud," Jody said, as much to herself as to Steve. She needed to stay focused on solving the problem at hand, not on irrational fear.

Steve pointed his light down and scanned across the tunnel floor. "Yeah, there's all kinds of footprints, going both directions. Someone must have opened the mine back up now that the water is drained out. Maybe there's still gold down here."

It sounded reasonable. Jody wanted to believe it, but she didn't. With each step deeper into the mine, her sense of dread grew stronger.

The passage wound to the right and opened up into a wider tunnel. The main passage bore straight left, easily ten foot in diameter. A smaller passage went in the opposite direction. Steve scanned his light to the right down the smaller passage. The silt and muck on the floor was deeper and unmarked by footprints. Jody closed her eyes, trying to orient herself to the terrain outside.

"This passage must lead to Lake Town. Most gold mines have both a horizontal entrance and a vertical shaft for ventilation. This was probably the main entrance at some point."

She opened her eyes to find that Steve had already redirected the light to the left. "Good to know, but no footprints that way. Professor H must have gone to the left."

They continued on and the passage began descending, winding its way through one blind curve after another. With each step, the mud became thicker on the floor and the smell of wet decay became stronger. A groan, almost too low pitched to hear, thrummed in the air around them, then disappeared a moment later. A few steps—a few seconds—later, and the groan returned, like the earth itself was groaning in pain.

Steve reached out to Jody and took her hand. She didn't know if he did it to comfort her or to comfort himself, but she didn't protest. The groan returned in regular intervals, and the smell of rotting organic material grew stronger as they trudged forward. Steve shone his phone light onto the ground again to make sure they were still on the right track. When he turned it upward again, they realized quite suddenly that they had emerged into a cavern that swallowed up the tiny LED beam.

The moaning sound was louder than before, and it was joined now by another noise: something scraping in the mud. Jody moved in closer to Steve and grabbed hold of his free arm. "Over there," she whispered pointing to their right.

Steve scanned his light in the direction she indicated and spotted movement, something on the ground. The scrapping noise intensified.

"Professor?" Steve whispered.

At first, Jody didn't believe it, but when she looked closer she saw it was indeed the professor, covered in filth, half-buried in the mud. His hands were digging at the muck around him.

"He's stuck," Jody said and she rushed to him, Steve right on her heels.

"Hold tight," Steve said as they both slid to a stop beside him. "We'll get you out of there."

The professor's feet and legs were completely buried in mud. Jody reached down to try and hook a hand beneath one of his knees to pull the leg free. Before she knew what was happening, the professor shoved her away with a feral grunt.

"What the hell are you doing?" Steve demanded, and when he shined his light onto the professor's face, they both saw it. He held the coin in his mouth, covering his teeth, and his eyes reflected red in the LED glow. He wasn't trying to dig himself free. He was *burying* himself. Steve reached out with his free hand to stop him, but the professor grunted again and slapped the phone out of his hand.

Everything went dark when the phone landed in the mud. Jody instinctively lunged at the professor, hands flailing in the dark to reach his face and get that dammed coin out. The professor flung her aside, though, and she rolled face down into the muck. The groan filled the cavern and her very being. Peripherally, she could hear Steve screaming, but all she could focus on was the groan. She forced herself up and opened her eyes. It was dark, but she could see it, the ten-armed serpent, shuddering beneath the surface of the mud in the center of the cavern. An eyelid opened before, revealing another eyelid beneath it, a membranous one that spiraled open. Dread filled her and she felt her head sag helplessly into the mud.

The screams are deafening, a chorus of pain, confusion. The only solace is in the center of it all, in the fleshy core, beneath the viscera, deep in the warm fluid that mutes away the screams. Sleep, sleep, she tells herself, though it's not her own voice. Sleep with me, she tells herself and sinks deeper into the flesh, into the warm void. I'm so tired. Must make the screaming stop. The eye beckons her nearer. Sleep. Sleep. Sleep.

It was only instinct that made Jody react and awaken. Something warm and firm grabbed at her thighs, and her body reacted, slapping it away and punching at it.

"Get off me, fucker!"

A giant worm-like appendage slithered off of her, leaving her half-buried in the mud. It was pitch black, but she could sense the creature retreating from her, focusing its efforts elsewhere, several feet away. The scraping and slurping of mud told her where Steve was. She pulled herself to her feet and reached behind her, finding the revolver still safely tucked away in her pants. She clicked the safety off and strode toward the struggling noises.

"Steve!" She dropped to her knees and groped outward with her free hand, finding his outstretched arm. She pulled him toward her, but the creature had his other arm, tugging him toward the center of the cave. She leveled the pistol and fired blindly. The groan became a roar, but the creature let go, and Steve came loose with a startled gasp.

"Steve! Are you with me?"

"I'm here. What the fuck is happening? Where was I?"

"We have to get out of here."

"The professor!"

"I don't know where he is."

She flailed around, one hand on Steve, the other still firmly gripping the pistol, but she was completely disoriented. She had no idea where the professor was, where Steve's phone was, or where the exit was.

"My camera," Steve said. "I still have it."

His flash bulb filled the cavern for a split second, but it was too bright, too brief to be of any use. Screams and shouts were filling her mind again, but no, they were real this time, she realized. And the cavern was becoming brighter with flickering orange light. *Brad Boy and Preacher Wilson!*

She blinked her eyes to clear her vision and took in her surroundings. She and Steve were kneeling in the muck. Immediately beyond them was a pit of quivering mud, the place where the creature with the membranous eye lived. She yanked Steve to his feet and away from the pit, spinning around, searching for refuge. There was only one exit, the way in which they had come, and that passage was growing brighter as Brad Boy and his gang approached. The professor was nowhere in sight. The only place to hide was along the nearest wall of the cavern, where an old mine cart was overturned onto its side. That's where she led Steve, and they ducked down behind the mine cart just as a crowd of people with torches filed into the chamber.

"Where they at? I heard a gunshot and screaming."

It was Brad Boy's voice.

"There's one," someone else said.

Jody stole a glance from behind the cart and saw Preacher Wilson and another man yank the professor from the mud. The professor gasped, and retched out the coin with a choking cough.

"Is he one of us now?" Brad Boy asked.

Preacher Wilson grabbed the professor by the head with both hands, pressing his thumbs against the professor's temples. He leaned his head back and began muttering in some unintelligible language. Every hair on Jody's body stood on end at hearing it. The creature in the pit groaned in response to Preacher Wilson's words.

At last it ended, and Preacher Wilson let the professor go.

"He is not ready yet. He needs more time with the Great One."

"We throw him in the pit then," Brad Boy said, stepping forward to grasp the professor by the shoulders.

Jody reacted without thinking. She jumped out from behind the cart with a feral scream and shot Brad Boy right in the head. The bird shot didn't kill him, but it stung like a motherfucker and stunned him. It bought Jody enough time, at least, to run up and shove *him* into the mud pit. When she turned around, eight assailants stared at her in stunned fury. Preacher Wilson was the first to lunge toward her, so she shot him in the groin. He screamed and fell to writhe in the mud.

The next man nearest to her growled garbled nonsense and swung his torch at her, but she was well out of his reach. She shot him in the face, and shoved him into the pit.

Push them all into the pit.

She moved mindlessly toward the next nearest man, shot him in the face, and hurled him into the pit.

Steve came swooping from behind the mine cart then, kicking out the legs of the man closest to the exit. Steve stomped the dude on the face and took his torch.

Jody leveled her gun at the next man closest to her and saw it wasn't a man at all, but a woman. *Well, why not?* The psychotic hag was missing most of her front teeth and was frothing at the mouth. Jody did her a favor and shot the rest of her teeth out. Into the pit!

Of the four assailants remaining, none of them seemed to have the courage to attack. "Oh Great One, save us!" a scrawny guy pleaded.

Jody leveled the gun toward his face.

"Jody! Stop it!"

Jody came to, staring at her old friend Ted.

Ted was gibbering like an idiot, though. It was Steve's voice that had brought Jody to her senses. "Jody, don't. Just leave him. Let's go."

Jody stole a glance left toward Steve and then back to Ted. She could hear groaning and a mass of mud churning over on itself to her right. What had she just done? She relaxed her finger on the trigger and held her free hand up in peace. "Ted, it's me, Jody. I don't know what just happened. Let's get of here and get help. C'mon, we can go together. All of us."

Ted stared at her for a long moment, his face twitching and contorting. He shuffled toward Jody tentatively.

"It's okay, I won't hurt you."

He squinted his eyes shut, twitched again, and when he opened his eyes all humanity was gone from them. "Great One, take me!" he screeched and hurled himself into the pit where the others were twitching and sinking beneath the muck to lie with the creature. At seeing Ted relinquish himself to the pit, the last two torch-wielding assailants followed suit and hurled themselves into oblivion.

Jody had to will her eyes away from the scene. Steve came to her, the last torch in hand, and pulled her away. Together they grabbed the professor, who still stood in a stupor.

"C'mon, Professor H. Let's get out of here while we can."

He stared at the pit for a moment—longingly?—but when they tugged on his hands he followed dutifully after them.

With the torch to light the way, they moved swiftly through the passage back the way they had come, and with each step, Jody felt the seduction of the pit weaken. The professor, too, regained more of his faculties.

"I saw it," he muttered. "It had me. That's why the valley was dammed up, to bury the creature, not flood the mine."

"Quiet," Steve whispered. "Not now."

"We're gonna get out of here alive," Jody said. If she said it out loud, it became reality. Didn't it?

When they reached the side passage, though, they heard more voices echoing down the vertical shaft. It was a cacophony of vowel-less babbling, human tongues twisted into bleating an inhuman language.

"Fuck, we're cornered," Steve hissed, dragging the professor to a halt.

"We *will* get out of here alive," Jody said again, tucking her gun back into her waistband. "This way."

She led them down the smaller passage, the undisturbed one she hoped led to Lake Town. The silt on the ground grew deeper and the passage narrower, tapering to the point that they had to hunch forward to proceed. Behind them the voices grew.

"The torch," Jody whispered. "Put it out or they'll see us."

"No way."

Jody didn't bother arguing. She snatched the torch out of Steve's hands and threw it to the ground, where it sputtered out with a hiss.

"This is a bad idea."

"Shut up and grab my hand. Keep hold of the professor."

"I'm here still," the professor said at hearing his name.

"Shut up, both of you."

She found Steve's hand and pulled him deeper into the passage, blind in the dark, probing in front of her with her elbow and forearm. The passage grew narrower around them, and then came quite suddenly to an end. Jody probed the sloping wall in front of her, feeling only wet mud that crumbled at her touch.

"What the hell is happening, Jody?"

"A dead end." They were screwed. The cave entrance must have collapsed decades before beneath the pressure of the lake water above it. Jody kept probing, desperate for a way out. She found a beam of wood, half buried in the mud. "Your camera," Jody said. "Take a picture in front of us."

"We already tried that. The flash doesn't stay on long enough to see any-thing."

"Take a picture and we can look at it on the screen."

"Of course. I'm an idiot."

The flash illuminated the mud walls around them briefly, and then Steve was holding out the LCD screen toward her. The photograph showed the wooden beam she had discovered, collapsed diagonally and covered in mud, barring their way. The photograph also showed several other beams, half-buried near the ground.

"This has to be the entrance," Jody said. "Maybe we can push our way through. Stand back." She probed the mud before her and found the beam again. She dug her fingers into the mud around and behind it, then yanked it toward herself. It budged, allowing her to get a better grip. When she pulled a second time, the beam came loose, along with a small avalanche of mud. She climbed up on the new pile of mud and used the beam of rotting timber like a battering ram, driving it into the mud in front of her. The soil crumbled away, and light leaked in

"Yes!" she yelped, and drove forward with the beam again, frantic to be free at last. The beam broke through the surface and fresh air and daylight bathed her face. She scrambled toward the opening, filled with elation. "We're getting out of here," she said, and then the ground collapsed beneath her and everything went black.

When she came to, Steve and the professor were standing over her, pulling away the soil and crumbled planks of timber beneath which she was buried.

"Jody!" Steve was saying. "Are you all right?"

"I'm okay," she said, but when she tried to push herself up, her ankle ex-ploded with white hot pain. "Fuuuck, my ankle!"

"It looks to be broken," the professor said, hauling the last beam away.

Jody was trembling and her forehead was already beaded with sweat. Shock, she knew, but she didn't have time for that shit. She hoisted herself up on to her elbows and peered back the way they came. The tunnel was a gaping, dark wound on the outer edge of the dried-up lake bed. The tree line was no more than thirty feet away, and up the hill somewhere in the trees was the other mine shaft.

"We have to get out of here," Jody said. "Whoever was going down the other mine shaft is gonna figure out where we went."

As if on cue, gibbering madness echoed toward them from the tunnel.

"Shit, we'll have to carry you," Steve said.

"No, we won't get very far that way. You go, get my Blazer and come back. Keys are in the ignition."

"You're sure?"

"Yes! hurry!"

Steve scrambled away toward the trees, and Jody reached up to take the professor's outstretched hand. He hoisted her up and gave her his arm so she could steady herself on her good foot. "Let's get away from the entrance," she told him, and began hopping away with his help.

The gibbering voices were growing louder. Jody tried to hop faster, but that only threw her off-balance, and she instinctively tried to steady herself by putting her bad foot down. She collapsed to the ground with a curse. The professor reached down to help her up again, but the ground rumbled beneath them as the creature in the mine groaned. The sky turned angry and red. *It must be smoke from a forest fire,* Jody thought at first, but when she spun on the ground to look to the sky in the west, she saw it was a solar eclipse.

"How the hell?"

The first of the mad folk stepped foot out of the mine.

"Nyrlp, flgrtrr," the professor gurgled above Jody. His eyes went blank and he turned toward the mine.

"Oh no you don't!" Jody said. She pulled out the pistol again and shot toward the professor, peppering his ass with bird shot.

"Aye-ahh!" He clutched at his bloodied ass-cheeks and spun around to face Jody, once again himself. "What the hell happened?"

"Help me!" she yelled at him. "They're coming."

How many shots left? She couldn't remember. Not that it mattered. There were a dozen mindless idiots shambling toward them already, and another stepped out of the mine every moment.

An engine roared and Jody looked up to see her Blazer barreling out from the trees to slide to a halt in the mud between them and their assailants.

"Hurry!" Steve yelled, his voice high-pitched and frantic.

The professor hoisted Jody up and into the passenger seat of the Blazer, then hopped in the back seat.

"Go!" Jody barked, and Steve punched it, spraying their attackers with four rooster tails of silt and mud.

Jody turned in her seat to watch the freaks and the mine disappear behind them as they tore ass across the lake bed. They skirted Lake Town, bathed in the red light of the eclipse. True to his word, Steve drove like a champ, straight into the sun as the moon slowly snuffed it out.

Jody was shivering and numb, exhausted beyond comprehension, but she couldn't push away what she'd seen and done in that mine. The creature with the membranous eye. How many had she pushed into that eye? It had consumed Ted. And probably Preacher Wilson. He was a blowhard who had turned his mother into a humorless Bible-thumper, but that didn't mean he was a bad guy. Even Brad Boy had deserved better.

"You still with us?" Steve asked.

Jody opened her eyes to see they were driving up out of the lake bed near the dam. The eclipse was full now, directly before them above the canopy of ponderosa pines.

"I'm here. You can slow down now. I think we're safe."

"Not until we get you to a hospital."

"Right, but you're gonna have to stop first and unlock the front hubs now that we're out of the mud."

Steve frowned at her, but once they were clear of the lake bed and on the dirt road again, he pulled to a stop. "How do I unlock them, exactly?"

"Just turn the hub switches all the way to the left."

Steve hopped out of the Blazer and disappeared from her line of vision as he knelt alongside the driver's side tire. Movement in the distance caught Jody's attention and she peered into the canopy of trees along the dirt road.

"Steve! Get back in here now."

Steve was already on the passenger side, unlocking the second hub. "What?"

"Back in the car. Hurry!"

Steve scrambled back around the Blazer and into the driver's seat just as a mob of people emerged from the woods on the dirt road. Hundreds of people from Georgebrook. Not just the local meth-heads and fuckups, but normal people, too. Jody recognized the attendant from the Gas'N'Go from that morning. The gal who worked the teller at her bank. The town librarian. All of them in a daze as they shambled down the dirt road toward Spider Camp and the mine shaft beyond it.

"No—what are they doing?" Jody whispered.

"It is the call of the creature in the mine," the professor said. "It beckons to them, just as it did to us. We have to get away while we still have the will to do so."

Several of the shamblers took notice of the Blazer sitting alongside the road and began coming their way.

"Shit, yes, go!" Jody told Steve. "Nice and slow and hopefully everyone will get out of the way. Everyone lock your doors."

Steve put the Blazer in drive and eased forward into the crowd. It was like driving through a herd of cows. They got out of the way, but slowly, some of them only after walking right into the grill of the Blazer. Some of them slapped at the windows, but for the most part they were content to keep walking down the road.

"Slow and steady," Jody said, more for herself than anything.

The crowd began to thin and Steve quickened their pace.

"I think we're clear," he said.

"No." Jody grabbed his arm. "Stop. It's my mother."

"What?"

"I said stop, dammit!"

He did, and Jody rolled down her window. It was indeed her mother, at the tail end of the pack, wearing a paisley house dress and still in her slippers. "Mom, stop. Get in. It's me."

Her mother tilted her head sideways and came toward the window. "Daughter. Come." Her eyes were milky and out-of-focus.

Cold fury filled Jody. She reached out the window and smacked her mother across the face, trying to snap her out of it. Her mother was unfazed.

"Daughter. Come. To the Lake Town. To be baptized in the warm embrace of mud."

"No!" Jody cried out reaching out again, but before she could grab her mother, Steve gunned it and they were speeding away. "No, stop!"

"I'm sorry," Steve said, "But she's gone. We have to get out here."

"I'm afraid Steve is right," the professor said. "There is no salvation for them. Not for any of us. Not after what we've seen."

"But she's all I have!" Jody sobbed.

"You're all alone now," the professor said.

The flatness in his voice cut Jody's tears short. Was he still himself? Was he back under the control of the ten-armed serpent? Either way, he was right. Jody was alone. Then again, she had been for years, she realized, and she'd survived this long.

TAXED

Scott William Taylor

Chief Larry Delafontaine stood beside Detective Stephens and looked through the one-way glass into the interrogation room at Tommy, sweaty and fidgeting. Larry could feel his revulsion tugging down the corners of his mouth and working in the muscles of his chin, and for the first time in years he was thankful Louisiana still had the death penalty.

"Has he said anything?" he asked Stephens, who couldn't take his eyes away from the twenty-seven-year old taxidermist on the other side of the glass.

"Nothing. Except he did say he'll only talk to you," the lanky man shifted his weight.

"He ask for a lawyer?"

"No, and thank God, 'cause then this whole f—" Stephens bit his tongue in mid-word and looked down. Larry knew Doug's new girlfriend hated the crude language used by Atwood County's entire police force. Some habits are nearly impossible to break.

"...This whole *insane* thing would just drag out longer," Stephens said.

"Can you do me a favor?" Larry asked as he reached for the interrogation room's doorknob. "Get me a Diet Coke and two Advils. My knee's killing me."

"Sure thing, Chief. I thought your knee was doing better."

"It was, but everything's fu—" Larry cut short the profane word in a show of solidarity. "Since this morning... well, a lot of things have changed."

Larry's hand was on the doorknob when Stephens said, "I... heard a little about all this at Tommy's shop from Neil Tarbet. Is it..."

Larry closed his eyes, trying to shut out the images that mention of "Tommy's shop" brought up. He fought to keep them buried. "Doug, it was the worst thing I've ever seen. Ever." Larry hoped that the note in his voice with which he ended the sentence would forestall any further questions.

"I'll go get your Coke and Advil." Stephens left Larry to do his job.

Larry opened the door and stepped through.

Tommy started from his chair. "Oh, thank God you're here!" Tommy said he blurted. Larry motioned him back into his seat. There was a small second table against the wall, near an electrical outlet, and Larry pressed the red button on the tape recorder on top of it.

"Tommy, you just sit tight." Larry pulled a cheap, government-issued chair out from the black linoleum table and took a seat across from the younger man. When he spoke again, his tones were measured and constricted. "And Tommy, I want to make one thing perfectly clear. It is taking everything that makes me human to not pull my gun and blow your damn head off right now. Do you understand?"

Tommy nodded, his breaths coming his short bursts. His lower jaw twitched and he eyes bore into Larry's. Larry knew the man across from him was terrified, but he didn't think it was because of what he'd said. He thought Tommy had brought that fear in with him.

"I do, sir. But I didn't do anything! I swear! It wasn't—"

Larry held up his hand.

"Tommy…" Larry took in several deep breaths. "Have you been read your rights and do you understand them?"

Tommy nodded.

"Good. Then you just start at the very beginning. Tell me the story, front to back. I'll stop you if I have questions. Understand?"

Tommy nodded again.

"Okay then," Larry said, and he could feel and the pain that pulsed in his knee begin to be mirrored by an equal sensation in his head.

"The beginning," Tommy muttered, his eyes darting back and forth across the tabletop. "The beginning… I guess it began two nights ago. Pete Johnson and Clyde Flatts just dropped me off—we'd spent some time at Lucy's Bar. We got home around 2 A.M."

"How drunk were you?" Larry asked.

"Just a little buzzed. I was expecting Dave Stoker to drop off a ram in the morning—he wanted a rush job and was going to pay top dollar so I didn't want a hangover to slow me down. You can ask Pete and Clyde if you don't believe me."

"I will. Then what?"

"I got up around 8:30, had breakfast and waited for Dave. Well, I wait for another hour, hour and a half, and he doesn't show, so then I check the drop-off box to see if he left the ram before I got up."

Tommy stopped talking and took several short breaths. His eyes darted around the room as if he expected something to attack him.

"You okay?"

"Yeah. Yeah." Larry saw Tommy's hands begin to shake and wondered if Tommy was about to confess. If so, Larry wasn't sure if he was prepared to hear it. "Just give me a second," Tommy said.

"Take your time."

After a few moments, Tommy spoke again. "I saw that the latch had been tripped so I knew something was there. I thought it must be the ram and I opened the box.

"Except it wasn't no ram. I don't know what the hell it was—still don't."

This wasn't the story that Larry was expecting, and in spite of the fact that he believed the man across the table from him was a murderer, he found himself intrigued by what Tommy was saying. Here was a taxidermist, after all—young, but experienced nonetheless. He'd probably seen everything that had flown, swam, walked, galloped or wiggled across south Louisiana.

"What did it look like?" Larry asked after Tommy failed to speak.

"It looked like a squid-thing. I mean, it had a squid head, but it had limbs almost like arms and legs."

"So, human?" Larry reached into his breast pocket and withdrew a small writing pad and a pen that hooked to the spiral binding. He wrote the word *squid*, then crossed it out and wrote *meth lab?* He made sure Tommy couldn't see what he had written.

"Almost—kind of like a baby, but more grey, like the primer color on my dad's Jeep—imagine what you'd get if you crossed a person and a fish, but with… you know, arms and legs."

A knock on the door made Tommy jump. The door opened and Stephens came in with a Diet Coke and two Advils. "Here you go," Stephens said and put them on the table, keeping his eyes off Tommy.

Larry looked at Tommy. Something had changed in the past few minutes. A small crack appeared in the hard shell of hate he had for the taxidermist.

"Hey," Larry said to Tommy. "Ah, you need anything?"

"No, no. I'm good."

Larry nodded to Stevens and the officer left, closing the door behind him.

"So, you found a squid-human thing," Larry said as he popped the pills and took a drink. "Then what did you do?"

"I took it in the shop and cut it open."

"You did what?" Larry said, stopping the second Advil halfway down his gullet.

"Yeah, I thought maybe Dave changed his mind and wanted *this* thing stuffed instead of a ram. So I skinned it, threw the innards in the trash and built the form. I had never built anything like it. It wasn't like any animal I've ever seen. The hide was like rubber, all slimy and tough. I was going to tell Dave—or whoever dropped it off—that I was going to charge him extra, just for the pain-in-the-ass project he'd given me."

"This animal, you don't know who sent it? Was there a note or anything?" Larry asked.

"No, but that's not unusual. Everyone knows that they can drop off a raccoon or boar and I'll get working on it. They usually stop by that day or the next and let me know it was them that dropped it off." Larry remembered seeing the drop-off box just outside Tommy's taxidermy shop, even remembered opening the hatch and looking inside.

"We didn't see any squid-thing in your shop. What happened to it?"

Tommy stared at Larry and bit his bottom lip. He then began to nervously tap his fingers on the table.

"Stay with me, Tommy," Larry said. His knee throbbed, and his head was beginning to pound. The Coke and Advils felt like they were just sitting in his stomach, wondering which way to go. "You good to continue?"

Tommy nodded.

"I got done with it around four or five o'clock yesterday. I didn't want to go nowhere in case Dave or whoever came by to pay up. Since I was going to be there, I started working on a swan for Todd Cummings that I'd been putting off.

"I was a couple of hours into that when I must have dozed off. It was dark outside when I woke up. That's when I heard something. It sounded like someone rummaging around in my scrap pile near the truck. I went and retrieved my 30-06 and that's when they came in, all three of them."

Larry jotted notes as Tommy spoke, but he stopped and looked at Tommy. Larry saw a look of pure terror on the man's face. It was so pitiful it almost made Larry forget what he had seen earlier in Tommy's shop. Almost.

"Tommy, who came in?"

"Huh?"

"Tommy!" Larry snapped his fingers. "Who was it that came into your shop?"

Tommy stared straight ahead as if he watching a vision only he could see.

"There were three of them," Tommy whispered.

Tommy's eye twitched.

"Did you recognize any of them?" Larry waited to write down either a name or the word *unknown*.

Tommy locked eyes with the detective and beads of sweat began rolling down his unshaven face. "Wasn't anything to recognize."

Larry lifted his pen. "Say again?"

"I mean, there was nothing to recognize. They weren't human."

"Not human?" Larry circled the *meth lab?* comment.

"Chief Delafontaine. I'm telling you I stood in my shop and saw three *things* come inside and they weren't human."

"Well, what the hell were they?" Larry felt pressure in his temples as the blood pumped in his veins just below the skin.

"I swear to God, I don't know," Tommy said.

"What did they look like?"

"They were all over seven feet tall. They had huge squid heads, like the thing I cut up, but huge!" Larry saw Tommy's eyes shifted rapidly back and forth. "They were all over seven feet tall..."

"You said that already," Larry interrupted.

"Yes, I did. I did. They walked on two legs, like people. Their torsos and arms were like humans, too, but those heads and their eyes... I am going to have nightmares for the rest of my life about their eyes."

And how long will that be? Larry wondered. "Okay," he said. "So, these tall squid-headed things came in. Do you think you can describe them to Frank when we're done so he can draw them?"

"Oh yeah. No problem. And I can describe the little one, too."

Larry had forgotten about that one. "Good. We'll have you talk to Frank in a bit." Questions swirled inside Larry's head. Nothing made sense. He needed more answers. "How were these three things dressed? I mean, were they clothed like people too?"

"No—they were naked, as all nat-ur-al as God made them. If God did make them."

"What did you do when they came in?"

"I just stood there, gun hanging down. I was scared shitless—I couldn't move. They came in and walked straight to the squid-thing that I had stuffed. That's when I thought it must have been a baby of one of those big creatures. That made me sick to think that I had carved up and prepared a baby one of those things." Tommy dropped his head.

"Then what happened?" Larry asked. Tommy sounded sincere. He sounded like he was saying exactly what he remembered happening. But there was no way this actually happened. There were no such things as giant squid-men roaming around Atwood County, Louisiana.

"They all walked over to it and kept looking at each other. It was like I wasn't even in the room, thank God."

"Did they say anything?"

Tommy gave Larry a puzzled look.

"I mean, did they make any noise?"

"Nothing—they didn't talk at all. They made no sound. They just kept looking at each other, like they were communicating, but without words. "

"So... didn't say anything," Larry said and wrote the same on his pad. "Then what happened?"

"They stood together, looking at each other for a couple of minutes. Then one picked up the baby squid-thing and put it under his arm, and he and another one of them left. The last one walked over to me. It came right up and stopped a few inches from me."

Tommy's hand began to shake again, followed by his other hand. Soon Tommy's whole body begin to twitch.

"Tommy." Larry raised his voice. "Son—snap out of it!"

Tommy stared straight ahead, but didn't stop shaking.

"Tommy!" Larry roared and slammed his fist on the table, breaking the trance in Tommy's eyes.

"Yeah?" Tommy said, his voice weak.

"Tommy—I need you to tell me what happened next."

After a moment, Tommy spoke. "This thing stood and looked down on me. The tentacle things on its head began to shake, like what a rattler does when you get close—except no rattles. And the smell—oh! It smelled godawful! Like it had been dead for weeks! That baby thing didn't smell unusual at all, just a little fishy like you'd imagine—not like *this* thing."

Larry watched Tommy as he spoke, head pounding, and wondered what had happened to his bullshit alarm. After twenty years of interrogating suspects, his gut was honed to detect falsehood when he heard it—usually. He'd been with Tommy for twenty minutes and any moment he expected his gut to sound the BS alarm. But the moment for catching Tommy in a lie never came. There was *no way* Tommy was telling the truth, but Larry was damn sure the man across the table from him wasn't lying all the same.

"Did it touch you?"

"No, no. It just stood there looking at me. And those eyes. They were black and yellow, like a catfish, but big. Lord help me, they were big. All I could do was stand there. It was like its eyes paralyzed me so I couldn't move. You know, like a trance or something. I couldn't see its mouth under those squid tentacles but I imagine, if it wanted to, it could have opened wide and ripped my head clean off."

"How long did it just stand there?"

"I don't know, man. Maybe five minutes, or fifteen, even though it only felt like a few seconds. I think it could read my mind. I really do. And its arms were huge; it could have killed me right then and there. I doubt my gun would have left a scratch on that tough grey skin. I knew how tough it was, even on the baby one."

Tommy paused again, slumped forward with his forearms on the table. He looked physically and emotionally exhausted. "You, ah..." Larry said. "You need to take a break?"

"No way—I want to get this off my chest. Then maybe I can forget this nightmare ever happened."

Good luck, Larry thought. "Okay, then. Go on."

"Like I said, we were just standing there. Then I saw the two other things come walking back into the shop, but this time they were carrying... they had with them..."

Larry knew what Tommy was going to say. And he knew why the taxidermist couldn't finish his sentence. Tommy began to cry.

"They carried in..." Tears fell freely from Tommy's eyes. They landed silently on the table's black linoleum.

"Son, I saw it too. I was there. Just say it."

"They were carrying Ross Phillip's three-year old son, Jack. Except... Jack..." He stopped talking and closed his eyes tight, but the tears continued to slide down his cheeks.

"Tommy," Larry said in as kind a voice as he could muster. An hour before he'd wanted to kill Tommy himself after he'd seen what was in the taxidermy shop. Now, things had changed. "You can stop..."

"The boy was naked. Jack was naked and sliced up the center and stitched together using, I don't know—it looked like twine or something. And his eyes... oh God! His eyes were gone. There was nothing, but..."

Tommy began to cry harder. His shoulders rose and fell with each sob.

"They just dropped the boy on the table where I had had that squid-baby. They just dropped him. The big monster looked over at Jack, then back at me, and then it walked away. All three of them—they left. I broke down after that, just knelt on the floor and cried. After a bit, I called Laura in your office. God, Chief, I know this sounds crazy, but there's no way in hell I would have done anything to that kid—no way. So, you can throw my ass in jail or even kill me if you don't believe me. I wouldn't mind. Really, I wouldn't."

Tommy bowed his head. Larry picked up the small notebook, slid the Bic pen back into its spiral cocoon and put them both back in his breast pocket.

"Tommy, we're going to have you go talk to Frank, and then I'd like you to meet with Dr. Farnsworth. He works with people who have seen... things. I'll give him a call and you and him can talk things over. How's that sound?"

"Good, I guess. That sounds good," Tommy said wiping tears away with the back of his hand.

"All right. You know we've got a lot to check out with this and I've got to give Ross Phillips a call so you just sit tight and Detective Stephens will take care of things from here on out, okay?" Tommy just nodded.

Chief Delafontaine rose. The cheap chair screeched as the metal feet scraped on the cement floor. He nodded to the one-way mirror. A click echoed in the room as the locking mechanism tripped, allowing him to leave. Miraculously, the man felt no pain in his left knee.

THE GEARS TURN BELOW

SM WILLIAMS

Emmett Parson came to the house looking for treasure, and almost as soon as he walked through the door, he kicked over a soup can full of old tobacco juice. It didn't help the appearance of the room, especially since there had been a layer of mold on top of the liquid, but it didn't hurt much either. Most of the juice had immediately run under an old gas tank from a tractor that had been cut in half by a torch, and it would soon blend in with all the other stains—oil, ground-in manure, other unidentifiable things—on the floor of what Emmett supposed would be called the living room.

Emmett edged his way between a pile of truck springs and a teetering stack of cogs toward a couch and an old easy chair, both stained and sprouting stuffing from dozens of holes. There was a gap between the two pieces of furniture, leaving a spot on the floor that was clear and almost clean. It was situated for the best view of the old TV that sat atop a milk crate, and from his visits as a kid, Emmett recalled it as Uriah's chair. He shook his head. It had never been a tidy place, but he didn't remember it being this bad. It looked like the state troopers had pushed some of the junk aside to form a lane so they could haul Orson through from the bedroom, and Emmett couldn't imagine why they'd left the can of tobacco spit next to the front door.

The smell in the main room was bad, but it was worse in the bedroom. None of the Speakman boys had ever bathed enough to make a secret of the fact that they worked on a farm, and when you put four of them together, sharing a bedroom—hell, sharing a bed—things got unpleasant. The mattress was stripped of its bedclothes, probably by the state police, Emmett figured, since it wasn't like the Speakmans to bother changing sheets. The saggy mattress was full of stains and scorch marks from cigarette ash. It was a wonder the boys hadn't all burned up in a fire before dying for other reasons. Emmett had brought a sleeping bag just in case he wanted to stay and keep an eye on things, but there was no way in hell he was staying in the bedroom. Even driving back to a town big enough for a hotel was losing its appeal. The idea that he was going to find what he was looking for here suddenly seemed ridiculous. He could make it all the way back to Newark before it got too late. Get some dinner at Top's and forget this whole thing. Try to put Uncle Jake's obsession behind him.

The bedroom was only slightly less cluttered than the front room, though the clutter had been kicked around by everyone going in and out. There was something odd about it, though, Emmett noticed just as he was about to head for fresh air.

The scraps and leftover parts and twists of rusty wire in the bedroom weren't piled, semi-organized here. They were formed into... things. Things like sculptures, or maybe devices, though what the devices could have been made to do, Emmett couldn't say. He picked one of them up, and turned it over in his hands. It was a thick rusty washer arranged against a large drill bit so that it would slide up the spiral of the bit, hauling a piece of wire that was in turn attached to a cog meshed with other cogs. He spun it for a moment, watching the cogs turn. It was clever, if pointless, and when he looked up, he noticed dozens of other pointless machines around the room crafted from scrap and junk. Some were versions of the same twirling object he held, others had their own mysterious purposes. He had a vision of the four brothers sitting up in the bed over long winter nights, manufacturing the little devices by the light of the single dingy lamp in the room. Or they might have made them in the other room, pulling the parts they needed from the piles, then brought them here to where they slept.

The sound of an engine outside made Emmett realize he'd been standing in the foul-smelling room for a long time, staring at the little creations. He picked his way back through the mess and onto the sagging front porch in the cool upstate New York autumn.

It took a moment for Emmett to see the black Mercedes in the driveway. Like Emmett, whoever had driven it in had needed to weave through tractors and other farm vehicles slowly rusting in place—some so old they seemed to be melting into the dead grass—as well as piles of rusty angle iron, jumbles of frayed cable, and sprawls of oil tanks and axles. The junk started in the front yard and continued out through the forty yards or so between the house and barn out back.

At least some of the junk had been there when he was a kid. Uncle Jake had always sent him out to mess around in the maze of stuff when they visited. Of course, Jake had always had his own motivation for sending Emmett out to explore. He'd go in and talk to the brothers, plead with them, cajole them with a bottle of Old Crow. And when he came away empty-handed and drove them home, knuckles white on the wheel of his truck, he'd quiz Emmett about what he'd seen, what he'd found. "You're my right hand, Emmett," he'd say, "I'm counting on you." But he had never found what Jake was looking for.

Emmett realized that the door of the Mercedes had opened in well-oiled silence and a thin, balding man was standing near it, looking up at him.

He was wearing a thick wool sweater with a fleece vest over it. "Hello," he said cheerfully.

"Can I do something for you?" Emmett asked.

"Mr. Parson?" the man asked. Emmett nodded. "My name is Laurel, Justus

Laurel. I represent parties interested in buying this farm."

Emmett eyed him for a few moments. "You're the one who made an offer last week."

Laurel inclined his head. "For the parties I represent, yes."

Emmett turned slowly, taking in the farm. "You offered three grand an acre for this." Laurel nodded again as he turned back. "Why?" Emmett asked.

"Real estate speculation," Laurel said blandly. "As you can see, it isn't much of a farm, but combined with some other purchases we've made in the area, we may be able to make some money selling residential lots."

"Well, maybe that's what I'm planning to do myself," Emmett said. "Clean the place up and build a few houses."

For the first time, Laurel's smile faded. "I wouldn't recommend that," he said. "Cleaning up this place could be very unpleasant. And I think we both know you don't have the assets to start building spec houses. Even if you did, it wouldn't be as lucrative as it would in Peekskill. Land speculation around here is best left to the locals."

Emmett came down off the porch. "I was a local, once," he said.

"Ah. Of course," Laurel replied, smiling again. "You were related to the Speakman brothers. Third cousin, was it?"

"Second cousin once removed."

"Of course," Laurel said, his expression communicating what he thought of the familial ties between second cousins once removed. Maybe he thought it was a relationship not worth inheritance.

"Funny you don't know that already, what with you knowing about my finances," Emmett said. "Or that I work out of Peekskill. I live in Newark, after all—that's where you sent the offer."

Laurel's smile faded again. "Due diligence, Mr. Parson. I research business deals I'm involved in. I assumed it would be uncomfortable for you to work as a private investigator in Newark. You'd constantly be running into former colleagues in the police department, after all."

Emmett walked closer, trying to back Laurel up, but the smaller man refused to be intimidated. "You really have been nosing around," Emmett said.

"I prefer to call it 'due diligence,' as I said."

Emmett eyed the smaller man for a moment. It wasn't good, the fact that someone could check into him without his noticing. "Maybe I should do my own due diligence," he said at last. "See what's up with you."

Laurel chuckled. "I'm sure you're better at it than I am. But not much to find, I'm afraid. I'm just a local fellow, with roots in the area. Hence my interest in the land."

"Land's not for sale."

Laurel shrugged. "Contact me if you change your mind."

Emmett stood in the driveway, watching him leave. He shivered in the cold breeze, realizing he'd just made up his mind. Someone—Laurel or someone he worked for—wanted the farm bad. Emmett didn't buy the story about real estate speculation for a minute. Which meant that Uncle Jake had been right.

There was something valuable somewhere on the Speakman farm.

He turned to look at the house he'd inherited. A hundred years with only the occasional half-assed repainting had left it, like the barn, a mottled gray-brown that blended into the autumn landscape like it was trying to hide among the piles of junk. It would take months to search the place alone. *Roots in the area,* Laurel had said. Well, he had some roots himself, and maybe they could help him out.

Emmett couldn't decide if he was proud of how fast he found Dan Ryan, or disappointed by how predictable his old friend was. After all, last time he'd actually seen him they'd both been sixteen, and done their drinking in parking lots or snowplow turnarounds on back roads. That had been when he'd lived not far away, and spent all his time with Uncle Jake. But Dan had stuck around, even without Jake to keep him busy, which was the first part of Emmett's prediction. And he was the kind of guy who spent Wednesday nights in a crummy bar like Murphy's on US 20—that was the second guess that had paid off, and Emmett hadn't even had to check more than one bar.

It wasn't hard to spot Dan, either—he was a little thicker around the middle, and his hair was a little longer, but that was about it. Emmett slid onto the stool next to him at the bar.

"How you doing, Dan?" he said.

Dan turned and stared for a long few seconds, his eyes just slightly glassy. "Emmett?" he said at last. "Emmett Parson? Holy shit, what are you doing back in town?" Emmett didn't reply—just watched as the gears turned in Dan's head. "Hang on, it's the Speakman farm, ain't it?"

Emmett nodded, and looked up as the bartender wandered over. "Bud."

"Your uncle Jake up here too?" Dan asked.

"He died three years ago," Emmett said. Just one more piece of unfairness. Jake had been a big bear of a man, someone without a gray hair even into his fifties, who looked like he could snap most men in half without trying. All four of the Speakman boys had looked eighty by the time they hit fifty, like they were used up before their time. But every one of them had outlived Jake, and apparently the only thing that could kill any of them was each other. Went to show the benefits of not giving a damn, Emmett supposed—it was a wonder Jake hadn't been hit with a heart attack like the one that finally killed him a lot earlier, during one of the times he was yelling at the brothers who just grinned vacantly at him until it was time to wander off and milk a cow or something.

"Hey, I'm sorry to hear that," Dan said. He took a drink of his beer. "It wasn't right, him having to leave town, anyway. No one ever proved anything, right?"

Emmett shook his head.

"But he did better for himself out east anyway, right?" Dan said, and leaned in conspiratorially. "Easier to move weed, right?"

"He switched to cigarettes, mostly," Emmett replied. At Dan's blank look, he added, "Running them up to Canada."

"Oh," Dan said, and nodded sagely. "That makes sense. Taxes, right?"

"Uh huh."

"You take over the business, did you?" Dan asked. "After he died?"

Emmett shook his head. Some asshole from Detroit had moved in to take over, as it happened, though he was happy to keep Emmett on the payroll. Maybe if they'd found the Speakmans' hidden money, Jake's operation wouldn't have been so tenuous when he died.

"I'm a PI now," Emmett said. Dan stared for a moment, then laughed. "What?" Emmett asked.

"Nothing," Dan said. "Nothing. Hell, you always were ready to do some regulating, I guess." He laughed again. "Remember when Jake had us teach that drunk driver out in Stockbridge a lesson? I thought we were going to just bust up his headlights, and then you set that fucking Chevy on fire." He shook his head. "I guess you always were one for law and order. In a way."

"Yeah," Emmett said. He was just as glad that Dan hadn't heard that he'd been a cop for a while. Anyway, all his "clients" since the internal affairs investigation were the same people Uncle Jake had worked with. He was just more under their thumb now than he had been as a cop.

"You planning on doing some investigating?" Dan asked. "Look into what happened?"

"Seems like the troopers already figured it out."

"Oh, I don't know," Dan replied. "Lotta folks seem to think there are still some questions."

The bartender returned with Emmett's beer, and he took a pull. "Not sure it makes much difference now, who killed who. Since they're all dead."

"Yeah, I guess," Dan replied. "But good to see you back." He stared down at the bar. "I miss those days, raising hell with you." He looked up. "You planning on selling that farm, or what?"

"Maybe, but I want to clean it up first, go through the stuff there."

Dan barked out a laugh. "That'll take a while."

"You've seen the place?"

Dan took a swig of his beer. "Me and everyone else around here. Swung by after they hauled Orson's body out."

Emmett grunted. "Well, that's why I was looking for you, actually. Wondered if you wanted to help me go through the junk."

Dan drained his bottle. "Maybe."

"I'll make it worth your while."

Dan flagged down the bartender. "I'll want some help. That's a hell of a job."

Emmett frowned. He didn't like the idea of people he didn't know poking around. But Dan was right—it was a huge job. "Only if you know someone reliable."

"Jesus, Emmett, you need someone to haul trash around for a couple days.

You ain't gonna get the cream of the crop."

Emmett sighed. "Fine. But no meth-heads."

"Sure," Dan replied. "I'll find you someone real trustworthy."

The rented dumpsters arrived first, the big engines and clanging metal outside jolting Emmett out of an uneasy sleep on the couch. He stumbled out to sign the rental agreements provided by the driver, who was staring around at the yard in awe. As the trucks left and Emmett headed back to the kitchen he noticed that it had at least warmed up since the day before, and felt almost like spring again. He'd had the foresight to bring his own coffeemaker and coffee so he didn't need to use the percolator encrusted with old coffee, but it took ten minutes to find an outlet in the kitchen that actually worked. There were more scraps of metal and junk covering all available counter space, and it looked like one of the Speakman brothers had been working on quite a project on the table with its sticky vinyl tablecloth—something that rolled around on wheels salvaged from a shopping cart.

He found himself staring at it as the coffee brewed. His sleep had been constantly interrupted, and every time he'd woken up he'd realized he'd been dreaming of machinery. Tedious, unsettling dreams that had him trying to fit together disparate pieces of junk that didn't want to fit together, somehow turn them into working machines. Obviously, he'd been looking at what the Speakmans had been working on too much.

He jumped at the sound of an engine outside, and took a sip of the coffee that had appeared in his hand at some point. It was cold, though he didn't remember even pouring it, and he frowned as he made his way back through the front room and onto the porch.

Dan was climbing out of an old Chevy pickup, wearing camo fatigue pants and a greasy ball cap. Another man, both tall and fat, was easing his way out of the passenger seat, making the truck rock on its springs. He spat a stream of tobacco juice onto the ground before he'd even touched down. Emmett wasn't too happy about that, but it seemed silly to object, with months-old spit cups scattered like landmines around the farm.

Dan strode across the dead, matted grass, his shoulders held too high in a way Emmett remembered from the old days, like he was heading for a fight. He was smiling, though, as he gestured to the big man trailing behind him. "Emmett, you remember Homer Fields?"

"Name's familiar," Emmett said, and it was, sort of.

"Well, he was a few years behind us in school," Dan said. "Knows how to work, though."

Homer nodded to Emmett before turning his head to spit again. Dan gestured to a woman still sitting in the bed of the truck, glaring at all the junk like it had insulted her. She hadn't wanted to be squeezed in up front between Dan and Homer, Emmett figured, and he couldn't blame her. Homer had probably taken up most of the cab, and Dan wasn't above copping a feel if the opportunity presented itself. "That's JT Quinn," Dan said. "My fuckin' truck started acting up last night and I had to take it to her. She fixes cars, see, but she works construction for old Mickey Randall, too, sometimes. You remember him?"

Emmett shook his head.

"Well, anyway," Dan said as JT vaulted out of the truck and approached. "She said she was looking for work, so I told her to come along. Since she knows construction and shit."

She was lean, with short blonde hair, and a full sleeve of tattoos running up her left arm—various tats that looked to have been laid on over years with no theme. As she approached, Emmett saw she also had a stud in her nose, and an eyebrow ring. Dan had found quite a crew, he thought, as Homer turned and spat another stream of brown liquid. At least they both seemed a bit too calm to be tweakers.

"So you just want us to get all this—" Dan gestured around the yard, then jerked his head at the dumpsters "—into those?"

"Basically," Emmett replied.

Dan looked around again, hiking up his trousers. "You want us to keep out anything that looks valuable, if we run across it?"

"I'll be working with you," Emmett said.

Dan nodded, a funny smirk on his face.

"How about the barn?" Homer asked.

"Lotta stuff in there," Emmett said. "We can get to it after we clean up the yard." He'd taken a look the night before, hoping against hope that he'd find the valuables there, but there was too much junk inside to even move around easily, all dominated by an old Buick with its hood open and most of the engine gone in pieces. And anyway, it would have been a terrible place to hide anything, back when the farm had been active and it had been full of cows.

"What about the house?" Homer asked. "You gonna need us to clean up the blood in the house? I think you oughta pay us extra for that."

"Ain't no blood," Dan said, a disgusted look on his face. "Amos and Uriah suffocated Orson and Pace."

"I heard Pace attacked Uriah with a sickle," Homer said. "Cut him up something awful, that's why Amos beat him up. That's why he died right after, too. Blood loss."

Dan snorted. "How do you explain Orson? He was the only one dead when that salesman came knocking. And Pace wasn't beat up—he was just in a coma there, next to Orson in the bed. Neither of them were that bad off, is what I heard. Just one of them dead and the other on the way."

"Not what I heard," Homer said. "I heard Uriah was bleeding something awful."

"Him and Orson was sitting in there watching *Law & Order*," Dan said, gesturing toward the house. His voice was rising, his shoulders coming up as he spoke. "How the fuck is anyone gonna do that if they's all cut up?"

"I heard *Futurama*," Homer growled. He wasn't backing away from Dan like most people would have, and Emmett had the feeling he was watching a ritual the two men had performed many times—he only wished he knew whether they usually came to blows, or just liked squabbling.

"I heard *Nova*," JT said from where she leaned against one of the rusted tractors. "Who the fuck cares?"

Emmett had heard *Wheel of Fortune*, himself, but he was inclined to agree with her. Dan rounded on JT, still looking pissed off like he might just go after her instead of Homer. JT met his eye with the bored expression of a mountain lion who isn't all that hungry at the moment, and after a few seconds, Dan turned back to Homer, relaxing slightly. "Yeah, who the fuck cares," he said. "Point is, Amos and Uriah was just out there watching TV while their brothers were in the next room. Fucking creepy, but they wasn't bleeding all over the place."

Homer looked over at Emmett. "That so?"

"Uriah's chair is missing," Emmett said. "Could be they took it because it had blood on it, I don't know."

"There you go," Homer said, triumphantly.

Dan stepped closer to him. "That don't prove—"

"Jesus *Christ*," JT said, as she stooped to pick up a massive old spring from where it lay near the tractor. She flung it at one of the dumpsters, a nice toss from where she stood, and it clanged out of sight.

"Yeah," Emmett said loudly, as Dan turned toward her, "let's just get moving on this. Weather's too nice to waste time arguing about those guys."

Dan turned with a scowl. "Whatever you say, boss."

The cleanup went uneventfully for a few hours, all of them sweating in the unseasonable heat, until Emmett noticed Dan standing still, staring at one of the piles of junk. As he walked over, Emmett realized that it wasn't just scrap—it was... organized. Something built from junk, like all the little things in the bedroom, but bigger. The main piece was an old axle from something small, a riding mower maybe—in the bedroom, the smaller versions had been made with long bolts or small pieces of rebar. One end of the axle had been burned off with a torch and replaced with a collection of cogs, and where inside the bedroom the pieces had wire, this used some rusty lengths of chain. Emmett couldn't quite figure out how it would do anything, but somehow he could see it turning, spinning a flail of rusty links that would do... something.

"What the hell is this?" Dan said quietly.

"Is that bone?" Homer asked, coming up behind them. "Where'd it come from?"

It *was* a piece of bone, Emmett was pretty sure of that, held to one of the cogs with a few screws. If the device *did* manage to spin somehow, the chains would slap against the bone with every rotation.

Emmett glanced off toward the collapsing barn, recalling a time when Amos strode past him as he sorted through a pile of galvanized pipe. "Got some business in the barn, young Emmett," he'd said on the way past. "Come along if you want to watch." Then he was off, his long beard streaming behind him, he was walking so fast. One of the pigs had started screaming a few moments later, inside the barn—a noise Emmett hadn't even known a pig could make. Uncle Jake had appeared and hustled him into the truck about then, but Emmett had seen Amos in the rear view mirror as they rolled out, standing in the barnyard, grinning and waving a blood-covered hand.

"It's a farm," Emmett said. "They had lots of livestock around here."

"What happened to all the cows and stuff, anyway?" Dan asked.

"They were getting kind of low on cows even back when I was visiting," Emmett said. "Years back." It was one of the things that had convinced Uncle Jake that the Speakman boys had to have money socked away somewhere —he'd mutter about how they didn't have enough of a herd left to make a living, especially when he'd been busy doing his own accounts, totting up how much he'd made on weed and fencing things here and there.

"Huh," Dan said, still staring at the device. "What would this thing do, anyway?" He turned. "What's this for, JT?" he said over his shoulder.

"The fuck should I know?" JT asked. She was leaning against one of the dumpsters, showing no desire to get closer to the device.

"You're some kinda mechanic, aren't you?"

"I ain't the kind who works on machines made out of piles of junk," JT snapped.

Dan laughed, and turned back to the thing. "I've seen your truck," he said, "but if you say so." He hesitated for a moment, then turned to Homer. "You want to give me a hand with this?"

"You oughta maybe leave that for right now," JT said. "We can get the loose stuff first." Emmett looked up at her, along with the other two. "Might turn out to have some value," she said.

Emmett looked back at the pile of rusty parts and bone bolted together, and back at JT. He found himself nodding, even though it didn't make much sense. He expected Dan to object just out of contrariness, but he'd already backed away from the thing.

"Whatever," Dan said, and grabbed a beat-up rim from a stack of them nearby. For another few hours, they worked in a tense silence, filling up one of the dumpsters, then broke for lunch. They ate in the bed of the truck— Emmett didn't have much of an appetite to begin with, and the smell inside the house would have killed it. There was a picnic table out back, but it was covered with pipes and a snarl of cable, so the bed of the truck worked okay. Emmett just wished it wasn't so close to the weird device Dan had found, because he kept finding himself glancing over at it.

"That all you got to eat?" Homer asked once as he looked over, making him jump.

"Huh?" he said, looking down at his handful of trail mix. "Oh. Yeah. Need to get to the store."

"Probably ain't eager to use the kitchen in there, huh?" Dan asked. "Them

Speakman boys weren't much for hygiene, I hear." He took a huge bite of his sandwich. "I got a cousin that works at the Big M in town," he said through the mouthful. "The Speakman boys would roll in once a month or so on their tractor to stock up, and they'd have to spray Lysol all over the place soon as they left, just to knock the smell down."

"Hey," Homer said sternly, and jerked his head at Emmett. "He's related to 'em."

"Yeah, no offense, whatever," Dan said.

"None taken," Emmett replied.

"You know them well, did you?" JT asked.

"Not really," he said. "I just came out here now and then with my uncle. Like, once every few months." Was that right? The visits had kind of run together, in his head. "Pace was always nice to me, whenever I showed up. He liked to recite these little songs he made up.

The gears turn behind you
The gears turn underneath
The gears have clever axles
And also they have teeth

"Pace had been big on mechanical stuff, even back then."

"Yeah, I heard they were nice enough," Homer said. "People were surprised by the whole murder thing." He took a long swig from a bottle of orange soda. "Lotta folks say Amos got railroaded, like the cops pushed him into confessing something he didn't do."

"Ah fuck, an hour ago you were saying he strangled one of his brothers who'd hacked Uriah half to pieces," Dan said.

"I was just saying what I heard," Homer said. "And anyway, I was right about Uriah being all cut up—the chair was missing."

Dan shook his head. "Whatever."

They went back to work after eating, Dan and Homer bickering as they dragged trash around. Several times, one or another of them ran across another of the weird constructions. Two of them looked a lot like the first one they'd found, while another seemed to incorporate a piston that would have worked a set of cogs if it could have moved, or if much of the arm connecting the piston and cogs hadn't been made from a long piece of bone. Each time, they all four gave the things a wide berth, continuing to haul armloads of loose junk metal back to the dumpsters.

By the time the sun was sinking on the horizon, they'd filled both dumpsters, and Emmett called the rental company and arranged for an early pickup the next day before counting out the money he owed everyone for the day's work.

"See you all tomorrow?" he asked.

"Sure thing," Dan said. "I'll be here, anyway. Am I picking you two up again?" Homer and JT both nodded, and Emmett felt a vague sense of relief. He'd been worried everyone might bail on him. But they were nowhere near done, and he hadn't yet found whatever the Speakman boys had been hiding.

* * *

Emmett spent the next few hours searching the house, but he didn't find any secret compartments full of money or piles of jewels or gold bars. The junk piled everywhere didn't make it easy. The first time a mouse darted out from under a pile of trash he nearly had a heart attack, but by the fourth one he barely reacted. Finally, he gave up. As it got dark it was too hard to see much anyway. Of the lamps in the house, the ones that worked were scarce and the bulbs were layered in grime. He could easily be working his way right past some evidence of a hiding place. He'd just have to keep on with the original plan, get things cleaned up outside.

It was nearly full dark when he drove into town and found a diner. He sank wearily onto a stool at the counter, feeling the day's work now that he had a moment to think. He ordered a burger and sat, staring off into space and thinking about machinery. The burger landed in front of him what seemed like seconds later, jolting him back into the diner.

"Thanks," he muttered, realizing he had no appetite. He picked up the burger anyway and began to chew, as the bell over the door jingled and the waitress greeted a new arrival. Emmett saw a Stetson hit the counter next to him, and turned his head just enough to take in the sheriff's deputy uniform on the man settling on to the next stool. He took another bite of the burger, even though it tasted like plaster to him now. Law enforcement uniforms made him twitchy, these days, ike any Podunk sheriff's deputy could see "dirty cop" written across his back.

"Anything new, Terry?" the waitress asked, setting a coffee cup in front of the deputy.

"Seems like all the lawbreakers are quiet tonight, Marge," Terry replied as she filled the cup. "Nothing much going on all day 'cept for some work out at the Speakman place."

Emmett carefully picked up a fry and popped it into his mouth, resisting the urge to hunker lower on his stool.

"That right?" Marge asked. "They finally wrapping that up?"

"I guess," Terry replied. "Troopers handled all the property stuff. I only noticed 'cause JT Quinn's out there. I like to keep an eye on her, 'cause, well, you know."

"Oh, yeah," Marge replied. Emmett realized he was staring off into space as he listened, and took a drink of his water. He would have dearly liked someone to explain why it was so obvious that a sheriff's deputy was keeping an eye on JT, but of course everyone except him in the goddamn diner already knew why, so there was no need to discuss it.

"Who even owns that place now?" Marge asked. She was leaning on the counter as Terry eyed the menu.

"Someone related to Jake Parson," Terry said without looking up.

Marge made a disgusted noise. "Parson. You oughta run them out of town, whoever it is."

"Can't do that, Marge," Terry said mildly. "We're not talking about Jake himself, after all."

Marge snorted again. "You know as well as anyone that every member of that family either terrorized folks for Jake, or were useless layabouts."

Emmett gritted his teeth, though he wasn't sure why he was so mad. Most of his family *had* been useless, after all, content to live off Uncle Jake's largess, and Emmett had said so to their faces often enough. That's why they'd all packed up and followed Jake when he'd had to leave. That or they were afraid what might happen to them without Jake and Emmett to protect them, after years of strutting around like they owned the county. The fact that Jake had chosen Emmett for a more active role had always set him apart, made the rest of the family jealous.

Terry laughed. "It ain't like the Speakmans were angels, themselves. I'll have the meatloaf." He tucked his menu back into its wire holder.

"So the State Troopers say, Terry," Marge said. "The Speakmans were pushed into confessing. Amos wasn't the sharpest guy out there—you put him a room with a detective like they did, he'll sign whatever you put in front of him. The man could barely read, and if you said something he didn't understand, he'd just agree with you. And Uriah, well, it just isn't right what they did, hauling him in to the barracks when they should have rushed him to a hospital. You can tell me he signed any confession you want, but I'll bet you any money it was written up after he'd already keeled over."

"Far be it from me to defend the troopers from a charge of fabricating evidence, Marge, but how did Uriah get so injured, if it was all a misunderstanding?" Terry asked, sounding amused.

"He said some machine caught him," Marge said. "Didn't you hear that? Happens often enough, on the farm. Pace lost most of his arm in a thresher years back. And you know those boys weren't much for doctors."

"Uriah might have died from blood loss, but what about Amos?" Terry asked. "He was fit as a fiddle, and he just killed himself in jail. Explain that, if it wasn't remorse."

"None of those boys were 'fit,'" Marge said. "They'd all been pretty much used up. And all his brothers were dead or in comas or whatever—it's no wonder the poor man killed himself. He told them—the last thing he said was how if he couldn't keep an eye on the farm he'd be best off dead. His brothers and that farm were all he had. They should have been keeping a better eye on him." She turned to slide Terry's ticket into the rail for the cook, then shook her head. "I don't know why they all loved that farm so much, but they did."

"Well, that farm's the problem of some no-account relation to Jake Parson now," Terry said. Emmett carefully chewed a fry and thought about how the deputy would react if he broke a glass on the counter and stabbed him in the neck with it. He ate another fry. Knowing the kind of glassware diners used he'd probably be stuck banging the glass on the counter until they hauled him off for making a nuisance of himself. *Be smart about how you go about getting justice*, that's what Jake had always said.

Marge leaned back onto the counter and lowered her voice to a conspiratorial tone. "You going to keep an eye on the place, are you?"

Terry heaved a sigh. "Doubt it's worth my time. Nothing worth a plug nickel out there, nothing to get the criminal element stirred up. Even if your pal Amos did dang near kill someone once over a piece of it, a few years back." He took a sip of his coffee. "Had his brothers helping, too. That's your innocent Speakman boys."

"Yeah, yeah," Marge said, moving off down the counter to fill someone's coffee cup.

Emmett managed a few more bites of his burger, thinking. He could feel the deputy staring at him, sizing up the guy he hadn't seen around before, as Marge slid a plate of meatloaf on to the counter. He stood and dug some money out of his jeans. Tempting as it was to pay with a credit card just to see the look on Marge's face, now was a good time to keep his head down. He walked out to his car and sat for a few more minutes, still thinking, then pulled out his cell phone.

He still had one or two friends in the department. None of them would really stick their neck out for him, but doing a little research for him was a small enough favor.

Emmett pulled up near the dark, looming forms of the dumpsters and pushed open his car door. It had been getting steadily cooler as the night wore on, temperatures dropping to something more seasonal, and he hurried toward the house, smelly as it was. Not that it was really much warmer inside. The only way to heat the place was an old woodstove in the main room, and he didn't have any firewood for it. He took a jacket from his bag on the couch and put it on before finding himself staring at the one clear spot on the floor where a chair had once been, thinking about the last time the Speakmans had been in the room.

The prospect of searching through the house again wasn't a fun one. He could look around in likely spots outside, he supposed. The barn again, maybe. But it was cold outside, and dark—he'd need to use a flashlight. He took a deep breath, which was a mistake. But an ammonia tang under the smell of manure and rotten food and old cigarette smoke made him pause. Back in the day, there had been dozens of cats prowling around at all time—they'd been half-feral, but Pace had treated them all like pets, as best he could.

Where had they gone? He supposed the county could have taken them, but could they have gotten them all? The smell of cat piss remained, but Emmett hadn't seen a single feline. He should have noticed the absence earlier, when it had become clear how many damn mice were running around the place.

He shook his head. Maybe if he looked at the devices scattered around he'd find some cat bones, but it wasn't important. It was just something else that made the house unpleasant, was all—both the absence of cats keeping mice down, and the ghostly reminder of the time they'd been around hanging in the air. Sleep, that's what he needed. He could turn in early and get up early, and do a little looking around in daylight before Dan and everyone showed up. But as achy as he was, he was in no mood to try to sleep in his bag on the couch again, to lie there listening to mice running around and en-visioning machinery.

He walked slowly through the house, glancing at the little devices scattered everywhere. Now that he knew what to look for, he could see a sort of theme tying them together even when they weren't obviously the same, as well as similarities to the larger versions outside.

He glanced out the flyspecked window toward the thing Dan had found near the barn, even though it was hard to see much by the light of a cres-cent moon. A flicker of motion caught his eye. One of the shadows out there moved.

The shadow disappeared, then reappeared again some ten yards away, and Emmett leaned closer, squinting out the window. He couldn't make out any detail, couldn't even tell if it was a person or an animal. He lost track of it again, and after staring hard for a few more seconds, he stepped away and started for the next window, immediately tripping over a toolbox on the floor. The next window with a view of the path the shadow had taken was as small and dirty as the first one he'd been looking through, one of only two stingy windows in the main room. He caught another glimpse of movement, but had no more luck figuring out who or what it was.

He stepped back, glaring around the room. There wasn't a single working exterior light on the house or the barn. He had no idea how the Speakman boys had managed the goddamn cows in the winter, when at least one milk-ing would have been done before sunup.

Since there was no lock on the front door, he settled for shoving a milk crate full of huge bolts in front of it. Maybe there was a coyote out there, may-be that was why all the cats had gone. And if there was, maybe it might have gotten used to hanging out in the house on cold nights—couldn't have con-vinced him otherwise from the smell, anyway.

Or maybe someone else knew the Speakman boys might have something hidden. Emmett didn't think they'd have much luck looking without a light, but it was an unsettling thought. He made his way to the couch and rooted to the bottom of his backpack for the pistol he had there—a Glock 19 he'd gotten to replace his service weapon when he was pushed out of the depart-ment. Emmett had never had to fire it except at the range, but if some hillbilly thought he was going to snag the Speakman brothers' money out from under him they'd have a surprise coming. He tucked the pistol into his waistband and returned to the windows.

Several times, he thought he saw something—moving, always moving. The piles of junk all over the farm created a tangle of deeper shadows, and what-ever or whoever it was kept sliding from view into them. The moon set after a few hours, making it even harder to see, but Emmett had a sense it was still out there. He considered going out for a look, or just shouting—a shout would probably scare off a coyote, he thought. But if it was someone from town, searching for the Speakman boys' treasure, he didn't want them to know that they'd been spotted. He kept watching, moving from window to window, for a long while.

Emmett started awake to a metallic clanging from outside. He sat up, blinking, and for a moment he felt disconnected in time. The sun was fighting its way through the two grubby windows. Again, he could hear the clanging from the dumpsters outside, and again, his thoughts were fighting past visions of machines, gears and cogs.

But he was sitting in one of the lumpy old easy chairs in front of the TV, still wearing his jacket, not lying in his sleeping bag on the couch. He'd sat down at some point, and fallen asleep. He pushed himself up and the Glock fell onto the floor with a clunk. He winced, and picked it up before stretching his aching back. After a moment's consideration, he tucked the pistol into the jacket pocket and shambled out the door.

The new, empty dumpsters had been dropped off, and the rental company was loading the old ones onto trucks. He signed the paperwork, and he was standing in the drive, trying to get his sludgy thoughts in order, when Dan's pickup pulled up. Despite the cold, JT was in the bed of the truck again, although today she wore a sweatshirt that concealed her sleeve of tattoos. Apparently Homer wasn't enough of a gentleman to offer to ride back there, though he'd probably offered to allow her to squeeze in next to him in the cab. He and Dan were bickering as they climbed out, so Emmett could see why JT had opted to slump sullenly in the open air. She clambered out as Dan and Homer approached.

"They weren't no Satan worshipers," Dan was saying, "no matter what Ezra got up to."

"All I'm saying, is everyone knew Ezra did some crazy shit, back in the fifties," Homer said. He looked up at Emmett. "Ain't that right?"

"What?" Emmett asked. "Who's Ezra?"

Both Homer and Dan stared at him with incredulous expressions for a moment. "The Speakman boys' father," Dan said at last. "You didn't know him?"

"He died in '63 or '64," Homer said, "but you never heard of him?"

Emmett shook his head. "By the time I was coming around here, it was just the brothers."

"Huh," Dan said. "Well, he was a smuggler. Gunrunner, I heard."

"He was more than a smuggler," Homer said. "He was a Satanist, or some damn thing. Word was, you'd see lights out here at all hours."

"Yeah," Dan said, "because he was smuggling shit."

"Lights," Homer replied. "Not people coming and going."

"Because the people who'd be coming and going didn't stop in town, you dumb—" Dan stopped at a loud clang. They all turned to see JT looking at them as she picked up another hunk of metal. She turned and threw it into the dumpster, then turned back to regard the three of them again.

"You think you're pretty fucking smart, don't you?" Dan asked.

"'Cause I'm tossing shit into a dumpster?" JT asked. "Yeah, I'm really exercising my brain power over here."

Dan took a few steps closer. "We're just trying to talk."

JT picked up a few pieces of rebar. "So talk." She turned her back on Dan and threw the rebar into the dumpster with a loud clang.

Dan took a step toward JT, his fists clenched.

"Dan," Emmett said sharply. Dan turned slowly. "Maybe we all oughta get to work."

Dan showed his teeth. "Sure thing, boss." He bent and grabbed an armload of rebar himself and dragged it toward the dumpster. Emmett began picking up scrap as well, keeping a wary eye on Dan as he worked. The atmosphere was even more tense than it had been the day before, but Dan managed to avoid coming to blows with JT, or even arguing with Homer as usual. JT seemed a lot more interested in working than talking. Maybe she just had a better work ethic, but maybe it was something else. Could that have been her last night, prowling around the farm? It seemed like she might have an idea about the Speakman boys' money, anyway, if she knew about the smuggling rumor. Uncle Jake had never mentioned Ezra, but now it seemed likely he'd known about him. Funny that Emmett had never thought to ask why the Speakmans were supposed to have money socked away, but then he'd been a kid back then. He'd accepted things more easily. Things Jake told him, anyway.

Between thinking about that and trying to keep an eye on JT, Emmett had grabbed one of the weird devices of cobbled-together junk before realizing what it was. It was an uneven pyramid made of different kinds of pipe this time, with two cogs suspended in the middle. They were meshed, looking ready to turn against each other if only there had been something to power the whole thing. The cogs used pieces of bone for axles, suspended from the pyramid frame with lengths of rusty chain. He noticed something about the bone as he carefully released the device.

"Shit," JT said with feeling behind him. He exchanged a glance with her and realized that she'd seen the same thing he had. The two bones weren't from a cow, or pig, or even a cat. Emmett was pretty sure one was a radius and the other an ulna—two pieces of someone's forearm.

"What is it?" Homer asked, spitting out a stream of tobacco.

"Nothing," Emmett muttered. "Just creepy." He thought back to the time he'd visited with Uncle Jake and they'd found Pace Speakman with the left sleeve of his filthy flannel shirt pinned up.

"Jesus," Jake had said. "What happened to you?"

Pace mumbled something that might have been "nothing much"—you could generally only make out about every fourth word Pace said.

"Thresher," Amos had said loudly. "Goddamn thresher got him."

Jake had looked back and forth between the two brothers for a moment. "Well, Christ, you need to be more careful."

Both Amos and Pace had nodded in that agreeable way of theirs, and that had been that.

Emmett shook his head. "C'mon. Let's get that loose stuff—"

His phone rang, making him jump. He gestured vaguely toward the dumpsters as he took a few steps away. The caller ID said it was Tony, his friend from the old department.

"Got some information for you," Tony said when he answered.

"Yeah?" Emmett asked, turning away at a metallic clang from the dumpster.

"Took a while to find anything about the Quinn woman—it was a long time ago. But you said 'JT', and there's a record for a 'Jane Temperance Quinn' who lived where you are, and served a stretch in New Albion."

"What for?"

"Aggravated assault. Beat some guy half to death with a length of pipe when she was eighteen."

Emmett looked up to see JT tipping a tractor rim into a wheelbarrow. "That so?"

"Yep. Now, the Speakman brothers, lots about them now, of course, but I went back a few years before the murders. Found a report with the sheriff. Seems they got called out for a disturbance. Someone from the historical society that had come by to check out their silo."

"Their what?"

"Their silo. They were putting together some kinda calendar of old grain silos in the county—don't ask me why anyone would buy something like that. Sounds like the Speakman boys objected."

Emmett turned again to look at the old silo next to the barn. It was one of the concrete stave models that you saw all over the place—curved plates of concrete bound by rings of steel so it wouldn't bulge out from the weight of silage, all capped by a rusty metal dome. It was picturesque, in a way, Emmett supposed—the vines climbing up the side were all dead now but maybe in the summer they would have added some color.

A memory struck him. Uriah saying, "Don't go near the silos, boy. Silos is terrible dangerous things." He hadn't thought much of it at the time, because of course, grain silos *were* dangerous. You heard stories all the time about someone being sucked into the grain and crushed, or passing out from the lack of oxygen in them, or a fire exploding from the grain dust if there *was* oxygen. But the grain silo had never been part of his searching, had it? He'd been focused on all the weird junk, not a silo that was like fifty others within a few miles.

"Emmett?"

Emmett blinked, and focused on the phone again. "Yeah?"

"That help you?"

"Yeah. Yeah, I think it does. Thanks." He thumbed off the phone and followed the others as they headed back toward the dumpsters. "Let's toss this in and knock off for the day," he said.

Dan looked up at the sun. "Already? It's early yet."

Emmett nodded. "Have some errands to run. Anyway, it's Friday. You guys probably have something you'd rather be doing."

"Well, hell, you don't need to be here," Dan said. "We can manage without you."

Emmett shook his head. "No. No, we'll just get this stuff, then pick it up Monday."

Dan shrugged. "Okay, boss."

Emmett stood on the front porch watching everyone drive off. He could see JT staring at him from where she sat in the bed of the truck until it finally dipped out of sight. The cold of the day was starting to sink in, but he didn't bother going back inside, instead heading for the silo.

It looked like half the silos in the county—the ones that weren't blue-painted Harvestores, anyway. Maybe a little shorter than most, but nothing strange about it. Emmett had only a vague idea of how silos worked, but he knew they had a series of doors running up the side to allow access to just above the level of silage, no matter how high it was piled inside. The doors were on the far side of the silo from the barn, all but the lowest protected by a semi-cylindrical cowling that ran up the silo.

Before he tried the door, Emmett made a circuit around the silo, looking for anything odd. He couldn't see anything, and it seemed like a high-traffic area to hide something. Would it make sense to hide something *inside* the silo? Maybe, as long as you didn't need it in the winter, when it would be buried under tons of silage.

He returned to the door, a wooden portal a few feet square held shut by two metal levers. He could see the whole series of doors running up the side of the silo when he poked his head under the cowling. The rings of metal bands holding the structure together doubled as ladder rungs, apparently, but not ones Emmett wanted to climb. He grabbed the lever on the lowest door and pulled. At first, it didn't want to give, but after a minute of tugging, rocking his weight back and forth, Emmett got the hinge to move with a rusty squeal.

The hatch swung into the silo easily, and Emmett could see a mostly bare concrete floor, dusted here and there with silage. He wondered how long it had been since the Speakmans had actually added fresh grain to the silo. The only light was what washed in through the door and through a few holes in the metal dome high above. He jogged back to the house for a flashlight, feeling a growing excitement.

The silo was eerie, once he'd clambered inside. There was a smell of mold underlying the vegetative scent of old grain, and any shuffling sounds he made echoed up and down the space. He scanned the floor first, seeing nothing but bare concrete. The concrete continued up the walls, staves fitted together almost seamlessly, nothing but the odd piece of silage caught here and there to see. The only thing that really broke the smooth surface was the series of hatches running up one side.

Emmett ran the beam of the flashlight slowly along the hatches, seeing nothing unusual. After ten minutes, he dropped the beam and stood, thinking. There was nothing here. No hiding spot on the floor, no bundles lashed to the inside walls near one of the higher hatches. Unless the Speakman boys had sealed something under the concrete floor, there was nothing hidden in the silo.

He crawled out of the door and replaced the door, lost in thought. It had been a longshot, he supposed. Just because the Speakmans had gotten into some trouble because of the silo didn't mean anything. They'd been crazy, after all. He wouldn't have been surprised to find that they'd gotten into all kinds of trouble with the law, except that he'd have heard about it through Uncle Jake. Uncle Jake had always kept close tabs on what was happening with the sheriff. It was how he knew who in the county needed some correcting that the authorities weren't up to delivering—drunk drivers, wife beaters, troublemakers. And it was how he'd known Anna Whittington was going to be a problem.

Emmett shook his head as he walked away from the silo. He didn't like thinking about Anna Wittington. The point was, if the Speakman boys had been causing all sorts of trouble back in the day, Uncle Jake would have known, and he'd have put a stop to it. He couldn't even remember Uncle Jake bringing the incident up, or talking about silos, except for the time he'd...

Emmett stumbled to a stop, halfway to the house, then turned slowly and looked down across the cow pasture sloping away from the road. Except for the time he'd been picking on Pace about all the grain storage the brothers had for a couple skinny cows, and Pace had gotten so upset he'd had one of his fits. They'd ended up leaving early, Uncle Jake even more pissed than usual—he didn't like displays of weakness.

But that wasn't the important thing. *Don't go near the silos, boy. Silos is terrible dangerous things.* That's what Uriah had said. Silos, plural. And he hadn't been talking about silos in general—he'd been talking about the two silos they had on the farm, the two silos Uncle Jake had thought would together hold more grain than they'd need.

Emmett stared across the pasture, scanning it slowly. Now that he was looking carefully, he could see some tall irregular hummocks here and there amongst the stones and shrubs dotting the dead grass. He had an idea they were more of the devices they'd been finding as they cleaned up, covered in dead grass. Which was odd, but not what he was looking for. He could see it in his mind's eye, though. Not a silo like the one near the barn, but a stone structure even older—squat, surrounded by vegetation, and looking like it had been there for a million years. Too far away from the barn to be really practical for grain storage, but the kind of silo that someone putting together a calendar of rustic photos would fall all over themselves to get a picture of.

There. A clump of taller shrubs near the stream that ran across the pasture. He couldn't see the old silo, but he was sure that's where it had been, years ago. He strode back past the newer silo and the barn, toward the pasture. There was a spot where the three strands of rusty barbed wire fence had been forced down, yanking posts on either side out of plumb and making a handy gap to walk through. It wasn't like the rest of the fence he could see was standing straight and neat, of course—there were plenty of other places where the posts leaned drunkenly.

Emmett tried to think back to when the fence line had actually needed to contain cows, but he couldn't recall exactly on which visit he'd gone from seeing a few of them to none. There was a sort of trail cutting across the gap, a worn path in the dead grass, and he glanced back to see that it led toward one of the devices near the barn. In the other direction, the path ran almost parallel to the fence, curving slowly into the pasture toward one of the little hummocks he'd seen earlier, off to his left.

He ignored the trail, heading straight for the stream and clump of shrubs off in the distance. He lost sight of the shrubs once or twice as he dropped into dips in the landscape, but now that he had an idea where he was going and it wasn't hard to stay on track.

The whole structure had collapsed—that was why he hadn't noticed it. As he got near, he could see that what was left of the walls stood no more than four feet tall, and was hidden by shrubs. It hadn't fallen long ago, judging from the lack of grass growing over the rubble. What mortar there was between the rocks was dry and crumbling, and it was a wonder it stayed up as long as it had. Not that it had been very tall to begin with, though now that he was close he could see that it had been a good twenty feet in diameter. He glanced back toward the barn. It really was too far from everything to be much use for storing grain. He was out in the middle of the pasture, and he could look down the slope a quarter of a mile to where the Speakmans' hay field started. He could see a few more of the devices the Speakmans had built down there, he thought, on either side of the divide between field and pasture.

He started around the outside of the structure, then paused. He could swear he felt a faint vibration, in his gut more than his feet. He cocked his head, and thought he heard a faint grinding or scraping, almost beyond his range of hearing. He shook his head and continued forward. There was a gap in what remained of the crumbling wall, perhaps where a door had been. A doorway that tall didn't belong in a stone silo, but Emmett no longer thought he was dealing with a silo.

Most of the silo had fallen to the outside, leaving the flagstone-paved area inside mainly clear. One of the stones in the center of the floor was different, though.

It was a lighter color than the rest of the flagtones or any of the stones that had been part of the structure's walls, for one thing, and it was polished and smooth, as if it had avoided hundreds of years of weathering. It was big, three or four feet across, and cracked deeply down the middle, revealing blackness underneath it. There was faint, weathered writing carved in it.

He crouched and ran a hand over the rock. The writing wasn't English, or anything he recognized, and for a moment his attention was drawn to a more understandable carving on one side—an image of a candle. It was the only pictogram there, and he returned his attention to the writing.

While he couldn't read it, after a while he felt like an understanding of the text was working its way into his head, despite the crack in the rock that had separated the writing into two pieces, and destroyed a few characters.

The sound of an engine jerked his attention away from the writing and he looked up, experiencing a moment of disorientation. The light had changed, and dusk was well under way. How had that happened? He blinked, looking toward the sound that had caught his attention.

He couldn't see much of the road from where he was behind the wall and the shrubbery, but it sounded like a car or truck that could use some tuning. No one ever went by the farm by accident, since the road dead-ended a few hundred yards on, but maybe it was someone who'd gotten lost, or someone indulging idle curiosity. Or maybe it was a sheriff's deputy. He frowned. Or JT, come back to nose around. After another moment, the sound of the engine dwindled, and Emmett knelt for a closer look at the rock and what was underneath it.

It was hard to make anything out in the deep shadow beneath the narrow crack, but gradually he realized he was looking at the teeth of a cog. Most of the cog was out of view, and it just didn't make sense for a cog to be there, underground, so it took a while to comprehend what he was seeing. But gradually, he became certain of what it was. A cog, and below it what he thought was a piston. The piston disappeared into the gloom of the well, or cavern, or whatever it was. He couldn't make out how the two were related, but they looked like they'd meet up just under where the rock, with its inscription, blocked his view. He could barely see any of it, really, especially in the fading light, but he had the sense of a machine that extended far below where he crouched, and to either side under the silo, then out into the pasture. He wasn't sure how he knew it, but he was suddenly sure that the engine was immense. As he watched, the cog turned. Or he thought it did—the light was too witchy to be sure, really. Probably it hadn't. He was just imagining it.

He grabbed the edge of the crack and tugged, but it didn't move at all—it was sunk into the floor around the outside edge, meeting the flagstones smoothly. More, he had a sudden feeling that he shouldn't try to move the rock if he could, that... something didn't want him to. He sat heavily next to the carved rock, and rubbed a hand over his head.

The whole cleanup, bringing in Dan and everyone else, had been pointless. That was his first thought. What he'd been looking for wasn't concealed in all the junk in and around the house. It was right here, by itself out in the pasture. This was the secret the Speakman boys had been concealing. And it wasn't money. That was his second thought. He should have just sold the land as soon as he inherited it, and walked away with whatever he got.

Except...

He looked down at the broken rock, and the gap in it that was now almost pitch-dark. Except that this was more important than money, more *valuable*. That's why the Speakman brothers had spent all their time constructing tributes to what was below him, things that did the best they could at simulating it. He even though he understood why Pace might have wanted to include his arm in one of them. He found himself looking at his own arm in the gloom, and nodding slowly.

He shook his head violently.

No. No, he needed to think. The Speakman boys had been at it for years, trying to match the engine down there, and they'd always been pretty handy, good at fixing stuff and cobbing together machinery. They'd kept a couple tractors running for years using nothing but the random junk they could scavenge, after all. They hadn't been too smart, any of them, and maybe he could do a better job than they had in time, but he needed to think, needed to practice, at least before he started incorporating his own bones into the machinery he was going to build.

He felt a sudden pang for the two dumpster loads of materials that he'd sent away the day before. But there was still plenty left in the dumpsters now, or in the barn and around the yard. He could think of a few things he could use, now that he knew to.

He ran a hand over the rock, rubbing the little pictogram of the candle, the one recognizable element to the carvings, the one element that didn't fit. Finally he stood and started back up the slope, along the stream. It seemed like it would be a good idea to get back before dark, at least. By the time he reached the little house it was a black shape against the horizon. He made his way in, flicking on a light in the main room, then found himself continuing on into the bedroom. By the light of the single dim lamp, he looked over all the little devices scattered throughout. He could see, now, how they were connected to the larger machine buried under the pasture. They were imperfect copies of the mechanism, he could tell that even though he'd only had a glimpse at a piece of the huge engine. But they had something to them, and he shuffled through the scattered junk, picking up one, then another, to give them a closer look.

It wasn't until he tripped over another of the ancient cans of old tobacco spit that he paused, looking around and wondering how much time he'd wasted. There was an old, nicotine-stained clock on the wall, but its hands weren't moving any more than the one out in the main room. He pulled out his phone, and found that the battery had died somewhere along the line.

Shaking his head, he made his way out of the bedroom, realizing that he was exhausted. He hadn't eaten since dinner the night before, either, not that he had an appetite. He was so tired he was getting... distracted. Forgetting to charge his phone, losing track of time. He'd had to unplug the little CRT television to plug in his phone charger, and he left his phone there charging and sidled his way through piles of metal back to his sleeping bag.

He had turned off the light and was just wriggling down into the bag when he paused. He didn't like being asleep in the house, with its lack of locks. Not with… everything going on. The front door was the only entrance to the old house, and it didn't even lock. He eased out of the bag with a half-sigh, half-groan. It wasn't like his car was any colder than the house, or less comfortable for that matter, and at least it locked. He got his shoes on, and pulled on his jacket, the Glock in one pocket pulling it to one side, and made his way out onto the porch with a flashlight and his sleeping bag.

The moon was down, and he wished that told him something about what time it was. He was feeling adrift as he looked up at the few cold stars peeking past the clouds, not knowing what time it was. He felt like he didn't know *where* he was anymore, either. His car was nothing more than a dim form among the other dim forms in front of the house. Now that he looked at it, it seemed even less secure than the house. Anything could creep up and look at him through the window while he slept.

After a few moments, he made his way down the steps. He walked around the corner of the house and into the back lawn. He needed the flashlight to avoid what junk was left there, thanks to the clouds, but soon he was at the barn. The beam of the light showed the big sliding door slumped tiredly on its tracks. He didn't bother trying to slide it open, just pulled the spongy wood of the door out a bit so he could squeeze in.

The variety of junk in the wide, open space of the barn made shadows bounce around crazily in the beam of his flashlight, and he kept having the sense something was about to jump him. It was a relief when he'd climbed into the back seat of the old Buick and he could flick off the light. Then it was so dark that he could easily imagine whatever popped into his head, out in the dark, but once he'd struggled into the sleeping bag, the weight of the Glock he held made him feel better.

He actually remembered the day the Buick had been moved into the barn, now that he thought about it. Just an old junker that Orson had hauled in with a tractor while Uncle Jake yelled at Uriah. "What the hell are you spending money on something like this for?" he'd asked. "This barn's for cows, and you ought to be replacing a few of them. For Chrissake, none of you even has a driver's license."

"Didn't pay for it," Uriah said, and spat a stream of tobacco. "German fella in Stockbridge just wanted rid of."

"We need the parts," Amos added. "Gotta fill the gaps." Emmett shook his head in the dark. He didn't know what Amos had meant by filling gaps, but the Buick had apparently been the thing that kicked off the barn's slide from housing livestock to being a depository for junk.

Emmett shifted on the seat, wishing again that he knew what time it was. It felt like he'd lost a lot of time, first in the old silo, then in the Speakman brothers' bedroom. Tired as he was, in fact, it seemed like he was just waking up. Had the Speakman boys felt like they were half-asleep sometimes? He kind of thought they had. Uncle Jake had spent a lot of time cursing the way they acted disconnected, made it hard to get through to them. It was that engine under the ground, somehow, that did it. Emmett still felt the compulsion to work on machinery, like they always had, though it wasn't so bad now. Had he really been planning to use his own bones in a machine?

No. No, that didn't make sense. Still, he was going to have to give everything some serious thought in the morning. In the daylight.

He jolted awake from a dream where he'd been arguing with Amos and Uriah in the main room of their house. Emmett kept gesturing to the bedroom where one of their brothers was dead and the other dying, but they just nodded absently, and tried to look past him at the TV playing *Jeopardy!* (not *Wheel of Fortune*) while their hands worked at making little machines. Amos had just shaken his head and said, "You gotta keep workin', Emmett, you want to stay ahead of it."

Emmett blinked, wondering why he'd woken up. Maybe just the fact that sleeping in the back seat of the Buick was twisting up his back.

A car door slammed outside.

Emmett sat up, groping for the Glock. It was still pitch-dark in the barn, so it wasn't like he'd overslept and everyone was arriving to get back to cleaning stuff up. They weren't coming back until Monday anyway. He awkwardly wriggled out of the sleeping bag and groped for his shoes. He strained so hard to hear any little noises that when there was a loud bang he jumped and hit his head on the window.

It had been the front door to the house, he thought. He eased the door to the Buick open and stepped out. He didn't dare use his flashlight, so he had to shuffle carefully across the barn, feeling his path ahead, to avoid stumbling over anything.

He made it to the sliding door and squeezed out. It was nearly as dark outside as it had been in the barn—all the stars were gone. But he could see a light in the bedroom window of the house, and as he watched a silhouette passed in front of it.

Emmett froze for a moment, then made his way slowly across the yard toward one of the barely visible piles of junk. The light in the window flicked out, and a moment later the front door slammed again as he crouched near the pile. With the light inside the house out, Emmett couldn't make out much of anything, but he thought he saw a shadow near the barn a moment before the big door squealed on its tracks. A flashlight beam flickered from inside the barn as it was played around the area. After a minute or two the light flicked out, and the rusty door complained again.

Emmett gripped the Glock tightly where he crouched. He could see *something* near the barn, a spot blacker than the surrounding darkness, and he was tempted to take a shot. But he couldn't make out any details—the shadow was jumping around, appearing, disappearing, looking like two shadows.

After a bit, he thought he detected the shadow moving around the opposite side of the barn, toward the pasture. A light came on as whoever it was flicked on a flashlight out in the pasture. It was JT, most likely. Or maybe it was someone else, but in any case he thought he knew where she was headed, and for a moment he thought about following her. She had no right to what was buried under the pasture, no right at all.

He gave himself a shake. No, he had to do the smart thing. He waited a few minutes to be sure she wouldn't double back, then made for the house. Even in the starless dark, he could see that his car was the only one in the driveway. JT must have parked down the road so she could come in quietly. That meant the car door he'd heard had been her checking his car. His legs went a little rubbery at the thought that he'd almost been sleeping there while she crept up on him.

He climbed onto the porch and turned on his flashlight, keeping it pointed low with one hand curled around the lens as he made his way into the main room. The end of the charging cord for his phone sat atop the TV, but the phone itself was gone. He looked back at the end table near the couch. His car keys were missing, too. So JT hadn't wasted her time in the house.

Emmett found himself smiling in the dark. Well, if she was going to force his hand, so be it. He'd have to be careful, but he hadn't liked the idea of letting anyone mess around with his machine anyway.

He flicked off the flashlight as he walked past the barn. He could feel a cold mist rolling in, which turned JT's light into a diffuse glow far off into the pasture. He shoved the flashlight awkwardly into his pocket and checked the Glock as he started forward.

He could see where JT had stopped ahead from her light, but that was about all he could see, so he had to move slowly over the uneven ground. Despite his care, smacked his knee painfully against something in the dark. He groped across the object, feeling a length of chain that gave a bit when he pulled on it. One of the strange devices the brothers had made.

Emmett froze at a noise, something that sounded like metal on stone. He peered at the glimmer of light, trying to make something out. The noise came again, from off to his left. He whirled, and thought he saw a dim shape, something just a bit blacker than the surrounding dark. It was really just a suggestion of motion, there then gone.

He staggered back a step, holding up the pistol. JT might have brought help. Or maybe someone else had gotten wind that the Speakmans were hiding something. He took two more steps back up the slope and crouched, slowly moving the Glock back and forth.

The noise came again, closer this time, a scrape and a click. His grip on the pistol tightened, but he couldn't make anything out. The scream, when it came, startled him so badly that he would have fired if his finger had been on the trigger. There was a second scream, and he was already running before he could figure out where it had come from.

He ran headlong through the dark until he finally, inevitably, put a foot in a groundhog hole and went sprawling across the dead grass. He lay there for a second, catching his breath and feeling a sharp throb in his ankle. Finally, he rolled onto his back and sat up, head cocked to listen. The screaming had stopped, but he could hear *something*. A scraping noise? It was very quiet, just at the edge of hearing, so he might be imagining it. He wasn't even certain where he was—the glow had vanished at some point, and it was as if he was floating in space, with no point of reference.

He'd kept hold of the Glock, but he'd lost the flashlight. It was probably for the best. He wanted to know where he was, but more than that, he wanted to remain hidden. He looked around, trying to spot the flashlight beam, but there was nothing. It was off, or cut off from his view. Emmett drew his knees to his chest, hugging himself for warmth, and waited.

He wasn't sure how much later it was, but he gradually became aware that he could see a tuft of tall brown grass not far away, near a dull gray rock. Colors were back. The sun wasn't up yet, but it was near, not that he'd see it through the thick fog that had risen during the night and now obscured everything more than twenty feet away or so. But he could tell what direction he was facing, at least.

He stood painfully. He was shivering, but also stiff and sore, a bad combination. It was better now, though. Now that he could see. Even with the fog, things seemed safer. He walked a few brisk circles, trying to get his blood flowing and loosen his throbbing ankle. What was the next step? He still didn't have his phone or keys, so trying to get help would mean a long walk. With the fog, though, he didn't have to worry about being seen by anyone still prowling around the farm.

That same fog made it hard for him to know where he was in relation to the house, but the road was uphill, he knew that much. He'd only been walking for a minute when he heard a metallic rattle from up ahead. It made him more nervous than it should have, and he felt the Glock going sweaty in his hand. He advanced slowly, hearing the rattle again.

He thought he was getting close to the road when a stray breeze shredded some of the mist and the barn suddenly loomed out of the fog to his left. The rattle came again, near the barn, and he made for it, placing his feet carefully and keeping the barn between him and the noise.

He got to the barn and eased around it, and there she was, half-obscured by mist. JT, hauling a wheelbarrow up to the silo—the newer one that he'd checked and found empty. The wheelbarrow rattled again as she dropped the arms—there were a few things in it, including a shotgun, with its barrel peeking over the side.

Her back was to Emmett as she stepped forward to examine the lowest doorway. Emmett raised the Glock, in the grip they'd taught him back in the force, and started forward slowly as JT tried the door. He was just getting into comfortable range for a pistol shot when JT straightened and turned toward him.

He froze, finger on the trigger. She reached back and grabbed a sledge-hammer from the wheelbarrow, and turned back to the door without seeing him in the mist. He took a few more steps toward her as she tapped the rusty levers holding the door shut.

Once you're sure, you act, Uncle Jake had always said. *Once you know someone is a real threat, you do what you need to do, and you don't hesitate, because that's when things go wrong.* Anna Wittington had been a threat. One of her cousins had tried to muscle in on Jake's weed business, and word was she was pissed about Emmett burning the guy's house down for it. Pissed enough to think about going to the police.

And JT was even more of a threat than Anna had been. She had a record, and she was prowling around with a shotgun, and she'd been out there last night, trying her damnedest to kill him, most likely.

He took a few more quiet steps forward as JT opened the door with a squeal. He was only a few yards away now, and if she hadn't been so focused on the silo, on the treasure she thought was in there, she would have sensed him.

No hesitation. He raised the Glock a few inches. JT bent, peering into the silo. *Once you know someone is a real threat, you do what you need to do.* He let the pistol drop slowly until it was pointed at the ground.

JT ducked through the hatchway and stepped in, dragging the sledgeham-mer behind her.

Emmett let out a breath. He stepped forward, and in one motion grabbed the door and pulled it shut.

"Hey!" JT said from inside as he slammed the lever home, latching the door. "Hey!" she shouted again. "Parson, is that you?" Emmett let out an-other breath and looked at the wheelbarrow. It held a bunch of junk—rebar, some pieces of two-by-four, a bucket, in addition to the old shotgun. He didn't know what JT had been planning, but he had some time to think about it now. He tucked the Glock into his jacket pocket and grabbed the shotgun.

Now that JT wasn't a threat, he could start down the road without worrying about her. But he could also check out the machine again, and suddenly he wanted to take another look, make sure she hadn't damaged it the night be-fore. He started down the slope through the pasture, ignoring the muffled shouts from inside the silo.

A thought fluttered through his head, something that nagged at him. Some-thing about the silo, and JT. If she'd been to the old silo, why had she... the thought fell apart on him. It was getting hard to think, and it didn't matter anyway. He could figure it out when he went back to deal with her.

As he walked, her shouts faded, either because she'd given up or because they were swallowed up by the fog. Even the normal sounds of birds and ani-mals were muffled, after all. As he neared the old silo, though, he finally heard something—a faint wet, sliding noise. He raised the shotgun as he walked, slowing his pace even further. A dim shape emerged from the mist, a low, hunched form.

A faint breeze pushed the mist away, up ahead, and Emmett stumbled to a halt, the barrel of the shotgun dropping. Dan was crouched on the ground just outside the ruin, his back to Emmett. The rest of the scene came to Emmett in a series of flashes. Blood spattered across the rocks. Homer lying on the ground. A pile of Homer's entrails nearby.

Dan was holding one of Homer's massive arms up, working at it with a knife. Emmett could see a flash of white bone, and he realized that another white and red object nearby was a bone from Homer's other arm, already mostly stripped of flesh.

Emmett must have made some kind of noise, because Dan whirled, still in a crouch, and in one motion he'd scooped up a shotgun and leveled it. For a moment, neither of them moved. A grin slowly spread across Dan's face. "Drop it, Emmett."

Emmett glanced down at the shotgun in his hand. Maybe he could bring it up and shoot before Dan got him, or dive back into the mist. But Dan was holding the shotgun steady in his bloody hands. He tossed the gun to the ground.

Dan grinned wider as he stood. "Good, good," he said.

"What have you done?" Emmett asked.

Dan glanced back at Homer's mutilated body before returning his gaze and tight grin to Emmett. "I need bones, Emmett, you know that. He was arguing with me about it." He gave Homer another flicker of a glance, and his smile turned sly. "I think he mighta thought he was gonna get *my* bones."

"That was you last night, both of you snooping around."

"Yeah, where the heck were you?" Dan asked.

"And Homer screaming."

Dan shrugged. "Yeah, like I said, we had a disagreement. But I gotta hand it to you, Parson. I didn't realize what you had here, not really." He barked a laugh. "Me and Homer just thought it was money."

"So did I," Emmett replied.

"That right? Huh." Dan laughed again. "Well, we know better now, don't we?" He gestured with the shotgun. "Come on over here."

Emmett took a few reluctant steps closer to the ruin that was Homer.

"I gotta get on with this," Dan said, one of his sticky red hands coming free of the stock of the shotgun with an audible sucking noise so he could gesture at Homer. "Need to get something built, right?"

"Right," Emmett said slowly. Involuntarily, he glanced over the low wall at the hole in the ground, though he couldn't really see anything in the shadows.

"Those Speakman boys were smarter than people gave 'em credit for, weren't they?" Dan said. "Out here all these years just drinking that machine in. Extending it, kinda."

Emmett nodded. "I guess. But they never killed anyone."

"How do you know?" Dan asked. "They got those things built in a big circle around this thing, all using bones. Who says they're all from cows? Besides, there at the end, what do you think they were up to? Amos and Uriah were all set to use the other two."

"Is that what you have planned for me?" Emmett asked.

Dan grinned. "Well, Emmett, you gotta admit, it would be nice to get some use out of you."

"We used to be friends, Dan."

"That was a long time ago, before you killed the Wittington girl."

"That was Jake, not me!" Emmett snapped. He might have helped bury her ten feet deep with a backhoe, but Jake had done the killing, dammit. "Anyway, what did you care about her?"

Dan shrugged. "I don't care about her. But you all decided to leave town after that, bigger and better things. Didn't invite me along, even though I did as much for your uncle as you did."

Emmett stared for a moment, then shook his head. "If you kill me, someone else will take over this land. You won't be able to come around here."

Dan snorted a laugh. "That what you think? You think anyone's gonna stop me from coming out here?"

Emmett glanced at the ruin. "Look, why don't we go back and talk at the house? It's easier to think there. The machine—" He broke off, and stared up toward the house. He couldn't see it, couldn't see more than a dozen paces, but he could imagine the house and barn, and more importantly how they felt.

"What?" Dan asked, his voice suspicious.

We need the parts to fill in the gaps. You gotta keep workin', Emmett, you want to stay ahead of it.

"Hey," Dan said, jerking the shotgun. "What is it?"

"Dan, those things they built aren't tributes to this machine, they're protection from it."

"The fuck you talking about?"

"Look around. None of the things they built are close to here. Most of them are back near the house, and there's more up ahead. They circle around this place, like you said."

"So what?"

"Those things, they block something. Don't you feel it? Don't you feel the difference between here and back at the house?"

Dan shook his head. "That's just because the house is too far away. The closer you get to the machine down there, the better."

"No, it's—"

"Shut up," Dan said, raising the shotgun to his shoulder. "Time for you—"

"Hey, Parson!" came a shout from up the slope.

"Shit, is that JT?" Dan asked.

It was JT, though Emmett was damned if he knew how she'd gotten out of the silo so fast.

"Parson, get up here!" JT shouted. "Something you need to see."

"What the fuck?" Dan asked. "Is she that hard up for work? Came out on her own?"

Emmett shrugged.

"Guess we better see what she wants," Dan said. He grinned. "Maybe her bones'll make better machinery than yours. Her being a mechanic and all."

"Yeah," Emmett said, starting to turn.

"Hang on," Dan said. He stepped forward and, holding the shotgun in his right hand, he patted Emmett's side with his bloody left hand. "Think you're pretty smart, don't you?" he said, pulling the Glock out of Emmett's pocket. He tucked the pistol into his waistband and shoved the barrel of the shotgun into Emmett's back. "Let's go."

They walked through the mist for a few minutes, and Emmett considered diving into it. Even if he got out of sight, though, Dan could bring him down blind with a spray of buckshot. He kept walking.

One moment, there was nothing but mist ahead of them, then a dim shape appeared, and in another moment it resolved itself into JT, standing next to one of the strange devices. She had her sledgehammer thrown over one shoulder.

"Hey," said Dan, and Emmett saw a look of surprise cross JT's face.

"Well, shit," she said. "I shoulda known."

"You really need this job, huh, JT?" Dan said. "Driving out here on your own on a Saturday."

JT looked over at Emmett. "There's work to do."

Dan nodded. "There is, JT. There is."

JT sighed. "You parked your truck somewhere else. I thought I was alone here."

"Yep," Dan said. "Came in last night. Gotta get up pretty early to fool old Dan Ryan."

"I also thought you could hold it together for a few more days."

Dan's eyes narrowed. "The fuck does that mean?"

JT shook her head. "Never mind." She looked over at Emmett again. "I had to bust a hole in your fucking silo, Parson."

"Uh huh," Emmett said, eyeing the sledgehammer.

"You really don't know what's going on here, do you?" she asked.

"I'm starting to figure it out."

JT nodded.

"Well, JT," Dan said, looking over at Emmett himself. "It don't really matter what he—"

He broke off as JT moved. He swung the shotgun to cover her, but she didn't even move toward him, just brought the sledgehammer off her shoulder and swung it in a wide arc over her head. It connected on the device where a cow femur was bolted to a leaf spring, a solid blow that shattered the bone and knocked the whole thing over.

"What the fuck, JT?" Dan said, taking a step closer.

"You'll want to save your ammo, Dan," she said, dropping the head of the sledgehammer to the ground.

Dan's eyes narrowed over the shotgun barrel. "What's that supposed to mean?"

JT tipped her head down the slope, and Emmett heard a clicking noise in the fog. It was the noise he'd heard the night before, but faster, somehow more purposeful.

"What the fuck is that?" Dan asked, shuffling back a step.

JT didn't answer, just took a step back herself. Dan still had the shotgun trained on her, but before he could fire, it was there.

Emmett wanted to think that what he saw coming across the pasture was a trick of the fog and his lack of sleep. He couldn't quite fix it in his mind anyway—it seemed put together wrong, in a way that should have been impossible. But it advanced, in a stuttering way—now creeping a few inches, now crossing several yards in a blink—and the closer it got, the harder it was for Emmett to convince himself it was an illusion. It was short, he thought, then immediately dismissed the idea—this thing wasn't human, so how could he say whether it was short or tall? But it walked on two legs, possibly three— Emmett rubbed eyes gone watery from looking at it and the way it didn't seem to fit the world.

The one thing he was sure of was the gears—gears and cables acting as joints and tendons. He could see them because so much of the innards of the creature were exposed, like it had been flayed. Gray skin gave way to bone, and cogs made of bone, and tendon-like cables. Several of those cables ran outside the thing's legs, yanking the limbs up and down in its jerky stride that made a bony, grinding, clicking sound. It had at least two arms ending in jagged bone, with more cable-tendons ready to yank them, and a mouth made of two bone gears, meshing so they'd drag anything that got near into its wide maw.

Dan swung the shotgun toward it and fired. Emmett was pretty sure he'd managed to miss, despite the close range and the wide spray of shot. He pumped the shotgun as the thing turned toward him, and fired again. This time he hit it—Emmett could see chips of exposed bone and pieces of gray flesh fly off the thing. But it didn't seem to slow it down much, because it came forward in a convulsive, twitchy leap.

Its limbs jerked forward, yanked by exposed tendons winding over bone pulleys, and Dan fell in a spray of blood. One bone spur had slashed across his throat, nearly lopping off his head, and the other sent the shotgun flying.

The creature paused, bending to poke at Dan's corpse with what looked like curiosity. Then, with a jerk, its head snapped up to look at Emmett. Emmett stumbled back a step, seeing the thing's limbs tense as tendons pulled taut.

JT appeared behind it, swinging the sledgehammer in a wide arc as she came. She took the hammer on a full circle of a swing over her head before turning a graceful pirouette on one work boot and bringing it around again to slam into the creature's leg. There was a loud crack of exposed bone and Emmett thought he saw a cog soaring away as the thing fell.

It was up almost immediately, spinning and lunging clumsily at JT, who backpedaled away. One leg hung at an angle and Emmett could see a bone cog turning uselessly, a cable-tendon gone slack. That slowed it down, but it seemed to feel no pain as it went after JT. She held the sledgehammer up as she backed away, and Emmett saw a splinter of wood fly off the shaft as she blocked its swing. Another swing hit the sledgehammer again, and JT staggered and nearly fell.

Emmett wasn't even sure how he'd gotten to Dan's body, but before he was sure what was happening he'd yanked the Glock out of Dan's waistband. It was like he'd just stepped out of the academy, and was working a drill, on one knee with the Glock held in the two-hand grip.

He wasn't sure how many shots went home, since the thing didn't really seem bothered by them. A few must have hit, because he saw chips of bone and spurts of black liquid flying off it. The shots didn't seem to do much more than get the thing's attention, though, and it turned from JT and began to lurch toward him. Emmett staggered to his feet, still firing. In mid-step, the thing seemed to figure out a new way to move, one that worked better with the broken leg. It somehow jumped off its good leg in a convulsive motion, clearing four feet in one twitching leap. It staggered as it landed on the broken leg, then gathered itself for another jump. Emmett stumbled backward, tripped and sprawled on his back, sending a shot straight into the air.

It jumped, landing where he'd been standing just as Emmett realized he'd used his last shot. The action of the Glock was racked open, and for a moment he just looked at it stupidly. The creature loomed over him, bony arms swinging wide.

There was a boom, and it twitched violently in a spray of buckshot.

JT, just a few feet away, pumped Dan's shotgun. "Come on, sunshine," she said, and fired again. It began to speak as it jumped toward her, in a horrible language that could somehow pass over cog-teeth. The words made Emmett's knees feel weak, made him want to puke, even though he couldn't quite understand the meaning.

JT felt the words too, judging from the grimace on her face. "None of that, you motherfucker," she said, and stepped forward, right up in its face. Its arm came up, but before it could grab her she fired into its mouth from about a foot away. That shut it up, but it had already started a jerky leap, and it slammed into her, bearing her to the ground.

If the thing had possessed more normal joints, it would have carved her up in a few seconds, but it had a hard time bringing the long limbs yanked around by cable-tendons to bear. For a moment, both sharp bone spurs hacked at the ground near JT, and she threw her head back and forth to avoid them.

She was pinned, and while the thing's mouth was ruined from the shotgun blast, the cogs still ground together, skipping now and again as they hit missing teeth. Its gray flesh, what there was of it, had been torn apart in several places as well, and was dripping a thick black liquid onto JT.

JT grunted as she grabbed one of the tendons operating the thing's arm and yanked it to one side. The arm folded up as the creature tried to brace itself and it rolled to the side, off JT. She sat up and pumped the shotgun as it turned and lunged, gears on its head turning, trying to get hold of something. JT gave it the barrel of the shotgun.

There was a grinding noise as its maw drew the barrel in, then she fired. This time, its head was blown almost free of the body, and JT scrambled to her feet, covered in the black gunk that had sprayed from it. She staggered over, pumped the shotgun again, and fired down at it.

It went still and seemed to start rotting almost immediately, going soft and losing all the sharp, geometric outlines.

Emmett and JT looked down at it for a few moments. Finally, JT let out a breath and looked at the mangled end of the shotgun barrel, shiny with gouged metal. "Shit," she muttered, and handed it to Emmett. She hauled her filthy sweatshirt off over her head and used it to wipe the black gunk off her face.

Emmett stared at her sleeve of tats for a few seconds. "I don't think I noticed that tattoo before," he said, gesturing to a small blue candle with a red flame on her wrist. "Kind of hidden by all the other ones."

JT showed her teeth in something like a smile.

"It wasn't an accident, you coming out to this job, was it?"

JT shrugged. "Not hard to fuck up Dan's truck. Barely rolls as it is."

"So, that thing," Emmett said, looking over to where the creature had been. It had rotted completely away, which was unsettling. "That thing. The Speakman brothers were keeping that penned in all these years?"

JT shook her head. "That's just something that came over when they finally tried to fuck with the engine, I figure. What they were trying to box in was an engine, not that I've figured out where the fuck that is."

"It's in the old silo, down there," Emmett said, gesturing down the slope.

"Well, shit," JT replied. "Come on. Work to do."

He expected her to head for the ruins, but she went back up the slope toward the barn. After a moment, he knelt next to Dan's body and gingerly fished his keys and cell phone out of his pockets, then jogged after her.

"Those Speakmans were tough bastards, I'll give 'em that," JT said over her shoulder as he caught up. "I don't know when the hole opened up, but it's been a while, right?"

"I'm not sure," Emmett replied. "But it may have been a few years since something started leaking out of it."

JT shook her head. "I couldn't have held out that long. Fuck, Dan Ryan back there couldn't last a goddamn week, and he was only here a few hours a day. Guess it's a good thing those boys were handy with scrap. Sounds like they kept making the best of things even after our little friend back there showed up and got a couple of them."

"So all of these... totems kept it contained?" Emmett asked.

"More like they kept things distracted," JT replied. "Fucking weird way to deal with it, but I guess it worked, sort of. You can see how they'd want to make machines that reminded them of the thing back there. Kinda dumb luck that they distracted the engine, too."

They arrived at the silo, and Emmett could see the hole JT had busted through the concrete. It would have been a tight squeeze between the iron bands.

"You thought there was something up with this silo, too," Emmett said.

JT glanced back at him. "We got someone in the sheriff's department," she said. "He thought it might have been important to the Speakmans. We only started asking after we finally figured out what was going on down here. Not that anyone told me about the other damned silo." She grabbed the wheelbarrow and started back down the slope. "Where's my fucking shotgun, by the way?" she asked.

"Back down near the old silo. Uh, Homer's there. Dead."

JT nodded as if she wasn't surprised. Neither of them spoke as they walked, and in a few minutes they were back at the ruined structure. JT looked over Homer's corpse for a few seconds, and shook her head. "Danny always was an asshole," she muttered.

Emmett barely heard her. He could feel the machine below his feet—working, grinding away to do... something. He wanted to know what that was. He wanted to look at it again, do something for it.

"Hey," JT said loudly. He looked up, realizing she'd been trying to get his attention for a while. She tossed him a plastic five-gallon bucket that had been in the wheelbarrow. "Go fill that up."

Emmett stared at her for a few seconds, then slid the Glock into his jacket pocket, dropped the shotgun, and took the bucket. He walked to the creek and held the bucket in the water. He could hear the sound of metal on metal as he filled the bucket, and when he returned, JT was inside the structure, pounding rebar into the ground to anchor a wooden frame around the cracked stone. The wheelbarrow was next to her, with nothing but a bag of concrete mix left in it. JT crouched next to the hole in the rock, now surrounded by the framework. Emmett watched as she draped the hole with a piece of fine metal mesh, and anchored it to the edges of the wooden framework with a staple gun.

Time seemed to have jumped again, and suddenly JT was on her feet, dusting off her hands. "Sometimes people overthink things. Laurel wanted to get a team out here with a stone cutter to set up a new *obex*, but I was like, 'there's a stream out there—just send out a bag of concrete mix and a template.'" She walked to the wheelbarrow, pulling out a pocket knife. "Of course, you know how it is—you come up with an idea, and next thing you know everyone's like, 'Great idea, Jane Temperance, how soon can you get that done?'" She slit open the bag and dumped the contents into the wheelbarrow. She tipped in some of the water and began mixing with the shovel. After a few minutes and a little more water, she seemed to have it to a consistency she liked, and she began shoveling it into the frame that surrounded the broken rock.

"That's not doing anything," Emmett said tightly as she smoothed it out.

He couldn't see the crack in the rock anymore, or the machine, but he could feel it running. It was okay. He could always crack the concrete later, and anyway the machine didn't want to be seen.

"Take it easy," JT said. She picked up something from the ground, a piece of cardboard with pieces cut out to form what looked like nonsense characters. She held it up so the light shone through the cutout for a moment, frowning, then spun it around.

Emmett felt a lurch in his stomach—he still couldn't have said what the characters spelled out, but they suddenly created something unsettlingly close to meaning in his head. Whoever had made the template hadn't bothered with the candle pictogram this time, Emmett noticed. "There we go," JT said, and lowered the cardboard onto the wet concrete. She flexed her hand, wincing. "You mind doing this?" she asked. "Kinda jacked up my fingers wrestling with that thing."

"Doing what?" Emmett asked.

"Just trace those characters into the concrete," JT said, standing up and flexing her fingers again. "I don't want it to get all shaky."

"Uh, okay," Emmett said, and knelt in front of the template. He could feel the machine as soon as he touched the concrete, sending a vibration up through his arm. It was certainly running, he thought as he traced the first character, gears turning beneath him, cranking implacably along. The longer he was in contact with the concrete, hovering just above the engine, the clearer the picture of it in his mind. For a moment, he thought he was about to grasp the real purpose of the thing. He felt like he was falling and floating at the same time. Then the meaning of the characters in front of him started to worm their way into his head, pushing out the truth of the engine, blocking it with something even more horrible.

He traced the final character and sat back with a gasp. He blinked, realizing that a pressure that had been building for days in his chest was suddenly gone. He looked down at the writing, complete and unbroken, unlike the carving it covered. His eyes watered, and he looked away, at the flagstone floor.

"What does that say?" he said, wiping his finger off on his pantleg.

"Fucked if I know," JT replied from behind him. "Best you don't think about it too hard."

Emmett stood and turned. JT was standing near the broken-off wall, holding her shotgun not exactly pointed at him, but not at the floor either. Her finger rested casually near the trigger guard. The finger didn't seem to be bothering her anymore.

"So," Emmett said. "It's safe now?"

JT laughed. "Fuck, no. This ain't ever going to be a comfortable place to live, no matter what's on top of that hole. Christ knows who set this up in the first place. Someone set a ward over this, probably two, three hundred fucking years ago, and somewhere along the line we lost track of it. Next thing you know people are living here and going fucking nuts, passing along a few tricks that get more confused every generation. We didn't even know about it until things went completely to hell and the Speakmans all died." She shook her head. "Fucking disgrace."

"So that guy Laurel was trying to get this land back to keep an eye on things," Emmett said.

JT tapped the chamber of the shotgun. "Yeah. Who knows how long before they fuck it up again, but yeah."

Emmett tried to keep his gaze from dropping to JT's trigger finger. "Why not just destroy it?"

JT sighed. "Partly because it ain't really *there*. That's why it screws people up so bad. Because it's impossible for it run here, but you can still feel it doing its thing. But also because some people want to use it."

Emmett was about to ask how someone could use the machine, but he was pretty sure knowing more about what was going on was a bad idea. "Sorry about before," he said instead. "The... silo. There's been someone hanging around here the last few nights. Dan, I guess. Or that... thing. I thought it was you. Didn't know you, and I did some checking up, heard about your record."

JT nodded slowly. "That was when I tried to get away from... all this." She took her left hand off the stock of the shotgun to hold it up, displaying the tattoos. Or one of them, anyway. "It didn't work out."

"It can be hard to get free," Emmett said. "I thought there was money here, but I don't need money, not that bad. I wanted it because Jake wanted it. It can start to seem like you want things that other people tell you to want, after a while."

"Yeah," JT said after a few seconds. She lifted the shotgun so the barrel pointed to the sky. "Yeah, you oughta tell Laurel you decided to sell this place after all, and you oughta do it over the phone from back in Jersey or wherever." She looked around. "Laurel's got people who are real good at making dead bodies disappear, and they're gonna have some work to do. Once they get on a roll, they're like to reduce a few variables and simplify things so they can just clean up another dead body or two and not worry about what leftover people who are still alive might get up to." She leaned the shotgun against the wall, then began tossing tools into the wheelbarrow. "Tell him you ain't even been here for a few days—you just hired us and went home. Hell, tell him that asshole Dan stopped returning your calls, and you figure it ain't worth the trouble if he's just going to not show up."

"You'll back that up?"

JT looked him in the eye for a moment. "Laurel's got his way of doing things, and I got mine. You took a shot at that fucker back there when I needed a distraction."

Emmett let out a breath. "Okay. Yeah."

"I'll stick around, clean up the rest of this stuff."

"Thanks."

"But, you know, it's Saturday."

Emmett blinked. "Yeah."

JT nodded. "Yeah, so I was wondering if you could pay me time and half for all this. Especially since you don't need to pay Dan and Homer now."

Emmett stared at her for a moment. "Uh, sure," he said at last. He reached back and found that he still had his wallet. He started trying to do the math, count out the right amount, then gave up and just shoved most of the bills he had at JT.

She tucked the money into her pocket and picked up the arms of the wheelbarrow. "Thanks," she said. "Laurel, he'll tell me just to be satisfied with saving the world, but that shit don't pay the bills, you know?"

Emmett nodded absently, and followed her as she turned and headed back toward the house.

SLICKER

ROBERT J DEFENDI

Carlin Reese had two broken yolks, one headache, and zero bars on his phone. He winced as he mopped up the last of the eggs with a bit of toast and tried to be as subtle as possible as he took in the other patrons of the diner. They all stared into their meals, pushing food around as if ignoring him. At least three glistened with clammy sweat, even in the air conditioning, their skin the texture of freshly washed squid. Something was wrong here. Carlin tasted something bitter on his tongue and realized, unexpectedly, that it was fear.

"Enjoy your meal?" The waitress was a middle-aged woman whose face was a memory of beauty supported by load-bearing makeup. She smiled in exhaustion, the basecoat cracking under the strain of being polite to a New Yorker, like fractures in drying mud.

Carlin cleared his throat and ignored the furtive stares of the other diners. For some reason, he was acutely aware that there were seven of them and one of him.

He looked the woman in the eye. "So the Lone Ranger and Tonto are standing on a mountain," Carlin said, checking his phone one last time for a signal, finding none, then pulling out his wallet. He didn't see a phone-pay scanner anyway. "The Lone Ranger looks north and says, 'Tonto, what's that to the north of us?' 'Five thousand Indians,' Tonto says."

Carlin started to pull out a credit card, but he didn't see a card reader either. He pulled out a hundred-dollar-bill instead, flopping it down. "So the Lone Ranger looks to the west and says, 'What's that to the west of us?' 'Five thousand Indians,' Tonto says. 'What's that to the east of us?' 'Five thousand Indians.'"

Carlin scanned down the counter, across a shifting ocean of flannel and bad hygiene. The men glanced back at him with flat glares, then at the waitress as if they wanted her to leave, then down at their meals. They looked for all the world like a group of men preparing to do something drastic. Either waiting for the last witness to leave or for a signal of some kind. He scanned the group to find the leader. "He finally looks south and says, 'What's that to the south of us?' 'Five. Thousand. Indians.' The Lone Ranger looks around, the panic just starting to sink in and says, 'It looks like we're surrounded.

What are we going to do?'" Carlin cleared his throat. "And Tonto looks at him and says, 'What do you mean "we," white man?'"

Carlin paused for the laugh, but none came. One of the men farther down the counter whispered, "That was kinda racist."

Meanwhile the aging waitress just said, "I can't change a hundred."

The hell she couldn't change a hundred. She'd taken in more than a hundred while he was eating. Still, best just to get the hell out of Dodge.

The glares radiated down the counter and he wondered distantly if any of them had ever eaten a city boy on one of those big hick farms they probably had. He needed to get back in his car and back on the road. Next time he got hungry on the road through Oklahoma, instead of stopping he'd eat his coat.

And as he considered the men, the whole image seemed to flash. One moment he looked down the counter, the diner exactly as it should be, the next he was a few stools down, and while the same people were there, they stood in different positions and wore different clothes.

Everything flashed back. Carlin grabbed the counter to steady himself and shook he head. A wave of fear washed over him, so powerful it seemed to resonate through the room. His headache pounded, blinding. He needed to get air. He squinted his eyes. What the hell had just happened?

"Keep the change." He gathered his Armani wool-cashmere coat and started for the door. One of the men started to move, but another put out an arm to stop him. *That* was the leader.

"Why you tell that joke?" the leader asked. He was stocky with dark hair well-groomed and moussed, in flannels so sharp they had an actual crease. Carlin blinked at him. He and this man were like night and day in size and breeding, but the hick's hair was almost identical to Carlin's own.

His eyes scanned the rest of the yokels and landed back on the waitress. "I have no earthly idea."

He pushed out the door and into the parking lot of the Ozark diner. Green trees crowded the winding mountain road on either side, the parking lot and diner cut out of the living wilderness. A cool breeze took the grill stink out of his nostrils as he moved to his Cadillac Escalade Hybrid. He opened the back door and hung his coat on the hanger he kept there, then moved to the driver's, tapping the voice assist on his headset. Lexi beeped.

"Lexi," he said, the words conveyed to the phone in his pocket via the magic of Bluetooth. "Take me to civilization."

"The nearest town is 430 feet away," the digital assistant said in his ear. *"Pull out onto State Road—"*

"No," he said. "*Real* civilization. This place is a shit hole."

"I'm afraid I can't help you with that," Lexi said. Stupid phone app.

"How far to St. Louis?"

"Three hundred and fifty-two miles."

He slid into the driver's seat and said, "Take me there."

The instructions played over the headset, and he tried to start the Escalade, but nothing happened. He tried again. Still nothing. Completely dead. He pulled out the phone. Lexi processed the navigation app on the screen, but he still had no bars.

"Dammit," he said, staring back at the diner. "Dammit!"

It took ten minutes for Carlin to work up the energy to open the door to the Escalade, and by then his headache had somehow gotten even worse. He didn't want to walk back into that place, but he really didn't have a choice.

He spent about five more minutes doing the ritual "no signal" dance, trying to find a location where the phone could contact a tower, but no matter how high he stretched or how he hopped, the phone didn't so much as ping. Lexi must be working off the new internal cache instead of the central Lexi servers. If he wanted to make a call, he'd have to find a land line.

He slid out of the SUV, but left his coat in the back. It was a cool autumn day, and the altitude left the air uncomfortably chilly, but it wasn't truly cold. He strode back to the diner, cringing at what the loose asphalt must be doing to the soles of his patent-leather shoes.

He pushed through the door and into a solid wall of disdain. The low hum of conversation ceased the moment he broke the threshold and all the flannel jockeys turned to look at him. The stocky leader in the freshly pressed flannel stood next to a gangly blond man who looked like Alan Tudyk with about ten grand less in lifetime dental care.

Their eyes fell on him, flat and emotionless, the way that creepy kid in the fourth grade had looked at bugs. It was like stepping into seven twin beams of… no, not hate… animal indifference.

And another flash. This time the faces of all the patrons were missing. In their place glistening, bloody muscle. The gangly one's intestines spilled out onto the floor and the well-groomed one knelt nearby, forming them into strange symbols.

Everything flashed back and Carlin gasped. His headache gnawed at the back of his eyes, scratched the inside of his skull. His heart pounded in his chest and he aborted his move for the counter, instead turning and riding a wave of fear in the direction of the rest room, the gazes burning his skin.

Light gleamed off the metal bands that surrounded the edges of the counter and tables as he moved under the ponderous judgment of the uneducated. He needed to get out. Out.

He pushed into the hall at the back of the diner and through the door into the rest room, then pressed his back against the door and gulped air.

Jesus Christ, what was going on? Was the headache making him see things? Was he having a psychotic break? It had to be fear, but while only one of them had seen the business end of a washing machine, they were just people. They weren't monsters. All that staring had just spooked him. His mind was playing tricks.

But then he remembered them all pretending not to stare, their expressions minuets of gathering hate. The image of the one man moving to head him off at the door before the leader had stopped him. Then, with that clarity that comes from hindsight, he realized what had really scared him.

None of them had eaten their meals.

Seven men, all ordering lunch, and then playing with their food as they watched him out of the corners of their eyes. His head pounded and his stomach plummeted. Still, why go through all of that and then just let him leave?

Unless somehow they knew his Escalade wouldn't start.

All right, Carlin. Get a hold of yourself. This is a diner in broad daylight. Just walk out there and demand to use their phone. They aren't going to just jump you *en masse*. Are they?

He eased the door open.

"It's a Grand Old One," one of them was saying in a soft drawl. Great, they were Republicans too. "We don't have a choice. We ran out of options days ago. You heard as well as I did. The stars are right. *Now.*"

Carlin stopped, the door cracked. The men sounded just a few paces away.

"I know, I know, I know. Are you sure you're ready?"

Oh God, it was some sort of homo-hick-rape party after all. He knew it. All these backwoods yokels were the same. He needed a way out of this. His headache throbbed. The fear was so powerful it seemed to batter him from all directions.

"I'm ready. You're sure that SUV won't start?"

"I cut all three positive twelve-volt cables. I do this for a living."

No wonder he hadn't seen the blond one when he'd been eating. The man must have sabotaged Carlin's vehicle and ducked around the building when he'd left.

"Yeah, yeah. I'm sorry. I didn't mean to challenge your professionalism." They used big words. Probably overcompensating for a sub-standard education.

"We just need his entrails," one of them said. "Quick, quick, like a bunny."

Carlin stumbled back away from the door. He slapped into the hard tile of the opposite wall. Entrails. *Entrails?* Oh God, oh God, oh God.

He squeezed his eyes closed. He couldn't breathe. Entrails. They weren't going to rape him. They intended to *kill* him. This was some sick, backwoods voodoo or something. Ozark magic. Superstitious nonsense, but that wouldn't keep him alive as his bowels spilled out onto the tile. He had to think.

All right. They would come through the door fast and hard. It wasn't that long ago he'd rowed crew in college, and while it pained him that they wouldn't put him in a skill position, they'd let him man the center because he'd been big.

Why hadn't he kept in shape?

Shut up, Carlin. Think. You're big *enough*. They'll come through ready for violence, but the others might not be prepared. If you can take them out fast, you might stand a chance.

His eyes cast about and stopped on a metal trash can. He quickly eased the bag out of it and onto the floor, then took up a position by the door, the can held up like a rock.

Carlin, you aren't just a hedge fund manager. You are a goddamned monster. You are the product of generations of breeding. Your ancestors conquered swaths of Europe. Embrace that. Let out your inner barbarian.

The door swung out and the barbarian surged, the fear a living thing inside him, giving him strength as he smashed the can down on the head of the tall one and driving him into the stocky one. A hooked knife glittered as it bounced clear, but it scattered under the stall, and the conqueror in him told him that the only thing he had was initiative. Going for the knife would mean death.

He charged out of the bathroom, hitting the first hick he saw low in the belly with one shoulder, just like when the frat had played football in the yard. He managed to take the guy off his feet and barreled them both back into another one. Carlin and the stumbling hicks drove out of that hall and into the diner proper.

The plaster-faced waitress screamed and her hillbillies cried out, but Carlin managed to throw them back into the others, then cut left and out the door.

The Escalade was no help. No time for his jacket. Cars only passed on the road once every few minutes. His first job was to escape.

He cut right, throwing himself into the woods.

Fifteen minutes later, Carlin crouched in a bush, watching the road. No movement. His headache had eased off, and all he needed to do was not be spotted by the locals before a car came along. Simple. He was well hidden. Uncomfortable as hell, but that was a small price to pay for surviving.

They were trying to kill him. Just like in all those stupid movies. Who would have believed that? Evil, full-on black-magic-practicing yokels in the woods. They'd never believe him at the microbrewery.

Just relax. Be calm, Carlin. You can get out of this. Just hitch a ride. You are a well-groomed, fashionable man, poorly dressed for the weather. You look exactly like someone who would offer a large reward. Flag someone down. Get to the nearest law enforcement facility.

He shivered and things moved in the underbrush beneath him, heard but unseen. The sunlight shone beautifully through the trees, falling in pools of green and gold on leaves and flowers. Diffuse swarms of insects gleamed over the road itself. He waited and his legs cramped and he prayed for the sound of a car engine.

That very sound rose in the distance. Carlin leapt to his feet and charged out into the pavement just as an old, beat-up truck came around the bend of the treeless cut of a road.

Carlin waved his arms in the air, trying to make eye contact with the driver. The truck didn't slow, and as it grew closer, the engine roared in sudden rage.

Oh shit, oh shit! Carlin threw himself out of the way, the truck passing so close that the wind gave him lift as he flew into the woods. He landed in a hard roll but he'd been the youngest of four brothers. This wasn't the first time he'd been thrown down a hill.

"I see him!" a voice called behind him.

He turned to see a fashion calamity in flannel, shouting into a hand-held radio. As the man pulled a rifle from the cab of the truck, Carlin turned and spun.

Crack!

Bark flew from a tree, shattered by the impact of a bullet. Carlin yelped and pushed himself harder, darting between trees. He couldn't keep the topography in his head but he tried to move with the trees between him and the shooter.

He had to get out of here. Tears filled his eyes as he ran, only mostly from the wind. This was the First World. One didn't just get hunted for sport on the road to a major U.S. city. All he'd wanted to do was stop for a meal. Ease the long drive with a little break. What the hell was going on here?

Three more shots rang as he ran, and he cut perpendicular to them. Think paintball, Carlin. You rock at the executive paintball retreats. How do you lose the enemy in Capture the Flag?

Simple. Run somewhere they don't expect.

He slipped and fell four or five times, his shoes finding no purchase in the wet, decomposing leaves of the forest floor, but finally he collapsed up against a tree. His limbs shook with exhaustion, tears burning his eyes. Sweat soaked through his shirt and it wouldn't take long before that bled heat out of his body in the chilly mountain air. He wasn't dressed for this. He wasn't ready for this.

All right. What did he have at his disposal? He was dressed poorly, but it could probably be worse. He couldn't trust the road, so he had to walk. He started to shiver, but it wasn't cold enough to be life-threatening, and if he kept moving even the cold wouldn't be too bad. So those two problems would cancel each other out if he just had a destination.

He checked the phone. Still no bars.

He put it away and reached up to his ear. The Bluetooth headset still hung there, even after the roll and the dodge. A bit of good luck. Dear God, he didn't think that anything could go his way. He didn't dare activate Lexi on speaker.

"Lexi, I need the location of the nearest law enforcement authority."

"*Searching.*"

He almost hadn't downloaded the Lexi update before leaving. If he hadn't, he wouldn't have offline mode while his phone wasn't able to contact the central Lexi servers. The perks of always needing the newest and the shiniest. It didn't just keep you ahead of the Joneses. Sometimes it kept you ahead of frothing, entrails-craving murder monkeys.

"*Located,*" the voice said in his ear. "*The nearest Sheriff's department is 1.8 miles away. The nearest Highway patrol facility is 2.3 miles away.*"

The idea of a Sheriff's department screamed "locals" to him. He wouldn't trust some hick Deputy to take him seriously even if they didn't know the people in that diner. No, Highway Patrol would pull from a state pool of talent. "Take me to the Highway Patrol."

"Turn around and walk .21 miles to the road and get back into your vehicle."

Dammit. "Lexi, switch to hiking mode. I'd like to walk." Please be a preloaded feature. Please be a preloaded feature.

"Switching to hiking mode." Thank God. He didn't remember downloading the hiking maps. A second moment of luck. Lexi continued, *"Head east for 1.5 miles, skirting south around Hillings Hill."*

Carlin started off.

"You're walking west."

Carlin turned around and headed the other direction.

When he'd caught his abusive mother cheating on his father, he'd gotten proof and managed to make sure his father got custody. When his new Southern stepbrothers had beaten him mercilessly, he'd learned to lie in wait and to return the pain sevenfold. When his college girlfriend had dumped him and posted those pictures on the internet, he'd buckled down, exercised ten hours a week, joined crew, and been accepted into a frat. When he'd been passed over for his second promotion at work, he'd learned that being the best at his job wasn't enough. You had to *appear* better than everyone else, and that meant dressing the part and tearing them all down. This was what made him a man not just worthy of respect, but a man who *demanded* respect.

Carlin Reese was agile. He had never been the man necessary to face the challenges before him. His genius was that he *became* that man when necessary.

Become the man who can survive this.

Lexi estimated that an inexperienced hiker would take fifty-five minutes to make the hike to the Highway Patrol. Carlin did it in forty-three.

He came up on the building from the back side, not trusting the road. His shoes slipped every other step on the wet underbrush of the building's hill. He was more a quadruped than biped but with mud slithering through his fingers and soaking through battered knees, he finally clawed his way up to the parking lot.

The building was blond brick and glass. Two cruisers sat out front, just visible around the corner from where Carlin stood. He took a deep breath and stumbled around the building until he could see through the giant windows.

A man in a Highway Patrol uniform and shiny brown hair stood as he saw Carlin, his face flashing through confusion to concern to professional helpfulness in rapid succession. He waved for Carlin to approach even as he moved around the desk and headed for the glass side door to let him in.

Carlin pulled on the door but it was locked until the deputy hit the bar on the inside. Carlin stumbled in, the heat like an embrace as he broke the plane of the doorway.

"Oh thank God," Carlin said and started to shake. "I thought I'd never find the place."

"Did you get lost?" the officer asked. He seemed to be trying to process why Carlin had come to the building from behind. "Your car go off the road?"

Carlin's headache returned. "They're trying to kill me." He hadn't realized how exhausted he was until he could finally rest.

The deputy guided him into a chair. "Sit down. Tell me who's trying to kill you."

"Locals," Carlin said. "This is going to sound crazy, but I think they're in some kind of cult. They want to sacrifice me for some sort of ritual."

The Officer perked up at that. "Raymond!" he shouted. "Raymond, you were right..."

A second Highway Patrol officer stepped out of the back, still buttoning his shirt as if he'd just come on duty. Short and stocky, his shirt pressed and perfect. His eyes dark and searching. It was the leader from the diner.

"...He came right to us," the officer finished, pulling his gun from his holster.

The barrel of the gun yawned, so huge it could swallow worlds, and Carlin had to stop himself from leaning out and catching the edge of the desk. He had to stand perfectly still. He couldn't set them off. They had him. His body couldn't contain the fear. It bounced back and forth, like waves, between him and the stupid, grinning officers, off the walls. His temples pounded, almost as bad as at the diner.

"You can't have my entrails." All right. That was a stupid thing to say.

"Hi, Carlin," Raymond said, "That's your name, right? Carlin?" He smiled broadly, but there was something off about it, like a creature playacting at being a man. "I'm Raymond. This is Nathan," he gestured at the officer.

Raymond wasn't wearing his belt. Nathan started to reach behind, presumably to grab cuffs. He moved slowly though, deliberately, as if he wasn't comfortable in his own skin.

"I'm really sorry about this," Raymond said. "Carlin, there's something we need to get out of you."

"I'll bet," Carlin said. Keep them talking. Talking has never failed you. "You are part of some sick cult and you're going to use my guts to summon something."

"Nathan!" Raymond said. "No handcuffs, remember? The iron."

"Right. The zip ties are in the back." Nathan nodded at a door and Raymond moved for it, not taking his eyes off Carlin.

"I don't know what this is about," Carlin said, "but I'll pass."

"We all have to make sacrifices, Carlin," Raymond said. "You shouldn't resist. That will only make things worse. You know what we mean. We look toward the future. You can make that future happen." He reached the back and slid through the door. "This is for the best."

"The best. Right."

Nathan's shoulders telegraphed his alertness. His eyes wide and wild. Why hadn't he pulled the trigger? If they just needed his intestines...

"You can't kill me here," Carlin said in realization. They needed to truss him up and move him somewhere. Maybe his intestines weren't enough. Maybe they needed to be fresh.

"The Grand Old One cannot come into this world," Raymond said, stepping back into the room with a zip tie in one hand. "It isn't too late. If you come willingly, I promise your sacrifice will be worth it."

Trying to stop something, not summon it? "I don't know what Republicans have to do with this," he said. "I'm a fiscal conservative and a social progressive." It didn't matter what their delusion was. Who cared if they thought they were killing him for good or for evil? They were still murderous bastards.

But Raymond was squinting at him. He smiled. "Ah. Grand Ol' Party. You made a GOP joke." He nodded as he walked across the room. "Funny. But no. A Grand Old One is a creature so old and so dangerous that its existence endangers everyone for miles. Maybe many states away. We aren't murderers, Carlin. You aren't either." He started forward with the tie, gesturing for Carlin to put his hands on his head. "We just need to open you up a little." He grinned wildly at his own joke. "Think of the children. It's a glorious future we see, Carlin. They will sing your praises for generations. If you submit."

"Tell that to my entrails," Carlin said, putting his hands on his head. He couldn't do otherwise with the gun, but he couldn't let him bind his wrists either. He had to do something.

Raymond nodded. "All right, fine, we're murderers, but if we don't finish the ritual soon and unravel the spell, it will come. It doesn't care about us or our families. It doesn't care about yours. But you already know that, don't you. Deep down." His face twitched and the good-ol'-boy personal almost cracked, but then it returned, like a carnival mask layered over a puppet made of bones. He looked at Carlin's stomach and giggled. He actually giggled. "Deep down. Get it? Get it?" His eyes flashed wild for a moment, then his face became composed. "If you come with us willingly, we'll finish this. Don't embrace the fear. Defy it. This is the right thing to do. Trust us." He smiled in what he probably thought was a reassuring manner. "We're the police."

Okay. Okay. Carlin was starting to get a feel for it. "You're insane."

"Oh sure," Raymond said, grabbing one of his hands and wrenching it around behind him. "A sane man couldn't save the world. The sane men have already broken completely. It's best if you just let go. Lean into the insanity. It's the only way to keep your survival instincts from playing into *its* hands."

"You don't have to be crazy to work here," Nathan said, "but it helps."

Raymond started to pull his other hand around and Carlin drove his head back into the man's face. Raymond jerked back, losing control of Carlin's wrists. That was easier than he—

The gun jumped in Nathan's hand.

The pain exploded in Carlin's arm before he registered the sound of the shot, a sudden explosion of agony and shock. Carlin didn't react coherently, but the wound didn't immobilize him either, and there are two primary reactions to mortal assault: fight and flight.

Carlin fought.

He screamed and grabbed a lamp with his good right arm and hurled it into Nathan's face, running before he had time to think. He charged straight at one of the tall windows, wondering if he had the strength to shatter it or if he'd just bounce off.

But he needn't have worried because through the window the tall gangly one was just getting out of a Fire Department SUV and pulling up a rifle, a huge bruise on the side of his head where Carlin had pounded him with the trash can. Seeing Carlin charging him, he raised the gun and fired, destroying the intervening window, but glass must have deflected the bullet just enough. The shot missed.

Carlin flew through the falling shards and into the tall one just as the man fired again, putting a bullet in Carlin's shoulder. Carlin barreled into him, smashing them both into the SUV. Then he changed direction slightly and threw himself off the hill and back down into the wood. Two more gunshots fired and one of them caught him in the other shoulder.

And then he tumbled down the hill, came up stumbling, all but blind with fear, delirious with pain, and took off into the woods.

Carlin's headache snapped and vanished. He looked up the hill at the High-way Patrol building. Then a pain exploded in his arm and he almost cried out. His head swam. Sweat poured down his face and soaked his shirt. His heart pounded, his ears roared. What was going on? Just a moment ago he'd been running, with three bullet wounds. Hadn't he?

He felt his shoulders, expecting to find shattered bone and pierced lungs, but the skin was smooth and unbroken. And yet he had a tear in the soft meaty outer deltoid of his left arm, right where Nathan had shot him. Had he just imagined everything with the Highway Patrol? Was it a premonition? If not how had he lost the other two gunshot wounds? If so, why did he still have the third? What the hell was going on?

A cry rose from the building and a moment later the tall gangly one with the bruise appeared, holding the rifle. He stared down into the woods and Carlin drew back, hoping they couldn't see him. The hick scanned the woods, but didn't seem to make out Carlin in his hiding place.

With a flash, the smooth skin of the man's face vanished, replaced by a pulpy yellow mass, like pus dried in the noonday sun. Then another flash and the skin vanished completely, the man's face a mass of glistening red muscle and exposed eyeballs, a massive personification of pain and twitching help-lessness that lifted its head to the sky and screamed.

And then normal again, the scream of pain turned into a call over his shoulder. Carlin took the opportunity to pull back farther into the woods, and when the man looked back, he raised his rifle and fired a shot into the tree Carlin had been using for cover a moment before.

"You see him, Jimbo?" Raymond called out, still out of sight.

"He's down there," Jimbo, the gangly one, replied.

Carlin took off into the woods, tapping his headset with his good arm. "Lexi, tell me you have a signal."

"I have a signal, Carlin."

"Dial the nearest metropolitan police department," he said.

"I'm sorry, Carlin, I do not have a signal."

Well, he had ordered her to tell him she had a signal. Dammit. "Give me a satellite view of the area." He pulled out the phone and looked at the overhead map. He could see the Highway Patrol, a ranger station too far away, and between… "What is that?" It looked familiar, somehow. He tapped it.

"A local feature," Lexi said.

It looked like a cabin. "Lead me to it. Hiking mode," he said, then tucked his phone back into his pocket.

What had happened at the Highway Patrol? Had the entire thing been a premonition, somehow leaving him with one out of three wounds? A hiccup in time that had only mostly reset the damage from the gunshots? Something else? And why did he keep having these horrific visions?

No answers. Only questions.

Sounds of pursuit rose behind him, men shouting back and forth, feet crashing through underbrush. Carlin pushed forward, moving more quickly through the bushes. After a moment he found a trail and started along it. He'd be harder to track on the packed earth than crashing through pristine bushes, right?

His heart pounded. The slow leak of his life's blood down his arm left him dizzy and slightly nauseated. He could taste terror like copper and bile on his tongue. They were going to kill him. He didn't stand a chance. They would shoot him to death and they'd rip out his entrails and if he were really lucky, they'd wait for him to die first. The image of that hooked knife rose in his mind's eye, piercing his tanned abs, plucking his still glistening bowels from his belly in a moment of exquisite agony.

No, Carlin. Stop being the man who can't survive this. Become the man who can.

The sun set as he stumbled ahead of his pursuers, their sounds like hounds on his heels. He tore off a strip of shirt and tried to make it into a makeshift bandage, but he didn't think that it did much good. Heat bled away and the cold, the sweat, and the blood loss left him shivering in the night.

Don't die. Keep moving. You aren't going to freeze to death. You are going to get out of this.

His stomach plummeted as he approached the cabin, with its dark windows and foul stains, reaching up the log walls like grasping fingers, clawing at the ceiling. The windows gaped and there was a smell, like something in the woods had started to go rotten. There was something wrong with that cabin. His skin turned to ice. If he entered that cabin, all of this ended. He didn't know how he knew that, but he fought the urge to vomit.

"Carlin!" someone shouted, distant in the darkness. Carlin looked around, but in the now-black wood the sound bounced around. A woman's voice. She continued, "So fitting that it ends here, isn't it?"

The cabin sat in a clearing of rotting leaves scattered with a few fallen branches. He could smell something else now, under the rot. Something metallic.

"The others are coming, Carlin, but I knew this was where you'd come. This cabin's been in my family for generations."

The windows stared at him like gouged-out eyes. Lifeless. Hollow. Grotesque.

"I've radioed for them, Carlin. They are converging on this spot. Give up. It could all be over. Do the right thing. Let go."

Why did the woman's voice sound familiar? Ah. Yes. The waitress from the diner. It was all so clear now. The men in the diner hadn't been wishing she'd leave. They'd been looking to her, not Raymond. Waiting for the signal to attack. The woman with the load-bearing makeup. The mastermind.

She was trying to get into his head. He needed to stay calm. If he dashed out into the clearing, he'd be shot.

A gunshot sounded in the night. A bullet bounced off a tree, but not close to him. She fired at shadows.

"I've lived here my whole life, and you come here, try to ruin everything. My grandmother used to take me to this cabin. I would sing as she cleared the traps and skinned the animals. As she taught me the old magic. As she told me about the Grand Old Ones and the Ancient Gods and the ways of the primal wood. I'd help her sort guts and eyes and brains, scoop them two-handed into the waste bin." Her voice turned wistful. "I used to sing."

Carlin circled the cabin quietly. If he kept moving, maybe he could nail down her location, but the cabin pulled at him, like a chain, and he a good dog, circling. Testing the range of his leash.

Her voice rose, strangely beautiful, a ponderous, slow tune, like a dirge.

"Mine eyes have seen the glory of the coming of the Lord..."

Gunshot. A bullet ricocheted off a tree about thirty feet away. Carlin cringed and froze as her voice, haunting with its subtle southern drawl, echoed around the woods. It shifted slightly as she sang. She was circling as well, looking for that angle that would bring Carlin into full view.

"...He is trampling out the vintage where the grapes of wrath are stored..."

Carlin had almost made it around the building now. A bat flew overhead, too-tight skin drawn over a skein of bones and gristle, beating into the night. The dread of the cabin pulled at him, like a fishhook in the deep-body fascia of his torso. He had to see the raincoat. He didn't know what raincoat that was, but he knew it would make sense when he saw the front of the building. He needed to know if the raincoat were hung up or spread out. What did that mean?

"...He hath loosed the fateful lightning of His terrible swift sword..."

The wound in his arm stopped hurting now. The cold no longer touched him. The corner of the building rotated slowly in his view. He could almost see the front. Almost. The dread rose in him. His throat clenched. What was he going to see?

Another gunshot—this one far away. "…His truth is marching on…"

The door slid into view, half in, half out of shadow in the pitiless moonlight. Black… gaping… hungry. But closed. The yellow raincoat hung on the frame, and for some reason, the sight filled him with rage.

The bleeding had stopped on his arm. The door was his world, drawing him forward, implacable. Undeniable. Irresistible. He took a step toward the door. Another. She kept singing. He didn't care.

A bullet crashed into his leg, and he ignored it. Another shattered rib and tore lung, but it was inconsequential. Another bullet and another.

Then the gunshots stopped for the moment, lyrics echoing down through the forest as woman presumably reloaded.

The yellow raincoat. What did it mean? Why did the cabin call to him? He could smell death and metallic stink. He looked at the door below the tape, no, not tape, a raincoat. No, tape. His mind changed the tape into a rain slicker, but he could force himself to see the truth. The black and yellow tape, hanging from the frame. The stain. Blood. Something had been slaughtered here, staining the bottom of the door and the stoop.

And for some reason, he thought, Good.

"Carlin," Lexi said, "you have returned to this location. Would you like to add it to your favorites?"

Returned? He'd never—

He looked at the tape. No, raincoat. No. Yellow police crime scene tape. It hung, torn where it was attached to one side of the door, a fragment of yellow on the opposing side of the frame. Once sealing the world away from what was inside, someone had clawed the tape away to try to get through that door. To the crime scene. He looked at it…

…And saw the door, clean in the daylight on some other day.

And he saw the diner, but different patrons, him eating a different lunch.

And he saw the diner again, Raymond in his Highway Patrol uniform, watching him suspiciously, the woman with the load-bearing makeup staring, whispering a charm of protection. The magic resonated in his chest, but it was so weak, he couldn't do anything but laugh, their fear pounding as a headache burned in his skull…

And he saw these woods during the night as he moved through, dragging a thrashing victim by the hair, almost to this cabin.

He understood now. He hadn't imagined the events at the Highway Patrol. Time hadn't reset. He'd merely… willed the two worse wounds away. He'd been too weak to do the third, and his mind couldn't handle it. He hadn't understood.

Carlin gasped and he was back in the now. "Lexi, how many times have I been here?"

"Seven times."

The gunshots started again, ripping through his body, but he was too close to his source of power now. He ignored them like so many flies, drunk and bloated on corpses. His headache raged.

"Lexi, what day is it?"

"February sixth."

No, that wasn't right. He'd left his house in January. He should have arrived in Chicago on the 27th. He had business there. Business. He had just stopped at the diner for a meal. He hadn't been here a week…

No. He'd walked out of his job. He'd come here. Why would he even *be* in Oklahoma on a trip from New York to Chicago? He didn't understand. It was as if he were sleepwalking, drawn to the perfect place. The place for his real work to begin.

He touched the door and the protection magic sensed him, began to rally to tear him in two like whoever had been the source of the bloodstain, the person who had torn aside the crime scene tape, desperate to get inside. And then the magic of the door recognized him. It withdrew.

Ah. Yes. That's why they needed his entrails. To undo the ward on the door. To disturb his work inside.

"He's entering the cabin!" he heard Jimbo scream in the distance. The rest had arrived. Their fear pounded like a migraine in his head.

The woman still sang, the lyrics punctuated by the shots. "…He died to make men holy, we must die to make men free…"

"We need his entrails!" Raymond screamed.

"I'm out of rounds! I need a bigger gun!"

"Oh, God. Oh, God, he's going to do it. He's going to finish it!"

Carlin frowned. He looked down at his bullet-ridden body, but already the wounds had closed. He looked back at the woods. He could feel their terror, pounding in his skull. Ah. Yes. He'd forgotten. That was the last ingredient of the ritual.

Years ago, he hid under his abusive mother's bed as the dark voices whispered to him that if he just waited for his father to beat *her*, he could use her terror to cast a control spell. Then it would just be a matter of forcing her into an affair with that neighbor who always leered at her. He'd catch them and get the proof, so his father would divorce her. Or beat her to death. He was good either way. His father only beat whores, after all.

A year later, standing over those goddamn Southern stepbrothers with their fucking hick accents, the baseball bat rising and falling until their terror pounded in Carlin's head hard enough to split his skull, then listening to the dark voices again as they explained how to use the boys' blood and fear to bind them in a spell that would never allow them to speak of this to *anyone*.

As an adult, hiring black thugs to attack a coworker at night, then watching from the shadow, a tissue with the coworker's DNA in one hand as he waited for the sweet headache as he sensed their fear, ready to cast a spell of ill fortune.

Today the fear, not his own, just feeling like his own, flowing off the men who attacked him in the diner, giving him strength. More fear, from the

Highway Patrol, just enough to heal the gunshot wounds...

And his entire life, the whispered voice, always in and out of his mind, his constant companion, forgotten moments after it had spoken. *"The stars were right at the time and place of your birth,"* it said. *"You will be my vessel, and one day, when the stars are right again, my door. You will be the man I need you to be."*

Oh. Right. He was opening a door.

He pushed the door to the cabin open.

His spell had worked, keeping these low-born hicks out of the ritual area over the week he'd spent hunting victims. He'd made just enough mistakes that the townspeople figured out it was him, so he could lead them back here for the end.

He stared at the bodies inside the cabin, bloated with rot, their organs dark and glistening, the effluvia of their seeping wounds used to draw symbols that twisted and wriggled, taunting him, whispering terrible things. Dirty things. Horrible things. He giggled. Right. Raymond was so right. He should have seen it all along. Just so very right.

This was all much easier if he just let go.

"You don't have to be crazy to work here!" he called out to the hicks as they charged his position, fear rolling off them in great, delicious, head-pounding torrents. "But it helps!"

Then he became the man he needed to be. A moment after that he became the Thing with No Name. A moment after that he roared.

And then he devoured them all.

A BROWN AND DISMAL HORROR

Jaleta Clegg

"There she is, Cletus. Ain't she a beauty?" Skipper waved his hand over the top of the battered steering wheel. In the distance, a ramshackle cabin crouched on the side of a hill as if it expected to slide into the gully below at any moment. The accompanying outhouse looked much sturdier and more securely positioned, straight and tall on a flat spot of ground surrounded by shaggy pines. Skipper gunned the engine, ground the gears, and let the pick-up roll down the rutted dirt road.

"You sure the still is up there?" Cletus sucked the gap where his left bottom bicuspid used to sit.

Skipper bounced the truck through a series of potholes before answering. "Sure as shootin'. Got me a batch of 'shine just last month from it. We got us enough corn to cook up a double batch this time. My granpappy knew what he was doing when he built it. It'll last 'til Judgment Day and then some."

The truck slalomed through the gully at the bottom, spewing sand from beneath its tires before lurching up the bank on the far side. A plastic grocery bag slid under Cletus's foot.

"What's this, Skip?" Cletus hefted the bag and its load. "A book? This don't look like your usual reading material." The book was thick, bound in strangely delicate pale leather. Arcane lettering flowed across the front, penned by hand in dark brown ink. Discoloration from an old water splotch spread like leprosy from the bottom corner.

"It's for the outhouse. Feel that paper. Ain't that the softest you ever felt? I grabbed that from a dumpster behind that university what done closed last winter. They had a whole pile of old books just tossed back there. I got more in the back, but that book's got enough pages to last us the whole season."

Cletus flipped the cover back. A faint odor of decay and rot clung to the pages. He ran his fingers over the title page. The letters were strangely shaped, square and full of odd angles, as if the person who had penned them suffered from some strange affliction of the musculature system that caused bizarre twitches. Almost as if terror were infused in every pen stroke.

Cletus whistled. "That is the softest I ever felt. Better than that Charmin paper Lucie Mae is always after me to buy."

"We're living like kings this weekend. No women, no rules, and plenty of 'shine to keep us warm." Skipper pulled the truck to a stop in front of the cabin.

Rosebud, the hound who had patiently waited out the bumpy ride in the back of the truck with the bags of feed corn, bounded out before the dust had time to settle. She woofed once before relieving herself on the nearest patch of meadow grass.

Skipper and Cletus banged their way out of the truck, doors slamming and shedding more dust from the rusted body of the vehicle. They grabbed the bags of corn, hefting them over their shoulders as they headed behind the cabin to the hidden shed half-buried in the hill.

"Let's get her fired up," Skipper said as he pulled the door open on the shed. "We'll get the 'shine cooking then do us some hunting. Steak for dinner?"

"Long as it ain't possum or squirrel again." Cletus dropped his bag on the floor of the shed. "I got to go test out that new paper, if you catch my drift."

Cletus headed back for the truck where he pulled the book from the front seat. He crunched his way across the loose grit to the door of the stately outhouse. Rosebud bounded up to him, wagging her tail until she caught a whiff of the book. She backed away, a whine building in her throat.

"Just an old book, girl. Don't you worry none." Cletus waved the book at the dog.

Rosebud broke into a long howl before disappearing into the underbrush next to the porch of the cabin.

Cletus studied the hole where the hound had fled. "Huh. Just old paper full of dusty old words. Nothing to be scared of." He stared a moment longer before answering the increasingly urgent call of nature. The outhouse door banged shut on his heels.

He checked for spiders before sitting on the wooden seat, polished by several generations of bottoms. Sunlight drifted through the obligatory crescent moon cutout in the door. Dust motes danced in the beam. The light shone on the ancient text. The lettering on the cover beckoned, tempting Cletus to explore the pages within. He hefted it into his lap. His fingers strayed over the odd words. His lips moved as he attempted to sound out the name scrawled beneath the title.

"'Mis-ka-tonic.' Huh. Sounds like an imported beer."

He flipped to a random page. His fingers picked out words as he stumbled his way through the unfamiliar lettering. The syllables fell from his mouth, awkward and angular and unfamiliar. The afternoon air stilled in the outhouse, as if a giant beast held its breath. Though the autumn sunshine was bright and warm, a chill slithered up through the hole beneath.

Cletus finished the final syllable. The invisible presence loosed a sigh, a breath of frigid air that stirred the dusty motes and set them dancing. Cletus gave a final grunt before ripping the page from the book. He slammed the book shut, then shoved it onto the ledge beside the seat before he put the soft page to good use, dropping that into the hole when he finished.

The door banged shut behind him leaving nothing but a lingering odor to indicate his recent visit. The dust motes settled to a slow drift. An icy chill rose from the dank hole beneath the seat. The words had been spoken. A portion of the man had been given to the Elder Gods. Not the most desirable portion, but it had been many long years since their slumber had been disturbed by anything mortal. Any sacrifice was better than no sacrifice.

The darkness beneath the seat swirled into life. A strange light grew deep in the hole, a glow of darkness that sucked in joy and warmth and radiated desolation and the chill of the nether worlds. The dust motes drifted into the strange not-light where they joined the whirling blackness in a spinning dance. The fetid smell of freshly used outhouse rose on the icy column of air generated by the swirling mist.

Dust motes coalesced into a flat disk, sparkling against the backdrop of black energy. Any light that penetrated the outhouse hole was sucked inside, smothered and devoured by the strange emanation. The disk spun and grew into a portal just above the brown streaks on the crumpled page.

A slender tentacle tip emerged from the disk once it had enveloped the bottom of the shaft. The tentacle twisted, probing delicately at the dirt lining the sides of the hole. It rose like a swaying dancer towards the sprinkling of dust still floating in the late afternoon light leaking through the crescent moon cutout of the door. The suckers lining one side of the limb slid upwards, tasting and sampling the organic matter of the hole. The tip of the tentacle paused to inspect the round wooden seat. It slipped over the polished wood, barely touching the surface, before riffling the pages of the book.

Three other tentacles emerged from the portal, swaying as they rose beside the first. All four twisted their way up the narrow shaft. The first reached for the crescent moon on the door of the outhouse while the others felt their way up the dirt shaft. They writhed as they moved, sinuous and undulating through the spreading pool of inky dark.

All four tentacles stopped abruptly, their dance rudely interrupted by the constricting ring of wood. They surged upwards, straining to break free, only to jerk to a halt again without making progress. They pulled back, becoming thicker, squat and fat just above the hole. Their bulk blocked retreat.

The limbs stilled while the the agency behind them thought through the dilemma. Dust motes danced over their purplish gray and green mottled skin. The last rays of the sun flickered through the crescent moon, splattering over the monstrosities in freckles of light. A hiss, like escaping steam from a kettle, rose from below. The tentacles slithered to the back of the outhouse in a vain attempt to escape the light. A vapor of darkness leaked out between the tentacles, but the constricting hole limited how much could escape between the fat lengths of suckered flesh. Light and dark battled in the outhouse while the appendages writhed helplessly and the sun slowly sank below the horizon.

The light vanished into a twilight glow. The tentacles relaxed, then began to curl through the space. They slid along the wood of the seat and felt the bench to either side.

The door banged open. Skipper stood outlined against the sunset, his head turned towards the cabin. "Check the boiler. Should be all clear." He turned to face the outhouse as Cletus shouted a muffled reply.

The tentacles reached towards Skipper. The suckers puckered open and closed at the scent of his warm, human flesh. They stopped short, plugging the narrow opening. The tentacles flopped in a desperate attempt to break through the wooden ring crowning the seat. A pink flush crept into their flesh.

Skipper froze at the sight of the flailing mass. His mouth hung open, his eyes wide. He slowly closed the outhouse door on the horror. He peered inside through the crescent cutout, his eye glowing white in the dusk.

"Cletus?" His voice broke like a teenage boy's, squeaking high into soprano range. His eye disappeared from the cutout. Rapid footsteps headed away in the direction of the cabin and the still.

The tentacles redoubled their effort to emerge from the hole. They shot upwards, straightening with an almost audible snap. The wood of the outhouse creaked but held firm. They jerked back, then up, repeating the sequence rapidly. The outhouse trembled, but Skipper's granpappy had built solidly.

The tentacles coiled around each other, their tips exploring the outhouse and everything they could reach. One riffled the pages of the book, but without a mortal to read the words and provide the sacrifice, it held no assistance. Cletus had provided a very low-quality sacrifice, not nearly powerful enough to break free of the outhouse prison.

The tentacles stretched, thinning as much as they could. The lowest one pulled back through the seat, straining to slide past the other three. Slime oozed from the pores of the rubbery skin. A thick sucking noise filled the outhouse. Writhing flesh and suckers twisted and bunched until the boneless limb finally slithered back into the hole beneath the seat. The other three tentacles followed in quick succession.

Dust motes floated above the hole, swirling lazily in the fading light. The toilet seat rested above a pit filled with impenetrable blackness that now oozed anger and frustration. A sense of impending doom built in the gathering night.

Lights bloomed in the woods behind the cabin as Skipper and Cletus fired up the old kerosene lanterns in the open shed that housed the still. Their voices floated through the evening air.

"I tell you, it was one of them giant squids, like Bobbie Lee saw on that TV show last month."

"How would a giant squid get into the outhouse?" Cletus' voice dripped with sarcasm.

"We ain't drunk yet, so I know it weren't no hallucination. Maybe it swam up the river and crawled inside. Octopuses and squids can do that, you know."

"No they can't. How 'bout you show me this giant squid? Prove it ain't no shine talking."

They fell silent. The darkness in the outhouse churned faster.

"You chicken?"

"All right, I'll show you I ain't no liar and I ain't no chicken, neither."

Two sets of footsteps crunched along the path to the outhouse. The door was flung open. Skipper and Cletus both stared inside.

"Idjit." Cletus slapped Skipper upside the head, but not very hard. "Let's get back to business. Those valves was leaking. Maybe tightening them will fix it."

"It was there, I tell ya. Tentacles as big as my legs sticking up out of the seat."

"Pull the other one." Cletus turned away.

Skipper followed, protesting and waving his arms as he described the horror he'd encountered. The door banged shut on their argument. Their voices retreated in the direction of the still.

A single tentacle rose above the seat, sliding in a circle as if tasting the wood. The darkness beneath boiled up in a froth of not-light. It spilled over the seat, engulfing the tentacle and the interior of the outhouse. Scrabbling noises came from the hole accompanied by squelching and squooshing. A hairy limb with too many appendages emerged from the inky blackness. Fur bristled then settled into a thick coat over ropy muscles. The rest of the creature emerged from the hole, sliding through as if molded from jelly. Once free, it solidified into a thick torso, four short limbs with stubby toes, and a head heavy with jowls and teeth. Red eyes burned in deep sockets. It fumbled with the door a moment before tearing it off the hinges with clumsy paws.

Rosebud, the hunting hound, let loose a long howl from her hiding spot under the porch. She bolted for the truck and leaped over the side to cower in the back.

The creature drew in a long breath, sniffing deeply of the mountain air. It wuffled once before answering Rosebud's howl. The sound was laced with centuries of despair and loneliness. It was the cry of a soul, lost and tormented, doomed to wander the cold wastes of the netherworld forever. But this soul had found a way to the mortal realm, and a body of semi-flesh. The body jiggled as the creature moved, as if the flesh were not fully solidified.

"What in tarnation was that?" Cletus crept from the back side of the cabin, lantern held high.

"That giant squid, I tell ya." Skipper followed with a shotgun clutched in his hands. He aimed at the outhouse and the shadowy form hunched in front of the still open door.

"Don't shoot, idjit. It's 'Bud." Cletus knocked the shotgun barrel just as Skipper squeezed the trigger. The blast tore through the bushes to one side of the outhouse. The creature dove into the trees on the other side.

"What did you do that for?" Skipper glared at his friend. "That wasn't no dog!"

"It wasn't no giant squid, neither."

"You saying I'm a liar? I saw a giant squid in there!"

They turned to face each other as they continued to shout. Skipper waved the shotgun for emphasis. Rosebud whimpered in the back of the truck. The creature melted into the shadows of the benighted forest.

The not-light swirled once more inside the outhouse. Twists and spirals of mist coalesced into flapping wings, a murderous beak, and glowing yellow eyes overflowing with hatred and evil. A giant bird flapped through the dangling door into the night. Skipper and Cletus were too involved in their argument to notice.

The mist gave a final swirl, flinging a cloud of stinging, biting flies into the mortal realm. The portal beneath the seat sputtered. The tentacles slithered back into the netherworld. The opening gave a final spark of not-light before snapping shut with a loud sucking sound. The sacrifice, after all, had been small and of low quality. The evil bird screeched as the hairy beast let loose another howl. They, at least, were free in the mortal realm. The cloud of flies descended on Skipper with bloodthirsty vigor.

"What in tarnation? Dadgummit!" Skipper smacked flies with reckless abandon. His wayward hand slapped Cletus upside the head.

"Idjit!" Cletus slapped him back. "Put that gun away before you blow your fool head off. Let's go. We need to get new valves for the still or the shine is just gonna run out onto the ground. Unless you want to stand there and fill each bottle by hand all weekend."

"Why ain't these flies biting you?" Skipper's voice slurred as his lips swelled from bites. He bit one unlucky insect in half as he talked. Ink-black smoke puffed from its corpse and swirled out between Skipper's teeth. "Gaw! That was foul. What are these things? Ow!" He smacked another into oblivion as it bit his ear. He also hit himself in the head with the barrel of the shotgun.

Cletus yanked the gun free from Skipper's hand. "Get in the truck. I'll drive." He whistled for the dog. Rosebud stuck her nose barely over the edge of the truck before burrowing back under the piles of old tarps and random junk that covered the bed.

The two men climbed into the cab and slammed their doors. The engine roared to life. Gravel peppered the clearing as Cletus gunned the truck up the hill out of the little hollow. Their bickering voices faded into the distance. Silence fell, punctuated only by the buzzing of the swarm of evil flies.

The monster slunk out of the shadows into the moonlight. Fur bristled along its back. It sniffed the air, then loped after the truck. The bird waited only a moment before flapping after, heavy wings beating the night air.

The flies remained in the clearing, a buzzing nexus of evil holding vigil over the outhouse.

* * *

"It's watching me."

"What?" Skipper turned his head towards his wife. Or where he guessed she would be. The fly bites had swollen grotesquely, pulling his face into a puffed and distorted caricature, and his eyes were bare slits.

Bobbie Lee gestured out the door with the bag of frozen peas in her hand. "That bird. Gives me the shivers. Just sitting in the tree, staring." She plopped the bag of frozen peas on Skipper's face.

"Probably just a crow. They do that sometimes." Skipper settled back in his worn recliner. It creaked, but held.

"Too big for a crow. Maybe a turkey? My da used to tell stories 'bout hunting turkeys with his granpappy."

"If it's a turkey, we should shoot it. Turkeys make good eating."

"Maybe I should." Bobbie Lee crossed her arms as she stared out the window at the bird.

The creature ruffled its wings, raising them slightly so the breeze caught the feathers. Its eyes glinted red even in daylight. It shifted on the branch, which bobbed under its weight. Clawed feet with wicked talons clutched and flexed on the wood. Malevolence hung in an almost palpable cloud around the manifestation of the Elder God's servant. It flicked tail feathers and hissed.

Bobbie Lee flipped it the bird before turning her back. No oversized crow was going to intimidate her. She returned to her dish washing, but kept half an eye on the plants in the vegetable patch beneath the kitchen window. Crows liked to eat her garden. She wasn't going to stand for that. No sirree. Those birds could go eat what grew natural in the hills. Or they'd find themselves on her dinner table, crow or not.

Something thumped on the roof. Claws scrabbled over the shingles. Bobbie Lee paused, dishrag dripping soap bubbles onto the counter. Whatever it was screeched, not a noise a crow usually made. It was more like fingernails scraping across a blackboard, except much louder. Made her skin crawl, that was for certain.

Wings flapped and snapped, heavy and huge. The evil black bird dropped into view right in front of her. It fluttered and glided to an ungainly landing right in her strawberries. She threw the rag into the sink.

"Oh, no you don't," she muttered as she swiped bubbles from her hands.

Skipper kept his shotgun loaded and ready near the back door, just in case. This was a 'just in case' if Bobbie Lee had ever known one. She stomped over to the door. Her hands closed over the worn wooden stock of the gun. Buckshot should take down that oversized crow, or turkey, or whatever it was. She yanked the door open and stepped outside.

Her apron flapped in the breeze, ruffles dancing in the sunlight. The bird twisted its head to stare. Bobbie Lee raised the shotgun as she took two steps forward. The thing hissed, beak gaping unnaturally wide. A long round thing emerged from the bird's throat, green-black scales glistening along its length. It raised a snake head, complete with forked tongue and fangs. The bird hopped towards her. The snake coming out of its mouth swayed side to side, eyes black as sin locked on her face.

Bobbie Lee shivered. The thing was an abomination, that was for sure. What kind of crow or turkey kept a snake in its beak?

One of the bird's clawed feet ripped up her cucumber vine, the one that almost had enough 'cukes for a batch of brined dills.

"Don't you touch my garden," she ordered. She sighted down the muzzle of the shotgun.

The snake head hissed. The bird deliberately raised one foot, claws spreading over her pepper plants. The eyes of both snake and bird watched her, baleful pits of absolute madness. Some part of Bobbie Lee's brain noted that the bird had three eyes in its head, but that didn't matter, not when her peppers were on the line. No one and no thing touched her prize bells.

The claw raked down towards a plump green pepper. Bobbie Lee's finger squeezed the trigger. The gun kicked back into her shoulder. Buckshot sprayed her garden. The snake head exploded. The bird thing squawked as it flopped backwards.

Bobbie Lee advanced on the bird, stepping delicately around her plants. She paused long enough to check the pepper. Buckshot had grazed the topmost bulge but the rest was intact and unblemished.

The creature fled into her corn patch, wings flapping as it ran. Leaves rustled as it barreled through the stalks. The clawed feet tore up chunks of earth in its haste. The dead snake flopped and bounced out the side of its beak.

Bobbie Lee recocked the shotgun, loading the second round. No crow, no matter how bizarre or creepy, was going to destroy her garden. She'd defended it from raccoons, weasels, rabbits, pigeons, deer, and even a bear once. This one wasn't going to succeed either. She followed the trail of squawking destruction through the corn and out the other side.

Trees clustered along the bank of the creek below her garden, wild plum and willow mostly. They made a thicket of narrow branches impossible for anything so large and ungainly to smash through. The bird turned to face her, backed against the hedge.

Bobbie Lee raised the gun and took aim.

The thing fluffed up its feathers, drawing in all the power of the Elder Gods. The mere sight of its gaze should have reduced the mortal woman to screams of panic. The touch of its mind should have invoked insanity. But the power was weak. The sunlight flickering on the water and through the leaves distracted it. And bird thoughts kept intruding on the mind of the servant of the Elder God. The body that should have been immortal dripped blood from numerous wounds. Pain twisted like thorns in its flesh. It pulled in power and released a feeble attempt at controlling the simple mind of the human woman.

The gun barrel lowered slightly. Bobbie Lee watched the bird-thing, sympathy growing in her heart. It was hurt and almost cute. An urge to drop to her knees and snuggle it wandered through her mind.

No. She shook the errant thought from her head. It was butt-ugly and it had ripped up her cucumbers. The gun snapped back up and fired.

Buckshot tore through the creature's face, obliterating the three eyes and the rest of the snake. The feathers flapped raggedly as it staggered backwards. The clawed feet snagged on a root. It tumbled backwards, sprawling in the dirt under a plum tree. Its claws reached up, grasping at nothing. The dark evil that had spawned it shuddered free, dissipating into the glare of the afternoon sunlight. The bird shivered once more before lying still.

Bobbie Lee lowered the shotgun and squinted at the carcass. It wasn't shaped like any bird she'd ever seen before. But it was close enough to a turkey.

"Waste not, want not." She grabbed the feet and hauled the body up. The neck flopped loosely. Blood dripped from the mangled remains of the head. "Definitely a meaty one. This should cook up real nice."

She whistled as she strode back to her house, apron flapping around her, shotgun in one hand, dead embodiment of evil in the other. Black feathers drifted on the breeze, forlorn and lost.

"Momma, there's a stray dog out there." Billy Joe pressed his nose to the screen door.

"You hush. Probably some fool thing your daddy dragged home." Lucie Mae flicked the TV volume up another notch. *Jeopardy!* would be on any moment. She didn't want to miss a single question. "Where is your fool daddy anyway?"

"Took the truck back to Skipper." Billy Joe's voice was mushy, distorted by his lips moving against the screen. "Looks like a hunting dog."

"Cletus won't be home 'til long after sunset then. Stand around jawing all day, if'n I don't smack him into moving." Lucie Mae settled her house dress around her pudgy knees as the opening theme song played on the TV.

Billy Joe watched the black shape in the yard. It moved on four legs. It looked sort of like a dog. Therefore it must be a dog. He wanted a dog more than anything. He'd tried to keep Rosebud, but his daddy made him walk her all the way over the ridge back to Skipper's house. The thing snuffling in the bushes outside had to be a dog, one without an owner. A dog who needed him as much as he needed it.

The gathering twilight, along with Billy Joe's bad eyesight, made it difficult to see the animal. The outline seemed to waver. Was that a long tail, with plenty of fluffy fur, or a whip-thin tail that coiled like a scorpion's? Fluffy, Billy Joe decided.

The beast outside yipped in surprise as its tail suddenly grew a thick coat of fluffy black fur. It whipped its head around to stare. The human inside had power—a simple power, true, but simple belief was the most dangerous kind. Hard to corrupt and hard to twist, simple belief made humans dangerous. The beast swung back towards the door, a growl rumbling low in its throat.

Billy Joe pressed closer to the door. The latch creaked. He glanced over his shoulder, but Lucie Mae just slouched deeper in her chair, attention fixed on the quiz show. She'd never notice if he slipped out. He was, after all, almost eight years old. He even went to school and could read. He knew about dogs. And he wanted one more than he wanted anything. He reached for the latch.

"Billy Joe, don't you go wandering out into the dark. You might get eaten." Lucie Mae's voice snapped him to a stop.

"I see Daddy's truck a-comin'," he lied. "I was just going out to meet him. Help him with chores." The creature—dog, he told himself firmly—the dog's ears pricked up. Big pointed ears, not floppy hound ears. More like a German Shepherd. He'd read about them. Big beautiful dogs with black and tan coats, fluffy tails, and pointed ears. They were loyal and helpful and wondrously good at biting people who made fun of you. Billy Joe would love to have a German Shepherd bite all the kids who taunted him because he couldn't see very well. Wasn't his fault he thought that that flock of pigeons was a spaceship.

The beast yipped again. Its body was changing, reshaping itself into something new. This was not supposed to happen. It had manifested in its usual form, mostly, but the sacrifice had provided very limited power and the portal had closed before it had fully materialized, leaving it still partially fluid. But the human child should not have been able to reshape its form. It shook its head, pointed ears flapping. The fluffy tail wagged behind it.

Billy Joe wriggled the latch on the door. Lucie Mae shouted answers in the form of a question at the TV. Billy Joe snapped the latch up, pushed the screen door wide, and darted out into the evening light.

"Billy Joe, you get back here!" Lucie Mae's voice followed him.

Billy Joe kept going towards the black animal. His momma wouldn't follow him, not for another twenty minutes until her show was over. Plenty of time for him to make friends with the stray dog and claim it as his. She couldn't take it away from him if he'd already made it his friend. And if she tried, well, he'd just have to cry until she gave in.

The black creature crouched, growling, as the boy approached.

Billy Joe smiled. He could see the black and tan coat of a German Shepherd. "Nice dog. You're a good boy, aren't you?" He held out his hand, just like the books said. He squatted down, crouching as he got closer. He waddled like a mutant duck towards the beast. "You want to be my best friend, don't you? We'll have so much fun together. We'll play fetch with sticks and go on long walks and chase rabbits. You'd like that, wouldn't you?"

The beast choked on a growl. He really would like to chase rabbits and fetch sticks. And romp in the fresh air.

The creature shook its head. The boy had power, great power.

"Here, boy. Come here. We'll get you some nice tasty dinner. Maybe a bone you could chew. You can sleep in my room." Billy Joe waddled closer, hand outstretched.

The beast raised a red light in its eyes. Evil oozed from every pore, only to be stopped by the fur coat and wagging tail. He was a dog and the boy was his master and he loved his master. No. It shook its head. The Nameless One was its master. The beast had manifested in this world as a harbinger of chaos and madness that the Elder Gods would bring when they came. Their servant was here to open the gate.

"Who's a good boy?" Billy Joe rubbed the fur over the beast's eyes. "You like that, don't you?"

The beast closed his eyes and thumped his tail. He did like what the boy was doing. His body solidified into the form of a dog. The brain resisted. He was not a dog, not a friend and servant of the human child. He was a servant of the Elder Gods, bringer of destruction. But the scratching behind his ear felt so good. His back foot thumped in time to the scratching.

Footsteps crunched down the gravel drive. "Billy Joe? What you got there?" Cletus called as he approached.

"I found me a dog, Daddy. A German Shepherd." Billy Joe kept scratching.

The beast tried to growl, but it came out a whine. His tail thumped in the dirt. He rolled onto his back, exposing his belly to the boy with the magic hands who knew all the right places to scratch.

Cletus stood over his boy, staring at the dog squirming in the dirt. "Well don't that beat all. What's a German Shepherd dog doing out here?"

"I don't think he has a home. Can I keep him?"

Oh, yes, the beast wanted the boy to keep him. He wanted it so much. His tongue flicked out, licked the boy's arm. Wait, no, this was all wrong.

Billy Joe giggled. "He likes me! Did you see that? He licked me."

Cletus leaned closer, staring at the dog's eyes. The red flickered deep within, then died. Cletus harrumphed deep in his throat. "Something ain't quite right," he muttered.

Billy Joe rubbed the dog's belly. The beast squirmed, unable to contain the joy of being accepted by the boy. His tongue lolled out of his mouth.

"He's a great dog, Daddy. I'll name him Horace. That's a great dog name, isn't it?" Billy Joe's smile spread over his face and spilled over. He turned the full power of it on his father. "I'm sure he's all alone out here. Can I keep him? Please? I'll take care of him real good."

Any objections or lingering doubts in Cletus's mind were destroyed by the sheer force of Billy Joe's happiness. "'Course you can keep him," Cletus found himself saying. "Let's get your momma. Skipper and Bobbie Lee invited us over to eat turkey with them tonight. Caught the bird in their garden today. Biggest turkey I ever saw, but it sure smelled good coming out of the oven." He draped his arm over his son's shoulder.

"Hey, boy, Horace. Come on." Billy Joe whistled, summoning the dog.

The beast rolled over and bounded to his feet. His tail wagged furiously as he trotted behind the humans. He was Horace, the German Shepherd dog. He always was, and always had been, Horace. He had lived for this day when he would meet his master, Billy Joe. And he loved Billy Joe more than anything.

* * *

The flies buzzed in tormented circles over the outhouse. The tiniest thread of darkness still leaked from the portal beneath the seat. The presence of the Nameless One filled the small building, though no physical manifestation protruded.

The time was not yet. Both servants were gone, one to grace the top of a table, the other to lie beneath. The humans were too strong, the servants of the Elder Gods too weak.

A breath of black mist stirred the pages of the ancient book as it lay beside the wooden seat. There would be other pawns, other sacrifices, other chances. Other offerings with perhaps more power. The location was not ideal, but one took what one was given. The presence withdrew to a barely felt chill while the flies buzzed over the seat. It could wait longer. It had waited centuries; what were a few more?

The Elder Gods were nothing if not patient.

THE PEOPLE OF THE OTHER BOOK

Robert Masterson

"The People of the Book" refers to those persons and prophets represented in the three primary texts of the Judaeo-Christian-Muslim tradition: The Old Testament or Jewish Torah, what Christians call The New Testament, and the Koran of Islam. Of course, there are other, even older books which may not mention people at all...

> Pallas, Daniel. *The Necronomicon Cults: A Study in Ecstatic, Organic and Manufactured Religion.* Aziz: Three Lobed Press, 1986. 235. Print.

But the idea that ideas themselves can be dangerous—that true wisdom comes from fervent faith, and that independent thought can lead you down a dangerous path—is an old one, and one that has sometimes led not to bibliophilia but bibliophobia, a fear that reading is perilous, particularly reading certain arcane and occult books.

> *The Journal of Rutgers Library.* "Forbidden Words: Taboo Texts in Popular Literature and Cinema" by Stephen Whitty 2014

I couldn't believe what the old man said. I wanted him to say it again.

"Say't agin," I told him.

"Ah set, 'If yah want you some money so gotdamn bad, go get yah some.' Go dig up some of that money in the basement if yah want money so gotdamn bad, gotdamn it," he snapped. The old man snapped, barked, hollered, and yelled a lot. It was that or he was mute.

"What money? Yah got money. Inna basement?" I couldn't believe it or him.

"Hell, yeah, Ah got money inna basement. Burred inna wall ahind one of them big ol' clown pitchers. Been there fer years."

I just stared at the twisted up old fuck, an old man knot of wasted human life just too furious to do anything other than rage. And drink. And use drugs. My old man was quite a guy in quite a few ways, but money-stasher was a new one on me.

"How much money we talkin' about?" I asked.

"Twelve fuckin' thousan' skins," he answered. "Yah shit."

"Yah got $12,000 buried in the basement? What the fuck fer? Why the fuck yah do a stupid thing like that?"

"So you and yer retard brother couldn't never get yer greedy fuckin' paws on it."

"Why yah telling me now?"

The old man clamped his mouth shut, his face collapsing around his tooth-less hole.

"Ah'm serious, old man. Why yah telling me only just now?"

"Ah got muh reasons."

"Such as…? Ah mean, how long've yah been sittin' on this stash of cash?"

"Long 'nough," the old man answered. "And Ah got me some reasons. That's all yah need to know."

And, yeah, we found the money. Down in the basement in a hole in the wall behind the third picture we tried, the third choice out of all the clown paintings down there and it was right where the old man said it would be. Or, rather, what was left of it—a rotten, rat-shredded, moldy wad of slimy scraps and fiber. If you ever want to know what $12,000 looks like, do not ask me. All I can tell you about is what $12,000 looks like after my wet-brained, drug-addict old man hides it in a wet, dirty hole in our cellar's wall and doesn't tell anybody about it for ten or eleven years. That's not all we found, of course, but finding those sludgy lumps of cash pudding was awfully disap-pointing.

Mixed there among the clots of slimy black money were the bones of a child, the skeletonized remains of a little girl, a little girl around 12 or 13 years old, a little girl named Sharon Lebanon from my last class in my last year of school, a kind of cute girl who wore a TV-star cardigan sweater. There she was, yellow bones and ragged shreds of ragged skull hair and super-white teeth, some scraps of clothing, and that cardigan sweater with the sweater-belt tie.

Tobias stood there for a moment looking at the money-slop and the rest of it; then he just *bolted* upstairs. I mean, he spun around and he was pounding up the steps and the next thing I heard was his heavy boots thumping across the floor above and the meat-sounding smack of his close-fisted blows to the old man.

"Yah stupid, worthless piece a shit," Tobias's voice, though muffled, was clear and the space between each word was filled with the sound of another blow. "Yah… insane piece a… fuck… shit."

Stuff like that. I couldn't hear much of anything from the old man, but that was not in any way unusual. I can't remember the last full sentence I heard him speak aloud before tonight and I'd stopped reading his little notes years ago. They didn't make sense anyway when I did read them. "Cancer dog at the back door," I remember one of them said; "Claws and beaks are all you eat," was another one. They were like fucked-up fortune-cookie fortunes or something, like those notes in those little cookies at that Ho Ho Palace those gooks made up in to town.

There's a story about the old man and a television like there's a story branching off of everything other damn thing that ever happens. The old man was out, had been gone for a week, a not uncommon practice of his. He'd disappear for a day, a couple of days, a week, and once for almost three months. He'd come up home flush with money and bragging about his wise choices, he'd come home with a chain of catfish or a hindquarter of venison bragging about his woodcraft skills, he'd come home tattooed and puffed up on some kind of promotion he'd got because he was such a gotdamned good Book Keeper, he'd come up home busted up and broke and hungover like hell behind his eyes not bragging at all, he'd come up home with a woman or a couple of men bragging that his sons adored him and that what was ours was theirs but to keep their hands of his. The lesson there for young children such as ourselves was that nothing lasts, that everything can be changed or ruined or taken away instantly for any reason or no reason at all. People come and people go. Attachment to people or things or the things people gave us lead to dull heartache, to the kind of disappointment the old man sanctified, a repetitive chipping away at things like "affection" and "security" and "hope." It was a kind of hollow understanding; a resignation to all foul things in the past, and all foul things in the present, and all foul things yet to come. Filth and disease wasn't just a lack of hygiene or antibiotics. It was in The Book. It was the fatalism, the certainty of the nihilism that replaced all hope in The Book and in the supplicant's heart. The father's braggart's ways and the money would both dry up. We'd eat fish and venison until it was gone and then we were on our own. Wounds would heal, the throbbing in his head would ratchet down to normal. The woman or the men would leave cursing him, in a flurry of violence, another loss to add to the losses already given up to The Book. And we, Tobias and me, we'd be right back where we always were no matter what he or we or anybody did.

One time, he came back grunting and puffing up the trace with the weight of a television set balanced on his shoulder. He said it was like radio with pictures, but since it had been a while since we'd had any radio except the radio the old man had jiggered to receive WCOB, "All the Hits From the Golden Age of Country" and that meant Hank Snow and George Jones and Patsy Cline and on and on, and one other station, all static and radio screaming that was also whispers of numbers, endless chains of numbers, or chanting or flute music and chanting, and none of it meant much to us. The old man would hunker over that radio set for hours sometimes and listen to that cryptic broadcast, listening and waiting, waiting and anxious.

I don't think it was our first TV, but it was our last TV. He improvised an old car battery to run the thing and turned it on. After that long warm-up period television sets used to make us endure as vacuum tubes (whatever they were) "warmed up," snow appeared, beautiful, shimmering, electronic snow. He twisted knobs and he angled what he called its "rabbit ears" and the snow kept falling with a cool, blue hiss.

"Gotdamnit to hell," he kept saying. "The man to the store'd said it work up here, that there were nuff TV signals going around to give everone a pitcher."

Tobias and I just watched from the corner of the room, the room for living, the living room, and thought the snow was the point. We didn't know about any pictures. I watched the faces in the TV snow emerge, each face an apparition with a story to tell, even if it just was one long, sustained TV snow-dampened howl of misery, pain, and regret. Other faces intoned TV snow pronouncements, statements, testimony, reports from Hell. The old man fussed and fumed and kicked and hollered, but miraculous, haunted snow was all he got. He fiddled with some of our aluminum foil and TV dinner trays and electrical tape, but he never got a picture. I wonder what we would have seen had he succeeded in pulling in whatever signal he searched.

Then, in his great obstinacy, he dragged his dump-pile Laz-E-Boy recliner directly in front of the TV and sat to watch the snow. And that was the last time I saw him outside the living room and standing up. Sometimes, he'd laugh like the machine was telling funny jokes. Sometimes, he'd lean forward with his elbows on his knees, pushing his face closer to the screen as if the snow people had become important and worth a more fuller attention. He spent the next 5 years in front of that television snow and, when the snow stopped, he spent another 3 listening to the cold hiss of the thing, messages still embedded in the its whispered hissing, and, when the hissing finally stopped, he spent the rest of his pitiful life staring at his own reflection in the curved glass screen, still laughing, still leaning forward, still occasionally calling Tobias or me or both of us in to see what he was seeing, but we didn't want to watch him watch himself in the brown-grey glass pointing at himself saying, "See? Ain't that the funniest thing?" or "See? Can you believe that?" or "See what them fools is doing? That ain't in The Book and, when the stars is right, they's gonna pay for their foolish ways," and we even thought we could never could see or hear the things he said he saw and heard, and we always said we did. We talked about it, Tobias and I, and we saw stuff in the TV, too, but we didn't see what each other saw and we never saw what the old man said he saw. And heard. He didn't even get up to use the outhouse except for shitting. Piss wasn't a good enough reason to leave his Laz-E-Boy, and piss dried up eventually. We had to go out to buy his meth and give it to him, we had to go out and find the cloudy moonshine he loved, but as far as I know, he never left the chair again. We took the plastic jugs of piss to exchange for plastic jugs of the opaque moonshine he drank like milk. Sometimes we would get mixed up as to which jug was supposed to hold what, a little snickering rebellion or revenge.

Tobias stood there for a moment looking at the money-slop and the rest of it, and I guess that included Sharon and I guess he had to look surprised and then he had to look angry, because he just *bolted* upstairs. I mean, he spun around and he was pounding up the steps and the next thing I heard was his heavy boots thumping across the floor above and the meat-sounding smack of his close-fisted blows to the old man.

"You stupid, worthless piece of shit." Tobias's voice, though muffled, was clear and the space between each word was filled with the sound of another blow. "You insane piece of fuck shit." He was repeating himself, but I suppose he thought it worth the emphasis.

It was a lot of stuff like that. I couldn't hear much of anything specifically from the old man, but that was not in any way unusual. I can't remember the last full sentence I heard him speak aloud and I'd stopped reading his little notes years ago. They didn't make sense anyway when I did read them. "Cancer dog at the back door," I remember one of them said; "Claws and beaks are all you eat," was another one. They were like fucked-up fortune-cookie fortunes from the chinky-dink take-out joint they run in town, Ho Ho Palace or something. Like one of those. Maybe I'm repeating myself. Maybe I'm just looking through time and space.

So, I just stood there in the basement leaning on my shovel, listening to my brother beat the crap out of our father, and staring at all that ruined money and the skeletonized remains of one of my childhood classmates from the days I went to school to sit in a classroom feeling like the worst kind of hillbilly I am. Sharon Lebanon disappeared when we were in the 8th grade, her folks moved away a few years later, and she slipped away from my memory. But I instantly recognized her sweater; it was not a particularly noteworthy sweater other than that I remembered it as hers. A cardigan thing with a belt, it had a geometrical pattern in gray and cream colors. I remember she'd been proud of that sweater, she'd seen ones like it worn by Hollywood movie stars in those magazines I suddenly remembered she'd always seemed to carry, how she always seemed to be pouring herself over the pictures, the pictures, the pictures of what she'd known she'd never be. She'd saved up her lunch money for a solid year and ordered it from the Sears Roebuck, and I could see her wearing it while she waited at the bus stop in the morning, steam from her warm breath pluming away from her mouth, could see her wearing it on warm spring mornings when nobody needed a jacket or a sweater, could see her wearing it as she walked the dirt trace to town in the summer, hot and sweaty and just like a picture in a magazine except the sweater was dirty by then and getting ragged in its hems. Obviously synthetic, it hadn't deteriorated much in eleven years. Sharon had, but the sweater hadn't.

Toby came stomping down the stairs from behind me.

"Asshole cocksucker," he announced. "Fucking useless perverted toothless piece a shit."

He was talking about the old man.

"What's he doing?" I asked Tobias.

"Fucking bleeding, man," Tobias answered. "Sitting there in his fucking Laz-E-Boy recliner, crying like a bitch, and bleeding."

"Did he say anything that made sense?" I asked.

"How the fuck should Ah know?" He answered my question with a question and I hate that.

"Did yah know about any of this?" I asked him.

"About the money or about Sharon?" Again with the question for a question.

I gently poked her ribcage under the sweater with the blade of my shovel. "Any of it."

"No," he said with his voice rising like that way people's voices rise up when they're lying.

I poked a little bit more.

"Then why'd yah ask? How'd yah know her name?" I wanted to know.

"Why did Ah ask what?" Tobias asked in that way people ask when they're trying to think up the lie they're going to tell next. Tobias was having trouble answering me straight on. "Know whose name?"

"Ah asked yah if yah knew about any of this," I explained to him. "Then, yah asked me, 'About the money or about Sharon?' If yah didn't know about this, if yah didn't know about her, why'd yah ask me which one?"

"Why'd Ah ask which one what?" This was getting painful. It was going to get even more painful.

"Why'd you ask me which one—Sharon or the money?"

Tobias just stood there, blinking and thinking, while he tried to figure out what to say next. He already knew it was too late and the shovel in my hands was connecting with his nose, splitting it open with a gush of crimson, before he could frame his next stupid question. Toby sat down hard on his ass on the basement floor next to the pile of worthless cash and what was left of Sharon Lebanon.

"Yah fuck," I told him. "Yah fuckin' knew. Didn't yah?"

"Glub?" Toby answered through his already blackening, swelling lump of a nose and the gush of bright blood. "Glub glum glub?"

"Stop answerin' my questions with more questions, you peckerwood asshole," I told him and smacked the top of his head with the flat blade of my shovel. It made a dull ringing sound and vibrated in my hands, kind of like a bell if a bell was a shovel.

"Ooowww," Toby moaned and at least that sounded like a statement. My family had suddenly gotten very big on beating up on each other. Again. Some more.

* * *

I'm the big one, the overgrown and overlarge one. The old man says its my Whateley blood showing, but I have no idea what that means. Tobias is the the little one, kind of goggle-eyed and him with a receding chin like that, it's a shame, really, to be so ugly, but the old man says it's just the Innsmouth Look, that the blood of the Deep Old Ones will always tell the tell, but neither of us, Tobias and me, know what that means. The old man says it's all in The Book, and we just have to take his word for it. It sounded to us like the old man spent a lot more time with Yankees than he'd mentioned outright.

The old man wasn't always a toothless, meth-addicted, alcoholic. There was a time, I remember, when he was just old. He'd swagger off on one of his adventures and come home with a jug and a bunch of fellows from some-place, say maybe the Ku Klux Klan. They'd drink from the jug and holler, shot guns at targets or just up into the trees. They'd build a bonfire at night and try to grill some meats and someone would always have a cooler or two brought up from the town. They were always slapping the old man on the back, urging him to drink, telling him what a right kind of guy he was. And the old man would believe them and he would dovetail their kind of childish, dress-up hatred into the doctrine of The Book, and he would begin to preach. The general drunken, homo-erotic gunplay and grab-ass would die down until all were gathered by the flames of the bonfire, until all anyone was hear-ing was the snapping of the bonfire and the old man, up on some milk crate or beer cooler or some such, preaching the gospels of The Great Old Ones, the ones who wait in the spaces between the worlds, the ones who were here so very long ago and who long for a day precipitous for The Return, that salvation lay in giving up all hope, in abject hopelessness, in the certainty of ash and dust.

That would kill the party—the old man up there in firelight preaching the end of the world in fire and water and tentacles, the Klansmen packing up their Klan shit and driving their Stars & Bars pickup trucks out into the night, an orgy of tail-lights in the darkness for those who watched them leave. Even then, I knew. If you were too crazy for the Klan, you were crazy like nobody's business.

Same thing happened with the American Nazis. And a whole mess of biker gangs whenever a newish club passed through the Gap, he'd be there sling-ing his racial hatred thing gleaned from The Book, that after The Return in furious indifference, the god-things would begin The Clearing. He'd start in on blood this and blood that, and that was usually all it took. Those types, those Klansmen and Nazis and uber-patriotic motor-cyclers, the bass fisher-men and the serial killers, the already damned, the eager to be damned, and the innocent, always took the old man to be talking racism and eugenics and the science of white superiority. They acted shocked and betrayed when they finally understood the old man's philosophies of purity and annihilation. A lot of times, they'd call him a Satanist or a devil-worshiper, and in his own, even patient way, he'd try to explain that all that Iron Maiden, Alister

Crowley, Manson Family crap was crap, that true Satanists were as wrong-headed as Christians in their worship and abjection to just another bunch of fairy tales and boogey men who just didn't exist and neither did their heaven full of fluffy clouds, speed boats, and magic wings, nor their hell of flame and pitchforks and devil-men with horns and pencil mustaches who would some-how punish everyone not like them forever. No, the old man was talking about a judgment, yes all right, The Biggest Judgment of them all, but it was from beings beyond comprehension, beyond their Jesus and their Book of Revelation, entities unto gods themselves who cared nothing for anything ex-cept themselves. If they, the old man's Elder Gods and Ancient Things, even if they did that, cared only for themselves, they did so in a way beyond the human mind to understand. What to us might seem like senseless torture, degradation, anguish, pain, and suffering might to Them be a most trivial but necessary scientific experiment. Or not. We could not, were not equipped, to know such things.

Among the old man's pantheon were those who cared not even for them-selves, for there was also great and humanly inconceivable madness and im-becility among these most high, those nonetheless still omniscient, omniscient and oblivious, oblivious and, if not, malevolent toward mankind in the way mankind was malevolent toward the cockroach and the ant, then completely unconcerned by or, occasionally, delighted by the carnage and the havoc that followed them, the terrible dreams they inspired, the loathsome behav-iors they evoked. In the grand scheme of things, there was no grand scheme, and none of it, none of the delight or the pain, the triumph or the fall, the innocent or the perverted would matter in the least.

The old man preached Cassandra-predictions, Cthulhu got the Pacific, Dagon got the Atlantic, the Black Goat in the Woods with Ten Thousand Young had been bleating since the birth of cruelty, and we were all, all all all of us destined to die die die in their frolic for no good reason and there were nothing anybody could do about it ever. Forever.

The old man preached that Heaven, if it ever even noticed we were alive beneath its awesome arc, that Heaven itself hated us with the kind of hatred people could work up over any number of things, insects and other races be-ing examples, perhaps not equal in human eyes, but anyone who followed him, followed the old man, followed The Book, wouldn't want or need eyes for The Clearing or The Aftermath. We'd, he'd, they'd be screaming with the joy of the skinned-alive, the gratefully tortured for unknown reasons toward unknowable goals.

If someone is too crazy for alcoholic, drug-addicted, leather-wearing, vio-lent, racist, sexist, homophobic, patriotic, America-First outlaw bikers, that person is too damn crazy. The old man actually scared folk like that, scared their women with their unwise clothing choices, scared the babies the women held in their arms to screaming for no reason and placated by no bottle or song or threat of a beating.

Children of all ages screamed and ran from the old man, and he pretended they didn't exist. At best, if forced to, if compelled by some social circumstance to acknowledge the presence of a child, the old man treated it, boy or girl, toddler or teenager, as if it were an imperfect adult, a simple man or a simple woman who did not yet understand enough of the world to understand their own understanding to be a falsehood and a chasm of lies. The old man treated children as he treated everyone with his certainty they were doomed. Too crazy. It's the way he raised us, so I guess we were used to it.

I'm leaning on my shovel only now I'm in the kitchen and maybe that's something The Book does to you over the years. There's this looping that goes with knowing what's in The Book or at least what the old man says in The Book. Nobody got to read The Book but him, but hearing him talk about it or preach about it or watching him work the smudgy science that comes from The Book was enough to scare most everybody from even wanting to want to know The Book or to have The Book know the reader.

But, it's the looping thing, the way my thoughts or actions will seem to have a specific goal or object clearly visible, how that goal or object becomes cloudy, until I will find myself almost precisely at the beginning. That is most disturbing. I'd begin a bedtime meditation on the world behind the world, the places where numbers are, at best, suggestions; where integers and square roots become colors; where all angles curve and where all curves have malicious intent; that place in mathematics where the Hounds hunt, composed of sentient numbers and hungry; but then I'd be back in my bed again, no wiser for having actually seen non-Euclidian geometry, damned, perhaps, to see the world behind the world and not only survive, but retain my sanity. Of course, the question of sanity had to asked and in some way answered, especially after we, Tobias and I, had grown, had lumbered and skittered toward our manhoods, and it was time to put some cards on the table, and the first card we wanted to play was "Are We Crazy?"

"Crazy?" the old man cackled and it didn't help his case. "We's the ones *ain't* crazy. We's the ones know the truth of this world and the next world and The Book. Yah ken see that, cain't ya? With yer own two eyes, cain't yah see that? *Them're* the ones what're blind. *Them're* the ones runnin' from the truth of the world and the truth inna Book. Yah can see that, cain't yah?"

But, some mornings my mail-order underwear would be inside out, and I'd know that when I was sleep-thinking about the world on numbers and angles, when I was sleeping and thinking and seeing how to tear this world apart, someone was messing with my privates—my weird, messed up privates. Was it crazy to consider that fair trade? That insight and knowledge cost molestation and degradation? It fit with the teachings of The Book. What was I to make of all that?

By 9th grade, the schools around here have something called gym and gym is different than Physical Education, often called PE. In PE, which I now understand to be for little kids, we, the children, wore our school clothes and sneakers, if we had them. Since Tobias and I never had them, we wore our regular shoes, but it didn't matter really for each of us was both terrible and hopeless at games and sports. Still, in gym, we were required to wear a gym uniform of jockstrap, gym shorts, t-shirt, white socks, and sneakers. No Substitutions Were Allowed. In that gym class, the boys all had to sit on wooden benches and take off all of their clothes and take showers. That meant that every boy could see how clean or dirty every other boy's underwear might be, what kind of crust had grown in this boy's and that's boy's white briefs gone gray and brown, elastic sprung to nothing, just a rag, really, wrapped around a prepubescent groin to hide the shameful, shaming things grown overlarge and ragged there.

So, it being 9th grade and all, I dropped out of school. Tobias, never one to put off the inevitable no matter if it was a beating or the last drop of lemon-lime soda in a 2-liter plastic bottle, Tobias dropped out of school, too. Technically, him being only a 6th grader and everything, he wasn't allowed, but, considering that I already had made my intentions clear and considering that no one really wanted Tobias cluttering up the public education system for another two to three years, they accepted that we two backwoods brothers were finished with school.

And here I stand with the shovel in my hands in the kitchen of my house and I've looped all the way back to the moment here, and I don't know if a minute has passed or if it has been hours; that is the nature of The Book and the looping thing. I don't feel violated. Yet.

So, every Saturday night and Sunday night at midnight, the old man would drag Tobias and the mother and me down to the basement for services. We didn't get to go to regular church, to tent revival church, to church-sponsored events like summer camps, ski trips to god-knows-wherever-there-was-snow, sock hops, cake-walks, skate night, "Baptism and Basketball," or before or after school prayer groups. Beside sports, religion was the only way to meet girls in our school, town, county, and for all I knew the country. All we had was The Book. There was no point to girlfriends in The Book and no potluck suppers to meet them.

"Them's that gots their ways'll stick to 'em," he told us. "Them's that got diff'ernt ways keeps diff'ernt ways. This here family been blest and curst in ways them's with those ways an't never unerstan' nor care ta. It's we's with our ways and Our Book gotta keep the day unholy in our devotion to them what's been here an' them what's comin' back," he told us.

And, every one of those nights we had to kill something. Something small, like a rabbit or a woodchuck, or something big, like a dog or some neighbor's stolen goat. We had to drink the warm blood, smear the blood on the walls according to his directions and extra-careful not to smear any of those clown paintings all the while he kept mumbling and grumbling stuff he said he was reading from The Book. He made us dance. It was all in The Book. A million billion trillion angry insects would buzz in our ears, what sounded like a million billion trillion angry corpses got inside our heads tearing each other apart, trying to tear us apart, a million billion trillion maggots, each one gone long mad, and the million billion trillion parasites that each maggot carried in its soft body. All insane, all buzzing, all trying to drag us down into their bedlam. That, also, was apparently in The Book.

After the old man's brain got wholly melted from the meth and the moonshine and from The Book, he stopped the cellar services.

"T'aint needed no more," was his excuse. "The Book says we's done with that now."

I think he was just too wasted to care anymore, and if those Star Things and Elder Gods and Night Gaunts he was always talking about gave a shit, they didn't show it to us. The Book said they never really paid us much mind, anyway, and that to them the way we served They That Had Been and They Who Were Coming was just ignorant, that we were to them as inconsequential as the microscopic parasites that rode the worms feasting on the fly-blown corpses they also ignored beneath the cataclysm of their passing. The joy of The Return, according to The Book according to the old man, the only joy for man, any man, every man, on The Day of The Return, was oblivion. Anything less would be beyond imagination, and even The Book wouldn't or couldn't say anything particular about human survivors. We prayed for an exalted, ignoble and ignored, quick death.

So, I just stood there in the basement leaning on my shovel, listening to my brother beat the crap out of our father, and staring at all that ruined money and the skeletonized remains of one of my childhood classmates from the days I went to school to sit in a classroom feeling like the worst kind of hillbilly I am. Sharon Lebanon disappeared when we were in the 8th grade, her folks moved away a few years later, and she slipped away from my memory, but her bones brought a sharp pain to my many-times-broken heart. I instantly recognized her sweater for no other reason than it had been hers. It was a cardigan thing with a belt, I think they called them "Shetland" sweaters like the pony. It had a geometrical pattern. I remember she'd been so proud of that sweater. She'd seen ones like it worn by Hollywood movie stars on TV and in those magazines I sadly remembered she'd always seemed to carry, always seemed to be pouring herself over and into their pictures, the pictures, the pictures of what she'd known she'd never be. I bet her nice room in her nice house was covered with photos she'd clipped from these magazines and taped up like talismans, like portents, like signs of what could be. She'd saved up her lunch money for a solid year and ordered it from the Sears Roebuck, and I could see her wearing it while she waited at the bus stop in the winter's mornings, steam from her warm breath pluming away from her mouth. I could see her wearing it on warm spring mornings when nobody needed a jacket or a sweater, could see her wearing it as she walked barefoot down the dirt trace to town in the summer, hot and sweaty and just like a picture in a magazine. Its Sears synthetic fibers hadn't deteriorated much in eleven years. Sharon had, but the sweater hadn't.

Tobias came stomping down the stairs from behind me.

"Asshole cocksucker," he announced. "Fuckin' useless perverted toothless piece of shit."

He was talking about the old man. It had become a theme.

"What's he doing?" I asked Tobias.

"Fuckin' bleedin', man," Tobias answered. "Sittin' there in his fuckin' Laz-E-Boy recliner, crying like a bitch, and bleedin'."

"Did he say anything?" I asked.

"How'n fuck should Ah know?" He answered my question with a question and I hate that.

"Did yah know about any of this?" I asked him.

"About the money or about Sharon?" Again with the question for a question, and I wasn't liking it any better.

I gently poked her little pelvis under the sweater.

"Any of it?" I was trying to give him a chance to be truthful.

"No," he lied.

I poked around little bit more and adjusted my grip on the shovel handle.

"Then why yah ask? How'd yah know her name?" I wanted to know.

"Why'd Ah ask what?" Tobias was having a lot of trouble answering me straight on. "Know whose name?"

"I asked you if yah knew about any of this," I explained to him. Again. And I looked at the little girl corpse and ruined money as a demonstration. Again. "Yah asked me, about the money or about Sharon?' If yah didn't know about this, if yah didn't know about her, why'd yah ask which one?"

"Why'd Ah ask which-un one what?" These questions were painful to endure.

"Why'd yah ask me which one—Sharon or the money?"

Tobias stood there blinking, blinking and thinking, while he tried to imagine what he'd say next. He knew it was too late but he was trying. The shovel in my hands hit his nose flat, splitting it open before he could frame his next stupid question. Tobias sat down hard on his ass next to the pile of worthless cash and what was left of Sharon Lebanon.

"Yah fuck," I told him. "Yah fuckin' knew, didn't yah?"

"Glub?" Tobias answered through his already blackening, swelling lump of a nose and the gushing bright blood. "Glub glum glub?"

"Stop answerin' my questions with more questions, you peckerwood asshole," I told him and smacked the top of his head with the flat blade of my shovel. It made a dull ringing sound and vibrated in my hands, kind of like a bell if a bell was a shovel.

"Ooowww," Tobias moaned and at least that sounded like a statement. We were making progress.

***

I thought about Sharon Lebanon for a second. A flood of quick memories followed my recognition of her sweater: Sharon on the school bus sitting next to Deb Skinner and talking about boys; watching her dance with another boy at an 8th grade sock-hop about 6 weeks before she disappeared; Sharon in 5th grade crying when she got 2nd place in the science fair because she had worked on her project entirely by herself and the winner, Little Fat Mike Tullman from town had so obviously gotten help from his father, a machinist down to the county Parks & Recreation Department. I remember thinking it wasn't fair. I hadn't gotten any help from the old man, of course, but my project sucked. I can't even remember what it was, maybe some last minute thing with lima beans or food color or something. I couldn't believe Sharon had been in my basement this whole time. And I had almost forgotten about her. I'd almost forgotten her name.

Tobias was curled on his side on the dirt floor.

"Anything else Ah need to know about?" I asked him, ready to kick him if it even sounded like he was going to ask another question.

"Nobe," he straightforwardly answered me. "Nuh-ting else."

I looked down on the little corpse and damned if it didn't appear as if there were tooth marks on the long bones of her little legs. The old man hadn't always been toothless; before the meth fucked up his mouth, he'd had quite a set of choppers.

"Yah sick motherfucker," I told him.

"Imb inna *Book*," he whined.

I kicked him for that. Hard.

I was standing in the kitchen sort of leaning on my shovel. I can't imagine how lonely it would be for someone to not have blood kin, people who aren't just like you but are actually part of you and you are a part of them. As much as I hated every single one of my family, I couldn't imagine my life without them.

We'd talked about blood a lot amongst each other.

"Ain't no gotdamn joke," the old would preach at midnight services. "It's jest true. Blood is thicker'n water and thicker'n mud an' that means they ain't no kind of bindin' or no kind of holy oath that'll put yah closer to no other human in this world or any other world than the blood yah share in yah veins. That's why I married your mother and that's why the blood inside yah boys is holy."

That last part doesn't make a lot of sense, but the first part rang true. Even monsters have mommies. I always wondered where ours, our mother, had gone. We, Tobias and I, talked about blood a lot, but we never talked about mothers. That's kind of weird, I think.

I remember standing there in the hallway and being just a little kid but still having this vision of how we are as a family, how we are like a silver ring or a group of interlocked silver rings and no matter which ring you set to follow

out of the group, you always loop back and find yourself tangled up in someone else's silver ring. That's the family for sure. The reason the rings are silver
is that gold don't tarnish. Says so in The Book. Tarnish is a kind of corruption.
Corruption is what keeps us pure, keeps us welded tight. It said so in The
Book.

Tobias was still moaning. I was sitting in the sick heart of the rancid rat's
nest we called our home and I was just sick of us all, tired and sick and bored
and infuriated and deeply saddened by our lives. There I was surrounded by
illness, decay, and deviance with a pile of rotten cash and the corpse of my
childhood sweetheart down in the basement and I just didn't know what to
do anymore.

"Lem has a girlfriend, Lem has a girlfriend," Tobias chanted while he danced
circles around me.

I lunged at the gadfly, narrowly missing a grab at his winter coat.

"Shut up, you fuckin' li'l brat," I tried to command.

"Lem and Sharon, sitting in a tree, F-U-C-K-I-N-G," Toby sang as he
dodged a punch-kick combination. "First comes love, then comes marriage.
Then comes Lem pushing on a baby—OW!"

Tobias rubbed his thigh where my boot had left the beginnings of a good-
sized welt. I was able, in general, to land only 1 blow in every 6 attempts, so I
tended to make them count when I could. It was the same strategy the old
man used to raise us boys on beatings.

All the way to home, Tobias limped in front of, behind, and alongside me
in a manner both mocking and defiant though he made no further vocaliza-
tion. I scowled, though not at my brother's teasing. In fact, I scowled because
I did not have a girlfriend in general and that Sharon Lebanon was not my
girlfriend specifically. Tobias's teasing reminded me of that fact and, since I
truly wished that Sharon *was* my girlfriend, that the we truly were f-u-c-k-i-n-g,
in love, getting married, pushing baby carriages, and since I knew that something like that was never ever going to happen, Toby's teasing ignited a slow
red fire in my head and in my heart that, once smoldering, would be hard to
dampen. What had started as love was already becoming rage.

"I HATE HER," I roared at my brother as if that would stop the mockery.

We slammed into the house, dumped our coats and tattered schoolbooks
onto the jumbled pile of clothing, hunting gear, odd bits of wooden things,
odd bits of metal things, and trash that piled by the back door, the kitchen
door. Walking into the house was walking into a wall of overheated, moist
air heavy with the odors of butane gas, piss, stale cigarette smoke, rotten
food, old grease, and unwashed bodies. Those smells were just one of the
reasons I would remain without a girlfriend; among many other things, the
way those smells clung to us was off-putting to our peers. We jealously suspected that other households hid secrets just as foul as our own; the usual
backwoods foulness of abuse, madness, and violence. The only difference,

we hoped in our impotent squalor, was that other households merely applied Lysol to the stink with more vigor. And for that, we hated those other house-holds and the children reared in those households for having the luck, if not the blessing, of good hygiene and the USDA food-group pyramid and some-thing to kill 99% of all germs. We could have accepted and lived with the foul secrets, for foul secrets were part of all the life we'd ever known, but good food and clean clothes would have made a difference and to be denied such simple amenities infuriated the both of us.

"Where's the fat bitch?" I asked my brother as he looked inside the barren refrigerator.

"Probably stuffing her fat face," Toby snickered.

"I'd like to know with what first," I said. "An' if it ain't someone's stank pecker, if it was some kind of human-like food, then I'd like some, too."

"Fat chance," Toby laughed. "Get it? 'Fat' chance?"

I reached behind to idly swat at and miss my younger brother.

"I get it, asswipe."

"Got any money?"

"You wish."

"No shit, I wish."

"Well, shit in one hand and wish in the other. Watch which one fills up first."

"Quit trying to talk like the old man. It don't suit you."

"Well, what are we going to do?"

I closed the refrigerator door. My stomach was knotted with hunger and shame, my feet burned in my stinking boots and unwashed socks, my hair hung in greasy, knotted ropes across my crusted eyes. I honestly didn't know how much more of this I could take. Later, I would be just as sadly surprised to look back and see just how much more it had been.

I came wobbling into the room for living, the living room, the room for not watching broken TVs dry and spent and just damn exhausted in ways I'd never been dry or spent or exhausted before, in a way that told me I was done, I was well shet of this life, and I knew. I just knew.

"I'm leavin', Pa," I told the old man. "I'm leavin' here for good."

That roused him and his head twisted away from his imaginary TV pro-grams and his dead eyes searched the room for the sound of me.

"You ain't leavin' nowhere, boy," he screeched to me. "You *cain't* leave. You ain't got it in yah. Ain't no leavin' in The Book."

"The Book," I sneered and his milk-filled eye-sockets locked onto me from the sound of my voice, a sound and a voice not either of us ever heard be-fore. "They ain't no Book. That's just one more a your lies, the line of dirty lies you been stuffin' in our heads afore we was even old enough to know the dif-ference. They ain't no damn Book. There's that book you wave around and holler 'bout, but there ain't no *BOOK*."

The old man's head snapped around as he took to fumbling and groping and clawing under his dirty crotch.

"Ain't no Book, is it? Ain't no Book? Then what'n all holy hell is *this?*"

And he held something up in his hooked hands, a pile of something, a wad of something that looked to be something that looked like it was maybe a book, maybe a dictionary or volume 9 of an encyclopedia nobody read or cookbook or any damned thing had been once been some kind of book afore he took to sittin' on it all day and all night watching his empty TV with his empty eye-holes. Who knew how much piss had dribbled through cotton and denim and corduroy and Laz-E-Boy stuffing over the years and onto that stained leather and wad of dirty paper, how much piss and liquor it had soaked in, had swallowed up to arrive at such a sorry state. If it had once been a Book, a leather-bound and gilt-lettered Book, it wasn't no Book anymore. It was just another ruined thing in a ruined house of ruined folk.

"Ever'things inna Book here," he cackled. "Ever'thing that ever was and ever'thing that'll ever be. It's all inna Book, and you leaving here just ain't in it."

He opened the sodden mass and, since I reckon he'd memorized the foul thing, he run his finger down a sticky page.

"My name is inna Book. Yer ma's name was inna Book. Even yer retard brother's name inna Book. Your name, mister, your name ain't inna Book. Every damn thing we ever done is inna Book, every damn thing. But, not you leaving, nossir. Nossir. You ain't leaving in The Book at all, at all, Not even one per gotdamn cent."

He stabbed at a place there on the ruined page.

"Read it yerself. If you ain't leaving inna Book, it means you cain't do nothin' about it, means you ain't even been outside The Book, and how can you leave a place if you ain't never been no where?"

It almost made sense. I looked over his shoulder quite as you please to see what he was pointing at. My mouth fell open. I still don't know or much care if the old man was crafty or crazy, bluffing or blasting scattershot in his wet-brain, but my mouth fell open like cat's mouth falls open in the cartoon pictures when the cat sees the mouse driving a steam-shovel. The only thing I could read, clearly read, the only thing on every sodden, rat-chewed page, the only word that filled every messy, nasty paper *was* my name. Not the name they'd given me. Not Lemuel Josiphat Beane, not the name I'd used to go to school with, not the name that floated through the air around me like some swarm of busy, biting bugs, but my real name. The name that told me who I was and why The Day of The Return *would* be a joy for someone such as I, how from wind-ravaged peaks I would hold The Book aloft in Welcome as the sand scoured me down to clean bone, bone to be reformed and reborn in ways both pleasing and enraging to Those Who Were Coming.

It wasn't a regular name, neither. It wasn't any Fred or Bill or Lucian or Michael-on-a-Cross. It wasn't even human, but I saw it and I recognized it and I could say it my head as clear as clear could be. Clearer. I could have said it aloud, could have screamed it aloud and blown that house to bits, could have started the mudslide that started the end of the Earth, but I held my voice. I held it like I'd hold one of those nuclear bombs.

I snatched the dirty thing from the old man's dirty claws. He tried to snatch it back, but couldn't I was so fast. He made those wanting, those scared and lonely wanting noises in his throat, but I was way past giving him my attention. I was just staring and reading my own true name like it was spelled out electrical. I put that name in my mouth, and I said it out loud, real soft-like, trying it out. I sounded fine, just fine to me, and it fit my mouth and it fit me like something store-bought.

The old man's whimpering dried up when he heard me whisper my own true name.

I said it again. I said it louder. I prized apart some pages, and I could see my name everywhere in that Book. Every page, loud and bright, my real name.

"What're you doing?" he spoked.

"Imma reading my name to you, old man. Imma telling myself what you never told me. Imma cutting through the lies and the shit and blood you've been spilling, and Imma telling you what's in your gotdamned Book. How you like it? How's it sound now, you gotdamned wretch?"

"Oh, my lord," he whispered.

"Your lord, what you been thinking ain't no lord, no lord got nothing to do with it, got nothing to do with me no more, no how," and I knew that Book just set me free that very minute.

"Nonononono," he scratched out.

"Oh, yes, you miserable liar. Oh, yes, and oh, for sure. Ain't nothing in this Book *but* my name now," I snapped, turned those stuck-together, piss-soaked pages. "This here Book ain't yours at tall. This here's *my* Book, and you've been hiding it from me all these gotdamned years like you was trying to hide that money, like you was trying to hide that poor little gal's little gnawed-on bones. You can't hide nothin'. You can't hide nothin' no more. It's come out now. It's all come out today. And today is the first day of a new day and ain't no day gonna be the same forever now, not the same at all."

"But, it's my Book. It's my Book. My Book," his voice rising to girly-girl highs. "You gonna wreck it; you gonna wreck it all, ain't yah? Yah gonna wreck it?"

"Gotdamn right, I'm gonna wreck it. Seems it me some things need wrecking. It *was* your Book, old man, but it ain't your Book no more. Maybe your name was in this Book once, but it ain't no more. Maybe this here Book was telling you what to do, and you didn't do it. Maybe this here Book was saying to wait for me to find it from you, begging me to take it from you and wring your damn chicken neck. I don't know, and I can't say I care no more. Maybe I took this here Book for me, or maybe this here Book has taken me. Maybe this here Book is taking me more and more, getting in my blood, changing my blood. Can't say I care. This here is the new day, the different day, and this here Book is The Book that's mine, that's been waiting for me to find it, that's been waiting to find me."

And I let my real name roll down my windpipe and fill me with the powers and the knowing and the darkness and the light it all carried with it all together in one piece. It was telling me everything that once happened and everything that was gonna happen if I'd just open up my brain to what it was telling me. I leaned down and whispered; I let a small piece of my name fall into the old man's ear.

"Oh, nonononononono," he whimpered and I laughed. He got to die from just hearing a whisper of a piece of my name. I had to hear the whole thing all the time. It didn't seem fair, so I undeaded the old man.

"nnnnooooooOOOOOO" he continued. I figured I could leave him like that for a while.

I took myself back to the room I'd taken to calling my own,

I went to my room. There had been a day I threw all of Tobias's junk out the window and told him to find another room, a cave, or a ditch to live in because I didn't care where he slept as long as it wasn't in what was from that day on my room. I sat at the junk-pile desk with three legs on the junk-pile chair with missing slats and began to read The Book. It wasn't in any alphabet I'd ever seen in my 9 whole years of public education, but I could read it like I was glassing a 4-point buck from a hundred yards. Clear. Frosty. Exciting. It was like the words and drawings and diagrams and figures and charts were just leaping into my brain and finding the places they fit, the places shaped like them, the places that had waited so long to be filled by those words.

"You got it all wrong, old man," I called to the mewling thing stuck back there in his Laz-E-Boy. "The stars ain't never gonna be right. You got it all wrong. Again."

I could see some sky out my window, and when I looked it was like heaven itself was changing, was rearranging, was shaping itself to be right, to be more than right, to be perfect. And it wasn't the stars I was seeing. The Book was telling me to look between the stars, and it was like looking at the sky with brand-new eyes. I could see. I could see everything. I could see the new, black constellations where there weren't any stars at all. The black spaces between the stars shaped themselves. The Bleeding Sow was one. The Coprophagic was another. The Prolapsed Vagina, The Malformed Sperm, The Flayed Bride, The Malevolent Idiot, The Entrails Speaking, and on and on and on they went until everywhere I looked and everywhere I didn't look was something new, something horrible, something wonderful.

I don't know how much time I spent at that window. It was long enough for the whole world to turn and for new black constellations to appear rising over the raggedy horizon. It was all the schooling I needed or would ever need just filling me up like dirty water, like vomit in reverse, and my eyes kept switching fast-like between the sky and The Book, and together they was my new teachers, and I was their best student ever.

I knew what I had to do. I put The Book in the satchel I'd made for hunting, bloodstained on the inside from all the dead animals I'd trapped or shot and carried home. A couple of shirts, some socks, and I headed into the living room to finish off the old man and all his ways of wrongness. Didn't take much. I just jammed my fist down his undead throat, all the way down his undead throat until his undead corpse couldn't make more than squeak with his pissy legs clobbering the floor like he was trying to dance one last dance. I grabbed onto something down there inside him, and I pulled and pulled until it came out wet and shining, and he was back to being just dead as dead could be. I couldn't help myself, but I smeared that foul glob of old man across my face like war paint and then I knew. I was at war. I was at war with the world as it was and as it would never be again once the battle really started.

I found Tobias back in the kitchen with a package of frozen okra pressed against his face.

"Naw wadda ya wan'?," he garbled.

"Not a gotdamn thing from you, brother," I answered and my steel-toed Red Wings knocked him to the floor. He made some "glub blub" noises when I started stomping on his face, and I just kept stomping until I'd stomped clear through his skull all the way to bloody linoleum, a Red Wing boot print where his face had been.

The Book said only the dead can really kill the dead. Tobias and the old man fit that description, and, after everything they'd put me through over the years, all the use and abuse and lies and plots against me since I was old enough to remember, I guess I didn't mind that they'd be all alone forever together. Forever.

I went down to the basement to retrieve Sharon Lebanon's bones, to stuff them into the game back with the extra clothes because The Book told me I'd need them, Sharon's little bones, and what I was to do with them when I needed to do the thing I'd need to do.

THE DIDDLEY BOW HORROR

Brad R. Torgersen

The little cabin was nestled so far back into the trees that Grover Petersworth could barely make out the light from the two windows built into the log framework on either side of the cabin's front door. Grover's shiny new 1962 business sedan crunched over the gravel as he rolled the car to a gentle stop directly in front of the packed-earth path that led up to the porch. There was a single, use-worn rocking chair resting on the wood slats that formed the porch's floor, but no moving shadows in the windows which might indicate that anyone was home.

It had been a long day of searching, and Grover wondered if he shouldn't turn around and head back into town. But now that he was finally here, an almost irresistible curiosity tugged him forward. Robert Jackson Lee Hill was a rather infamous figure in these parts, for the country folklore that swirled around Hill's youthful adventures. If anyone had ever shaken hands with the devil, it was said, that person was Bobby Jay Hill.

Grover turned off the engine to his sedan and waited, staring at the yellow glow that filtered through the trees. Who knew how long it might take to ask all the questions he'd written down? And there was no telling whether or not Bobby Jay would be in any mood to talk about his past. The country-bred teenagers who'd finally put Grover on the right path, had said that Bobby Jay was notoriously private. He might not like the sight of a stranger from the city walking up to his home. If Grover spotted anything that looked even a little bit like a rifle or a shotgun, he was running for the car.

There. A tiny bit of movement through one of the windows—the barest rustling of what looked like curtains?

Grover pulled a little liquor flask from his jacket—draped across the passenger seat, where it had been resting for the past three hours—and took a swallow. For courage. Then he opened the driver's door, slipped his hat and his jacket on, made sure his notepad was tucked securely in one hand, and began to walk slowly and deliberately toward the house of the man who'd supposedly gone to the land of the living dead and returned to tell the tale.

The porch slats creaked as Grover's black leather loafers touched the wood. He stopped for a moment, waiting to see if there was any additional movement from inside. The glass was filthy, to the point that the windows were translucent instead of transparent. The front door was partially shadowed in the lowering evening light, with only a simple wooden handle where a knob might have been.

Grover stared at the handle and felt his hands grow sweaty. Wiping them quickly on his slacks, he straightened his tie, breathed deeply three times, then rapped politely on the wood.

Nothing. No sound, nor any movement beyond the windows. Grover frowned, and politely rapped a second time. Then a third.

Grover sighed, and determined that he'd just have to retreat and make some additional inquiries. He turned on his heel to step off the porch.

The muzzle of the double-barreled twelve-gauge was a horrible shock. The man holding the weapon was stooped by age, with a face so wrinkled he could have passed for a dried-up apple. Bright, small eyes stared unblinking at Grover, while Grover instinctively put his hands up, palms facing forward.

Two hammers clicked back, and Grover felt the bottom drop out of his stomach.

"Damned bank," the old man with the weapon said, using a mouth that was missing too many teeth. "If I told you fellers once, I told you fellers a thousand times: my *daughter's* got the payment on the loan, and if anyone has a problem with it, they can go talk to *her*."

"No sir," Grover said, hating the tiny crack in his voice. "I'm not from any bank."

"You came from town, didn't'cha?" the old man barked.

"In a roundabout fashion," Grover said, marveling at the inky blackness he could see down the mouths of the two barrels.

"On'y men from town got the nerve to come out here," the old man drawled, "are the kind wantin' money. And in case you ain't noticed, money's somethin' I don't have a lot of these days, you hear?"

"I hear," Grover said, suddenly sensing an opportunity. "Which is germane to my reason for visiting you tonight, Mister... Hill?"

"You callin' me a kraut, son?"

"No, no," Grover said, taking a reflexive step backward, and bumping into the closed door. "I'm sorry. What I mean is, I've got a business proposition for a certain Robert Hill, who's rumored to reside at this location. Would that be you? Or should I head down to the main road and try a little further north? I'm so sorry to intrude at this time of the day. I've driven a long way to talk to Mister Hill, and it's important that I make sure I've got the right home."

The old man still hadn't blinked, nor had the hammers been lowered back into place. For all Grover knew, he was mere seconds from receiving two shells of buckshot between his front teeth.

"What kinda business you got with Bobby Jay?"

"I'd like to interview him."

"Interview? For what?"

"My name is Grover Petersworth, but you might know me better as G.P. Grayson, from the *All-American Weekly*."

The old man's eyes didn't register any recognition.

"I don't suppose the papers circulate this far from town?" Grover asked, again hating the tiny crack in his voice.

"Nope. And if you don't want things gettin' unfortunate, son, you'd best get off my porch and go back to your automobile, and get gone, you understand?"

"Absolutely," Grover said, "and I do apologize again for the intrusion. I imagine a man such as yourself values his solitude. So, if you don't mind lowering that shotgun, I'll be on my way."

The twin barrels slowly but surely dropped, until they were pointed at the porch.

"Git with ye," said the old man, who turned and spat off the porch and into the weeds and grass that grew along the edge.

Grover stepped carefully—but quickly—around the old man, noting the threadbare nature of the old man's bib denim dungarees. Very possibly they were the only ones the old man owned? Grover decided to try one more time to get a bite, and set the hook.

"If you don't mind," Grover said over his shoulder, "please pass the word that I'm very interested in meeting with Mister Hill, and that I'm paying generously for the opportunity—as well as for solid leads on Mister Hill's whereabouts."

"How much is 'generous' to you, son?"

"The *All-American Weekly* is world-class, sir. To get an exclusive interview with Mister Hill, I'm putting five hundred dollars on the barrelhead. More than that, if the interview is truly in-depth."

For the first time, the old man's eyelids fluttered closed, and then opened quickly again.

"That's a lot of money in these parts," the old man said.

"I imagine it is, sir. I imagine it is. Well, I'll see myself off now. Again, so sorry to have bothered you. I'll be staying at the—"

"Cash?" the old man interrupted.

"Beg pardon?" Grover asked.

"Got the cash on ye?"

"I'm from New York City, sir," Grover replied, suddenly realizing that his attempt to entice some answers from the old man might wind up with Grover face down in the gravel while the old man went through Grover's pockets, with the barrels of the shotgun pressing against the back of Grover's skull. "I'm not in the habit of carrying large sums of currency on me. However, I can have a cashier's check cut in town. Assuming I get what I came for."

The old man seemed to consider this information for several seconds, then his thumb, still on the hammers, gradually lowered them back into place on the shotgun's breach.

"Yah best be good on your word, son," he said. "If it's Robert Jackson Lee Hill you came to talk to, you found 'im."

Grover slowly turned around, and raised an eyebrow.

"I don't suppose you have any identification to verify that?"

"You handled yourself better than some other men who've had my shotgun pointed at their melons," Hill rasped, "but don't get cute. You got any way of proving you're who you say *you* are? I ain't never heard of no *All-American Weekly* and I ain't never read nothin' by no Gee-Pee Graystone, or whatever you said you was. Seems to me we got a fundamental question of trust that needs answerin' first. Since this is *my* land, I figure I got every right to shoot you dead, no questions asked. I already *done* you a favor, then, not pullin' the trigger. You gonna look a gift horse in the mouth?"

"Of course not," Grover said. "I apologize again, if I've further offended you, Mister Hill. Being from New York City, one learns to not be too credulous."

"What'n hell's that mean?"

"It means I'm nobody's fool, Mister Hill."

"That makes two of us, son."

"Good. Then I hope you won't mind me asking you some questions about the Diddley Bow Horror of '23?"

Now it was Hill's turn to reflexively back up, until he bumped into the front door.

"How in hell d'yah know about that, boy?"

"I'm the curious type, sir. Occupational necessity, you might say. Judging by your reaction, I think I've found just the man I came to see. Now—"

Grover took out his wallet and fished for a crisp, new fifty-dollar bill he'd reserved for just this occasion.

"—how about I make a small down payment, just to reassure you?"

Hill eyed the bill, which was now visible in the dusk only because of the yellow light coming out of the filthy windows.

"Ye can come inside," the old man said, turning and opening the door—which had not been locked, nor did it appear to have anything in the way of a fastener. "But I got to warn you first. If it's the Diddley Bow Horror you want to hear about, this is one story that's gonna stay inside your head long after you don't want it to. Trust me, boy. I've been living with it for forty god-forsaken years."

Grover had heard and seen a lot of disturbing things in his time—enough to be sure there wasn't much that could spook him. But the expression on Hill's face made chills run up and down the back of Grover's neck.

"We was just kids then," Bobby Jay said, his shotgun replaced in its customary spot over the fireplace mantle, and two oil lanterns burning at either end of the small, battered table that was positioned in front of the cold hearth.

"Fresh back from the war?" Grover asked, sitting across the table from his subject. The old man hadn't offered anything—no water, nor whiskey. He'd just taken and pocketed the money, then demanded that they get to work. This wasn't a courtesy call.

"The Big One," Bobby Jay said, nodding his head vigorously. "You might say I was a little more idealistic in those days. When news came that General Pershing was going to France, all us folk who grew up hearing about our grandpas who fought for General Johnston, or Stewart, or Longstreet, we couldn't wait to enlist—get our piece of history. Well, some of us got a little more 'history' than we bargained for, if you know what I mean, son? Left our bones in those trenches. Anyway, you shoot and get shot at, that changes ye. I came home and found I had a hard time talkin' to fellers who'd not seen what I'd seen. And some of my friends who'd gone over, they didn't like talkin' 'bout the war at all. Used to make me mad. Then I ran across Blind Izzy Brown."

"Who's that?" Grover asked, scribbling shorthand on the pages of his note-pad with one of the many already-sharpened pencils he'd stuffed into one of the inner pockets of his jacket.

"You knew about the Diddley Bow Horror, son, so how'n hell you never heard of Blind Izzy?"

"Would that be the same person as Isaiah Crawford Brown Washington?"

"That's him," Bobby Jay said, nodding. "He never did like going by that last name, since his daddy used to whup Izzy's ass until Izzy bled, so when he enlisted for The Great War, he used his mama's name. Anyway, Blind Izzy used to sit on a crate out front of the Flying Crow grocery, in town. You know it?"

"No," Grover admitted.

"Probably ain't there no more," Bobby Jay said. "Anyway, it was tough for us who came back from the war. There wasn't no work! Didn't matter if you was white or negro, them uniforms they gave us didn't count for spit. So we got on however we could, wherever we could, and even though Izzy lost his eyes in battle, the fact he could sing and play a tune made all the difference. Owner of the Flying Crow used to pay Izzy a lunch, plus some nickels, to sit out in front of that store and regale passersby. Mostly other negroes, you understand. They was in their own part of town. But working for the shipping company, I went everywhere the man needed me to go. And one day I'm off-loading freight from the back of the truck—out behind the Flying Crow—and I hear this sorrowful call to heaven, askin' for the Lord's mercy. I'd never heard such beautiful tragedy before. Izzy could make that cigar-box diddley bow of his play the perfect tune, to go with the words, and when he started singin' about how the war had changed him forever, I knew I had to go have a look."

"But I don't understand—how this ties into what happened in 1923?" Grover asked, impatient in spite of himself.

"You wanna hear the story I got to tell or not, boy?" Bobby Jay snapped.

"Sorry, yes, I do. But I want to be able to make the connection, for the readers. Isaiah Washington's whereabouts are unknown to this day. Some-how, he's tied into the events of October 19, 1923, but I don't know how or why."

"Keep your lip zipped, son, and you might find out."

"Of course. Please continue."

"Okay then, like I was saying, I'm off-loading freight, and I hear Izzy sing-ing and playing, and I figure this has got to be a man who saw the war the way I saw the war, so even though it meant getting bad looks from the truck driver, not to mention some of the negroes out in front, I went around and stood in front of Izzy's crate, and I just listened to him go. He had a dough-boy's metal cup sitting on the ground in front of his crate, and when I dropped in a nickel of my own—more'n a few nickels in that cup that day, mind you—he stopped playing, and his face pointed right at me, and he said he'd been waitin' for me."

"Waiting for you?" Grover asked. "Did you meet each other overseas at some point?"

"Nope. Negro troops was separated from us white doughboys back then. This was before General Eisenhower put us all together, after the last world war."

"Then I don't understand why he'd say what he said."

Bobby Jay laughed—a hard, bitter sound.

"You and me both, son! I told him he must have confused me for someone else—him being blind and all, and me not saying a word until then—but he called me by my full name, and he told me he'd been waiting since early morning for me to show up and drop my nickel in his cup. When I asked him how he could possibly know my name, he just aimed those dark glasses of his to the sky and said, 'The Lord provideth.' Izzy was always fond of saying that. Anyway, he had my attention by that time, so we got to talkin' 'bout where he'd been in France, and where I'd been, and the shootin' we'd done and which had been done to us—bullet from a Mauser caught Izzy on one side of the head, went through both eye sockets, and out the other side—and pretty soon I forgot all about my boss waiting for me in the truck. When the storekeep came out to tell me the driver was shouting my name, I dropped another nickel in Izzy's cup, and dashed back to work, before I gave the boss an excuse to pink-slip me."

"But that wasn't the last time you saw Isaiah Washington, was it?" Grover asked.

"Nope. The Flying Crow became a weekly stop for my truck, and every time we rolled in, I always took a few minutes to go out front and listen to Izzy play and sing. We'd talk a bit too. Eventually everyone who'd stared at us got used to seeing this dirty white boy in coveralls talking to a blind negro boy—both of us carrying on about the war—and it was alright. Even the boss driving the truck stopped minding, and he'd time our drop so that I could take a few minutes to sit and eat lunch with my new friend."

Grover's shorthand pencil strokes increased their pace, as he recorded de-tails to paper. Bobby Jay's tale was topical—so far—because of what was presently going on with Dr. King, who'd so recently marched on Washington D.C., and his evocative speech. The story of two First World War veterans—

separated by so much, four decades earlier, yet finding common ground—might run as a feel-good piece in the *All-American's* editorial section. But that would only occupy a few paragraphs, and couldn't justify the time and expense Grover had already taken tracking down Bobby Jay. What Grover wanted were specific details dealing with the emptying of an entire graveyard—supposedly through dark powers which had only been hinted at in the dispatch which had landed on Grover's desk one week earlier.

He still didn't know who'd sent the dispatch. But he'd made his name fleshing out unusual and extraordinary goings-on—putting fact to fiction—and people tended to send him leads all the time. When one seemed interesting or unusual enough, he investigated further. So he'd left the city, for a trip down South. Grover's plan was to eventually wind up in Cocoa Beach, where he could devote some time to covering the space shots going up from the Cape—the new two-man Gemini launches would begin soon. He could sell words on the space program to the *All-American* for top dollar, and get plenty of mileage out of interviewing the astronauts.

But first, there was Bobby Jay's slowly unraveling story.

"When did Isaiah Washington first tell you about the cave?" Grover asked, hoping to move things along.

"That came a few months later," Bobby Jay said, his mouth turning down in a distinct frown.

"How did it come up?" Grover asked.

"It was the oddest thing," Bobby Jay said. "I didn't figure Izzy for voodoo. This is South Carolina, after all. Not New Orleans. But one day my truck shows up, and Izzy's all bothered. Not playing his diddley bow. Not even singing. Just sitting out in front of the Flying Crow, his chin on his chest, talking about how the Lord's called him to go fight evil. When I asked him what that could possibly mean—him being blinder than blind—he pointed his face to the sky again and talked about how the Lord had been talking to him ever since he'd woken up on the hospital ship, headed back from Europe. Not being the superstitious type, I'd always shied away from getting too involved with Izzy's spiritual side. I mean, I appreciate a God-fearing man like any decent Christian ought to, but with Izzy, he had a special intensity. Seemed convinced that everything happened for a reason. God's secret plan, or something along those lines. Anyway, Izzy said he'd been shown a vision, about how the end of the world was near. About how the forces of Satan were mobilizing, and it was up to God's chosen faithful to stand in Satan's way. There was an old enemy coming forth, and Izzy had been shown where and when, and it was up to him to do something about it."

Grover's pencil was practically skating over the page now. This was more like it. The kind of lurid stuff he'd been hoping for. Not that he believed any of it, of course. But these were the kind of details that hooked readers. A small smile perked up the corners of his mouth, as he continued the interview.

"Not much a blind vet can do against any kind of evil," Grover commented. "What precisely did Isaiah think God wanted him to do?"

"He didn't know. That was the thing. He didn't know! But he was convinced of it. And nobody he told about any of it, would listen. He was in despair. That's when he grabbed me by the arm and made me promise to help him. Had it been any other man, I would have said no. But by that point… Izzy and I had an understanding. We were from different sides of the tracks, but the war kind of put us together—in our minds, at least. So I promised him I'd help, though I didn't know what'n hell that would mean over time. I asked him to describe this place he'd supposedly seen, and he gave such good detail, I knew right where he was talking about."

"The cave?" Grover guessed.

"Yup. Little cave, up in the hills. Nothing so great as Linville, in North Carolina. But a landmark just the same. When I was a teenager, we used to call it the Dead Man's Cave, because there's always been talk about how some Confederate troops holed up in there, fearing General Sherman's march on the South, and never came out again. We used to go in there and scare each other with spook stories, about how we might find the skeletons. But it was a lot of silly horse shit. At least until Izzy described the place so exactly, without ever having been there, that I began to wonder if the silly stories weren't true."

"So what did you do?" Grover asked.

"I made arrangements to take Izzy there, at the time and date he said we needed to be there. Damned tricky, that. Me and Izzy chatting out front of the store was one thing. Me and Izzy wandering around in the countryside, at a place where only white folk ever go? I had a revolver tucked into my coat pocket, that night—just in case. Didn't want any friendly citizens getting any ideas, if you know what I mean?"

Grover nodded. He may have been a Yankee, but he understood the old man's drift perfectly well.

"Was it just the two of you?" Grover asked.

"Yup. Just two damned fools, going for a little hike, in the middle of the night. It was a clear evenin', with a full moon. Almost didn't need the oil lamp. Izzy's feet seemed like they knew the trail, all the way to the cave mouth. I was stumblin' and kickin' into roots all the way, but Izzy stepped over that damned stuff like he was walking on a cloud. He barely said a word to me, the whole way. Just kept his hands on a rope I had tied to my waist, and which was also tied to his. I half-expected to drag him, but again, it was like he knew the way, without having to be told. It was just him, me, and that diddley bow of his."

"I'm almost ashamed to admit it, this late in the tale," said Grover, "but I'm not even sure I know what a 'diddley bow' is, Mister Hill."

"Damned New Yorker, ain't seen nothin' ever," muttered the old man.

Grover let the insult pass and waited for an explanation.

"Hell, son," Bobby Jay said, "it's nothin' more'n a cigar box with a broom stick jammed through it, and you take the wire from the broom's bristles and string it up tight from end to end, like a gee-tar."

"One string only?" Grover asked. "Seems like you couldn't do much with that."

"You never heard Blind Izzy," Bobby Jay said. "Man could make sounds come out of that instrument like you ain't never heard. A virtue... virt... Hell, son, help me here, what's the damned word for someone so good at playin', he's like the best in the world?"

"Virtuoso," Grover said.

Bobby Jay snapped his fingers, and actually smiled for the first time that night.

"That's the word! Blind Izzy was the virtuoso of the diddley bow. He had the neck from a glass bottle, that he'd broken off and worn smooth on the sharp end, and he'd run that bottle neck up and down the wire, twisting the little nut at the top of the broom stick to get the tension right, and make any note he wanted to come out of it. Plus he'd put this little warble in there— just a bit of play on the wire, wigglin' his hand just so. Man could play and sing forever, and make it so you were either smilin' and slappin' your knee to the tune, or you had tears coming down your face, because he brought the hurt out—and made it be beautiful."

"So he was good," Grover said.

"The best," Bobby Jay said.

"And he took the instrument along for... sentimental value? Comfort?"

"Nope. He said the Lord commanded him to bring it to the cave. He didn't know why. And at that point, I didn't ask. I figured we'd just spend a cold night at the cave mouth, waiting for whatever it was Izzy thought was going to happen, and when it *didn't* happen... we'd laugh it off, I'd get him back home, and that would be the end of it. That's what friends do for each other. You know? Let each other be crazy a little bit, until sanity sets in, then have a drink over it."

"So what happened? I know the police eventually asked you about Isaiah Washington's whereabouts. Though it doesn't seem like anything came of it."

"You saying it was *my* fault?" the old man hissed, suddenly rising halfway out of his seat. "You saying Izzy not coming back, is because of *me*?"

"No, Mister Hill, I don't want to imply anything at all. But I did some asking around town, before I came out here. I never ran across a store called the Flying Crow, but there are people who remember you—from the old days. Some people think you're responsible for Isaiah Washington's disappearance. I suppose that's another reason I'm here tonight. I'm giving you a chance to tell *your* side, since so many other people seem to have their minds made up."

Bobby Jay slowly sat back down, the expression on his shriveled-apple face growing even more bitter than it had been when he'd been behind the barrels of his shotgun.

"That's the problem with people," Bobby Jay said, diverting his eyes to one of the lamps, where he stared at the gentle oil flame.

"What's that, Mister Hill?"

"They can have all of the facts right in front of them, but if they want to decide something different—about you, about how it all goes, or how it all went—they'll go ahead and make up their minds. And there's not a damned thing you can do about it."

"Then help me understand, Mister Hill. The locals say you've lived out here, alone, almost since the day Isaiah Washington went missing. Doing odd jobs. Picking up work as you were able, but avoiding people for the most part."

"I know what they goddamned say," Bobby Jay muttered.

Grover waited.

"But I ain't goddamned crazy," Bobby Jay finished, after a lengthy pause.

"Then what *happened* at that cave?" Grover asked emphatically.

There was another lengthy pause, as the old man drew in a long, deep breath, then let it out slowly.

"Like I said, son, I ain't crazy. But what you hear next? It's gonna sound mad. And I don't mean angry-mad. I mean mad, like *madness*-mad. I said it before I let you in here: this is gonna knock around in your head long after you don't want it to. I reckon you've got enough to write up something for your magazine now, so you could leave, and not take anything with you that you don't want to take. So I'll ask, to be sure: You really wanna know the truth?"

Grover stopped writing. The old man's eyes had taken on an especially haunted quality, as the dim light from the oil lanterns wavered in the reflection of his pupils. There was memory there. Old, jagged memory. The kind of thing that hung around inside a person, occasionally cutting new wounds. For a moment, Grover considered ending the interview—simply to spare the old man a trip to a particularly painful moment in his life.

But... no. Grover was an investigator. He didn't flinch from the hard things which needed to be shown to the world.

"Tell me it all," he said, fishing a fresh pencil out of his coat pocket and poising it over a new page in his notebook.

"The bad shit started when the moon went down," Bobby Jay said.

"What kind of bad... stuff?" Grover asked.

"We sat there for three hours. Doin' nothin'. It got cold. I scraped together a little fire, but there was too much smoke and not enough heat, because the underbrush was all wet. You ever feel it when the air is so thick with water, you expect the fish will start swimming out of the rivers? That's the kind of night we had. So I poked at the fire and Izzy just sat there, with his black glasses off. Only time I ever remember the man taking his black glasses off."

Bobby Jay shuddered involuntarily.

"Was he disfigured that badly?" Grover asked.

"Man had a channel carved through his *face*. No eyes, no eye sockets, just a deep... gouge, straight from one side of his skull, through to the other side

—where his eyes *shoulda* been. I kept starin' at him, and was thankful for the fact that he couldn't see me starin'. Or… maybe he could."

"What does that mean?"

"I swear to God, son, it felt like Izzy could sense the whole place. He kept turnin' his head back and forth, back and forth, like one of those radars from the last war. I kept askin' him what it was, and Izzy wouldn't say nothin' to me. Just kept muttering about how God had told him to be there—at the cave. Then he'd stop, and bow his head to his folded hands, and whisper these little prayers. I couldn't rightly say what he was askin' the Lord for, but when the moon finally dipped out of sight, that's when I started prayin' too. 'Cause you ain't never seen nothin' like what I seen come up out of that cave."

"What?" Grover asked, his pencil's tip almost snapping on the pad.

"They was like… they wasn't men, and yet, they was men. Just… changed. Like you take a fish, and a snake, and a snail, and a man, and you mix them all together the way God mixed one o' them funny duck-billed beaver animals, but there weren't nothin' cuddly about any of the things that came up out of the cave. In twos and threes, they staggered up. Like they was bein' yanked on the end of an invisible chain. They had mouths like trash fish, opening and closing and opening again, and some of them walked on more than two legs, and most of them had arms that rippled and slithered like eels. They was hard to look at, because everything about them was just plain *wrong*. You ever see anything that just strikes the center of you as being completely unnatural, son?"

Grover didn't move. He wasn't sure he had an answer for that question.

"So they were alive?" he asked.

"To this day, I don't rightly know," the old man replied, in a voice so low and hushed, he was almost whispering.

"They came for us," he said, his hands clenched in his lap, "so I screamed, and I tried to run—but Izzy had his fist clamped like iron around my wrist. He wouldn't stand up, and he wouldn't let go. Just sat there, with his glasses off, his mouth scowlin' like he knew what was comin' up on us, and how horrible they were, but he wasn't about to leave. God still had a plan for him, and that plan included me. And as those things came into the light of our little fire, I prepared myself for something awful to happen. I didn't know what, but those things were so evil—you could *feel* the air turn cold as they got closer—I was sure in my heart that I wouldn't live through the night."

Grover had said it in the beginning: he was not a credulous man. And what he was hearing now definitely stretched the boundaries of believability to the breaking point. But there was nothing about Bobby Jay that seemed out of sorts. The man actually seemed more clear-eyed and composed than he had at any point since Grover had stared down the barrels of that shotgun. The old man absolutely believed what he was saying, and the conviction in the old man's voice was almost overwhelmingly compelling.

Grover forced himself to keep writing.

"You obviously did live," Grover said. "Did the things attack? Or did you ward them off? What happened next?"

"There were a hundred, at least. Probably more. Pale as corpses. And the smell... more rotten than a dead steer that's been left in the sun for a week. When that stench hit me, I hate to say it, son, but that's when I lost my supper. I doubled over on hands and knees and coughed up every last drop that was in my stomach. Somehow, Izzy wasn't bothered by it—though I can't say why. I'm told a blind man's sense of smell is better than a normal man's, and Izzy didn't flinch once. He just kept his hand wrapped around my arm."

"So what happened, since he's—"

"Shut up, boy, and let me finish. We was surrounded. There was no way out. And the fire was dying. I was certain once the last lick of flame left us, those things were going to move in. I started blowing on the coals, and tossing on wet leaves. But the things... they just went right on past us. As if Izzy didn't exist. And as if I didn't exist, so long as Izzy had hold of me. I watched them go for many minutes, all of them coming up out of the cave and spreading into the blackness of the night. Until something else came up out of that cave, too. And this most definitely was a man. Though I'm pretty sure he'd been dead a long time. What little was left of his uniform hung on his black bones like the tatters of a flag, and he had a rusted Confederate officer's saber in one of his bony hands. The orbs in his bony sockets were like red marbles, and they gave off their own light—hot coals. He felt even more *wrong* than any of the fish-things before him, and when his skeleton's face turned our way, I was sure I was looking at one of the devil's lieutenants, come straight from Hell."

"What did you do? What did Isaiah do??"

"We sat in stone-cold silence, watching this black-boned hellspawn walk past us, the leather on his boots flaking off and falling to the earth. Then Izzy was yanking me to my feet, and this time it was him leading me by the rope around our waists. I don't know how he could see in the dark, but he told me we had to follow the things, and especially follow their leader. Something still hadn't happened yet, and Izzy had to be there when it did, or all Hell was literally going to come loose on us. So I just stumbled along, keeping my feet as best as I could, scared plumb out of my gourd. We went like that for who knows how long, until suddenly we hit the edge of the old war cemetery —that's about two miles from the cave, and a mile outside town. With the moon down, it was still pitch black, but when we got to the cemetery, it was like the air itself started shinin' with its own light. A strange, cold light. The things were linin' up along either side of the graves, and they was makin' a terrible moanin' sound—with that black-skeleton feller standin' at the head of them all, his saber raised high. Like he was callin' the troops to order, or somethin'. And then, up out of the earth, the dead actually came! Men who hadn't walked the land in sixty years, rose up—as if the Lord Himself had commanded it. But it was plain obvious to even Blind Izzy that none o' this had anything to do with the Lord."

Grover waited, as the old man bowed his chin to his chest, and seemed to be catching his breath.

"What did Isaiah do?" Grover asked quietly.

"Izzy swung that damned diddley bow around on its rope, until it was on his stomach, and he started playing."

"He *played* the instrument?"

"And sang! Like he was back on his crate in front of the flying crow. Those things stood there, with fish-mouths going *yawp-yawp-yawp*, and the dead were coming up out of the land by the hundreds, and when Izzy began his tune, they all froze in place. And before long, they was swayin' back and forth, almost like you see them snake charmers make the cobras do, in the movies. Back, and forth, back, and forth."

Grover continued to experience a disconnect—between what he was being told, and what he could see in the old man's eyes. Grover had known liars before. In some cases, fantastic, world-class liars. The kind of people who spun fantastic webs of falsehood, for fun, and for profit. But he detected not a single hint of deception in Bobby Jay's words. The man believed absolutely every syllable that he was saying. And Grover had no choice other than to believe with him.

It seemed like the oil in the lamps was waning. Not much, but enough so that the light was beginning to soften, and the shadows around the cabin— single room, from what Grover could tell—began to deepen.

"Well," the old man said, "that black-skeletoned officer didn't take too kindly to Izzy putting a song-spell on the officer's hellspawn army, so he came for us. And when he raised up that saber to strike, I pulled out my pistol and started shooting. Six shots, three of them to the head. The black skeleton went down, but he didn't stop coming. I yanked on the rope to try to get Izzy to run with me, but discovered that Izzy had untied the damned rope, and was actually beginning to walk back the way we'd come!"

"You mean, toward the cave?"

"Yes! And he was singin' so loud, he was almost hollerin', and he was playin' that diddley bow the whole time, rubbing the glass bottle neck up and down, gettin' the strongest sound he could get out of that old cigar box. And the fish-things, with the dead, they *followed* Izzy. And no matter what that black-skeletoned officer did, he couldn't make them turn away. While he was tryin' to get back up, I dumped out my revolver and put in fresh shells, and went to work on him again. *Pop, pop, pop, pop, pop, pop.* I blew out one of his hips, so he wound up dragging himself along, using the saber as a crutch. And when it snapped, he went along on hands and knees, his bones making the most awful sound as they knocked and rattled together. It was like he didn't care about me. He only cared about Izzy's playin' and how the rest were followin' Izzy back to the cave."

"What happened then?"

"I shouted for Izzy. I asked him what'n hell he thought he was going to do, with that horrible host behind him. He shouted that he was going to lead them back to where they should be in the first place—under the ground. Hopefully, to rest for good. I shouted that he was crazy, and that he'd get himself killed, or worse. That's when he said the last words he ever said to me: 'The Lord provideth.' And then he and that host of undead things were moving too quickly for me to keep up. I tried to run, but I wound up putting my head straight into a tree branch, just outside the cemetery border. Next thing I knew, I was rolling over onto my knees, and there was dried blood down my face, and the light of the morning was coming up."

"Did you go back to the cave?"

"I tried to walk a few paces, and fell flat on my ass. Concussion, the nurse told me later. Of course, by that point, I was too exhausted to do much more than crawl back toward town, where the sheriff picked me up."

Bobby Jay stared down at his arms, which he'd folded tightly over his chest.

"And you never saw Isaiah again?" Grover asked gently.

"Nobody ever saw Izzy again. Not his family, not his friends, not none of us, you understand? I told the sheriff everything, of course. Knowing I'd sound like a damned fool. But what else could I do?"

"Surely there was *some* proof left behind. What about this… this skeleton officer you talked about?"

"When I took the sheriff back to the old war cemetery, we found the graves empty alright, and the broken saber. But no bones. Not even footsteps in the dirt. All those terrible undead things, shambling along, and not a single one of them left a print! There was just me and Izzy and the marks our boots had left. And me sitting in the sheriff's office for a whole day, trying to convince them not to lock me up, and not to put me in an asylum either. Since there weren't no body to be found, they couldn't rightly charge me with anything. They did take my pistol though, as evidence. Never got that back. It's still locked up in the county courthouse, I imagine."

"There was a trial?"

"Of sorts," Bobby Jay said. "Judge threw the book at me. For the unlawful disturbing of the war cemetery."

"Didn't they wonder what actually happened to the *bodies?* Didn't anyone ever go to investigate the cave?"

"I've been in that cave myself, since," Bobby Jay admitted. "More'n once. Just long enough to convince myself that however far Izzy went—leading those fish-things, and the dead who'd risen to walk beside them—he went deeper than I had the courage to explore. Izzy's probably still down there with them. And his diddley bow too. I sure hope to hell he was right. That the Lord did, in fact, provide. Taken up, like they say happened to righteous people in the Bible. Before it was too late. Anyhow, I always wondered what would have happened if the hellspawn had reached town."

* * *

The car ride was a silent one. Grover's wrist watch said that it was past three in the morning. If the moon had been out before, it was gone now. Only Grover's headlights showed him the road ahead. And every once in awhile, he thought he saw something lurking just at the road's shoulder. Which was nonsense, of course. Barring a few deer that might leap across his path, there wasn't anything to menace him on the highway. Nevertheless, Grover couldn't shake the sense that Robert Jackson Lee Hill's story wasn't yet entirely over. That somewhere, out there, Isaiah Washington's diddley bow was still playing. And that if it ever stopped playing... the creatures that inhabited that world—between the living and the dead—would stir again.

AT THE HIGHWAYS OF MADNESS

David J. West

That is not dead which can eternally drive
And with strange eons even death may not arrive

1. Midnight Rider

It was just past midnight when our—well he ain't exactly a hero, a man called The Squid—pulled off the highway in Wendover to get himself some coffee and diesel. His big black Mack truck rumbled into the Flying K with all the subtlety that a pair of brass knuckles has for a glass jaw. The anthropomorphic chrome octopus hood ornament on his truck held a deck of cards in one hand and a mud flap girl in the other. It's an awful strange ornament, but then The Squid is one strange dude, and the ornament was probably how he got his handle 'cause he sure wasn't in the Navy, leastways that I know of. Despite his being a long-haired weirdo outta Shakey City—that's Los Angeles for those of you that don't speak Trucker—The Squid's a pretty congenial fellow. He's forty-something and dresses for comfort in shorts and rock-&-roll T-shirts along with a favorite cardigan sweater from his longtime girl, Jeanie. The Squid's a generous tipper, he picks up hitchhikers and ain't afeared to give anyone that Nazareth or Deep Purple T-shirt off his back. Quick with a joke or a song, he's the kind of guy that always gets free pie and an extra smile from the waitresses, but he never lets it go to his head neither. Always on time with his loads, The Squid is always "Truckin it up." That's just the kind of trucker he is. You'd like The Squid, he's good people.

Anywho, it fell on April 30th or Walpurgis Nacht—that's "Witches Night" for a quick translation—back in 1986 that The Squid and his good buddy Ogre got themselves into a bizarre mess of trouble with a heap of near-impossible-to-believe repercussions, and this time it weren't The Squid's fault neither. You see, when he stopped off at that Flying K, he had no idea what was heading his way from so far off, and a man can sometimes get mighty surprised. But I'll take a step back now and just let the story unfold for you in its own way.

After fueling up, The Squid went inside the diner and sat himself down on a ripped vinyl stool at the counter. A waitress in a teal uniform with shockingly red hair looked him up and down. "What can I do you for, hun?" A lit cigarette dangled from her lips with a long cherry of ash teasing that it was about to drop.

"Java, darlin'. I gotta get to Denver by tomorrow afternoon."

She winked and poured him a cup. The fading cherry from her cigarette fell into the steaming black coffee. The Squid's eyebrows raised. She turned to walk away.

"Uh, ma'am? I'm gonna need a fresh cup."

"What, 'tain't good enough for ya, sugar?" she asked with a red-stained smile.

The Squid squinted, wondering at her teeth and deciding it must be lipstick. "No, I mean, yes. I need a fresh cup; your ash went right in the java. I don't mean to be picky, but come on."

"So?"

"So? So, I need fresh java. Come on, I got a long way to go and a short time to get there."

"Uh huh." She pushed the soiled cup a couple spaces down the counter and grabbed another from somewhere beneath. The Squid peered inside to inspect the potential lack of cleanliness as she poured it full. "Here you go, Your Majesty."

"Thanks, Toots."

She snorted at that and walked away.

Ogre, a tall beer-bellied trucker with a Dixie-flag ball cap, walked in, slapped The Squid on the shoulder and sat beside him. "You made her mad. Gotta watch out how you treat people, Squid. You can't go getting personal about how people run their business." He grinned wide, his smile framed with a Fu-Manchu mustache beneath tinted aviator shades that he never took off.

The Squid turned and shook Ogre's hand, answering, "The thought did occur to me, but I wasn't gonna drink that."

Ogre laughed, reached for the tainted cup and swallowed it, ash and all, then loudly belched.

A full body shiver wracked The Squid. "You're a sick man."

"Like Sun Tzu said, 'Whatever doesn't kill me makes me stronger.'"

The Squid shook his head, "Never mind, I ain't even gonna try and correct that."

"How's the highway been treating you?"

"Good, good. I gotta burn rubber to Denver and then pick up a load and get it to Tucson." He leaned up off his stool looking for the vanished waitress. "Where'd she go? Fix her weave? I need to order some grub."

Ogre nodded. "You catch more flies with honey than liquor, Squid. Plato said that."

"You have got to get your white-trash facts straight, my friend."

Indignant, Ogre spouted, "White-trash facts? Squid, I am the most well-read trucker on these highways. Don't make me draw you a picture."

The waitress returned and Ogre smiled at her. "Evening, ma'am. I'd like a dozen eggs and a side of bacon and do you have any…" Ogre glanced out the window and noticed the flagpole. His demeanor darkened. "Squid, do you see that?" He pointed an accusing finger outside.

"What?"

Ogre grimaced and sputtered, "Out there is a gold-fringed flag on that flag-pole! That is the flag of an Admiralty Court and here we are in god-fearing, five-wife-loving Utah!"

"Nevada," corrected the waitress, with the cigarette stuck to her heavy lip-stick.

Ogre frothed, standing up and shouting loud enough for the handful of other patrons inside to pause and look their way. "Last time I checked this was still America! Not a U.N. Charter stop-and-shop. Take that flag down now!"

The Squid put a hand on Ogre's shoulder. "You can't go getting personal about how people run their business. It's still an American flag. He's had a long day," he directed the last sentence at the waitress.

Ogre slammed the counter shouting, "No, this will not stand. I'm gonna give my diesel back! I'm taking my business elsewhere! You Commie sons of bitches!"

"Ogre, calm down."

"Am I wrong here?" asked Ogre, his breath coming in angry spurts.

Dark as it was outside, a bright flaring light arced overhead accompanied by a wretched grating noise akin to colossal nails on a titanic chalkboard. It turned everyone's attention away from Ogre's tirade. Appearing to be some type of rocket or craft, it tumbled violently in a downward spiral through the night sky. Green and orange flames backlit the grey smoke trailing behind like a twisted comet. The waitress's cigarette fell from her slack-jawed mouth.

Holding fingers in their ears, The Squid, Ogre and others stepped out the café doors to watch. The weird light sparkled and fizzed, turning a variety of colors as it cascaded eastward. It looked like it would hit just a couple miles away. Then there was a thunderclap and blast of brilliant green light. Dust fell from the eaves as tremors rippled through the truck stop.

Ogre slapped The Squid on the back. "That's right down I-80! Let's go take a look!"

The Squid glanced back to see the waitress picking her nose while pouring another cup of coffee. "All right, let's go look. We'll find somewhere else to eat."

2. Highway Star

Roaring down the highway, the Mack and Peterbilt headlights were weak compared to the twisting green fire that had beckoned in the distance. It seemed to The Squid that out here on the edge of the desert there were no stars, just a blackness hanging overhead like a bad dream. He had a bad feeling about all of this, but had to try and keep Ogre out of trouble. You gotta do what you can for good friends. But the boisterous redneck was driving as fast as his rig could go and The Squid had to stay above eighty to catch him.

It was farther than The Squid first thought. They were almost twenty-five miles from Wendover when they came to a huge furrow that had plowed into the salty desert. The rocket or whatever it was had hit a local landmark, or eyesore, depending upon your artistic interpretation. Something known as the Utah Metaphor Tree. The colossal steel and concrete monstrosity was leaning forty-five degrees crooked beside the highway with those same eerie green flames sputtering about like ghostly candles where shreds of steel and concrete had been cast off like dead leaves.

Ogre had made it there a bare moment before The Squid; he leapt from his truck and ran out into the enveloping darkness. "Hahaha! Look at that! It almost wrecked that damn tree! I hate that ugly thing!"

The Squid felt obliged to follow at a more leisurely pace, keeping his sweater tight about him against the April chill.

Ogre yelled out something unintelligible.

"What is it, man?" called The Squid.

No answer or sound but the licking flames that made shadows dance like marionettes.

"Come on, man, quit yanking my chain. Where are you?" shouted The Squid. He couldn't see much in the interplay between darkness and flickering lights. He felt a ripple of wind and a twinge of nausea, and wondered a moment if he was dizzy or sick. Then the feeling passed as quick as it had come.

"Hahaha! Look at that! It almost wrecked that damn tree! I hate that ugly thing!" shouted Ogre from the darkness.

"I heard you the first time, man."

"First time?" asked Ogre in a shout. "What are you talking about?"

"Yeah, yeah, where's the rocket?" asked The Squid, casting a look about the black landscape.

"I wish it had knocked that ugly piece of trash all the way over! Hey! It's over here!" shouted Ogre, running forward from the gloom. He stopped suddenly as The Squid caught up to him. "You gotta see this!" said Ogre, tugging on The Squid's sweater. "The Martians have landed."

"Come on, man. It's not alien. Must be an experimental rocket accident or something. Like the Challenger, man."

"Hell, no, Squid, lookit that thing. That is a bona-fide UFO right there. You ever heard of Roswell, Squid?"

"No. Should I have?"

Ogre's childlike glee went deadly serious. "It's only just the most radical secret the government has ever tried to keep from us is all."

A long silver object was half-plunged into the salt flat. Mist surrounded it. "It's a rocket, ain't it?"

"Damnit, Squid! Aliens crashed in the New Mexican desert. Lee Iacocca and the Bilderbergers have been trying to hide it from us for almost forty years! You need to read a book, my friend. And right here, right now, we are here to witness this one!"

"Iacocca? Outside of Wendover? Next to the damn Utah Tree? It looks more like a silver cigar."

"I'd call it more of a lozenge, but hey! Fate shines! I know exactly what we need to do. We have to take it!" Ogre slapped The Squid on the back.

"Ow! What, man? No, I've got a load to pick up."

Ogre spun The Squid saying, "You know what Julius Caesar would say here?"

The Squid shrugged. "'Et tu, Brute?'"

"Stop playing games, Squid! He said, 'Seize the day!' It's like his most famous quote, and that's what we are gonna do! We are gonna seize the day!"

"What? No, man," said The Squid, shaking his head. "I've gotta get to Denver."

"We are gonna pick up this thing and get the hell out before the Feds arrive to turn it over to the Illuminati and reverse-engineer it."

"That's crazy. The army handles this stuff. We can't do this."

"That's the beauty of it, Squid. You got a flatbed, I got a forklift. We can snag that thing before anyone's the dumber. I need to do this, dude. I need money bad. My mom has cancer."

"I have got to get to Denver, Ogre. It's important."

"No problem, we drop it off and hide it at my brother's place in the Four Corners."

"Your mom has cancer, since when? And you have a brother? You never told me that before."

"We don't talk much. He's a Jehovah's Witness."

"And the Four Corners, Ogre? That's not on the way to Denver."

"It's the scenic route, Squid. Try and be a team player here. We are doing this for truth, justice and the American way. It's the right thing to do. I need to do this. For Mom."

"No way."

"You love my mom. Help me."

"This won't fix that.

"It will if we sell it."

"That's crazy."

Ogre moved uncomfortably close to The Squid and looked him in the eye. "You remember that time I saved your life? How about that other time I pulled you off that mountain on I-90 over Butte? Are you just gonna forget all the times I caught the tab? Do you know how many times I have paid for your drinks? Two hundred and ninety-three times. Are you leaving me hanging now?"

"You counted?" asked The Squid, wrinkling his brow in disbelief.

Ogre frowned in response as if it was plain as day. "Two hundred and ninety-three times, Squid."

Shaking his head, The Squid responded, "I bailed you out of jail, that cost five hundred dollars. And you gave me snow chains once. Once. And that lifesaving thing? I wasn't drowning, man!"

"I couldn't take that chance, Squid. You owe me."

"No way. I have got to get to Denver."

"All right, all right. Just help me load it on your truck, and you take *my* rig to Denver and I'll meet you there by tomorrow evening. I need to do this. Will you help me? For Mom?"

Exasperated, The Squid nodded. Ogre was gone in a flash to get his fork-lift as The Squid looked closer at the wreckage. The silver cigar-shaped object was perhaps twenty feet long, smooth all over with no discernible seams or rivets. Amazingly, the impact had not scratched it at all. At its widest diameter it was around six feet and gradually tapered at each end to about a two-foot diameter. Except for the direction it was facing as it plowed into the ground there would have been no way of knowing which end was front or back.

The Squid touched the craft. It was surprisingly cold. Warm air coming off the Great Salt Lake met the cold surface and a mist swirled about in phan-tasmal caresses.

A long dark shadow moved in behind The Squid, cutting him off from the rig's headlamps. He turned suddenly, expecting a person to be right behind him, but it was just Ogre coming with the forklift. It was an odd feeling; he would have sworn someone was there but he didn't see anyone.

Ogre drove the forklift to the furrow and with a bit of skill and luck, got the forks under one end of the big cigar. He was pleased. "This sucker is light! I was afraid I couldn't pick it up. This is great! I'm gonna use the straps to put it on the trailer."

"You know, Ogre-man, what if this is, you know, just one of ours, or it's a missile or something? Maybe we shouldn't even be touching it. Like, what if it goes off or something?"

Ogre spun one end of the cigar out of the furrow and started on the other. "Squid, if it was gonna blow it would have done that already when it hit the Utah Tree *and* the ground. It's not a missile, it is the skateboard of the gods, my friend. You never read Daniken?"

"No, I never read Daniken. Come on, man, this might be dangerous and what if the army shows up?"

"Salvage rights, Squid. They're probably on their way but we got here first and if we take it, they'll probably just think it took off again or that it's not their problem to deny to the TV-watching zombie public anymore."

The Squid shook his head. "They don't forget stuff like this, Ogre-man."

Lights appeared on the highway and a car slowed to look at them. It was an older man in a yellowed Buick. "Do you need help?"

The Squid and Ogre looked him over, back to the gleaming silver craft caught in the big rig's headlights, and back to the old man. "No, we're good."

"What is that? Some kinda airplane?"

"Yeah, something like that."

"Anybody hurt?"

Ogre looked at The Squid, who was covering his face in his hands. "No sir, its fine, it's just a model for a movie."

"Oh? Which one?" asked the old man, excitedly.

"The next *Star Wars*."

"Never heard of it," said the old man, frowning. He threw his car into gear and drove off.

"And a good day to you, sir," said Ogre, waving the old man off dismissively.

"See, now there are witnesses that we messed with the Tree," said The Squid. "We gotta get outta here."

Attaching a long strap about one end, Ogre set to pulling the craft out of the furrow. "Relax, Squid, he thinks it's all part of a movie and that's the end of it. Like Freud said, sometimes you gotta break a few eggs to make a salad."

"What? Are you high?"

"Egg salad, Squid. Don't be naïve." Ogre finished tying off the strap and spun the craft fully out of the furrow. He then slowly drove it up to the trailer bed and lowered the forks gingerly, placing the craft on the deck. It didn't roll thanks to a few two-by-four nubs catching it along the center.

The Squid looked the cigar over and said, "He did ask one question right. What if there is someone hurt inside this thing?"

Ogre raised his eyebrows well above his shades. "Nobody is hurt. I didn't hear anyone crying for help, did you?"

"No, but that doesn't mean anything."

Ogre peered over the smooth silver craft again. "I don't see any doors. Maybe it's just robotic."

"So you jaw all you want about skateboards of the gods and now decide there is no chance of anything living inside?"

"Hey! This is my first time handling one of these, Squid." Ogre ran a hand along it. "It's cold. Maybe they're frozen inside and this is like a deep freeze sleeping bag."

The Squid rolled his eyes at that. "Are you sure you want this thing at your brother's, then?" The Squid held his hands out wide for emphasis. "What if whatever is in the sleeping bag wakes up? What then?"

"I was being facetious, Squid, just like Immanuel Kant. It's gotta just be a probe or something."

"And how does us taking it away help anything?"

"It helps us. I need to do this. For Mom. I'm going to make a fortune on this. Unless you've changed your mind and want in on this action? The choice is yours. Accept the golden goose or get out of the kitchen. What else do you have going for you as far as a nest egg is concerned?"

The Squid looked about nervously and blurted out, "Look, I didn't want to tell anybody yet, but the real reason I gotta get to Denver by tomorrow afternoon is Jeanie is gonna find out if she is pregnant and I wanna be there."

Ogre acted as if he didn't hear and tossed a strap to The Squid. "Well, this will only be a minute, I need your help on the tie downs. Come on."

"That's all you've got to say?"

Ogre stopped and pulled his shades down a hair. "What do you want me to say?"

"How about maybe, 'congratulations?' 'You're going to be a father, that's awesome,' maybe?"

"Sorry Squid, I can't relate, I'm shooting blanks myself. I suspect the whole 'father' thing is overrated anyway. This is a helluva world to bring a child into."

"You're an ass. I'm outta here."

Ogre, exasperated. threw up his hands. "Sorry, Squid man. Look, I'm glad you'll get to experience all that diaper shit and baby puke and nagging and settling down with a white picket fence and all that boring stuff. I guess I just didn't want to see you fade away like that. I thought more of you, Squid."

The Squid ran a hand alongside the bottom of the silver craft and snatched it back from the cold. "What the hell does that mean?"

"Just what I said, I'm gonna miss you."

"Miss me? That's not what you said."

"Yeah, I mean you'll be rotting away at home and I'll still be out here, a lone cowboy of the highways and you, you'll be at home withering away, is all."

"Is that what this is? You think you'll lose me as a friend? I'm still gonna truck, Ogre."

Ogre wiped away a tear. "No, I'm fine. I know you'll find something else to do, it's all right, I'm sorry for what I said. I'll be okay." He snorted and spit before wiping away yet another tear.

"I'm not playing your game, Ogre. This isn't about you."

"I'm sorry, man, I love you," said Ogre, slapping The Squid on the shoulder.

The Squid responded in kind, saying, "Thanks. Jeannie and I are gonna be happy."

Ogre nodded. "Yeah. She's made a lot of guys happy," he muttered under his breath.

The Squid wheeled and punched Ogre in the nose. Blood shot from the big man's nostrils. Ogre wiped blood from his face, grinned and punched back. Both men went down on the salt flats wrestling and cursing, kicking and spitting in anger. They missed the searchlight in the sky heading their way.

3. Gimme Three Steps

The Squid and Ogre beat each other black and blue. When the dust flying at them was far beyond a strong breeze they finally noticed the helicopter. A searchlight coated them like it was basting turkeys. A voice on a megaphone commanded, "Stay where you are! You are in violation of international law! Do not touch the TAV."

The Squid shouted into the wind, "What the hell's a TAV?"

"What'd I tell you, Squid? It's the U.N and the Men in Black! They want to steal it from us."

"From us? We don't own it!"

The megaphone continued. "Lay down on the ground. Keep your hands on your head. Do not move!"

"Like hell," answered Ogre, defiantly taking a step forward.

A three-shot burst from an automatic rifle made each man drop to the ground immediately.

"Try that again, Fat Boy!" taunted the megaphone.

The Squid and Ogre lay on their bellies on the salt flat. The helicopter backed away slightly from them and prepared to land on the side of the Utah Tree away from the direction it was leaning.

"Thanks a lot, man," muttered The Squid.

"I was just trying to tell you she gets around," said Ogre.

"No, you jackass! Not Jeanie! The Feds! We're going to jail."

"I need to do this. You with me? Look, I ain't gonna let them take this from me and Mom."

The Squid scoffed. "I don't think they're giving us much of a choice here, Ogre."

Ogre got up. "I'm not gonna let them steal our investment. Just drive the rig! Get the hell out of here! I'll hold them off!"

The helicopter touched down amidst a swirling dust storm.

"What? How?"

The megaphone barked at them, "Get back on the ground. We will fire!" Men barely visible against the search light jumped out of the helicopter and ran toward them.

"Trust me, Squid! I can handle Iacocca's goons!" shouted Ogre. "You just get our payload somewhere safe!" He pulled out a bowie knife and slashed the straps holding the craft. It dropped and hit the deck with an echoing gong. Ogre then threw his forklift in reverse. It kicked up dirt, racing backward into the dark.

The Squid jumped in the cab and threw his rig in gear. He put the hammer down. In the rearview mirror, he could make out little against the gloom and the blinding searchlight.

Men were shouting and many had drawn weapons. Ogre leapt from the forklift as it careened backward, smashing into the already tilting Utah Tree.

It was enough.

The Tree made a terrible groan and leaned left, then right, and slowly fell, smashing the unmarked black helicopter into road pizza.

"Two turds with one stone!" shouted Ogre, making a fist of triumph. Several shots in his general direction had him ducking and running to his truck.

A few of the undisclosed men continued shooting at Ogre and his rig, but that stopped as the helicopter exploded in an amazing fireball.

Ogre hopped into his cab and pulled away. Before he was out of earshot, he had to lean out the window and shout, "Suck it, Iacocca!"

A few miles down the road, The Squid picked up his CB. "Ten-Ten Mud Hen, you got your ears on? This here is The Squid, come on back."

"Ten-four, Squid."

"What's your twenty? I need to know what my back door looks like as far as Wendover goes. I am eastbound and down. Come on back."

"Copy that. Just passed the Bend-Over exit. Be aware there's a lot of Po-Leese back here and maybe some cocaine cowboys on your back door too. Lots of them and some G.I. Joes too. Everybody is running eastbound."

"Much obliged, Mud Hen."

"Ten-four. 'Sides, you got a triple-digit truck. You'll be all right. Just keep your nose clean."

"Ha! Copy that."

The Squid looked in his rear view mirror and worried about the bizarre craft. It wasn't tied down or covered, and soon as day broke everyone would see it plain as anything. And what if it vibrated or rolled right off the flat bed? It was round after all and the nubs along the edge couldn't hold it in forever.

Feeling like he had some distance between himself and the Feds, he pulled off an exit and grabbed some tarps and straps from his truck-box. He threw the tarps over the top of the craft, then the straps, and cranked them down quick as he could. Oddly, he could have sworn that thing had been cylindrical and symmetrical but now it appeared that the bottom was flat; it was resting gently on the bed, not capable of rolling at all. The Squid wondered a moment if it had squashed down a bit when Ogre had cut the straps and dropped it the last few inches into place. He touched the craft again, expecting cold, but instead of being freezing, it was almost as warm as the trailer itself.

He thought he saw a shadow moving behind him again. Whipping around, he waved the flashlight in all directions looking for whatever caused that unnerving feeling of being watched. But there was nothing except the night wind in this wide open land.

The bright moon overhead cast an eerie glow on the barren landscape. He was about to get in and drive away when bright lights bore down on him and, expecting the worst, The Squid raised his hands. A familiar horn blasting *Dixie* let him know Ogre had caught up.

Ogre leaned out his window shouting, "Hey, Squid! I showed those pukes! You shoulda seen that!"

"Damnit, Ogre, you almost gave me a heart attack."

Ogre jumped out and gave The Squid a hug. "Did you see that? I put those jack-booted sumbitches in their place! Hell's yeah, I smashed their unmarked black helicopter!"

"They're gonna find us."

Shaking his head violently, Ogre said, "Not if we haul ass!"

The Squid looked at the tarp-covered craft. "I still don't feel good about this."

"Had to be done, Squid. They pushed us into this and now we've got to see it through."

The Squid shook his head at that. "Maybe you should take my truck to your brother's and I'll get to Denver as fast as I can before they know where we're going. If we're lucky, they have no idea who we are."

"Yeah. About that earlier plan, Squid, my truck isn't gonna make it. They hit my tanks and I'm almost bone dry and we need to haul ass, so I'd better just ride with you and we'll leave my truck here. I'll get another later after I'm a millionaire, and after Mom's surgery, of course."

"Of course. And when in the hell will that be? The Feds are gonna impound it! They'll know it's yours."

Ogre walked around the side of the truck and opened the passenger door. "Well, like you said, they can try. But I'll have enough dough after this to get a new truck. I'm gonna take care of this. Give me a minute to snag my plates. Dispatch be damned."

The Squid stared as Ogre ran to the rear of his truck, then quickly ran back to his cab. "What the hell are you doing?"

"You ever been no-trace camping, Squid?"

"What? No! What the hell is that?"

Ogre pulled a bundle of dynamite out of his cab. "Get in your truck. I'm leaving no evidence behind; they won't have any idea who we are. I'll be dis-appeared like the real Jimmy Hoffa."

"You're insane."

Ogre frowned as he lit the fuse on the blasting caps. "Please be mature about this. We have nothing to fear but— Oh shit, run! Drive! I cut the fuse too short!"

They raced to the cab and jumped in. The Squid slammed the gears to get the rig moving. They had just pulled away by a hundred yards when Ogre's truck exploded. It was more shrapnel and sound than flames, but a twisted chunk of flying metal smashed The Squid's driver's side mirror. "Thanks a lot, idiot! Who knows what that did to my tarps or the craft?"

"Your precious tarps are fine. Besides, that thing is invulnerable—you saw what it did to the tree. Now those Nazis won't have any idea of our identi-ties."

The Squid shook his head. "You seriously think they can't piece any of this together? About who was driving tonight? Maybe they call all the dispatch offices? Or ask that nose-picking waitress who was there tonight?"

"No, dude, we're talking government employees here. They can't be both-ered with that."

"I hope you're right."

Ogre laughed and said, "I never said it would be easy, I only said it would be worth it." He then stared at The Squid for a long moment. "Well?"

"Well what?"

"Who said that?"

"You did."

"No, I mean who said it first? Who am I quoting?"

"I'm not playing your games, Ogre," said The Squid before he took a swig from a Mickey Big Mouth.

"Who said it?"

"I don't know."

"Come on, its important."

The Squid shook his head. "I don't know, man. Socrates?"

"Ha! No. Our Savior, FDR. He won us the Big One."

"Whatever."

"Do you not know the 33rd-degree President?"

"I know who FDR is, I just disagree, okay?"

"Really?" asked Ogre, with genuine shock.

The Squid shook his head. "So what are we really doing?"

"We're taking it to my brother's. He lives somewhere just southwest of Durango. We'll drop it off and you can still make it to Denver for the baby's delivery."

The Squid wiped his face and held back a retort. "We're finding out if she *is* pregnant, that's it. But I'm talking about the *thing*. We're taking who-knows-what's-in-there, to the Four Corners? I mean, what if there's something bad in there? Did you see *The Andromeda Strain?*"

"Don't make fun. That was based on a true story, Squid."

"I'm not making fun. I'm seriously asking the important questions and you're giving me bullshit quotes you don't know the real answer to and we might be transporting some diseased alien to your brother's place."

Ogre nodded and looked out the window. "Yeah, can we just be cool about this, please? Just drive."

4. Living After Midnight

A pink dawn rose behind the Oquirrh Mountains just as The Squid reached the Tooele exit. "This can't be right. What the hell, man?"

Ogre jostled in his seat and woke up. "What?"

The Squid smacked his dashboard. "I'm almost out of fuel."

"Yeah?"

"I fueled up at the Flying K, your U.N. Stop-and-Shop. That was a hundred miles ago."

"Did your tank get hit too?"

"I don't think so. I looked when I strapped down the craft, but that's not what is really bugging me."

"What?" asked Ogre, as he adjusted his ball cap and shades.

"It's dawn."

"So?" asked Ogre, wiping at his eyes.

"So? We picked up that thing just after midnight."

"Yeah, where you going with this, Squid?"

The Squid pointed at the brightening east. "It's morning! And we've been driving all night and we are only getting to Toolly."

Ogre slapped himself in the face a couple times. "Okay. Draw me a picture. What are you saying?"

"I'm saying, Ogre, that we drove all night to get maybe eighty miles. It doesn't feel like it, but it took us like eight hours."

"I coulda sworn you were doing more than ten miles an hour. What happened?"

"I was doing more than ten miles an hour! I've been doing damn near ninety. This trip takes just over an hour, and that's what it felt like to me. It should not be morning."

Ogre shrugged. "Missing time, dude. I've read about this."

"Lotta good that does me. What the hell happened?" The Squid pulled off the exit and pulled into the truck stop. He hopped out of the cab and put on his sunglasses. He then went to inspect the rear of his truck and trailer. Looking at his trailer he threw up his hands and cursed, "Son of a bitch!"

"What?" asked Ogre, jumping out.

"Not only did we lose a whole night and full gas tank, we lost the damn UFO!"

The tarps and straps were still there but the craft was gone. "This is some Twilight Zone shit, Squid." Ogre pulled at a tarp and strap, which were still secure. "Cheer up, Squid—on the bright side, no Feds can say we took anything extra-terrestrial last night. No evidence. No body. No case."

"I'd think after everything we've been through last night; you'd be a little more upset. What about doing all this for your mom's cancer?"

"My mom doesn't have cancer. Wasn't this mostly your idea?"

"My idea?" shouted The Squid. "Oh, that's just great."

"So what happened to the body we saw?" asked Ogre, earnestly.

"There never was a body!" yelled The Squid, pacing in a circular pattern.

"Well, we are completely in the clear then, aren't we?"

The Squid kicked his tires. "Oh, you think so, Ogre? Why did I let you talk me into this?"

"I don't remember," Ogre mumbled. "Everything is fuzzy from last night."

"Great. Exactly. You needed this for your mom, so I went along with it." He walked around the side of the truck and started pumping fuel. "This wasn't ever my idea."

"I'll just go get us some drinks and grub," said Ogre.

"Catch the fuel and a new side mirror while you're in there."

"Why?"

"Because your dynamite trick blew off my side mirror."

Ogre coughed loudly and pointed at the pristine side mirror. "Looks fine to me."

The Squid waved him off and pondered what could have happened. He had seen shrapnel shatter the side mirror. How was it still intact? He had fallen asleep at the wheel before a few times, but thank the Lord, he had never wrecked. But he had never lost a full night of driving before. It felt like the whole night went by in an hour, and now it was morning. Where had the time gone? Why did he remember that mirror being broken?

Ogre returned with drinks and snacks. "What do *you* remember from last night?"

"Nothing, just driving," said The Squid.

"Had to be something. What happened after I fell asleep?"

The Squid, took off his sunglasses and rubbed at his face. "Ugh. We hit some cross winds. But it shouldn't have taken this long. It couldn't have."

Ogre pondered, then he walked to the trailer and clambered up on it and started lifting up the tarps. "Look at this, Squid-man."

The shadowy outline of the craft was distinctly there almost like silver paint had been sprayed in that bizarre cigar shape, but tiny hairline tendrils of the mercurial ship also stretched out over the trailer, barely perceptible against the dulled steel. The Squid looked, then went to his cab and noted that they had spread everywhere, even encroaching onto the glossy surface of the Mack's black paint job. On a whim, he slid underneath and saw the silver veins entwined there too. "Where did that thing go and what are these lines everywhere?"

"I dunno, man, that's freaking weird."

"Great. That ought to help the resale value."

"You know what else is weird? The clerk inside said he saw that fireball last night when it was still way up in the atmosphere, he even felt the impact a little all this way and that the army and cops have been here all night. Guess they must have called ahead. Good thing they weren't here when we pulled in, huh?"

"Yeah, great, Ogre. Especially after you said they wouldn't have any idea who we were."

"Hell, if *we* don't know what happened, *they* don't know. They just had to call around after that spectacle last night and this is the closest service station so..."

A highway patrolman slowly pulled into the fueling station. He cast a wary eye at the two of them and they could see he was on the radio talking excitedly to someone.

"Let's get the hell out of here," said The Squid.

"Right," agreed Ogre, throwing his sack of snacks into the cab.

The Squid slowly pulled out of the station. The highway patrolman followed closely. "Dammit! He must have our descriptions!"

"Now, take it easy, Squid. Remember, we don't have the UFO, so they've got nothing on us."

"What about the damn tree, resisting arrest, smashed the helicopter and all that? I think they have a case."

"You're such a pessimist."

The highway patrolman was right behind them.

"I'm a realist, Ogre! You live in fantasyland, thinking you know shit about the world but you don't! You listen to conspiracy radio and dream that you have the inside scoop on things. But you don't get any of it right! And you even try to distract me by telling me my girl is a tramp."

"She is, dude."

The Squid reached over and smacked Ogre, the truck swerving while he did so.

"Well, now that Bear will have an excuse to pull us over," said Ogre.

Expecting to see the red and blues flashing, The Squid was surprised to see no trace of the patrolman in his mirrors. He had just been right behind them, hadn't he? The highway stretched back in a long straight grey line. Where could the cop have gone? The Squid had only taken his eyes off the cop for a second to hit Ogre. He kept watching the rear view for a long time but there was no sign. "That's not right."

"The hell it's not. Karma, dude," said Ogre. "We deserved to get away clean."

"But where did he go?"

"Who cares? We're in the clear."

The Squid wasn't so sure, but there was no denying that the patrolman was gone. They were only a couple miles down the road and the sun was already far too high in the sky for his comfort. It looked like noon, but they had only just filled up. "What time is it?"

"I dunno, lost my watch last night," said Ogre. "Does it matter?"

"Yeah, it matters. I have a schedule to keep and we're way behind."

Ogre scoffed, but smiled to make up for it and handed The Squid a beer.

"What?" asked The Squid, as he popped his open.

"Nothing, just that time is simply a construct of man. It's meaningless."

The Squid shook his head. "What? You have deadlines and schedules."

"Sure, but not by my making. That's all just to please someone else, and for what? We made pocketwatches so we could meet appointments with our social betters. What did we do before that? We gauged time by sun up and sun down. Not for me, if I have a say in it."

"Oh yeah, you don't! How else will anything get done?"

Ogre took a deep swallow of his beer. "Squid, come on. Before we watched the sun-up-sun-down thing, life was free and easy. We did everything for as long as it took and there was no stress. Time is an artificial construct we'd be better off getting rid of. It's such a stressful frame of reference."

"You're crazy."

"Am I? Does anything hinge on New Year's Day? Anything natural? Does any plant, animal, vitamin or mineral give a damn what day it is? What time it is? Of course not. So why should we?"

"Wait, you said before sun up and sun down. What the hell was there before that?"

"The purple dawn of creation, Squid-man. Everything was an Eden. We lay back and let fruit fall from the vine and into our mouths. We should live that way again. Back to basics. No worries."

"Uh huh. I must be losing it, your insanity is almost making sense and it looks like it's afternoon already and I know we've only driven about five miles and this has been the emptiest I have ever seen the highway. There's not another vehicle in sight."

"Must be some kind of Utah holiday. Maybe May-Day is Pray-Day? Yet another good reason not to recognize time."

The Squid shook his head. He was a little buzzed from beer on an empty stomach, but this was the strangest day of his life and it went far beyond Ogre's crazy ramblings and the cold beer.

5. Smoke on the Water

The Squid was looking at a dark cloud out over the Great Salt Lake. At first he thought it was smoke or mist but it rapidly changed shape and density. It grew darker by the moment, forming into undulating bizarre movements. He thought it was a UFO until he pointed it out to Ogre.

"It's just birds."

The big cloud of birds wafted about in the sky near Saltair. He couldn't tell what kind they were but guessed they were starlings flocking together in weird patterns. A few more miles down the road and could swear they were following. "That's weird."

"What?" asked Ogre.

"I don't see any other trucks or cars or anything on the road and those birds look like they are following us. Just looking at the sky, I would say it is three o'clock in the afternoon, but it was dawn when we filled up."

"See, I told you. Time is bullshit."

"And those birds are getting closer and they look huge. What are they?"

Ogre looked in the side mirror at the rapidly approaching shapes. They were indeed big. A whole lot bigger than starlings. "Hell if I know, Squid. Storks?"

The Squid grumbled. "Ha ha, very funny. I'm supposed to be in Denver with Jeanie right now. Don't talk storks to me, Ogre."

"Actually—"

The Squid reached to smack Ogre who ducked away. "Don't ever start a sentence with 'Actually' to me again! Got it!? I'm pushed to my stressing limits here!"

"It's not like storks really deliver babies, Squid. I'd think you'd know that by now."

"I know that, jackass; I just don't like being reminded of what I'm missing because of your needs."

"Please, this isn't about me. Without the UFO, we—"

"What?" The Squid threw his hands up off the steering wheel and the truck started to drift out of its lane. "I want to hear you say it."

But Ogre had gone deathly silent staring at the side mirror.

"Say it, Ogre."

"Can this rig go any faster?"

"Yeah, but you are gonna tell me."

"Just put the hammer down and get us the hell outta here!" cried Ogre, in a panic.

"What is it?" asked The Squid, as he looked in the rear view mirror while taking a swig of his Mickey Big Mouth. He looked at the bottle, then back to the rear view mirror. "What'd you slip into my beer?"

"Nothing."

The things flying after them in obvious pursuit and with dreadful intent were not birds. They did have wings, but beyond that all similarities ended in mind-shattering horror. These dark things were near the size of a man but looked more like black prawns or horrendous insects with multiple clawed pincers and wide fleshy heads covered in myriad throbbing antennae.

The Squid took another drink but spit it out as the nearest thing swooped down in front of the cab, narrowly missing being swatted into the windshield. Ogre rapidly rolled up his window. Another one of the creatures smacked into the side of the cab on The Squid's side but didn't get a grip and was knocked away.

"I'm gonna get my gun!" shouted Ogre.

The Squid nodded and put the pedal to the metal, kicking their speed up to over a hundred miles an hour. One of the bug-like creatures landed on top of the cab and scrambled over the top to the windshield. The Squid turned on the wipers. Ogre pulled a .357 Magnum out of his bag and aimed at the thing.

"Not my windshield, man!" cried The Squid.

"How else am I gonna hit it?"

"Reach around through the window!"

The Squid glanced in the rear view mirror and saw another creature on the trailer. And several more in the air catching up. The monster tapped a claw at the windshield, producing an awful ticking. "Shoot it, Ogre!" cried The Squid, sure that the thing would break and crash through the window at any moment.

"What if it bites?"

"Shoot it before it does!"

Ogre unrolled the window halfway, reached over and fired at the monster one-handed. The bullet hit it center of mass. The creature tumbled forward over the hood and down. There was no denying the bump as the truck rolled over the top of it. "Ha! Yeah!" shouted Ogre. "Where's another?" A scuttling sounded on the roof of the cab. And Ogre shot through the roof at the thing.

"My truck, man!"

"It was a dud! There's no hole in your truck!"

Then the monster was at the window. A hairy claw ripped into Ogre's forearm. Blood spurted out over the window and door. He screamed like a piglet but reached back with the pistol and shot the fleshy tendril-covered head. It split wide open and burst in something like powder or spores instead of blood. The cab filled with a smell like moldy bread after the pungent carnage. The body dropped away from the truck and tumbled down the freeway.

The Squid became aware of the dull red of evening and, concurrent with his panic, wondered how it was getting dark already. He coaxed a little more speed from the truck. At least three more creatures flew in their wake, but gradually fell farther behind as the truck sped into the gathering darkness. "Are you okay? Are they gone?"

Ogre shook his head, but couldn't say anything because he was biting down on a rag while wrapping a T-shirt around his arm.

"I can't stop the truck. Are you going to make it?"

Ogre nodded and spit out the rag. "I think so. What the hell were those things?"

"No idea. Maybe the UFO belongs to them. Maybe they want it back."

"Well, we can't give it back!"

The sky was fully dark and there were no stars against the blackness. "It's night already? Where are we? We should be in Salt Lake. How can it be dark already?"

Interstate I-80 merged with I-15 and they turned south. Still there was no traffic. "Where is everyone?"

"Maybe we're the last ones on Earth," said Ogre, "and everyone else has already been taken by those fleshy-headed mutants or aliens or whatever the hell they are."

The truck's headlights cut into the darkness only a short span ahead and both men cried out as they spotted the trio of the monstrous insectoids waiting for them atop a stopped car in the middle of the road.

"They think I'll stop, but The Squid doesn't stop for lot lizards from Pluto!"

"Yes, yes, yes!" cried Ogre.

The big black Mack crashed into the stopped car, tossing it from the interstate like a toy. The alien creatures exploded in a fungal powdery blast on impact with speeding well-made Pennsylvania steel.

"Yeah! Take that, you cosmic roaches!" shouted Ogre, leaning out the window.

"Are we going crazy?"

"You mean together?"

The Squid gestured at the night sky that was already showing a hint of the approaching dawn. "I mean, we see this falling star, it's a UFO, we pick it up just as the Feds get there, we get away and it's night, then it's day, and the UFO disappears from my moving truck."

"While strapped down," added Ogre, as he popped open another beer. The makeshift T-shirt bandage seemed to have stopped the bleeding.

"Yes, thank you. While strapped down. Then it's night again and those giant flying roach things come after us and its almost day again. And we haven't seen another living soul since we left the truck stop in Toolly and that highway patrol man disappeared on us right when he should have pulled us over. And finally, I want to say it has only felt like two hours, not two days!"

"I got it, Squid! We got sprayed with mind-control acid and we are tripping out from CIA experiments."

"Together? The exact same thing?"

"Okay, maybe not. Maybe we are dead and in Hell now. Lord knows I deserve it."

"That's more reasonable. Those roach things seem enough like demons," said The Squid as he flipped his headlights off; there was now a good mid-morning's light. The view was splashed pink and red sandstone. Where there should have been a city's urban sprawl going on for miles, there was nothing but strangely hued brush and rock beside the highway. "How's the arm?"

"It's all right, so long as it's not infected." Ogre swallowed hard, staring at the blank landscape. "If this is Hell, I'm kinda glad you're with me. No offense."

"None taken," said The Squid. The rig hit a bump and jostled them inside the cab. "I didn't see a pothole."

"We didn't hit another cosmic roach, did we?" Ogre asked, looking in the rear view mirror for any sign of giant roach roadkill.

"No. But this nightmare would get to anyone."

"You can say that again."

"Yeah. Maybe this is all a dream," postulated The Squid.

"You're so close," said a woman's voice, behind them. "And yet so far."

The Squid and Ogre each jumped and looked over their shoulders at the new passenger.

6. Under Pressure

She had a pale, sharp face framed with long straight hair, black as a raven's wing. Her dark eyes were deep wells that neither man could see into—they might be solid black for all either man could tell in the rapidly deepening twilight.

"Who are you? And how did you get into my truck?"

"Yeah, how'd you get in The Squid's truck?"

The Squid looked over his shoulder, back to the road and back to her, saying, "I just said that. She wasn't there a minute ago, was she?"

"No, dude, this is another one of these anomalous happenings like on *In Search Of.*"

The Squid raised a hand to quiet Ogre's input. "So who are you? What are you doing here?"

She gave them a coy smile and said, "My name is Shuarna."

"Have you been back there the whole time?"

"No. I had the opportunity to hitch a ride and I took it."

"Bad move, lady," said Ogre, as he took a long sip. "You're riding along with the Nightmare Express here." He looked to The Squid and said, "Unless she's a dream too." He reached out to touch her and she slapped his hand away. "She's real all right, Squid."

"I never said she wasn't. You sound like you've got some answers, Shawna."

"It's Shuarna."

"Whatever."

"Names have power. I suggest you respect that," she said.

"I apologize. Shar-Naaa. How did you get here and what can you tell us about this psychedelic trip? I gotta admit, I'm stumped, and even the Answer-Man here hasn't thrown out any proverb about it yet."

Ogre bristled. "That was uncalled for, Squid."

Shuarna moved a little closer. She was beautiful, with a petite hourglass figure. She wore a strange dark garment the likes of which The Squid had never seen before, with a deep open V-neckline moving between her breasts down almost to her navel. The Squid didn't know what to call it, having never seen the like before. If he hadn't been driving, he would have been staring. She smelled exotic like some distant shore from the land of dreams—perhaps like Black Lotus, he guessed, not that he knew what that was. Why did that thought even enter his mind? She was alluring but had a dangerous vibe about her, like a jungle cat. He wondered why these thoughts raced through his mind so quickly at her very presence. She had magically just appeared in his truck, and he thought he should be scared, but instead he was intrigued and maybe even pleased.

"You have something that does not belong to you," she said.

The Squid looked at Ogre. "Great. Are you a Fed? A Spook? Maybe an agent of Mr. Lee Iacocca?"

Shuarna gave hint of a smile. "I'm not from around here."

"What, Utah?" asked Ogre, who then shrugged at The Squid's frown.

"I dwell outside your realm. Your kind might call it the Aether."

"Aether realm?"

She half smiled again. "You have stepped beyond the bounds of your world and time with this stolen artifact."

Ogre shook his head violently. "Impossible. This is a bad trip, a bad dream, this isn't real, there has to be an explanation. That waitress slipped me a mickey."

"Believe whatever you want, it will not change the truth," she said. "I saw a moment I could phase and catch a ride with your vehicle, and I took it. That is when you felt my footprint."

"The bump back there?"

"The same."

The Squid looked at Ogre, then Shuarna. "Is the 'artifact' yours? You want it back?"

Her smile, while pretty, was disconcerting, as if her teeth were just a little too big and too sharp. "I merely wish to keep the balance of things. Your presence bordering into the other realms has upset them greatly."

"Them who?" asked Ogre. "The Illuminati? The Bilderbergers? The NWO? CIA? NSA? KGB? EPA?"

The Squid broke in, "Wait, what's this about presence and upsetting the talents of things? What do you mean?"

"Balance. You have upset the balance of worlds and dimensions by moving the artifact. It should have been left where it fell. It would have phased on in but a few moments. Now you are crossing realms of which you have no understanding. And in so doing you have attracted the attention of beings much less benevolent than myself."

"How? We're just driving down the highway."

She rolled her eyes. "This vehicle has bonded with and absorbed the artifact. One of the Shining Trapezohedrons."

"Huh?"

"This 'truck' has merged with the artifact and is now a vehicle that transcends the crossroads of realities."

"That's plural?" asked The Squid.

Shuarna nodded. "And with every movement, every revolution of its wheels, ripples in the subspace appear. With those ripples, even if you are but a drop of water skimming across an ocean, every time you touch down, *they* feel your presence, your violation of their space. They see you and they are coming."

"They who?"

"Any of a number of entities that walk this plane. Star Spawn, Outer Gods, Great Old Ones, Elder Things, Moon-Beasts, some you have encountered already. The Mi-Go attacked you, did they not?"

"Those giant flying cockroaches?"

Shuarna nodded again, "The Mi-Go just happened to be nearby. It was your own brand of human luck that these weakest of antagonists were but the first. You only survived because they grossly underestimated you. Next time they will surely have greater numbers and be fully aware of how to combat your vehicle."

Ogre sputtered, "I do *not* want to see any more of those damn bugs. What would they do if they caught us?"

"At the very least they would drive you mad, but likely enough they would devour you, and in this realm, that digestion and absorption would take eternities."

Ogre's eyes flared wide and, for once, he had no words.

"I have a better question," said The Squid. "How do you know all this, Shuarna, and why tell us? What's your stake here?"

"That is a better question. Move," she said to Ogre, who begrudgingly got up and gave her his seat.

"Anything for a lady," he grumbled.

"I want the artifact, of course. But if we stop, worse fates waiting will catch up to you. That's why I transported myself to your moving vehicle."

"Yeah, how'd you do that? Some kinda magic?" asked Ogre.

She gave him a patronizing smile. "I guessed where you would be next and I adjusted myself to that frequency and spectrum. Your enemies could potentially do the same, but the human mind is so alien to them that they have difficulty comprehending your motivations. It would be the equivalent of you anticipating where a buzzing fly might travel. As I have said before, they are following the ripples, your cosmic wake. They will eventually catch up. So we must end this race as soon as possible."

"Wait," said Ogre. "Are you saying we are the flies?"

"Compared to their power, intelligence, lifespan and power—you are less than flies."

Ogre rolled his eyes at that and mouthed *crazy* to The Squid.

The Squid ignored him, asking, "How do we end it, then? I want out. I sure don't want to meet anything worse than those bugs."

Shuarna reached out and touched the truck's dashboard. The Squid looked at the molded plastic and realized he could see the tiny silver veins spanning all over his Mack truck. Hairline fractals covered everything save himself and his two passengers. It was almost imperceptible until he really looked, and then he didn't understand how he could have missed it before.

"I will have to separate the artifact from the truck and take it to my own realm," she said.

The Squid looked in the rear view mirror to Ogre who made a grasping gesture with his hands and mouthed *big boobs*. "Shut up, Ogre."

Shuarna turned to look at Ogre. "Yes?"

"Well, uh, I was wondering, what about us?" asked Ogre. "Where will we be? What will happen to us when you do that?"

"Nice save, idiot," said The Squid.

"That depends on where we stop," she said. "I will do my best."

"For our sakes?" asked The Squid, giving her his best grin.

"Do not flatter yourself. This is for my benefit. I just don't seek to destroy you for this trespass as the Others will."

"Well, that's comforting."

Night had already come again, passing overhead as if they were but in a long tunnel. Faint cold light greeted them just beyond the horizon.

The Squid asked, "Why can't we see anyone else? You know, any other people?"

"You are traveling between realms; you are a ghost to them. From their perspective you disappear as soon as you venture outside their immediate perception. When you stop this truck you come screeching back into your own time and realm. But the destroyers will find you, and stopping only lets them get closer. Do you understand me?"

The Squid nodded. "I think I do. Are we still traveling our own highways? It looks the same except for the lack of other drivers."

"You still remain in your own realm in a sense, as if you have one foot in each world. But it is also bordering the Dreamlands, which will not be without its hazards."

"You mean like I'm almost out of fuel again?"

Shuarna shrugged. "I am not particularly familiar with your earthly vehicles, but yes, we must keep moving. So you need to feed it quickly, before any malevolent entities catch up to us."

The Squid smiled at her. "Feed? You really aren't from around here, are you?"

"We must keep moving and at our swiftest pace."

The Squid wiped his scruffy jaw. "So I gotta keep trucking because if we stop or slow down, monsters are gonna eat us forever?"

"Yes. Are you feeling the pressure yet?"

The Squid looked back in the rear view mirror at Ogre who again made the crude gesture and mouthed *big boobs*.

Without even glancing behind, Shuarna shot her fist back and struck Ogre in the face. His already tender nose shot blood out over his face and shirt. "I don't find you amusing. Don't press your luck," she warned.

"You're all right," said The Squid, with a grin. She smiled back. It was still eerie, like something was wrong that he couldn't put his finger on, but he was enjoying her company despite the grim tidings.

6. Gimme Shelter

The truck barreled through the night and into the grey day and back into the night. Sun and moon, stars and inconceivable constellations traversed the sky, washed into each other so much that they blurred the track of the cosmic sands through the hourglass. The kaleidoscope of color and night was nauseating to the men, though Shuarna seemed oblivious to the contradiction of light and time.

Ogre heaved an exasperated breath before asking, "Where are we, Squid?"

"I think somewhere near Spanish Fork."

"We gonna take the canyon or go down I-15?"

"I dunno. Shuarna?"

She pointed to the left but said, "Each way is much the same as the other. We'd best feed your truck."

The Squid pulled his truck off the highway and into a truck stop. The sunlight was harsh and bright as they coasted, but as he stopped in front of the pump and turned the truck off, night fell immediately as if a curtain had been draped over the sun. "What the hell?"

"Your perception of time matters not. Feed your truck, but let us be swift," said Shuarna, jumping out of her seat and walking toward the back of the trailer.

"Fill her up for me, Ogre. I gotta try and call Jeanie and see how she is."

"You think that's a good idea, Squid?"

The Squid scowled and muttered to himself but walked to the payphone. He dropped in a quarter and dialed the number.

It rang and rang. The Squid had to dial a second time before someone picked up. It was a man.

"Yo," answered the unknown male voice.

Raucous music blasted behind the unfamiliar voice and The Squid could swear he heard a woman in the background ask, "Who is it?" before cooing,

284 David J. West

"Hello?" said The Squid. "Who is this? Where's Jeanie?"

After a brief pause, Jeanie came on. "You got some nerve calling now."

"Jeanie! What's going on? Who's that there?"

"Why are you calling me now, Jeff?"

"Because I love you. You won't believe what happened to me—"

"You're right, I won't believe you. You disappear off the face of the earth for like two months without a word and you think we're cool? Ha!"

"Who is that at our place?"

"*My* place. And not that it's any business of yours, but it's Brad. Don't you ever show your face over here again or he'll kick your ass. I dumped all your stuff off over at Ogre's mom's. So thanks for all the good times, and drop dead." She hung up.

The Squid just looked at the phone as the dial tone blared. "Two months? She couldn't wait for two months?"

Ogre clapped him on the shoulder.

"I didn't even get to ask if she was pregnant or not."

Ogre looked away and said, "You dodged a bullet, dude. I always hated her."

"Thanks a lot. That's really what I want to hear right now, man," said The Squid.

"Well I thought since you didn't want to hear any of my proverbs, I'd help you feel better by letting you know she was trash. Always out gambling your money away and trying to pick up dudes behind your back. If she really was pregnant, it probably wasn't your kid anyway. Odds, dude. Cheer up."

Shaking his head in disgust, The Squid said, "I don't think a jackass like you has any idea on how to help people feel better."

"That was rude, dude."

"Oh, heaven forbid I offend Mr. Sensitive."

"You're hurting, I understand. I'm gonna let this one go," said Ogre, backing away.

The Squid cursed under his breath and went toward the truck stop to get something to drink. He needed to forget this whole mess; he needed to forget a lot. But right beside the door was a cork board with a smattering of notes, personals and ads, and glaring out like a slap in the face was an FBI wanted poster with his face along with Ogre's. They were unflattering pictures, probably taken from their old driver's licenses; it made the two of them look like criminals rather than the good-natured dudes they were.

"What the hell?" He tore down the poster and looked at it closer. The verbiage was vague and bureaucratic but there was something about them both being wanted for domestic terrorism, and a warning that they were armed and dangerous was in bold lettering at the top and bottom. "Oh, this is bullshit, man!"

"What is it, Squid?"

He handed Ogre the poster and asked, "Is the truck full?"

"Yeah, I just gotta pay."

"Better make it quick. I'm gonna ask Shuarna if she has anything figured out 'cause this mess is just getting worse by the minute."

"You got it, Squid," said Ogre, before he turned his cap backward and took off his shades. Looking terribly unlike himself, he strode inside.

The Squid walked back to the truck and called out, "Shuarna. You figure anything out?" There was no response, so he walked around the other side of the truck. There a black clad figure hunched, examining the back of the tractor trailer. It was tall and skinny with unnaturally long arms ending in obscenely long fingers which caressed the trailer bed. Dressed entirely in black flowing robes, it also wore a towering miter-like hat which only made it appear taller and more menacing. It had a nearly featureless black face, smooth and immobile as a mask but with glaring yellow eyes that flashed like a nova when it saw The Squid staring.

The Squid was so taken aback that he turned right around and rushed to the other side of the truck, wondering where Ogre's gun was. Was that one of those elder things after them?

Shuarna appeared from nowhere and took The Squid's shaking hand. "I did not mean to frighten you."

"That was *you?!*"

She half-smiled. "Yes. My natural form is jarring to your kind, I suppose."

"I'll say. I thought you were one of those 'elder things' you talked about."

Her half-smile sloped bigger. "They are much more frightening than me. I assure you."

"Yeah, I assure you," said The Squid, nodding and trying to get a hold of himself. "Did you figure anything out? Maybe you can separate my truck and that whatever-it-is? I need to get back to my life and get some things settled. Things aren't gonna be easy. I don't have the answers but we can't stay here, right?"

"No," agreed Shuarna. "We must keep moving. I cannot perform the separation here on this plane. We need to travel to a place where the barrier is thin, where I can work my enchantments."

"Uh-huh. How far is that?"

She smiled at him with a wicked grin.

The Squid shook a finger at her. "I get the feeling you're playing with us."

"I am, after a fashion. You humans have so much passion and emotion in everything you do. I admit, I enjoy seeing how far it will go. I wanted you to carry the artifact, the Shining Trapezohedron, for me."

The Squid frowned, "You are playing with our lives here? That's not cool. What do we need to do to fix this, and get back to life as I know it?"

"We must go toward the Four Corners, there is a place where I can unmake this cruel manifestation and free each of our prizes."

"What? How?"

"Would you understand me if I explained it? I simply need you to physically move the artifact."

Shaking his head and then a finger at Shuarna, The Squid said, "You didn't just show up in my truck. You were there the whole time, weren't you? I sensed or saw your shadow when Ogre was getting the forklift, didn't I?"

She shrugged.

"Maybe that bump we felt in the truck was you transforming from whatever the hell you are to this woman in front of me."

"Do you not find me attractive?"

"Sure I do! I am as red-blooded as the next man and you are mighty fine, but I think I may have learned my lesson about pretty faces and dark hearts."

She gave him that lop-sided grin again. "I swear I have no heart."

"So basically all the trouble I'm in is your fault. Why the hell should I trust anything you say? I am in a world of hurt in the 'realm' where I'm from, and it's all because of you!"

Shuarna looked deep into his eyes and said, "This is important. I need your help. What is done is done. We must finish this."

The Squid opened his own eyes wide in a mocking glare. "Are you trying to hypnotize me? This kind of playing with people's lives will not stand, sister."

"I had to try. You can't fault me for that, can you?"

"Yeah, I can," said The Squid, nodding. "I'm done with this."

Shuarna then swept her hand through the air between them, and faint blue lights appeared showing a map in midair. "Here is where we must go. Upon completion of this journey and the separation ceremony, you will be rewarded and I will set right all of the issues in your world."

"Uh-huh. And just why should I trust any of this?"

"You have no choice. Waste time disputing this with me, and things worse than the Mi-Go will come and feast upon your flesh."

The Squid put on his sunglasses and stood as tall as possible. "Yeah well, maybe that's just a chance we'll have to take, then. I don't like being played by anyone."

Shuarna's coy smile vanished.

"Ogre, let's roll. Without the lot lizard."

Ogre walked up carrying a brown paper bag full of beer and chips. "Serious, Squid? She propositioned you?" he asked, dropping his shades to look over Shuarna with his left hand while barely managing to keep the bag upright in the other. "Also, bad news, the clerk in there recognized us. Pretty sure he called the cops the second I walked out the door." He looked back and they all saw the clerk speaking excitedly into the phone, watching them.

Shuarna snarled at them, "You won't get far without me. The hunt for the artifact has only begun and only I can undo the merging of materia."

"Uh-huh."

Popping open a beer, Ogre asked, "You sure about this, Squid? She seems crazy as a road lizard, but I don't have any other answers."

The Squid grinned at Ogre for that. "For real?"

Ogre put up a finger. "I've still got opinions."

The Squid opened the door on his cab and, standing on the running board, said, "Shuarna, if that is your real name. I don't know that we ever got a straight legit answer from you."

"You need me," she protested.

"I don't know that anything you have said is true, so I think we're just gonna say our goodbyes and leave you here. So long!"

Shuarna scowled at him. The Squid scowled back as hard as his sunglasses would let him.

Then their standoff was shaken loose by a siren, and the red and blue flashing lights came into view seconds later.

"Uh, Squid?" urged Ogre, tugging on The Squid's shirtsleeve.

"It's all right. I figure soon as we start driving he's gonna think we disappeared just as much as we'll feel like he did."

"Not the cop I'm worried about."

"Shuarna ain't gonna do anything. If she was, she wouldn't be arguing with us."

She glared at them but had not moved.

"No, dude," protested Ogre. "What the hell is *that?* We gotta get outta here!" He pointed opposite from the oncoming police car and toward a big patch of swirling darkness. Black smoke was belching forth from a dumpster's retaining wall beside the service station. And there was an aura of dread accompanying the sight of it, a dread that needled at The Squid's very soul and made him feel so terribly small, vulnerable and alone.

"It is the Hounds of Tindalos! I *told* you there were worse things waiting!" said Shuarna. "Do not look directly at them. Let's all get in the truck and drive away, now!"

The Squid didn't protest Shuarna jumping in the cab with them. He fired up the rig without waiting for the glow plugs and threw it into gear. In the rear view mirror, he saw long lean shapes escaping swiftly from the inky vapors. They appeared lupine, but were exaggerated and skeletally thin. At least three of them ran out and paused a brief moment, scanning each and every way as if to catch a scent.

"The Trapezohedron is merged with your truck. It is confusing their senses. You may survive," said Shuarna.

Two Hounds were not confused and tore after the retreating truck, running alongside with long blueish tongues lolling. "Holy hell! Those things are ugly! Ogre, shoot 'em!"

"I can't see!"

Not knowing what else to do, The Squid wrenched the wheel hard to the left and took one Hound under the wheels. They heard an awful yelp and felt a bump. "Did that work?"

"It appears so," said Shuarna.

"Where is the other one?"

"Cheese and rice!" cried Ogre.

A twisted dog's head suddenly leered from the glove box, snapping its terrible jaws at them, it's long blue tongue slavering for their blood.

Ogre shot his .357 into the glovebox but the dog's head was gone.

"Where'd it go?"

Beneath the driver's seat, something bit at The Squid's shoe. He screamed, poured his beer on the floor and stomped his foot down, and again it disappeared. Breathing heavy, he pulled over and looked. Nothing.

"We have to keep moving or the others will find us!" shouted Shuarna.

"One thing at a time! We have to deal with this insane dog!"

The snapping jaws were popping from above the sun visor and then gone again.

"This is bullshit!" shouted Ogre.

Something behind ripped at Shuarna's dark shirt before disappearing again as a hail of Ogre's bullets riddled the cabin behind. Shuarna screamed, looking fearfully about.

"Sumbitch is playing with us," snarled Ogre.

"I'm going deaf with you shooting in here!"

"Well, do you want to get bit by an insane Labrador?"

Impossibly, the Hound's head appeared at the slot on the door handle.

"Open the door!" ordered Shuarna.

The Squid opened the door, just missing a bite from the snapping Hound. Shuarna threw a ball of light outside the cab, shouting, "Fetch!" The Hound leapt outside after it.

Ogre lunged over the top of The Squid and shot the Hound twice, just as it turned with the ball in its muzzle. Its body fizzled and melted away in a haze of blueish smoke.

"We have to get moving!" shouted Shuarna.

The Squid, started the rig and watched in his rear view mirror as the other Hounds, covered in a greenish light, did their terrible work back at the truck stop. They had torn both the officer and his car apart, then had turned their attentions on the clerk inside the shop. The Squid shut his eyes against the horror, trusting that the truck would remain on the straightaway for the next few seconds. "Did we make it away? Are they coming? Can I look?"

Shuarna was breathing a sigh of relief herself before answering. "Yes, at least for a time. They will keep coming, however. We must stay ahead with as swift a pace as we can manage. The Hounds of Tindalos come from the angles of time and are among several entities which are offended at your passing."

Ogre shivered and downed his beer in one great gulp before belching and asking, "Where did you say they come from?"

"They both exist and enter through angles. The corners of those walls around the garbage receptacle suited their purpose very well. We stopped for too long—we must be faster. Next time they will destroy your bodies while devouring your souls."

The Squid raised a hand from the wheel, "So, I need an answer, Shuarna. Are you with us? Or just using us? The way I see it, we gotta work together on this, because seems like you weren't able to fight those things off either on your own."

She looked away but admitted, "True. I need you to transport the artifact for me. I will help and try not to allow harm to come to you."

"Try?" he asked.

She smiled that grin again that simultaneously made The Squid uncomfortable and turned him on.

"I'll do the best I can."

The Squid looked her over. "I guess you're still with us, then. No more tricks or using your mental powers on either of us."

"What'd she do?" asked Ogre.

"Don't worry about it. It's over."

Shuarna nodded. "Agreed. But we still must head southwest, to where the barrier is thin."

"How long will this take?"

"Time is of no consequence here. It will take as long as your truck takes, though it is all relative to where in the realms we are."

"Sorry I asked. Just not my day, I suppose."

Ogre clapped The Squid on the shoulder. "You gonna be okay, man?"

"Yeah, you know, all things considered, I think I am. Something about horrible dog monsters coming out of corner-pocket dimensions, intent on devouring your soul, kind of puts things into perspective. I guess I'd just say I'm glad to be alive. No thanks to Shuarna here for putting us into the middle of this existential crisis."

"Squid. Don't judge," answered Ogre. He then turned to lay down on the sleeper. "I'm getting some shut-eye. I've had enough craziness for one day."

After they heard Ogre's snores, Shuarna put a hand on The Squid's and whispered, "Thank you. You won't regret helping me. This is important."

He smiled at her, melting inside.

8. Highwayman

They drove up a mountain with peaks that were not familiar: tall, jagged and glinting with veins of light near the zenith. A red dawn splashed bloody color across the granite face just before shadows washed over it once again, transporting them back into darkness. Colossal fir trees stood beside the highway where The Squid knew no such things had grown before. Several times it seemed to him that they actually waddled beside the road like giant penguins. "I am straight tripping," he muttered to himself.

"Things are different in the Dreamlands," said Shuarna.

"Is that where we are? I thought it was Utah."

"It is and it isn't. This truck has wheels in each of many realms at once. Our driving is the only thing keeping us from the claws of the Mi-Go and the tongues of the Hounds. There will be other trials but for now we are ahead of the game."

"A game? Is that what this is to you?"

Shuarna wouldn't answer.

"I'll take that as a yes." The Squid shifted as they slowed, heading up a steep pass. "Good to know. Any more surprises coming up?"

Shuarna shook her head. She looked ready to fall asleep.

"You look tired. Want me to wake Ogre up so you can have the bunk?"

"No, I am just feeling weakened at holding this together. Sometimes these crossings drain me. That, and creating the light ball for the Hound took my reserves down."

"Ogre! Let the lady get some sleep back there. Mind games take it out of her."

Ogre jostled in the bunk but did not awaken.

"Ogre! Get up and spot me!"

Now the big man mumbled and twisted out of the sleeping cab. He rubbed his face and put his hat and shades on before saying anything.

"I figure it's about time I let you take over," said The Squid.

Shuarna looked concerned. "Shouldn't we do this when we stop?"

"No, we've done this lots of times."

Ogre came up behind and put his hand on the wheel to The Squid's left. The Squid took his hands off the wheel and started to slide over with his foot still on the gas. Then in a flash he was over into the passenger seat and Ogre leapt into the driver's seat. There was only a bare second that someone's foot wasn't on the gas and the rig barely hiccuped at the pressure change.

"Now go get some sleep, Shuarna," said The Squid.

"Wake me before you stop."

"We will."

Getting comfortable as he could riding shotgun in his own rig, The Squid lamented the events behind and those ahead. Night and day were blinking back and forth almost once every minute. The time was passing so fast that he wondered if they would still be wanted men by the time this was over. If anything would be the same anymore. He had seen a lot of changes in his life already, and what if he was now some kind of trucking Rip Van Winkle?

Ogre interrupted his thoughts. "You know, Squid, I've been thinking."

"Yeah?"

"We handled those damn roaches, the 'Mi-Go,' with some truck splatter and my .357. I'm almost out of ammo and according to Shuarna we are likely enough to meet up with some heavier dudes."

"So?"

"So what I'm saying is do unto others before they do unto you."

"Huh?"

"We need heavier artillery, Squid. We need something with some kick, some punch, some wow!"

"'Some wow?' What the hell you talking about?"

"I'm talking about we arm ourselves with some big guns. We get something that will really put a hole in people or monsters or bugs or whatever," said Ogre, excitedly enough that he took his hands off the wheel for emphasis. As he did the truck veered sharply to the left and while The Squid was

convinced for a moment they would wreck and flip over, they found themselves on a dark stretch of highway completely different than where they had
been only moments before.

"Where the hell are we?"

"I dunno, Squid, I just took my hands off the wheel for a sec—" His hands
started to lift in demonstration.

"Don't!" commanded The Squid with a finger raised. "You keep hold of
that wheel until we figure out where we are."

While the landscape was familiar to both men, it wasn't part of where they
had been. The earth had gone from a hazy yellowed earth to a green and grey
stony desert with rolling hills arching ever higher with each passing mile.
Soon enough, pines were scattered about. Great mountains loomed ahead.

"Do you see a mile marker or anything?" Ogre asked.

"I haven't seen one since we left Toolly. I think this Dreamlands crap
erases them, at least from our perspective. I've been going off familiar land-
scapes, but this is not where we were in Utah. This is still familiar, though. I
think we must be somewhere past all that."

"Squid, somehow we are way past the exit we wanted."

"We missed the Price turnoff?"

"Oh no, long past that."

"Green River?"

Ogre shook his head.

"Crescent Junction?"

Ogre shook his head furiously. "Nope. We're way past all that. I think
we're coming up on the Eisenhower Tunnels!"

The Squid leaned forward examining his surroundings out the window. "I
think you're right."

"Too bad you don't need to get to Denver anymore."

"Shut up."

"Here we go!" said Ogre, as they plunged into the tunnel. While there were
overhead lights, not far inside they blinked out and then only the truck's
headlights granted any illumination.

"But this ain't right either, Ogre-man. Shuarna said to separate the thing
from my truck we have to go to where the barrier between worlds is thin and
she said that was down in the Four Corners. We gotta turn around."

"Do you see anywhere I can turn around, Squid?"

"We need to."

"Maybe after we get through to the other side."

The tunnel seemed gloomier now, as if the headlights could barely hold
back the darkness. They could no longer see the walls or ceiling lost in the
atmosphere of the black tunnel. The road, while still relatively flat, became
rough and uneven and every now and again Ogre had to dodge the truck
around outcroppings of stone.

"What the hell happened up in here, an earthquake?"

"Looks that way, Squid."

A great wall of cyclopean stone suddenly forced them to come to a complete stop, tires squealing.

"What is that doing here?" asked The Squid.

"Looks like its man-made. That's not from a cave-in or an earthquake. Someone put that there."

Shuarna rolled out of the sleeping bunk and asked, "Why did we stop?"

"We almost hit a wall."

The Squid argued, "That can't be a wall, we're in the middle of the Eisenhower Tunnel!"

Shuarna was insistent. "We must turn around and get moving. We cannot stand still! Every moment we stop his forces draw nearer."

"His forces?"

"We must get moving again," she urged.

"We gotta get turned around from this earthquake rubble."

"This ain't from no earthquake, Squid! Look at those stones. They're all different sizes and shapes, but they all fit together just right. That's man-made. That's a freaking wall!"

Shuarna moved between them to stare out the windshield at the dimly lit stones. "It looks like it curves slightly. Perhaps there is room to turn the truck around?"

The Squid shook his head, "No way, we're in the tunnel. There's no room for that. I've been here a thousand times before."

"It won't hurt to get out and take a look will it? Am I wrong on that?" asked Ogre.

"Fine. Let's look at how we will have to back up."

Shuarna took The Squid's hand. "Please be careful."

He smiled and nodded. "We'll hurry." They jumped out of the cab. It looked like she blushed but he couldn't be sure. He liked that.

The headlights still shone on an isolated section of the wall. The Squid held a flashlight he had retrieved from the glovebox while Ogre grabbed a spray can. They kicked some smaller rubble out of the way and Ogre spray-painted peace signs on a boulder with glow paint.

"Knock it off," said The Squid.

"I think we can turn around, but take a look at that," called Ogre.

Shuarna called out from within the cab. "I think you should return immediately and we should back out. I think we may be in the Vaults of Zin."

"What?"

"We are no longer on your earth. We may have crossed wholly into the Dreamlands. Come back now!"

The Squid shone his flashlight at her. "Dreamlands, my ass. This is a nightmare trip," he muttered, under his breath. "We're already out, we'll just take a quick gander."

"Look at this, Squid," said Ogre, as he ran his hands along the fitted stone. "These are fit so well together I can't even put my pocketknife in between them."

"Why would you want to?"

"This means something. I heard about a place like this before where strange cults did weird sacrifices."

"In the Eisenhower Tunnel?"

Ogre glared. "No man, weird places in South America. Macho Pikachu."

The Squid shone his flashlight farther out and up. He couldn't see the ceiling. He walked a short distance away. "This seems taller than I remember. That's why I think this is just a chunk of ceiling that fell and left it open up there." The Squid heard a shuffling sound from close by. He turned his flashlight at Ogre who was several feet away, examining the stones. The shuffling was getting closer; it sounded like rubber flapping on stone. The Squid spun the flashlight back the other way.

"Look again," said Ogre. "These are worked, molded stones. Tell me I'm wrong."

"There's something in here with us," said The Squid.

"Yeah, a wall. Just like I said. Tell me I'm wrong, Squid. Look at it."

The Squid backed away slowly toward the truck. "We better get outta here."

"Well since you can't say you're sorry, I guess retraction is the better part of valor."

A second shuffling sound came from another direction within the pitch black.

"I still hear it. Let's go," said The Squid, shining his flashlight back and forth.

"It's nothing, man. You wanna drive and I'll guide you back?" asked Ogre.

"Yeah," said The Squid, as he turned to walk back to the truck. Just as he wheeled, his flashlight caught a patch of black fur not five feet away. For a heartbeat, The Squid thought it was a bear, but as he brought the light higher he was not met with a bear's face but that of a hideous giant monster. Protruding eyes on short pink stalks leered at him beside a wicked vertical smile. Long curved yellow teeth chomped together as multiple paws as big as bucket seats lunged for him.

"What the fug is that?!" cried Ogre.

Shuarna shouted, "Gugs! Run! Run!"

9. Ace of Spades

Huge arms covered in swarthy black hair swept forward, crashing together. The Squid dodged, dropped and rolled. A massive foot stomped down at him as he rolled away with crushing blows, following his every move.

Ogre was already back in the truck and throwing it in reverse. A massive obelisk of stone crashed against the wall, splintering into a hundred shards just where the cab had been a moment before. "Sumbitch!" cried Ogre.

Another of the Gugs was picking up a second boulder to throw at the retreating truck. The truck's headlights outlined at least a trio of the gargantuan monsters moving silently forward.

The Squid got up and ran. He leapt and grabbed hold of the side mirror and got his feet on the running board. "Faster! Faster!"

Ogre nodded and backed the truck up as fast as he possibly could, but the Gugs were gaining.

The trailer rocked upward as the rear tires bounced over stalagmites they had missed coming in. The Squid almost lost his footing at that awful jarring but held on for all he was worth. Somehow he still had his flashlight. He swung it outward in the confusion and could not see the far side of the wall.

"Ogre! I think you have room to turn around! Do it and get us the hell out of here!"

The Gugs were almost upon them when Ogre stomped the brakes. The Squid used the opportunity to jump into the cab, just as a Gug slashed its terrible talons along the door of the truck.

Shuarna reached forward and slammed the air horn. The Gugs halted to cover what could only be their invisible ears.

Ogre threw the truck into gear and slammed it forward, hitting a Gug head on and knocking it aside. Turning in a tight circle, Ogre brought the truck and trailer around and hit the same Gug in the head again as it tried to sit up.

The truck sped up, now going forward, and pulled away, easily missing the crumbled stone and sprouting stalagmites in the beams of the headlights.

Dim red light from the brakes illuminated one of the monsters falling behind until the darkness swallowed all sight of it.

"I think we made it!"

Then a heavy crash sounded behind as a Gug leapt aboard the trailer, tearing across the bed with its black talons for traction.

Ogre swung the truck in a serpentine pattern to try and shake the beast loose, but to no avail.

"We have to get rid of it or it will crawl forward and tear us to pieces!" shouted Shuarna.

"Any ideas on how to do that?"

"Try to blind it!"

"Where's your gun, Ogre?"

"Nuh-uh. If someone is gonna do some shooting, it's me!" he said, leaping out of the way for The Squid to take the wheel.

The truck jerked back and forth, slowing the monster from coming forward more than a foot at a time.

"Hold her steady!" cried Ogre, as he struggled to aim out the side window.

He shot once, twice, three times without hitting the Gug at all. It crawled another five feet closer.

"It's getting too close!" The Squid shouted. "Shoot it!"

"Hold her steady!"

Ogre fired again and again, finally hitting the Gug in one of its eyes. It screamed mutely.

When it was only ten feet away from the cab, The Squid turned sharply, and the monster fell back a few feet.

Ogre shot again but missed. "Steady!"

The shaggy demon silently screamed its defiance as it crawled forward.

The road thundered beneath their wheels as death came for them.

Ogre took steady aim. The gun went click. He was empty and the Gug was nearly upon them. It opened its vertical mouth, and wretched sounds gurgled forth as a pink tongue wagged invitingly.

"I'm out," said Ogre, dejectedly.

The Gug took hold of the top of the cab. It held to the roof like an eagle gripping a fish.

"It will rip the roof off!" shouted Shuarna.

The Squid jerked the wheel back and forth, but with its grip on the cab, the Gug was going nowhere but inside.

"Where's the fire extinguisher?" called Ogre, searching under the seats for anything to use.

Shuarna clasped her hands together and a blue-lit appeared between them. She chanted strange words and her eyes lolled back up into her skull. She slumped and The Squid caught her with one arm, the other still on the wheel.

"I brought us out of the Dreamlands," she said in a whisper.

The smoothness of the asphalt beneath the tires met The Squid's ears. Lights above returned and he could see that they were indeed in the regular Eisenhower Tunnel. The wide open maw of the Gug was struck by steel-reinforced concrete, the ceiling much lower now than it had been in the realm of Gugs. Purple ichor splashed over the truck as the behemoth was broken and tossed from the tractor trailer.

They were all breathing heavily, and welcomed the daylight outside the tunnel as they headed back down the mountain pass.

"Is that what waits for us every time we stop?" asked The Squid.

Shuarna sleepily nodded. "Or worse."

"We have to get to your barrier-free zone and be quick, then."

She nodded again and then was asleep.

10. Hush

Shuarna slept but held The Squid's hand even while unconscious. Ogre raised an eyebrow from his seat in the back, but said nothing.

The highway became a long grey thread through the desert beneath an ever-changing sun and moon. The cosmic dance overhead no longer made them quite as nauseous, but it was still unsettling. It seemed even faster than it had been before, day and night trading places almost as fast as one could notice. They developed a system of pulling into gas stations and having one man run in and pay as the other rushed to fill their tanks. They had no more unwelcome encounters for three stops. It was the fastest they had ever moved like this. They made jokes about being an Indy 500 pit crew for themselves.

As Shuarna finally started to stir, The Squid said, "You know what is a pleasant surprise after all those things?"

"What?" answered Ogre.

"After fighting those bugs, running over that Hound and that Gug crawling all over us, I haven't seen so much as a scratch on the truck. Looks like we might just make it out of this unscathed."

Shuarna broke in. "The Shining Trapezohedron repairs itself, ergo the truck is repaired of any sort of damage that is accrued."

"Sweet! I was afraid she'd be ripped up after Ogre's dynamite, those flying cockroaches, the Hounds and the Gugs."

"It *was* torn apart. But the Shining Trapezohedron is especially powerful in the flux between realms."

"I'll drink to that," said Ogre, raising a beer. He yawned against the bright afternoon sunlight. "Where are we now?"

"Almost to Moab. You know, the whole 'Arches, red cliffs, Colorado River' thing?"

"Yeah, I think I stopped at a waffle house there once."

The Squid nodded, "Yeah, it was a good one, wasn't it?"

Shuarna blinked at them as if she didn't understand a word that was said.

"What is it?" The Squid asked. "You've never had a waffle? Look at her, Ogre, she's never had a waffle!"

Ogre leaned forward to stare at Shuarna. "Oh, we gotta remedy that."

Shuarna shook her head. "I do not understand your interest in what sustenance I have or have not had."

"You're in our world now, little girl. You've gotta try a waffle!"

"Don't call her that, man," said The Squid.

"I'm just having fun here, Squid. Thought we all were."

"I get it, just… you don't know her like I do."

Ogre was indignant. "Oh, you know her better than I do? We've all been in the truck the same amount of crazy time, my friend. You don't have any more experience on the UFO subject than I have."

"Jeez, Ogre, let it go. You don't know everything, Mr. Books-on-Tape."

"I knew it. Well, you're blissfully ignorant, my friend. Next time you need a candle in the darkness, don't come cursing me."

"See! You're not even getting your aphorisms right."

"Ha! I'm not, huh? You didn't even say it right, Squid. It's 'euphemism.' Am I wrong?"

The Squid just looked at him and shook his head. "Okay, forget it. But about those waffles." He turned to Shuarna. "We drop Ogre off to get waffles, I'll fill the truck, and you can go pay the attendant inside."

"Fine," said Shuarna. "I will try these 'waffles' if we can still be swift. We cannot risk anything catching up to us."

"It's a deal."

They slowed as they pulled into a twilight-soaked Moab. The moon seemed to slide with greasy ease across the vault of sky before disappearing behind towering cliffs of vermilion. Ogre hopped out as they came to a crawl beside the large A-framed waffle house. The Squid parked at the station next door and hopped out to pump his diesel. Shuarna strode into the station. Funny how quickly the whole bizarre routine had become, well, routine. Sometimes he wondered if this was all a dream he couldn't yet wake from, but the soreness in his legs from sitting too long and the sweat beading on his forehead all said this was real. Still, being with his best friend and Shuarna didn't seem so bad. He especially thought he's like to spend a lot more time with her.

"I gave him the entire amount. Fifty dollars?" asked Shuarna.

"That's good," said The Squid. "That ought to fill us up."

"Why did you tell Ogre that you knew me better than he does?" she asked, as she caressed his hand.

"I suppose because you admitted to me that you got us into this mess, and I've seen that other form of yours. I think you and I have a little more understanding, that's all. Maybe something more too."

She smiled at that. "I like you, Earthman."

"I like you too, Aetherwoman."

She smirked, again and he hated how much he loved that haughty smile. No matter the extra-dimensional madness, or the other-worldly form she reverted to; he was falling hard for her, and he cursed himself for it. He wasn't sure this was something that could ever work out, but how she looked in the moment was mighty nice.

"I'll never get used to that, but I'll take the compliment." He smiled. "Do you have anyone special to you where you are from?"

She looked sharply at him for that. "My father."

"Oh, no, I meant like another dude. Like me." He smiled again, though a bit awkwardly.

"There is no one like you. You are special to me, Jeffrey—" She blushed.

"Please," he cut her off, "call me 'The Squid.'"

She smiled at that and moved closer. Her eyes, though black and yellow, were enchanting, and The Squid was captivated. They moved closer together. Lips within inches.

A horrid cry broke their shared breath and the early morning stillness alike.

Shuarna drew back and pointed at undulating shapes swinging out of the deep blue. "Hunting Horrors! They serve him! We must away!"

"Him? Who?" shouted The Squid, as he yanked the gas nozzle out of the truck and dropped it next to the pump. He clambered into the cab and started the truck.

"Nyarlathotep!" she answered in a panic.

Swooping in ever closer, the three twisting black shapes looked nothing so much as thick serpents with bat-like wings. They spiraled through the air and between each other as they drew near. The Squid guessed them to be nearly the size of his truck and trailer.

He pulled away from the station. "Are they going to lose us as we drive?"

"I think so."

"What about Ogre? He's still in that waffle house!"

"They want the artifact; they will pursue only us until they have it. They will ignore him trapped in the past."

"I can't leave him stuck back there."

"You have no choice."

The Squid looked in the rear view mirror at the A-frame Swiss-themed waffle house. There was no time to wait for his friend before those winged fiends would be upon them. He saw Ogre stepping out the doors with bags in hand. He knew Ogre could plainly see the truck pulling away, was probably shouting at them. Ogre dropped the bags of waffles and then The Squid could see no more as the titanic Hunting Horrors flew low, blocking his view.

"Do you think he can see those giant flying snakes?"

"I don't think so—they are on another plane. But who knows?"

"You know all this stuff! That's why I'm asking you!"

One of the Hunting Horrors was right beside the truck, matching its pace. Its great black tail whipped out and struck, jarring the truck. The Squid barely kept control as they barreled through the center of Moab.

"When will we lose them?"

"When we fully phase into another time."

"When will that be?"

"In just a moment more."

The Hunting Horror's fat tail slapped the side of the trailer again, causing the back wheels to bounce over the sidewalk and cleave into a bike shop before wrenching back out onto the street.

The Squid realized he was screaming, "Holy Hell!" The only thing he could see in the side mirror was the terrible open maw of the black Hunting Horror, opening wider and wider. Tentacles writhed from a frill surrounding its head. Fangs longer than his arm gnashed together. Frothing green spittle from its mouth sprayed across the mirror, obscuring his view.

Shuarna leapt onto The Squid's lap, facing him. She took him in her arms and brought her lips to his. "Hush." She kissed him long and deep. A crunching sound collided with his ears outside to his left just as her lips met his. It sounded like twisted steel and flesh but he didn't know anything anymore.

He lost track of time and space. If the truck would have crashed right then and there and they were devoured by the Hunting Horrors he wouldn't have known. He wouldn't have cared. Everything was gone while in her embrace. There was no danger, there was no fear, there was no self; there was only the two of them entwined like a caduceus.

11. You Make Loving Fun

He was aware of driving again. They were cruising at top speed down the long road splitting a red and black land in half. Shuarna was beside him with a content look upon her face.

"If you think that was good, you really should have tried the waffles," he said.

She rolled her eyes. "I share my soul with you and you speak of food?"

"Man's gotta eat."

She smirked.

"But really what happened?" he asked.

"I am understanding better as we get closer to our destination how to use the power of the artifact. I was able to focus us away through time and space, but I did require some extra energy. Which you were kind enough to supply."

The Squid scratched at his goatee. "So was that just a necessary kick-start? Or did it mean something to you?"

"It was quite enjoyable."

The Squid's grin disappeared. "Anything else?"

"I'll get you some sustenance, if that is what you require to be pleased afterward."

"No, I get it. You got me. I'm not gonna be able to come out on top of this discussion. You win, Shuarna."

The road wound up and down through serpentine canyons. Weird rock formations sculpted by sand and wind appeared even stranger than anything The Squid remembered from previous trips. This having multiple wheels in multiple spaces was a hard thing to get used to. He needed to change the subject from the two of them.

"Do you think Ogre is going to be all right? Will all those things hunting us leave him be?"

"I believe so. The Hounds of Tindalos would be the largest threat. If they did not get his scent thanks to the Trapezohedron cloaking us, he should be fine."

"What about with the people in my own 'realm?' We're wanted outlaws, you know."

"I couldn't say for sure. By your own reckoning of time, perhaps a year has gone past already. They should not be looking for him in any aggressive manner. But he should keep his mouth shut."

The Squid grimaced at that. It was unlikely that Ogre would be able to stay quiet about the whole strange business. His friend was many things, but "discreet" was not one of the words he could claim any kinship to.

"You said you knew who sent those Hunting Horrors after us. Who was that and how do you know?"

"It is Nyarlathotep, the Crawling Chaos. He commands those horrors and many others, too different for your understanding and sanity. The Shining Trapezohedron is his and he wants it back."

"Who is he and what is it exactly?"

"It is beyond your conception."

"Try me. Don't I have a right to know?"

She gave him that smirk again. "The silver craft you saw was but a container. It was a protective shell to hold one of several Shining Trapezohedron stones of great power."

"So where is the stone now?"

"It and its container have been absorbed by your truck."

The Squid looked again at the tiny silver striations touching every part of the truck, from the steering wheel down to the gas pedal.

"I can separate them once we reach our final destination." She did a wave of her hand and the blue light map reappeared inside the cab of the truck.

The Squid scrutinized the map. "Okay. I think I know where that is." He looked her over and asked, "So, you stole it, didn't you?"

Her smirk vanished. Exhaling sharply, she said, "I did."

"So once you do your thing, and get it and the truck separated, are you gonna be okay? Or are all those monsters and cosmic what's-its gonna still be coming after you? Or me?"

"I will be safe. I didn't have time to do it right before. So I cast it through the aether, through time and space, and it landed beside you and within your world. Once I unlock its power, I will control reality strongly enough to vanquish any such being that opposes me."

The Squid stuck out his bottom lip and nodded. "That'd be convenient."

"Don't patronize me."

"Hey, you're the all-powerful, omnipotent-through-all-space-and-time sorceress, I'm just the driver."

She smiled again. "Yes, you are."

12. Crazy Train

They turned left at a crossroads that The Squid knew in his world was a town named Monticello, but there was no sure sign of it but a few derelict buildings and a strange glowing light somewhere off to his right. There was, however, a road sign reading *Route 666*. "Always comforting," he said.

The light and darkness above the highway careened over each other as flames sputtered alongside the road here and there. It was an ageless fire burning the sagebrush, blanketing a smoky residue over the warped environment. Several times The Squid thought he saw bizarre beings hitchhiking along the road but he didn't dare stop. None of them looked remotely human anyway. Most looked like kachinas he had seen at roadside souvenir shops in the southwest and others looked like werewolves and many were even worse.

"What are those things I just saw?"

"Denizens of these twilight lands. Gaunts, skin-walkers, ghasts and others who traverse the worlds between your own and the Dreamlands. They can't stop us."

The Squid tried to take comfort in that despite spying one of the werewolf things loping after them almost as fast as the truck was traveling. He was just starting to sweat about it being another opponent when the wolf thing abruptly veered off and was swallowed by the desert gloom. "You're sure none of those things will be trouble?"

"Even if they are eyes for Nyarlathotep, we are far removed from a linear timeframe. When they report and when he could send his servants are different things entirely."

"Hope you're right, doll face."

She gave that coy smile and said, "Of course I'm right. This has been a long time coming."

He kept driving, watching the sun and moon swirl after each other. Glancing back, he noticed that Ogre had left his cap behind. The idea struck him. "Shuarna, how can I communicate with others beyond this realm now?"

"We are outside your world; you can't communicate with anyone there."

"I want to try though, for fun."

"For fun?" She was puzzled.

The Squid picked up his CB. "Ten-ten, Ogre-man. You out there, come on back." Static met his ears. He hadn't truly expected anything but it had been a pleasing thought for a moment.

Shuarna said, "I told you there was no way—"

"I'm here, good buddy, when's your twenty?" The voice was undoubtedly Ogre's.

The Squid was shocked but thrilled. "Ogre? You're out there?"

Shuarna took The Squid's hand off the CB. "It must be a trick of Nyarlathotep. Don't answer anything more. Turn it off. This will only bring you pain."

"But it's my friend. I need to know he is okay."

She shook her head. "It's not him."

"You got your ears on?" crackled Ogre's voice. "Come on back. What's your twenty?"

Shuarna looked as fearful as she ever had.

"What's the harm?" asked The Squid. He took up the CB again. "How you doing, buddy? I'm cruising. Not sure where I am. Route 666 somewhere abouts."

"Something you should know, Squid. I'm expired. I didn't make it much past the waffle house. All those things caught up to me. It was a blur. I'm not even sure which ones took me down. There was a wide selection. But it's like I'm in the weigh station of no return, just waiting around like some kinda damn wraith."

"You're telling me you're dead but can talk on the CB?"

"Yeah, it's like it just appeared in my hand when you started talking."

"So I take it you didn't go toward the light?"

"No, man, I was kinda worried about stepping that way considering all the things I've done. Guess I wanted to see if I could get a second chance."

"You got it."

"But, man, I'm glad you're still trucking."

The Squid looked at Shuarna. "They got him! It's your fault!"

"I'm sorry," she said.

"Hang on, Ogre," The Squid snapped into the CB. "Shuarna, if this eighteen-wheeler can cross time and space we need to go back and get him. We need to get him *before* anything happened to him."

"That would be suicide. You would be as dead as he is. The forces must have converged upon him utterly."

"This might be crazy to you but he's my friend and we gotta try something. I can't just keep driving like this. I have to try."

She protested, "We are ahead of our pursuers. They don't know where we are or where we are going. We can make it, and I can work my enchantments. You will be free of these worries."

"Minus my best friend. No thanks. I'm driving and we are going back!" He pulled the truck to a stop as a strange kangaroo-like monstrosity hopped beside the burning highway. "What the hell is that?"

"It's just a ghost. Do as you will."

"So you admit it can be done?"

She nodded ruefully. "Yes, maybe, but we are more likely to lose everything."

"Don't fear the reaper, baby."

"I don't, but *you* should."

Into the CB, The Squid said, "Ogre, hang on. I'm coming to get ya." Pulling onto the sloping shoulder, he turned around, taking the truck back the way they had come. A pair of ghosts tried to quickly hop out of the way as he pulled the air horn but they weren't fast enough and he plowed over them. Gruesome grey fur and ichor splattered but there was no damage to the truck. The Squid nodded approvingly, "That's what I thought!"

"What?" asked Shuarna.

"Nothing, just I think I got a serious ace up my sleeve."

She shook her head. "There is no such thing as luck."

Barreling down the highway at breakneck speed, The Squid turned to Shuarna. "Yeah, well, did you know we could have gone back the whole time?"

"I had an idea. But I still say this is a terrible decision. You may not make it out alive and I could lose everything I care about."

The Squid shook his head, "I guess that's a risk I have to take. I couldn't live with myself if I didn't at least try."

"Your species does have such a primitive, alien mind. I'll never understand you no matter what my father tells me."

"Your father? What does that mean?"

She smiled a genuine smile. "He said I should try something like this sometime just to experience your kind's peculiarities. I know he didn't expect I would do such with one of the Shining Trapezohedrons, but still."

"Well, we truckers are a different breed."

"He meant humans in general."

The Squid pondered that and smiled. "I aim to please."

Waving her hand across the dashboard, Shuarna again brought up the blue light map. She pointed at a coordinate and said, "I can take us back to the place just before we vanished. We will pass ourselves on the highway. The Hunting Horrors will immediately turn on us as we try to get Ogre. Not to mention that this much chronological imbalance will surely set the Hounds on us, as well as anything else capable of arriving."

"Ourselves?" he asked. She bit her lip and he couldn't have loved her more.

"When I phased us away from the Hunting Horrors, something hit one of them beside us. I didn't see it and I wondered, and now I know it was a self-fulfilling prophetical maneuver. I think perhaps you are rubbing off on me, as you say."

"I never say that."

"I can't change your mind, can I?"

"No, why? You're telling me you think we killed one of those squid dragons with the truck, right?"

"Yes, but if Ogre was speaking to us as a specter then he died already, regardless of us going back. You must have, too."

The Squid, looked at her. "I won't quit, not now, not ever."

"You can't win against these odds. You will die."

He rubbed his chin and took a long pull on his beer. "The way I see it, I gotta do this. 'Sides why should I worry? I didn't answer my own CB call."

"Of course not."

"Well, Ogre didn't say I was with him in the weigh station to Hell."

"No, but—"

"So, I must succeed in rescuing him. This truck rolls through time and space, right? So we hit that squid dragon and we were speaking to Ogre, in between the time we rescue him." He nodded at that and took another swig, rather pleased with himself.

Shuarna was dubious. "We are striding between time and space, true, but none of that means you succeed."

"I'm deciding it does," he said, wiping his mouth on his sleeve. "Won't do any good to think anything else."

"I think the highway has driven you mad."

He shrugged. "I'm cruising. Let me know when we are almost there."

"You'll know soon enough."

An indeterminate amount of time later, after many revolutions of light and dark overhead, the truck started to shake violently.

"We're close," said Shuarna.

"You sure? None of this looks familiar," he said, glancing out the window.

"It never does from this perspective."

A flash of light and screeching sound blasted their senses. Then nearly filling the windshield was the open maw of a Hunting Horror, tentacles writhing from the frill about its head.

Honking the air horn and turning on all his lights, The Squid slammed the truck into the beast like a battering ram. Green and purple ichor splashed, coating the windshield. Some of the beast's ichor smoked away from the truck lights, wafting off in a stink. Turning on the wipers, The Squid saw a mangled black corpse tossed to the side of the road. The carcass of the Hunting Horror was demolished but there were so many more things waiting. The waffle house was coming up on his right, surrounded by all the denizens of his nightmares.

Ogre was standing out front, .357 Magnum in one hand, his to-go bag in the other. He was shooting at a variety of horrifying beings: unclean Gugs, tentacle-faced Moon Beasts, buzzing Mi-Go, the wraith-like Hounds of Tindalos, circling Hunting Horrors, and spiders the size of cars. Then all their infernal attentions were turned to The Squid and his approaching big black Mack.

"Aww, crap."

13. Hair of the Dog

"It is all the forces Nyarlathotep could muster at once!" said Shuarna, in a panic. "You can't escape!"

Slamming the truck into a lower gear, The Squid growled, "I ain't trying to escape!"

A pair of Gugs moved forward, standing taller than the cab of the truck. Hounds were behind them and so too were the awful toad-like Moon-Beasts.

In her fright, Shuarna reverted to her true form, that of a towering, black-clad, yellow-eyed titan. Crouching in the passenger seat, she looked like she might burst from her seat belt. "I won't be able to protect you! This is madness!"

The fearsome bestiary of doom closed in on the truck, momentarily forgetting their business with Ogre.

The Squid said, "Now, they'll see they're messing with a real son of a bitch!"

The Squid plowed right into the Gugs, Hounds and Moon-Beasts. Unholy grey fur flew and blue ichor splashed from the Hounds. The gigantic soft bodies of the Moon-Beasts were ripped open by the awesome truck as it spun about the lot.

Now the creatures scrambled to get out of the way, but The Squid succeeded in running them down left and right. A master of trailer control, he whipped the bed behind him, letting it skid across the gravel and pulverize his colossal enemies.

"It can't be!" exclaimed Shuarna. "You have harnessed the power of the Trapezohedron without me!"

The Squid turned sharply as he could, saying, "I had an idea that the truck was impervious to those things after I saw that nothing had really damaged it, even when that Hunting Horror slammed us into the bike shop." He spun about and rear-ended the last Gug. "I think we are bridging enough worlds, as you said, that we're made of denser stuff!"

A giant spider attempted to web the truck, but ate grill as The Squid slammed it into the wall of the waffle house.

A Hunting Horror swooped down at the truck. The Squid flipped on his lights and pulled the air-horn, and the brightness melted the leviathan like a hot sidewalk melts a dropped popsicle. A pair of Mi-Go gyrated through the air and were hit by the top of the truck cab, disintegrating in a putrid explosion of muck.

Ogre shouted, "Yeah! Eat that, you flying slug!" He shot his .357 at a retreating Mi-Go.

The Squid pulled up to Ogre. "Get in, man!"

Ogre clambered aboard. His hair was distinctly longer and greyer than when they had dropped him off.

"What happened to you?"

"Time," answered Ogre.

The Squid circled the truck and went over the top of another Moon Beast.

The Mi-Go congregated in a swarm high above and after a brief buzzing congress, fled into the depths of the approaching twilight.

A bruise-colored collection of blood covered the truck, along with Gug bits and hair, Moon-Beast tentacles, spider legs and even a broken Hound wrapped up in a wheel well.

"Is it over?" asked Ogre. "That wasn't so bad once you went all road-rage on them."

The Squid popped the truck out of gear and set the parking brake, then turned on his windshield wipers again to wash away more gore. "I don't see anything else coming at us. Seems like, you know, they learned their lesson."

"It can't be over," said Shuarna. "There is no way he would give up so easily."

"Easily? You thought we were toast, but I turned all these monsters into road kill."

She watched out the windows warily, then said, "It is the power of the Trapezohedron. It melded with your truck and gave to it the power. I never would have believed you could wield it."

"Is that so wrong?" asked The Squid, as he grabbed a doobie from the sun visor and lit up. "I feel," cough, cough, "pretty good about it."

"Gimme a toke," said Ogre.

Shuarna talked as much to herself as the two of them. "It is unheard of. A bare handful of mortals have ever been able to utilize the power of the Dreamlands. I underestimated you."

"Will you look at yourself," said The Squid, pointing at Ogre. "You look like you're thirty years older!" His friend had greyed considerably and sagged around the middle and jowls.

"I am, Squid. Time got weird after you guys left me. I've spent 1990 through 2016 in Moab, Utah. I shouldn't have taken so long to think to call you up on the CB."

"But I called you, and that was just an hour or so after we last saw you."

"Not to me, Dude." He pointed at the waffle house behind the idling truck. It said Ogre's in neon lights. "I decided to stay put and wait. I just didn't think it would take so long."

The Squid's smile dropped, "I'm sorry, man."

"No, no. I've made out all right. I own the waffle house and got myself a nice little woman named Dorothy. When tourist season hits, we do real well."

"Well, good, man."

"Please," interrupted Shuarna. "He is here."

"What? Who?"

"My father. Nyarlathotep."

The Squid's face was covered in surprise and he dropped his roach.

"Squid, who the funk is that?" asked Ogre, pointing at a tall dusky man in semi-Egyptian garb approaching the truck. A tall white crown was the only contrast to the black that clothed him, and in his hand was a twisted long scepter or staff. "His hat looks like a bowling pin," muttered Ogre.

"Shut up, man. Shuarna, is he pissed? Like, is he gonna think we kidnapped you or something?"

"No, he is angry I stole one of the Shining Trapezohedrons for myself."

Shuarna opened the door of the truck and stepped out. The Squid followed to stand by her. Ogre got out but hung back.

Nyarlathotep glared at them with piercing yellow eyes. "Well?" His voice sounded like it came from a deep cavern, echoing and dark.

"You said I should experience their realm for myself. This seemed a natural way."

"Thief," he said, coldly.

"You limited my choices. I did what you would have done."

"You will be punished." His staff shot up and a crushing force swept Shuarna to her knees. She was strangled and smothered as if by a great invisible hand.

"Let her go!" The Squid broke in.

Glancing at The Squid and Ogre, Nyarlathotep spun the staff in their direction and knocked their feet out from under them.

The Squid caught himself on his truck. He kept a hand on the truck's handle above the running board and challenged again. "Let her go!

Nyarlathotep focused an invisible force, beating down upon him but The Squid crawled up the rig's running board and managed to open the door. Once inside he started the engine.

His dark nemesis, Nyarlathotep, pulled Shuarna and Ogre to himself, their feet dragging across the pavement as he reeled them in. "Surrender to me," demanded Nyarlathotep.

"Don't think so," sputtered The Squid, still fighting the force that churned his insides with every breath.

Nyarlathotep raged and cast both Shuarna and Ogre to the side. The Squid's gaze met the Black Pharaoh's and neither flinched. More monstrous creatures appeared in his peripheral vision, and The Squid knew they were closing in on him.

Nyarlathotep stepped closer, sending shockwaves of power at The Squid. "Exit and kneel before me."

The Squid made like he just might step out, but then he grinned, dropped the gear on the truck and stomped the pedal. The big black Mack smacked into the Crawling Chaos like the hammer of the gods. The crown cracked and staff shattered. The monsters vanished as bright noonday light suddenly appeared. Everything looked normal again.

Nyarlathotep slowly stood and took a step back from his human antagonist.

Leaning out the window, The Squid said, "That's right, man. I can focus some of the Dreamlands' power myself and you can't ruin me." Ogre got up and stumbled to be next to the truck. Shuarna climbed up the running board, reached and put her arms around The Squid.

"It seems I must respect your power here," said Nyarlathotep.

"That's right. And I need you to leave Shuarna alone. She did the wrong thing for the right reason. She told me all about it. Cut her some slack, jack."

Nyarlathotep looked to his daughter with a piercing stare.

The Squid continued, "Hey, man. For what it's worth, no real harm was done. It's all good."

"Uh, Squid," broke in Ogre, as he kicked a broken Hound of Tindalos out of the wheel well.

"Well," said The Squid, sheepishly. "Those things started it. So I'm sorry if I killed your dog or whatever it was."

Nyarlathotep looked about and took in the gruesome carnage and broken monstrous bodies of a dozen Gugs, Moon-Beasts, Hounds and more, and he laughed, a deep malevolent roar without mirth. It made The Squid and Ogre terribly uncomfortable.

"You have tread where no man has before, and yet you do it with an ignorant impunity that has warmed my daughter in her own transgression. It would be a cosmic joke to punish you any further. So be it. Go your way."

"So we're cool?"

Nyarlathotep's gaze narrowed as his eyes were but slivers of light that shone beneath a black door to the abyss. "Yes, we are... cool."

"Am I free to continue?" asked Shuarna.

"Go thy way, daughter, tread the forbidden paths now that you have the key to cross the worlds without end. But do not cross me again." With that, Nyarlathotep turned and his shade vanished like an invisible door shut.

"Does that mean we can keep on trucking?"

Shuarna smiled. "I'd like to. There are many more realms to see."

"Then I'll fire her up and we'll get going."

14. Space Truckin'

The two men clasped hands and hugged one last time. "You take care of yourself, Ogre-man."

"Will do, Squid."

"We better get moving," said Shuarna, from the cab window.

"Where are you gonna go? What are you gonna do, Squid-man?"

"I'm just gonna keep on trucking with her. This Earth here ain't a time for me anymore." He fired up the rig.

"Seems awful dangerous, man. You don't know what other crazy shite is out there!"

"I know, but I'm gonna find out, aren't I?" he said, with a grin. Shuarna reached over and gave him a big kiss. "Living the dream, brother! Take her easy," said The Squid.

"Take her easy," answered Ogre, as he stood watching. The rig pulled out onto the asphalt and went down the road toward the sunset vanishing into a midnight-soaked blur.

So that, my friends, is how the man known as The Squid started space-trucking across the universe. I don't know about you, but I'm kinda glad he's out there, keeping an eye on things for all of us.

Take her easy.

CONTRIBUTORS

Jason A. Anderson was raised in Southern California before moving to Utah to attend high school. While a teenager, he conceived and began writing his teen adventure series, "The Starriders Saga." Never one to let grass grow under his feet, he continued exploring different story concepts and struck upon what has become the "SoulChaser Universe," which includes teen paranormal subseries, "The Jean Archer Quartet." Besides being a father and writer, his passions include theater production, fast cars, off-roading, rock'n roll, and Harley-Davidsons.

D.J. (Dave) Butler is the author of middle grade fantasy adventure *The Kidnap Plot* (Knopf, June 2016) and the blackpowder epic fantasy *Witchy Eye* (Baen, 2017). He is Acquisitions Editor at WordFire Press, and you can read more about him at *davidjohnbutler.com*.

Garrett Calcaterra is author of the YA fantasy series *The Dreamwielder Chronicles* and other works of dark speculative fiction. His short work has appeared in *Black Gate, Confrontation,* and *Arkham Tales,* among others. Garrett lives and writes in California. To learn more, visit *garrettcalcaterra.com* or follow Garrett on twitter @Gcalcaterra.

Jaleta Clegg loves telling stories, especially weird and silly ones. Or ones with spaceships and aliens and explosions. Or ones with swords and magic. Or pretty much anything that isn't quite the normal world. She writes mainly space opera and silly horror, but is branching out into high fantasy and steampunk fairies. Look for her work at *jaletac.com*.

Robert J Defendi was born in Dubuque, IA (in accordance with prophecy). He reads voraciously, if you consider audiobooks reading (which you shouldn't). He has yet to find, conquer, and rule a small Central American country (but I think we all know that's inevitable). He is neither Team Jacob nor Team Edward (he is sympathetic to Team Guy-Who-Almost-Hit-Bella-With-A-Truck). He shamelessly stole that last joke.

Steve Diamond is the author of the YA paranormal thriller/horror novel *Residue.* He is also the co-editor of the horror anthology *Shared Nightmares.* His short fiction was nominated for the Hugo Award in 2015. Steve writes for Ragnarok, Baen, Privateer Press, and numerous small publications. He founded and runs the review site *Elitist Book Reviews*, which was nominated for the Hugo Award in 2013, 2014 and 2015.

Born in Texas and currently living in Utah, **David Dunwoody** writes subversive horror fiction including the novels *Hell Walks, The Harvest Cycle* and *Empire*. Most recent is his post-apocalyptic dark fantasy *The 3 Egos*. His short stories have been published by such outfits as Chaosium, *Shroud, Gallery*, and *Dark Regions*. More info and free fiction at *daviddunwoody.com*.

Theric Jepson's lighthearted college-students-in-love novel *Byuck* includes a scene in which a monstrous subterranean god devours blind mermaids. His novella *Perky Erect Nipples*, however, contains nothing eldritch at all.

Robert Masterson is an award-winning writer, editor and teacher and the author of *Garnish Trouble* (forthcoming in July 2016 from Finishing Line Press), *Artificial Rats & Electric Cats* (Camber Press, 2008) and *Trial by Water* (Dog Running Wild Press, 1982), Masterson's creative work (both literary and horror), journalism, interviews, and creative nonfiction have appeared in numerous anthologies, journals, magazines, and newspapers websites throughout the world. An English professor at the City University of New York's Borough of Manhattan Community College campus, Masterson holds both a BA and an MA (with distinction) in English Literature from the University of New Mexico, Albuquerque; an MFA from Naropa University's Jack Kerouac School of Disembodied Poetics; and a weird little academic certificate from Shaanxi Normal University in the People's Republic of China.

Nathan Shumate is a writer, media critic, editor, small-press publisher, and assemblage artist. He has written (and gotten paid for) comic books scripts, screenplays, and various forms of fiction and nonfiction. He is the instigator and publisher of the Lovecraftian pulp space opera *Space Eldritch* anthologies. He also unleashed *LousyBookCovers.com* onto the world. His webcomic *CheapCaffeine.net* appears weekdaily. His latest book is *The Last Christmas Gift: A Heartwarming Holiday Tale of the Living Dead*.

Through two wonderful mentored research experiences, **Sarah E. Seeley** had the opportunity to work with dead sauropods and ancient odonates while acquiring her undergraduate degree in geology from Brigham Young University. She hopes to study more dead things in the future and contribute to scientific discussions about what makes life on Earth so amazing. In the meantime, she explores the bright side of being human by writing dark fiction. Sarah's stories appear in *Leading Edge Magazine* and various anthologies. Her independently published works include *Maladaptive Bind* and "Blood Oath: An Orc Love Story." She is an affiliate member of the Horror Writers Association. To learn more, visit her author blog at *SlithersOfThought.com*.

Scott Michael Taylor is a husband, father, writer, just your ordinary crime-fighting blogger, father of 4, husband of 1, owner of a dog, owned by 2 cats. He is the writer of the award winning short film *Wrinkles*, and writer of the upcoming feature film, *Edwin*. He blogs at *scottywattydoodlealltheday.blogspot.com*.

Brad R. Torgersen is a multi-award-nominated and multi-award-winning science fiction writer whose short fiction has appeared in numerous magazines and anthologies, and whose novels are published by Baen Books. A Chief Warrant Officer in the United States Army Reserve, Brad recently spent a year on deployment to the Middle East. Married for over twenty-two years, Brad is also a father, and has two decades of experience supporting technology in the healthcare industry.

Ian Welke grew up in the library in Long Beach, California. After receiving his Bachelor of Arts in History from California State University, Long Beach, he worked in the computer games industry for fifteen years where he was lucky enough to work at Blizzard Entertainment and at Runic Games in Seattle. While living in Seattle he sold his first short story, a space-western, written mainly because he was depressed that *Firefly* had been canceled. Following the insane notion that life is short and he should do what he wants most, he moved back to southern California and started writing full time. Ian's short fiction has appeared in *Big Pulp*, *Arcane II*, the *American Nightmare* anthology, and the *18 Wheels of Horror* anthology, amongst other places. His novels, *The Whisperer in Dissonance* (2014) and the Bram Stoker Award-nominated *End Times at Ridgemont High* (2015) were both published by Ominum Gatherum Media.

David J. West writes dark fantasy and weird westerns because the voices in his head won't quiet until someone else can hear them. He is a great fan of sword & sorcery, ghosts and lost ruins, so of course he lives in Utah in with his wife and children. You can visit him online at: *david-j-west.blogspot.com*, *twitter.com/David_JWest*, and *david-j-west.tumblr.com*.

SM Williams is an author of horror and supernatural thrillers who lives somewhere in Central New York. He has held jobs teaching, figuring out where things are, battling invasive insects (largely without success), and counting trees for NASA. More can be found at *internetmanifestation.com*.

If you enjoyed this book, check out some of the other publications from Cold Fusion Media:

SPACE ELDRITCH

Science fiction goes occult in *Space Eldritch*, a volume of seven original novelettes and novellas of Lovecraftian pulp space opera. Featuring work by Brad R. Torgersen (Hugo/Nebula/Campbell nominee), Howard Tayler (multiple Hugo nominee), and Michael R. Collings (author of over 100 books), plus a foreword by New York Times bestselling author Larry Correia, *Space Eldritch* inhabits the intersection between the eternal adventure of the final frontier and the inhuman darkness between the stars.

SPACE ELDRITCH II: THE HAUNTED STARS
Edited by Nathan Shumate

The cold of interstellar space is again closer than you think as eleven authors —including New York Times bestseller Larry Correia, Nebula winner Eric James Stone, Amazon #1 bestseller Michaelbrent Collings, and multiple Hugo nominee Howard Tayler—explore what happens when space opera meets Lovecraftian cosmic horror.

SHARED NIGHTMARES
Edited by Steven Diamond and Nathan Shumate

Twelve authors—including New York Times bestseller Larry Correia, #1 Amazon bestseller Michaelbrent Collings, Prometheus Award winner Sarah Hoyt, Campbell Award nominee Max Gladstone, and Hugo nominee Howard Tayler—take you to the dark side of the dream world, where phantasms and fears become frighteningly real.

ARCANE

Edited by Nathan Shumate

The first full-length anthology of this series features thirty stories by some of the freshest blood in the horror, dark fantasy and weird fiction fields! Included:

- An office worker returns from bereavement leave to find his workplace changing before his eyes…
- A priest excites his village to the greatest show of devotion to their god ever seen…
- A mortician sees all of his immaculate handiwork destroyed when his clients start rising…

ARCANE II

Edited by Nathan Shumate

This second volume of the *Arcane* anthology series presents twenty-one more stories of dark imagination. Included:

- A landlord finds something left behind by a former tenant, something with a will of its own…
- A bride explores her new husband's manor house, seeking the mystery that overshadows his life…
- A survivor of the apocalypse sees an insidious change infecting the few remaining humans…

Cold Fusion Media
http://www.coldfusionmedia.us